
THE OUTSIDER

BOOKS BY HOWARD FAST

The Outsider
Max
Time and the Riddle:
  Thirty-one Zen Stories
The Legacy
The Establishment
The Magic Door
Second Generation
The Immigrants
The Art of Zen Meditation
A Touch of Infinity
The Hessian
The Crossing
The General Zapped an Angel
The Jews: Story of a People
The Hunter and the Trap
Torquemada
The Hill
Agrippa's Daughter
Power
The Edge of Tomorrow
April Morning

The Golden River
The Winston Affair
Moses, Prince of Egypt
The Last Supper
Silas Timberman
The Passion of Sacco and Vanzetti
Spartacus
The Proud and the Free
Departure
My Glorious Brothers
Clarkton
The American
Freedom Road
Citizen Tom Paine
The Unvanquished
The Last Frontier
Conceived in Liberty
Place in the City
The Children
Strange Yesterday
Two Valleys

THE
OUTSIDER

Howard Fast

A DELL BOOK

Published by
Dell Publishing Co., Inc.
1 Dag Hammarskjold Plaza
New York, New York 10017

Dell ® TM 681510, Dell Publishing Co., Inc.

ISBN: 0-440-16778-7

Reprinted by arrangement with Houghton Mifflin Company
Printed in the United States of America
First Dell printing—August 1985

For the stranger, the newcomer, Benjamin Isaac Grace Fast,
welcome to this very curious world.
I greet you with love and I wish you joy and fulfillment.

PART ONE
1946

Rabbi David Hartman came to Leighton Ridge in the spring of 1946, six months after his discharge from the United States Army, where he had served as a chaplain in the infantry. The six months had been a mixed bag of sadness and happiness. His discharge, quickened by news of his mother's illness, brought him to her bedside only hours before her death. His father had died when he was a small boy, and his mother had raised him, cared for him, and adored him.

Five months later, he married Lucy Spendler, whom he had met a few weeks after his mother's death. Lucy was a volunteer worker in a U.S.O. coffee and doughnut store on Broadway in the Seventies. David came there to conduct evening prayers, a convenience for Jewish servicemen who desired to say the mourner's *Kaddish*. He met Lucy, a slender, pretty girl with rich brown hair and huge brown eyes, and saw something in her that reminded him poignantly of his mother. As for Lucy, she saw a tall, lean man, sunburned, with a pair of bright blue eyes, decent features, and a smile half-sad and half-delightful. He had a wide mouth, a high, strong nose, and a thick shock of brown hair, and the fact that he was still in uniform, with important-looking ribbons on his blouse, made him as romantic as a rabbi might be — at least to Lucy.

Lucy's father was a printer — more correctly, a Linotype

operator — at the *New York Times*. Her mother worked as a typist at City Hall, again, more correctly, the Municipal Building; and both her father and her mother were militant Jewish atheists. In spite of this bias toward God — for a Jewish atheist is more fervent in his anger and disagreement with God than in his disbelief — they embraced David Hartman and gave their blessing to the marriage. Which did not lessen their skepticism about David's ability to earn a living and support their daughter.

Talking with Rabbi Belsen, who headed the placement committee at the Jewish Institute of Religion, the seminary David had attended, David began to share the doubts of Herbert and Sally Spendler. "The trouble is, David," Rabbi Belsen explained, "that you are a very young man, not even thirty. Believe me, I would treasure that problem. Still and all, in this case, it creates certain difficulties for you. I know you're just married, and that calls for some sort of income. Certainly, we should have made provision for young men coming out of the service, but we were not equipped for that. I have three older men, men with families and children. So if you'll be patient, in perhaps another month — "

David nodded. He could exercise patience, but what he needed very quickly was a job.

" — unless," Rabbi Belsen added.

"Yes?" David asked eagerly.

"If you can live with this, David, there is a place. I can't put an established rabbi with a family in there. That's out of the question. But a young man like yourself, right out of the service, which was no picnic, I'm sure. You didn't sleep on silk sheets in the Normandy invasion."

David smiled. "No, I don't think so."

"All right. So listen. There's a town in Fairfield County called Leighton Ridge. In this town there are fourteen Jewish families, and they decided they want a synagogue and a rabbi. Now I must tell you, David, that for two weeks we have been trying to find someone to accept this assignment. It is no blessing. They will provide a house, which may or may not be fit to live in, and they will pay a salary of twelve hundred dollars a year. We might get that up to fourteen or fifteen hundred, but not any more than that, because, as they tell me, they will have to put down two thousand dollars cash for the house, with a mortgage of eight thousand more, and also another thousand dollars in cash for a synagogue, against four thousand dollars, although what kind of a synagogue you buy for four thousand dollars, I don't know."

"Where's Fairfield County?" David asked. His New York childhood in the thirties was devoid of any knowledge of Connecticut.

"Ah-hah, you don't say no immediately. A good sign. Fairfield County is in Connecticut. It runs north and east from the New York border maybe thirty, forty miles, and the way I understand it, Leighton Ridge is a town of perhaps four thousand people. You should know the worst. In the fourteen families, there are two Orthodox families and two Conservative families. They go along with the Reform movement because it's the only way they can have a synagogue. If there were three Orthodox families, they'd build a synagogue of their own. That's a joke, David."

"Yes. You know, Rabbi Belsen, when I went into the service, I had half-decided to give up the rabbinate, possibly to get into medical school. But then, after what I saw. I saw Dachau — I saw other camps — well, the pay doesn't matter. I told myself that I'd never question the pay."

Rabbi Belsen looked at David Hartman with new interest. He recalled David Hartman the student, vaguely, one among many students; the young man who stood in front of him was something else, a strong face but not without innocence, and as if graven and carved into the sharp angles of the face, eyes of great sorrow. He was quiet without being humble. He asked nothing.

"Yes," Rabbi Belsen said after a long moment, "this may be something right for you."

"I'd have to discuss it with Lucy. But — only fourteen Jewish families — is it one of those places where they bar Jews?"

"Not the way I understand it. America is a very large place, David, and there are a limited number of Jews. Fourteen is reasonable for a place like Leighton Ridge."

"You know, Rabbi Belsen," David said, "I'm only twenty-nine years old and I was born in New York, and do you know I've never been to Connecticut."

"Since you spent the past six years in the service and in school and in the Institute before that, it's understandable."

"Still, it's peculiar. I mean I feel very strange. I have been to North Africa, England, France, and Germany — but never to Connecticut. I suppose I'd need a car?"

"I would think so."

"I never learned to drive. I think Lucy can drive. I've never discussed it with her."

"Talk to her, David, and then we'll talk some more about Leighton Ridge."

But before David brought the proposal back to Lucy, who was still living with her mother and father, he stopped at the New York Public Library, found a history of Connecticut, and located the single paragraph devoted to Leighton Ridge. Historically speaking, Leighton Ridge was not terribly important. David discovered that it was one of the smaller Fairfield townships located in the northeastern section of the county, that it had been founded by Captain Egbert Leighton in 1771, at which time he was given a royal grant of eleven hundred acres for his service in the French and Indian War, that it was located on the high ridge of lower Connecticut, that its winters were cold and its summers salubrious.

"But can we live on twelve hundred dollars a year?" Lucy wondered. "That's only twenty-five dollars a week. They paid you more than that in the service."

"I had a larger congregation in the service."

"Fourteen families — "

"According to the custom, all we'd need would be ten. That would constitute a community according to Jewish law."

"It doesn't frighten you, does it?" Lucy asked him. "It scares me. I have to tell you that."

"A little. I mean not the way things overseas scared me. You know, I didn't expect them to hand me the Temple Emanu-El or anything like that, but I thought at the worst I could come in as assistant to some place in New York or Chicago or Los Angeles."

"I was there once. I love Los Angeles," Lucy said. "It's mostly always warm there. Leighton Ridge sounds cold. Even the name sounds cold."

"According to the book I looked at in the library, the temperature in Leighton Ridge varies in the winter between thirty-six degrees to a low of five above zero. But it's not the cold I mind. It's just that I never thought of anything like this. You know, you spend a lot of time in the service dreaming about how things will turn out afterward, when you get home. But this is so far removed from anything I ever dreamed of."

"You don't have to take it," Lucy said. "After three years with the U.S.O., I'm as good as any professional waitress or counter girl. I can get a job and so can you. And you told me they had offered you an instructorship in history at N.Y.U. We could get an apartment — "

"I'm a rabbi, Lucy."

"I know. I'm not asking you to be something else, David, but just to fill in with a temporary job until something good comes along in the rabbinate."

He kissed her. He did care for her a great deal. She was sweet and she was clever, and under the sweetness she had a hard core of determination. But she was also young and very much New York City born and bred, and it was not easy to explain to her what his experience in Europe added up to. He had not yet reached a point where he could talk about what he had seen in the camps.

"I think I have to take this thing on Leighton Ridge — if you agree," he added.

"I'll agree to whatever you want, David. But why?"

"I don't know. But it's been offered, and I don't think I can say no to Rabbi Belsen. And there's at least one positive thing. I'll be my own boss, not someone's assistant."

"Thank heaven for that."

"And you can drive a car, can't you? I remember you mentioning something about it."

"David, I drove a U.S.O. panel truck for six months."

"Good, good. You must teach me. There's no real railroad station closer than Westport or Fairfield, and they're both miles away."

The following day, David returned to the Institute and knocked at the door to Rabbi Belsen's office. The rabbi, whose white beard matched David's childhood notion of God, opened the door, stared at David moodily, and then motioned him into his office.

"Is something wrong?" David wondered.

"I hope not. You came to tell me you're accepting the post in Leighton. I'm worried. I went to a grocery store this morning. I haven't been to a grocery store since before the war. My wife does the shopping. I don't know how you're going to live on twenty-five dollars a week. It's not the same as it was in the thirties. I was thinking maybe we should establish some sort of minimum wage. A rabbi is human. I'll bring it up before the board."

"We'll manage," David said. "I have my discharge pay and some savings and Lucy has some, and there were the wedding presents, so we have almost five thousand dollars between us, and we can manage for at least a couple of years, and with all the guys coming out of the service and getting married and looking for a place to raise their children, the Jewish community up there has to grow. Who knows, in a few years I might have a congregation of a hundred families."

"I've seen stranger things," Rabbi Belsen said. "So you'll go to Leighton Ridge. At least there's plenty of fresh air up there. David, usually I don't give advice, but just a word or two. You must try to love your congregation even when they're least lovable — which can be frequently. Don't expect righteousness or even integrity. You teach it. And don't expect gratitude. It is very precious and in time it will come, but don't expect it. And when you come into New York, come to see me and tell me what's happening up there. I'll be filled with curiosity."

"Of course."

"Good. Now I have some notes here that I had typed up for you. First of all, the president of the congregation. There are only fourteen families up there, but unless you can live and work with and remain a friend of the president of your congregation, the fourteen families will be as troublesome as a hundred. His name is Jacob Osner — Jack, he calls himself. We had lunch when he came to the seminary to talk about organizing a synagogue — an intelligent and forceful man, but without sentiment, possibly a totally pragmatic man. German-Jewish grandparents, early forties. An advantage, David, you were both in the service. He was a colonel with the Judge Advocate. He has a boy of twelve years and a girl, I think, nine. Maybe part of what pushed him is that he wants the boy *Bar Mitzvahed* right there in Leighton Ridge. You're young, he's middle-aged, and maybe he isn't as tolerant as he should be. Maybe he is. I don't know. But, David, you must have him as your ally, never your adversary."

"I'll certainly try my best."

"All right. Now, the synagogue committee consists of three people: first, Osner, the lawyer, and incidentally his office is in New York, then Joe Hurtz, about the same age, has a men's furnishing store in Danbury, three kids. Osner tells me he had to have his oldest son, I think the boy's fifteen now, had to have him *Bar Mitzvahed* at an Orthodox *shul* in Bridgeport. He didn't like that. It's a funny thing going on there, maybe it comes from the war and the Holocaust, and maybe the same thing is going to crop up in a lot of other places, but it's like an angry demonstration that they're Jews. No, maybe not angry, maybe just determined. Where was I?"

"You were talking about the committee."

"Yes." The old man consulted his notes. "Yes, the committee. The third member is Mel Klein. He's in the garment business in New York, Kleinfrocks. From what Osner tells me, he's well fixed, which I guess is why they include him. Commutes every day to New York. So now you know as much about the congregation at Leighton Ridge as I do. Along with the *Shabbas* services and the high holidays, they will want a *minyan* for the mourner's *Kaddish* whenever it's required, which maybe you can escape from on occasion and maybe not. With only fourteen families, it will be mostly not."

"I've been thinking about it," David said, "and it just isn't possible that every Jewish family in that area joined the synagogue group. There must be others."

"You're absolutely right. According to Osner, there are other families. Some are mixed marriages, some are just uninterested or without any desire for religion. That's something you'll have to deal with. Maybe Lucy can teach Bible class. What kind of a family does she come from?"

"Jewish atheists."

"Still, she married a rabbi."

"She'd have to learn Bible before she could teach it."

"Why not? As long as she stays a chapter ahead. The Hebrew language instruction you'll have to do yourself — until the synagogue can afford a teacher. You still want the job?"

David nodded.

"I know a dozen your age who'd run from such a prospect. You want it, you got it."

"If they'll have me."

"They'll have you. There's no contest, David, no volunteers, no one else pleading for the job."

But when David spelled it out for Lucy that evening, after dinner at her parents' apartment, she looked at him in anguish and whispered, "Do you know what we're getting into?"

"Not exactly. But neither did I know what I was getting into in the service."

"This isn't the service, David. The war's over. And why do they want me to teach Bible class?"

"Because if you don't, I'll have to do it."

Lucy's mother, Sally, was in the kitchen, washing the dishes, and Lucy's father, Herb, was drying the dishes, and the door to the dining room was far from soundproof.

"Are you listening?" Herb whispered to Sally.

"I'm not listening and don't interfere."

"You heard."

"Don't interfere."

"She's your daughter, too. Not like we got seven kids. We got a daughter. One, period."

"So we got a daughter. She's married two weeks and already you want her divorced."

"That's nonsense. I don't want her divorced."

"Thank God. Just go out and find a boy like David."

"That," Herb whispered hoarsely, "is why my daughter has to live like a peasant in some godforsaken wilderness called Leighton Ridge."

"It's not a wilderness. It's a beautiful place only sixty-two miles from New York."

"How do you know?"

"Because I looked it up!" Sally whispered fiercely.

"So this girl brings home her date, and the father asks him what he does for a living and he says he's a rabbi, and the mother says, What kind of work is that for a nice Jewish boy?"

"That's disgusting," Sally said.

"It's just a Jewish joke."

"It's stupid, and do you know, I think most Jewish jokes are stupid, and as far as you're concerned, Herb Spendler, just don't interfere. Leave them alone."

In the dining room, Lucy asked plaintively, "Would you have married me, David, if you knew I never read the Bible? Worse, until Rabbi Belsen married us, I had never set foot in a synagogue."

"That wasn't a synagogue. That was Rabbi Belsen's study. And I knew Herb and Sally were atheists."

"It didn't upset you?"

"No. Should it?"

"I don't even know the difference between a synagogue and a rabbi's study."

"You'll learn. Meanwhile, we need a car."

"You really want me to teach Bible class?"

"It's good stuff, battles, orgies, adultery, onanism, love stories — "

"What's onanism?"

"First you read it, then we'll talk about it."

"You talk like the Bible's a study in pornography."

"And other things. The point is that the Jewish chroniclers who put it down spared no person and no act. They put it down the way it was. Of course, in the translation it's gussied up, and instead of saying he went to bed with her, they say he had knowledge of her, but you'll soon learn your way around."

Lucy's mother and father returned to the dining room at that point with cake and coffee, and Herb could not resist saying, "With fourteen families, Dave, suppose five of them resign? Bang. You're out of business."

"You're right. I have to find some backup."

"But first things first," he told Lucy, and the next day they went looking for a car. They ended up at Honest Joe Fierello's lot on West Fifty-second Street. Honest Joe had a cherubic face that inspired trust, and he had a two-door 1940 Chevy that could be had for two hundred dollars. "A hundred dollars a door," he told them, showing that he had a sense of humor as well as a sense of piracy. "Nineteen forty," he explained, "was the last year they made a good car, and compared to the garbage they're turning out today, this little beauty is a work of art, just raring to go. They don't make them like this anymore."

The newlyweds rode off in the small work of art, Lucy driving and David observing her carefully.

"Doesn't look too hard," he said.

"No, once you get the shifting sorted out and you're able to relax. Where to?"

"Let's look at our destiny, as long as we have wheels."

"Leighton Ridge?"

"Right. Do you know how to get there?"

"David," Lucy said, "I haven't the vaguest notion. I thought you weren't due there for another three days."

"It won't hurt to see what we're getting into."

"It may just mean losing a brand-new wife," Lucy said, "but if that's what you want and you're ready to risk it, we'll stop at a gas station and pick up a map of Connecticut."

They drove through the Bronx to the Hutchinson River Parkway, following it until it became the Merritt Parkway, and then turned north at the Black Rock Turnpike. They drove past a beautiful reservoir, miles along the reservoir's edge, and then the road climbed to the backbone of the Connecticut Ridge. It was lovely country, at its best now in the new spring, farms and spreading lawns and white Colonial houses. Finally, a small roadside sign told them that they were entering Leighton Ridge, and a few miles farther on, they were at the small common, which was surrounded by an old white Congregational church and three white clapboard houses, each with a center chimney to validate its antiquity.

"What a strange and lonely place," Lucy whispered. "We're a thousand miles from anywhere."

David was thinking differently, looking at a place as calmly beautiful as any he had ever seen, a village lost in time, clinging to a past that was gone forever, but clinging gently and without rancor. His conscience troubled him, this appeared to be such secure, safe harbor; but he felt that through the war years he had paid his entry fee to a secure, safe harbor, at least for a while, at least for long enough to work off dues paid. Yet —

"I don't have to take it," he said to Lucy, trying to sound light and indifferent. "Something else is bound to come along in the city, and Rabbi Belsen will understand."

"Oh, no, I didn't mean it that way. I'm not backing out of it."

"You're sure?"

"Of course I'm sure, David. You know how it is — where thou goest, I goest. I love the city, but that's where I've lived all my life. You have to give me time. This is a very new scene."

"All the time in the world."

She drove slowly through the township along winding roads, most of them unpaved except for oiled dirt. They parked for a few minutes in front of an apple orchard in blossom. The trees were perfumed balls of snow-white blossoms, a soft rain of petals dropping to the ground whenever a breeze touched them.

"Do you know where any of your congregation live?" Lucy asked him. "We might drop in on one of these strange Jews who live in a place like this."

He shook his head. He didn't like the notion of dropping in. Before the war, like Lucy, he had been a city boy.

They were staying with Lucy's parents at that time, sleeping in Lucy's old bedroom. The day after they had driven up to Leighton Ridge, they had a telephone call from Jack Osner, the president of the congregation.

"Rabbi Hartman?" he asked, his deep, aggressive voice placing him in an immediate adversary position.

David resisted the impulse to say "Yo!" After all, it had been Colonel Jack Osner. He contained himself and said, "Yes, this is Rabbi Hartman."

"Glad to talk to you, Rabbi. I understand everything has been cleared at the Institute and you're ready to put your head in the lion's mouth."

"Well, I wouldn't think of it precisely in those terms."

"No, of course. We are the most puny lion in the state of Connecticut. But we're all eager to meet you. When can we expect you?"

"I still have a few things to clear up."

"Before June, we hope."

"Oh, absolutely. Say three days."

"Good, good. Now we have a house for you, nothing very grand, but it's a roof over your head, an old Colonial building, dates back to seventeen seventy-one. We've been trying to get your home into shape and neglecting the synagogue in the process. But the congregation's so small, we can hold services for a while in various living rooms. You wouldn't object to that?"

"Oh, absolutely not."

"Do you have furniture? I hear you've just been married."

"I have my mother's furniture, yes. She passed away recently."

"Sorry to hear that. You'll have all our condolences. Tell you what, Rabbi. You'll have a fairly small kitchen, small dining room, living room, and two bedrooms. So plan your furniture to fit. All small rooms, I'm afraid. Best thing to do will be for you and your bride to come to our house early, say about noon. My wife — her name is Shelly — she'll show you around and you'll get a feel of the place. Have dinner with us, and we'll have a meeting of the committee after dinner and we'll put you up for the night. Order your furniture trucked out here the following day. How does that sound?"

"It sounds all right," David said.

"Then we'll see you on Wednesday. I'll send you a map for directions."

Standing beside David, Lucy heard Osner's booming voice without effort, and when the conversation was over, she said to David, "How does he dare talk to you like that?"

David shrugged. "After all, he was a colonel. I was a lowly captain."

"Hah!" Lucy snorted. "A colonel indeed! Judge Advocate! He probably had a snug warm desk somewhere in Washington and spent the war comfortably stateside on his fat salary." And then she added, "On his fat backside."

David regarded his wife with new interest. "Of course, we

don't know that he has a fat backside, but you know, Lucy, Rabbi Belsen gave me a lecture on diplomacy where our congregation is concerned. We have to try to love them all, and where it's impossible, we endure them patiently and with some grace."

"I thought that was Christianity, that business about loving your enemy."

"They're not our enemies, no one in the congregation. Anyway, they got it from us — the Christians, I mean, this love-your-enemy thing. Will you try, with Osner?"

"Love him? Come on, David."

"Like him. Try to understand why he does what he does. Also, he may be a very nice guy."

"Maybe so. In Macy's window."

"You're a strange gal for a rabbi's wife," David admitted.

"I get that feeling. David, you married a guttersnipe. Here you are, a beautiful guy and a rabbi, and I tell you that if Osner's a great guy, I'll kiss your ass in Macy's window."

"Rest easy. I know about Macy's window."

"Still love me?"

"Rest assured."

The following Tuesday, with David driving, having squeezed two driving lessons into two days, and Lucy carefully charting their progress on the map Osner had sent them, they managed to locate Jack Osner's home in Leighton Ridge. It was an old but large renovated farmhouse on a narrow, winding dirt road. Evidently, Shelly Osner had been expecting them to arrive at a later hour. In their desire to be on time, they had left New York early. Shelly Osner was slightly annoyed to be caught in an old skirt and sweater, but she tried to be both hospitable and pleasant as she explained that she had not expected them before twelve, and would they please forgive her? She was a tall, large-boned, good-looking woman, with light hair and blue eyes, and it was plain that she did not know what to make of this young rabbi and his pretty wife.

"Anyway," she explained, leading them into the living

room, "it's my fault, because it's eleven forty-five and I should have been showered and changed by now, and I mean it as a compliment, but you don't look much like a rabbi."

"I guess it depends on what you expect," David said awkwardly.

"Oh? Oh, yes. Well, do make yourself comfortable here while I shower and change. Martin will be here any moment. Please get the door when he rings."

"She's a dope," Lucy whispered when Shelly had gone upstairs. "Don't look much like a rabbi! She must take stupid pills every morning. Myself, I must have been taking invisible pills. She didn't even know I was here."

"She's trying hard to be nice. She's flustered."

"All over you."

"And you respond by being the sweet, pleasant person I know you to be."

"Absolutely. And who's Martin? She doesn't go into details. That's not her husband, is it?"

"No. Her husband's Jack. Just be patient. We'll soon see."

Immobile patience was not for Lucy. She prowled around the living room, a large comfortable place that had been created by knocking down walls and putting two rooms of the old farmhouse together.

"Whoever did it has a kind of taste," Lucy admitted. "It's got that museum look. Maybe she has a brain in her head."

The doorbell rang. Since no one else appeared, Lucy went to answer it. There on the doorstep stood a tall, skinny man of about forty or forty-two, straw-colored hair, a bony face, very pale blue eyes, and a long chin. He wore a turtleneck sweater under an old jacket, and he regarded Lucy quizzically but with pleasant admiration.

"I'm Martin Carter," he said, "and you must be Lucy Hartman, and that must be the rabbi, there behind you."

"Bingo," Lucy admitted. "You know everything about us. What about you?"

Reaching past Lucy, David shook hands with the man, who

said quickly, "Forgive me. I thought they told you. I'm Carter, the Congregational minister here in Leighton Ridge."

They all moved into the living room, and from above, Shelly Osner called down, "Martin, introduce yourself and explain. I'll be down in two shakes of a lamb's tail."

"What's to explain?" David wondered.

"Depends on how much they told you. I mean about the synagogue?"

"Only that it's falling apart," Lucy put in.

"Oh, yes. I'm afraid so, except that the roof doesn't leak, which is a positive note. You see, it's a hundred and seventy years old, give or take a few years." And seeing the expression on David's face, he added hastily, "No, they didn't tell you. We sold them the old Congregational church. I mean, to your committee. It's a very good buy, you know, comes with eight acres and adjoins the old parsonage."

"You mean they bought your church to use as a synagogue?"

"I do hope that doesn't break some law or synagogue ruling or anything of that sort. I was sure they investigated, and you know, it was a very important lesson for our congregation. You would have hoped that after the war and all that went with it, there'd be some understanding among my people of what anti-Semitism actually is. Not so. I had to preach a real hellfire and brimstone sermon — which is not my style at all — to break down the resistance of two of the deacons."

"No, there's nothing wrong with it," David said. "Churches become synagogues, and synagogues become churches. It's been going on for a long time. I just didn't know about it. Of course, I'm very new. And I suppose the parsonage is where we'll live?"

"Much better shape than the church, thank heavens. I'm sure you know a good deal about Congregationalists, Rabbi — "

"I'm sure he does," Lucy put in. "I don't."

"Well, we must all have a good long talk about that one day, perhaps an interfaith service of some kind. You know, Mrs. Hartman, we're the closest thing to your faith in Protestantism. Not that that doesn't leave a wide gulf, but we are the direct descendants of the Puritans, and we've marched with some pretty good banners. We came into being in a jailhouse in fifteen sixty-six, but that's a long story for another time. Meanwhile, welcome to Leighton Ridge, and anything I can do to smooth things over — well, just let me know."

At that moment, Shelly Osner appeared, dressed now in a bright plaid skirt and a white cashmere sweater set. "Martin, have you bothered with names? Rabbi Hartman is David Hartman, and his wife is Lucy."

"Done. Thought of it the moment I entered."

"And now, for heaven's sake, don't scare them off. We've had enough trouble finding a rabbi. Shall we take my car or yours?"

"Yours is larger," Carter said.

David was watching Lucy. He was intrigued by the fact that he knew absolutely nothing at all about this girl he had married, and even more intrigued by the amount he was learning and the speed at which he was amassing this knowledge. He was aware of her distaste for people who talked across her, and he wondered whether he would have to live with the fact of Lucy and Shelly Osner as intractable antagonists. Martin Carter was another matter entirely, and David had met and lived with, during his time in the army, enough Protestant ministers to understand that the cheerful, good-sport, playing-field manner was almost a part of their training, less a self-imposed image than an actual segment of character. Yet it failed to be a statement of Martin Carter's inner self. On this first contact, David liked him, but David did not easily exercise dislike. When there was some question of character, he would advise himself, rather sternly, to wait and see.

Rolling along in the car, David in back with Lucy and Carter in the front seat with Shelly Osner, who was driving,

Carter said, "Forgive me if I come off like some sort of tour-guide bore, but since they didn't bother to tell you that your synagogue is our old church, I can't imagine that they bothered to tell you much of anything about Leighton Ridge."

"Truthfully, my coming here was all done very quickly through Rabbi Belsen, who's in charge of placement at the Institute. He was my prof in comparative religion when I was a student there, and when one asked him a question, he would sometimes say, 'Go find the answer. God gave you eyes and brains. Use them.' I suppose he took the same attitude about my appointment here."

"And did you inform yourself?"

"Not very much, no. I found out that Captain Leighton had been given this place as a royal grant some years before the American Revolution. Not much more."

"There isn't very much more, you know, except that we do have the reputation of being the most New England town in Fairfield County, that is, in the picture postcard sense: beautiful old Colonial buildings, amazing stone walls, and an absolutely delightful landscape, except in winter, when it turns monstrous."

"Oh, the winters aren't so bad," Shelly said. "Great for snuggling down under the covers and doing what one does under the covers."

Carter laughed.

"Silly bitch," Lucy whispered into David's ear.

"Population just about four thousand," Carter went on. "A mixed bag, some families who have had their holdings since the old, old days — I might mention that once there was a good deal of small manufacturing here on the Ridge, using our plentiful water power, but when electricity came in, that washed out. No more manufacturing, but people live here who have plants in Danbury. Some commuters to New York, some young folks, writers, artists, potters, people who don't have to commute, a very mixed bag, and a good shot of bigotry thrown in. We're famous for our book-burning, which comes about almost yearly when some righteous, pious citizen finds something in his child's textbook that he objects to. Then he raises the very devil, and demands that the book be removed. And then practically the whole town packs into the new church — the largest hall in town — hanging from the rafters so as to speak, and we go at it hammer and tongs."

"That sounds pretty healthy," David said.

"It is. We're pretty well split down the middle, and that keeps the mental hoodlums in line."

"Why did you sell the old church?" David wondered.

"Not big enough. Also, not stylish enough for the current congregation. You know, David — you don't mind if I call you that, and you must call me Martin — people have very rigid ideas about the past. One of them is that all New England Congregational churches were built without steeples. Well, most were, because a congregation of stiff-necked Puritans regarded the steeple as part of a Papist plot to undermine Congregationalism. Some of these early churches wouldn't even permit a cross in their church, or permit it to be called a church. It was a meeting house. Well, a group of that persuasion built our old church in seventeen seventy-three. They had come over here from Rhode Island, where the citizens had permitted the construction of a small Catholic church as well as a Jewish synagogue, and when they built our church, they abjured the steeple and built a small boxlike affair instead. Well, my current congregation wanted a steeple — as they put it, a proper church steeple. Anyway, the old meeting house was too small. It can hold two hundred people, but only if they're squeezed in like sardines."

Yet when they pulled up in front of the building, David was struck by the simple beauty of the old church or meeting house. There was a sort of magical relationship between wall and window, and, strangely, one did not miss the steeple.

"It's a good, solid structure," Carter said. "It's framed with six-by-six oak beams — " He opened the door and let them file in, and then pointed to the beamed ceiling. "There, you can see the beams. No rot. Of course, it needs painting and new glass where the windows are boarded over, and you might want to do a few things inside, but essentially, it's all there."

"It's a fine building," David admitted. He had been a bit anxious over the possibility that there might be stained glass windows, but there were none, and he said softly, "Very *frum*, those who built it. Very *frum* indeed."

"Oh?"

"*Frum* — means very Orthodox, very strict in observance of the law. The old folks in the old country were *frum*. They would have looked upon me, a rabbi of the Reform movement, as an agent of the devil."

"I imagine the people who built this place were not so different," Carter said. "Very *frum*, as you put it. Proper. In our new church, we have a large brass cross behind the altar and a very healthy steeple. So you can imagine what my Puritan ancestors would have thought of that."

"*Frum*," Shelly said. "What an interesting word."

"As if she never heard it before," Lucy said under her breath, marching up the aisle to the altar. "Can we use this?" she asked David. "This old church. Is it proper?"

"The *bimah* is all right. And the altar? Proper? Sure, why not?"

"*Bimah?*"

"The step up. The platform at the front."

"I'm getting an interesting education."

"And I'm getting chilled," Shelly said.

"Just a few minutes more," Carter assured her. "I must show them the parsonage. It's small but pleasant," he assured Lucy. "Millie — that's my wife, Millicent — Millie and I would be living there, except that she's a local girl, and her parents passed away and left her their house. Big house, and we need it, with our kids." He led them across the lawn to the parsonage, a small white clapboard Colonial house; living room, dining room, and kitchen downstairs, and then narrow stairs up to three bedrooms. It was sparsely furnished with old maple and pine pieces, and there were rag rugs on the floors.

The two of them together were alone upstairs for a minute or so, and David asked Lucy what she thought of it.

"Beats me. I'm a stranger here, David."

"So am I. But I've been a stranger on earth since the first two Christian kids jumped me and beat the hell out of me. It's something you get used to, and in a way it has its advantages."

"Tell me about it some time."

"When we have more time."

"And meanwhile we worship in a Christian church and live in a Christian house and make love in a Christian bed — unless you bring up your mother's bed. This is lumpy."

"We'll bring up Mom's bed. And I don't think buildings partake of either faith or prejudice. Anyway, you're an atheist, so you shouldn't mind."

"I'm a Jewish atheist."

"Right. I'll try to remember that."

Washing for dinner that evening, in the guest bathroom of the Osner house, Lucy said to David, "Maybe I shouldn't dislike that pissy Shelly Osner so much. After all, she bounced around with us all afternoon and then got out dinner for how many?"

"Eight, I believe."

"Eight. And I'll bet it's delicious," Lucy said unhappily. "I'm a lousy cook, David. I've kept that from you because I never had to cook anything for you."

"Scrambled eggs this morning. Delicious."

"That's not cooking. And the Osners are putting us up for the night. That's kind of nice. I guess I have a lot of quick, dumb opinions."

"No. You're sensitive and you're worried. I guess I am too. I guess neither of us has ever been in a situation like this before, and if you feel that you can't hack it, tell me. It's not irreversible."

"David, they sent me down to a U.S.O. in Georgia. I spent six months there. If I could take that, I can take anything. And I kind of like that little house. I always wanted to live in a parsonage, ever since going on a Brontë bender at age fifteen. And I'll tell you something else, that sweet little house isn't insulated, and it appears to have some kind of primitive hot-air heating system, and everyone's been boasting about the wonderful cold winters — so we're going to have lots of fun trying to stay warm. Did you ever hear of bundling? That's an old New England *mishegas* I read about somewhere — "

"I think we'd better go down to dinner," David said firmly.

Having a cocktail before dinner, David and Lucy met the three men who would form the pro tem committee for the functioning of the synagogue. They also met the wives, but that was simply social necessity and not the purpose of the evening. The host and Shelly Osner's husband was a heavy-set man, Jack Osner by name, balding, mid-forties, a pair of heavy brows over small blue eyes. David had already learned that Osner had spent the war with the Judge Advocate and held the rank of colonel at discharge. He was part of a prestigious law firm, and the Osners maintained a small apartment in New York City. The two Osner children, Adam, twelve years old, and Susan, nine years old, were brought in briefly to meet the new rabbi and then disappeared. Osner brooked no nonsense around him.

"That boy has to be a *Bar Mitzvah* in about six months. You'll have your work cut out for you there, Rabbi."

Then the two other members of the pro tem committee and their wives were introduced. Joe Hurtz, about the same age as Osner, had a men's furnishing store in Danbury. His wife, Phyllis, a few years younger than he, appeared to be overly shy. She smiled and nodded and said nothing. Mel Klein was the oldest of the three, a successful dress manufacturer in New York, who kept extolling the local air and school system, as if to account for his presence there. Like Joe Hurtz, he had three children, and a bright-eyed, perky wife, Della, whom Lucy immediately liked. She was years younger than her husband — a round, pretty, and bright lady.

Dinner consisted of roast turkey and trimmings, served by a skinny, unsmiling local lady who, as Shelly explained, helped out when they had guests. The food was delicious, as was the wine served with the meal. Most of the conversation was pointed toward the rabbi, either directly or obliquely, as when Phyllis Hurtz finally spoke and informed Lucy and David that there was a kosher butcher in Danbury.

"I'm sure that's not very important for a Reform rabbi," Shelly Osner said.

"We prefer it," Lucy said loftily, which made David glance at her in astonishment.

"I hear you were with the Seventh Army," Osner said to David. "What division?"

"The Forty-fifth."

"They took quite a shellacking. Were you with them all the way?"

"When I wasn't too frightened to lift my head up. I got to love the smell of wet mud."

That drew a general round of laughter, and Osner said, "Joe and I were both in it, both of us old farts, but we both had commissions out of World War One. Just desperate for human flesh."

"I was in the D.F.B. in World War One. D.F.B. — defusing bombs. You know, a bomb or a shell comes in and it doesn't explode. At age nineteen, I was just crazy enough to volunteer for the double pay and the conviction that I was immortal."

"Very crazy," his wife said softly.

"This time, they pulled me in as a teacher. I spent the war at Fort Dix. Jack there had more sense. He spent the war at a desk in Washington."

"Someone had to. As a matter of fact," he said to David, "we have a very decent representation out of the congregation, five army, one air force."

"I don't think the rabbi wants to hear about who was in the army and who wasn't," Della Klein said. "I know this isn't a meeting — perish the thought that women should be invited to a meeting — but it is Wednesday and we've been talking about a Friday night Sabbath service, and where shall we have it and what do we need? Do we need prayerbooks? And where will Rabbi Hartman and his wife sleep? They can't sleep in that wretched parsonage with its lumpy beds, and anyway it's cold and smelly. So may I offer our guest room?"

"They'll sleep right here tonight," Shelly said firmly.

"As the mistress says," Della whispered to Lucy.

"And what about it, Rabbi," Osner asked, "could you do a *Shabbas* service Friday, day after tomorrow?"

"No reason why not," David said.

"We could have it right here," Shelly said.

"Our living room's much bigger," Della Klein said with particular emphasis. "You know everyone will come, and most will bring the kids, and then if word spreads to Redding and Ridgefield — "

"You're talking about ten Jewish families, if that."

"It could be thirty more. We might just have sixty or seventy people, and we certainly couldn't turn anyone away — could we, Rabbi?"

"I wouldn't want to — no, indeed."

"Then my house," Della Klein said decisively, looking firmly at Mrs. Osner and scoring.

"It makes sense," Osner said. "What about prayerbooks?"

"I can drive down to New York tomorrow," David said, "and pick some up."

"Would you? Wonderful. And I imagine there are other things we need, but no hurry. I'm in New York every day. As a matter of fact, no reason why I can't get the prayerbooks for you. There are at least five people in my office who spend the day doing nothing more important than taking coffee breaks."

"Perhaps I'd better go in this time," David said. "There are so many things to do. My Aunt Ana is moving into my mother's old apartment, but there are certain things there we'll need up here in the country."

"But you'll be back Friday on time?"

"Absolutely."

In bed with Lucy, in the guest room at the Osner house, David asked her how she felt about it now.

"A little better, I think. I liked Della Klein — only — what is it, David, does a certain amount of genteel charity go with this job?"

"How do you mean?"

"Her husband's in the dress business. She told me she realizes how hard it will be for us to get along on what they pay you, so I must feel free to go down there with her and pick up some dresses, on the house."

David sighed. "I suppose it comes with the territory."

"No good. But I do like her — in spite of the way she looked at you."

"Come on — how did she look at me?"

"Hungrily. I sort of like Phyllis Hurtz. But so shy. Her husband beats up on her."

"Did she tell you that?"

"Oh, no. No. He just looks like someone who would. Defusing bombs. Wow!"

"Someone has to do it."

"No work for a nice Jewish boy. Oh, the hell with the lot of them. Turn off the light and let's make love."

"Let's try to enjoy it, baby."

"Lights out."

"Starts now. Happiness at Leighton Ridge." He turned off the lamp and they both burst out laughing.

"Put on the light, David," Lucy said.

"Why?"

"I don't want to laugh in the dark. It's like smoking. No fun smoking in the dark."

David reached out, turned on the lamp by the bedside,

controlled his laughter, and asked Lucy, "Why, my love, are we laughing?" After which, he burst out laughing again.

"Because," Lucy managed to say, "the whole thing is so absolutely unbelievable. Here I am, Lucy Spendler, street-wise, smartass tough kid, product of P.S. Forty-six, Wadleigh High School, and Hunter College, the only girl on West One hundred and fifty-seventh Street who skipped five hundred and sixty loops of rope without ever snagging—"

"Five hundred and sixty? I don't believe it."

"Cross my heart and hope to die."

"Lucy, you're a rabbi's wife. No more crossing the heart."

"Then you're not supposed to call me a liar—and here I am out in this Connecticut Wasp wilderness, with all these tightass Jewish types trying to be country Wasps and pious Jews at the same time, and a husband making twenty-five dollars a week, and thank God he has a sense of humor. You know, years ago, when Pop had just started in as a printer at the *Times*, there was a point where all the copy boys were tied up, and Editorial was yelling for someone to come up and take a last-minute correction, so the printing foreman told Pop to run up to Editorial and get it. The editor, his name was Schiller or something like that, had scribbled out a paragraph to replace the one he had written before. Terrible handwriting, according to Pop. 'Mr. Schiller,' Pop said to him, 'can I tell you a story? It'll only take a minute.' Schiller said okay, and Pop then told Schiller his favorite printer story. It seems that when Horace Greeley was editor of the *Tribune*, there was only one old grizzled printer who could read his handwriting and set up his editorials. Of course, that was before the Linotype and everything was set by hand. So one day, the other printers took a chicken, dipped his feet in ink, and walked him back and forth over a sheet of paper. Then they gave the paper to the old printer, who wasn't in on the joke, and told him it was Mr. Greeley's editorial and he should go ahead and set it up. Well, slowly and painfully, the old man set up line after line of the chicken tracks, but finally he was stuck. So he took the paper up to Greeley, pointed to one of the chicken tracks, and said, 'Hate to interrupt you, Mr. Greeley, but that there word confounds me.' Greeley glanced at the chicken print and shouted, 'Unconstitutional, you old fool!' Now I must have heard Pop tell that story thirty times, and there was always someone broke up over it, but Pop says that Schiller never twitched a lip. He said to Pop, 'Why do you tell me this, Mr. Spendler? Is it a comment on my handwriting?' 'Oh, no, sir,' Pop said, 'I thought you'd be amused.' And Schiller said, 'Why should I be amused? Everyone knew that Greeley made a fetish of his so-called defense of the Constitution.' "

David stopped laughing and stared at his wife thoughtfully. "Are you going to tell me why you decided to tell me this strange story at midnight in this Connecticut wilderness?"

"Because you're a pussycat."

"That's a sort of compliment, I guess, but not a reason."

"You'll figure it out. You're pretty smart."

"Thank you."

"Do you want to turn me in? Do they have Jewish annulments?"

"Not tonight. You'd have to buy your way out, but tell me, Lucy, didn't it ever bother you, having absolutely no religion?"

She thought about it for a long moment. "I don't think it ever really bothered me. There were times when I felt a little left out of things, but the anti-Semitic kids on the block, the Irish and Italian kids — they beat up on me the same as on the Orthodox kids, and of course I didn't go around telling kids my mom and pop were atheists."

"It didn't trouble you — God, death, the universe?"

"I think men brood over those things. Women have enough sense to manage the business of living day by day."

"You know," David said to her, "you puzzle me."

"A woman should. That's what Mom told me. Keep your

secrets and see that he has enough changes of socks and under-wear."

"You're one of the most decent, straightforward, and ethi-cal persons I've ever known — "

"I'd much rather you said I was beautiful."

"That too. Absolutely."

"Then can we turn off the light and make love?"

He reached out and turned off the light. "Coming back to the city with me tomorrow?" he asked her.

"No. I'm going to clean up the parsonage and see whether people can live there."

"People have."

"So they say. No more talk, David."

David left Leighton Ridge early the next morning, enough of a neophyte driver to enjoy navigating the narrow, twisting Connecticut lanes. By the time he reached the Black Rock Turnpike, on his way to the Merritt Parkway, he felt relaxed and assured. In New York, he discovered that the prayer-books had increased in price since before the war. The money the congregation had provided would buy thirty books, which he felt would be ample, in spite of the enthusiasm at the dinner table the night before.

It was a glorious, cool, and sunny spring day, the trees in Central Park bursting into blossom. The people out on the crowded streets on this typically New York spring day had to experience the sun and cool air before it disappeared. His Aunt Ana, his mother's widowed sister, had moved from her wretched hotel room into his mother's apartment on West End Avenue. She could barely manage the rent out of her small trust fund and Social Security, yet she begged David to let her hold on to the apartment. It was not large; she had always loved it; and it had a single window from which you could see the Hudson River.

"Of course you can have it," David assured her. "And if you need money, you must let me know." Although what help he might be in that area he couldn't imagine.

"You'll want the furniture," she said wistfully.

"Absolutely not. Only the bed and the chest in my room. And perhaps some dishes and pots."

"I have plenty of those," she said with relief. "That's all in Martha's basement." Martha was the third sister. "But I sold my furniture. I was such a fool, such beautiful things. But tell me, David, I hear already you have a congregation and a synagogue. Isn't that wonderful, just out of the army and it should happen so quickly. Your mother, may she rest in peace, would be so happy." Ana was a small woman, with a round, pudgy face. Her eyes filled with tears as she spoke about David's mother. "For her to walk into a synagogue and see her son on the *bimah* — a big synagogue, I'm sure. I hear the German Jews built wonderful synagogues there a hundred years ago."

"In Hartford and New Haven, Aunt Ana. Not in Leighton Ridge. The congregation bought an old Congregational church."

"A church, David?"

"It's a small wooden building. They didn't buy the religion, Aunt Ana, just the building."

"It's a sin, David. It's wrong."

"Aunt Ana, believe me, it's not a sin. You remember Rabbi Belsen. He's a very important rabbi and scholar at the Institute. I'm going to telephone him and let you talk to him — just so that you won't think I'm doing something pretty awful."

He watched his aunt as she had her telephone conversation with Rabbi Belsen. At a point, she began to cry again. "He's a sweet man," she told David. "He said such nice things about your mother."

David spent the rest of the day packing dishes and pots. One of the congregation, Moe Saberson by name, had a large appliance store in Bridgeport, and he had offered to send down his truck and his two large sons, age seventeen and age fourteen, to take care of moving the bed, chest, and dishes from New York to the parsonage. For all of the fact that he was being paid on the scale of an itinerant cotton picker in the most backward state of the South, David had the additional bonus of being surrounded by people who desired to solve his every problem. Of course, the only problems that had arisen so far were either financial or logistical, but at least some of them had been solved. And the day had been so wonderful, in terms of the weather, and he was so deeply in love with his new wife and so delighted with the challenge of Leighton Ridge that nothing could dull his exhilaration.

And underlining everything every day was the enormous fact that the monstrous, unspeakable war that had gone on for endless years was over.

He stayed with his aunt in his old bedroom that night, and the following morning he loaded the prayerbooks into the car and started off for Leighton Ridge. Just inside the Leighton line, a policeman in a patrol car waved him over.

"You've lost one of the screws off your rear license plate," the officer said.

"Oh? Sorry. Will I lose the plate?"

"It'll hold. There's a service station up the road. They'll put another bolt onto it."

When he told Lucy, she shook her head hopelessly. "It's my fault, David. I shouldn't have let you go. You're not entitled to drive alone until you have a license, which you don't have, but that cop looks at honest faces. You do have an honest face, sort of. Well, come let me show you." She had scrubbed the little house clean. "Della Klein came by; otherwise I would have been marooned here. She took me shopping. Four miles to a proper grocery store and butcher — would you believe that? The girl's dear. I don't care if she looks at you the way she does. Anyway, she's happily married."

Lucy had roasted a chicken for dinner that night, and with it she put out baked potatoes, string beans, salad, pickles. In the dining room, there was a Pembroke table as old as time and four rickety chairs.

"Ware chairs," she explained.

"How do you know that?"

"Millie Carter stopped by. That's the parson's wife. I've got to rethink my whole life in this crazy place, David. To me, the parson's nose was always the turkey's ass. Anyway, Ware chairs are old and important, and this Millie Carter's a knockout. You're going to flip over her; one of those tall, skinny blond types, short hair and smart as a whip. Nice. She brought home-baked bread and pie. She decided we were both sold into theological bondage before the age of reason, but we're survivors. She's got two kids, and he only makes twice what you do. And by the way, they heard about you doing the first service tonight, and they want to come and bring a few friends. I told them it was all right. It is, isn't it?"

"I don't see why not," David said. "But you know, I don't have a real sermon. I've only made a few notes."

"You'll be great."

"How do you know? You never heard me preach."

"I love you. That's enough for me."

"I wish it were enough for me."

Someone was knocking at the front door, and when Lucy opened it, there was Mel Klein, fat, bald, perspiring, and wiping his face with a large handkerchief.

"Sit down. I'm just cutting Millie Carter's pie. Carrot pie. I never heard of it before, but it's delicious."

"I'll have a piece of pie. Fine. I haven't even eaten. Good *Shabbas*, Rabbi. First time. I feel real good about that, but on the other hand we have a large problem."

"Coffee?"

"Yes. Sure."

"What's the problem?" David asked him.

"I'll give it to you quickly, because we have just under an hour to work it out. I offered my house because our living room is big, seventeen feet wide, thirty feet long. That's pretty big for up here on the Ridge, where the old houses have small rooms. Well, we got ten dining room chairs, eight bridge chairs, some kitchen chairs, and the couches and stuff. I figured Joe and Jack could bring some more bridge chairs. We got fourteen families. Even with all the kids and if everyone turns up, that's got to be less than sixty people. But look what happened. It's the way the war winds up. The kids come out of the service, they get married, and they find a place up here in Connecticut, and most of them know which way is up and they're looking for a Reform synagogue. And there aren't any — no closer than New Haven. So let me tell you what's happening, Rabbi. Freddy Cohen, he's got this mechanized garden thing, and he works over in Ridgefield and Wilton. He spread the good word, and he thinks we'll have at least twenty from there — if they don't spread the word. Four families in Redding and three in Brookfield. Could we say no to them?"

"Absolutely not," David said.

"And Herbie Nathan — he's got this army surplus store in Westport — he's been spreading the word to everyone who comes in there. He got an old copy of *Yank* with a story about you, Rabbi, and he tacked it up on the wall of his store, and he figures we could get anywhere from twenty to thirty out of Westport and Norwalk. But let me tell you something, if those clowns figure they're getting a free ride right down the line, they're mistaken. They got to join and pay their dues. And now listen to this, Jack Osner's got a partner in his firm lives in Greenwich. Greenwich, Connecticut. I didn't know there was a Jew alive living in Greenwich. But there it is, and this Greenwich type is coming with five people. He got very exact directions from Jack. So now tell me, what do we do with maybe a hundred and fifty or two hundred people?"

"That's wonderful," David said. "That's absolutely wonderful."

"It's wonderful. What about my living room? I feel I'm a good Jew, but that still can't squeeze a hundred and fifty people into my living room."

"We'll use the church."

Mel Klein shook his head slowly, wiping the perspiration

from the folds in his neck. "David, you're a nice boy and I like you. Impractical — that's a rabbi's privilege. We can't use the church. We don't own it."

Lucy slipped away from the table. Confused, David asked, "Why? We bought it."

"We bought it. Which means we signed a contract and put down ten percent. The same with this house. How could we know how long it would be before we found a rabbi? All right. We found you and we set a closing date. Monday, three days away. All right, you and Lucy are maybe sleeping here tonight. No big *tzimmes*. But if we put two hundred Jews into a church we don't own, Arnold Sloan and Charles Winter are going to blow their tops."

"Who are Arnold Sloan and Charles Winter?"

"Two of the coldest *farbissener* anti-Semites you ever ran into. Also, they're deacons in Carter's church."

"Deacons in the church? But why?"

"Because Carter is a remarkable man, and he plays the game the way England does, a proper balance of power. When we proposed to buy the church and the parsonage, Sloan and Winter fought him tooth and nail, claiming that we were opening the door for the anti-Christ, whatever the hell that is, and give us an inch and we take a foot and before you know it, the whole Ridge will be crawling with kikes. That's the word he used, and when Marty Carter exploded, Winter — has the biggest estate on the Ridge — Winter says he was down in Washington and Truman used the same word for the lice who infest New York, and if the President of the United States can talk that way, he has the same privilege. That's why we can't use the church until we close, because Winter would like nothing more than to call the cops and empty the building in the middle of the service."

"Could he do that?" David asked.

"Why not? It's his building."

Lucy came back into the room and told them she had telephoned Martin Carter.

"When did you get a phone?" Klein asked, puzzled, nodding his approval of Lucy.

"Today. Martin will be here in a few minutes."

When Carter arrived, David summed up the situation. "I think that's great," Carter said. "My word, it's like an act of faith. Two hundred people! David, we only hit that figure on Christmas and Easter."

"I don't think it'll ever happen again. But can he break up the service and order us out of the church?"

"He cannot!" Carter answered angrily. "There are other deacons. He has one vote. Sloan has one vote. We have outvoted them twenty times, but even if they outvoted me, I would take it to the congregation. We are a Congregational church, not a tool of bigots and fools!"

"And if he comes in and raises hell?" Klein asked.

"I'll be there. My word, Mel, if there's one pledge I made to myself, it's that Leighton Ridge will not become another Greenwich."

"And how did you get the telephone?" David was asking Lucy. "Other people wait for weeks."

"The perks of the cloth, Millie calls it. Tell them it's for the rabbi and they hustle it right along."

Klein was worrying about the lights. "If there's no electricity in there, Marty?"

"It's there. You get back home and start sending your people over this way, and David and I will take care of the church."

Lucy found a bucket, some old towels, soap, and two brooms. Martin was still sweeping the aisle while David and Lucy worked frantically to get some of the loose dirt off the pews, when the first of the congregants began to arrive. All three gave up and went into the tiny parson's refuge or study — too imposing a word for a room seven feet square.

"You'll want it lit, won't you?" Carter asked. "The sun will be setting in about fifteen minutes or so."

"Oh, yes — yes, indeed. Lucy, I forgot about the prayer-books. In the trunk of the car."

Lucy dashed off for the prayerbooks. Carter switched on the lights. Jack Osner joined them in the parson's refuge, where he picked up on Klein's worries about Congregational objections.

"You're all my guests," Carter told him. "There will be no objections."

David was unfolding his robe. Osner held it for him to slip his arms into the sleeves, and then he put a small velvet cap on and placed his prayer shawl, his *tallis*, over his shoulders. He felt strange, divorced from himself, outside himself, watching apart from even himself as more and more people crowded into the already crowded parson's refuge, Lucy to assure him that the prayerbooks were being distributed, Joe Hurtz to report a count — two hundred and eleven people and more coming, every pew in the little church packed solid — Della Klein asking for more prayerbooks. There were no more. Shelly Osner squeezed into the tiny room, surveyed David, and told him that he looked positively beautiful. David, smiling, uneasy, kept nodding.

"I think he ought to be alone," Mel Klein said, with surprising sensitivity. "Let's give him a few minutes alone."

Then they emptied the room, and David drew a deep breath, and then another and another. He said in a whisper, "I am a priest of the dead." He had taken time that morning, before returning to Connecticut, to write a three-page sermon, and now he took it out of his pocket, glanced at it, and then crumpled it and threw it away. Then he walked out onto the *bimah*, the little platform at the front of the old church, and said, almost harshly, "We will begin with the greeting to the Sabbath. We have too few prayerbooks, so try to share them." He looked at a sea of faces, and wondered what was wrong with him. Almost all of them were young, the kids he knew and had known for years, at Fort Dix, in England, in France, who had come here from all over Fairfield County because they heard there was a rabbi in Leighton Ridge and because it was Captain David Hartman of the 45th Infantry Division, and because someone had stuck up an old story from

Yank on the wall of an army surplus store. Inwardly, he groaned, Oh, shit! Why that damned story? And then he recalled, all in a flash, the time Colonel Patman informed him that he was going to put him in for an M.O.H., and he had lost his temper and called the colonel names that could have replaced the medal with the stockade; and now here he was in Connecticut, conducting a Jewish Sabbath service in an old Congregational church that was packed with young ex-G.I.s and their wives, and the whole thing became so ludicrous that he almost burst out laughing, which he knew he would have done had Lucy been there to meet his eyes; and yet it would not have been laughter-funny but laughter-what-am-I-doing-in-this-insane-world?

He felt better after that passage of inner turmoil. Tonight was properly primitive; no choir, no sanctuary, no hand-inscribed roll of the Torah, the five holy books of Genesis, Exodus, Leviticus, Numbers, and Deuteronomy; only himself and the congregation, the parson's podium, and a silver goblet of wine. And when at last it came time for him to speak, to preach, David said:

"My dear friends, I was going to plead time and the pressures of these past few days as a reason for not writing a sermon, but it would not be a good thing for me to begin a rabbinate with a deception. I did write a sermon of sorts, but it was no good, and I threw it away because it said nothing of real meaning or importance. I am not sure that I will ever learn how to say things of real meaning and importance, but I'm only twenty-nine years old, and that's no time to give up hope, is it?"

They were grinning at him. His manner was gentle and deferential and sweet, and he appeared to be totally unaware of how gentle and sweet it was.

"So, if you will, instead of a sermon I would like to tell you something about myself and how I came to be here. That's important. I don't want to have any secrets." He looked around the old church. "I feel somehow that we're in a good place. Congregations have sat and given thanks to the Almighty in this church for almost two centuries, and from what I've been able to learn, those old Puritans were not so different from us. So, if you will, we will thank them for their gift of a house of God — just a moment of silent prayer."

He closed his eyes for a few seconds, and when he opened them, the congregation had quieted and there was not even a rustle of sound from the children.

"I went to the Institute," David continued, "not because I had a calling, as the Christians say, but because my mother, may she rest in peace, desired it so ardently. It was a good education, and my mother was a widow and quite ill. I had to face that fact, and I decided that after the seminary I'd put in a few more years of school and become a physician or a teacher, which was the way my thoughts went at the time.

"The war intervened. I enlisted and broke my mother's heart. But there are enough of you in this congregation wearing that funny little pin which we call a 'ruptured duck' to understand what motivated me. Even today, so soon after the fact, it is becoming difficult to recall the nature of that cloud of horror that Adolf Hitler and his Nazi movement cast upon the world.

"I am not going to bore you with any account of my life in the United States Army. Suffice it to say that I was a chaplain in the Forty-fifth Division, Seventh Army, and a trail of horror and human suffering and courage and fear led us finally to a place outside Munich that was called Dachau. That was just about a year ago, on the twenty-ninth of April, nineteen forty-five. It was also an eternity ago in another world.

"I was with one of the first rifle companies that went into the place. I can't truly tell you what I saw there, as much as I might want to. There are bits and pieces of the horror, like standing at an open mass grave and staring at the stiff, naked bodies of those who had been murdered and cast there, and trying to breathe through the terrible smell of decaying flesh. Pieces of memory like that, and I still wake up at night, moaning and frightening my poor dear wife.

"But there is one part of the memory as clear and lucid as if it had happened only yesterday. With a couple of G.I.s, I was walking toward one of the prison buildings, when the liberated prisoners began to come out. They didn't come out running and leaping to greet their new freedom. They came out slowly, tentatively, as if they were afraid that this might be another grotesque trick. They were walking skeletons, inhabiting filthy striped and ragged suits, bearded, fleshless agony walking, dragging their feet, blinking.

"I stopped, and the two kids from the company who were with me, they stopped, and one of them was a Jewish kid from the Bronx who had gotten three commendations already, and he was one of those crazy, brainless kids who will go up against anything, a rifleman, and he began to cry, and through his tears, muttering, shit, shit, shit — and I say those words here in this house of God because if there is a God, he will understand that prayer, because it was a prayer — and we just stood, watching them and waiting. They came up to us and stopped, and we could smell the stale, unwashed odor of their bodies and clothes, and because we were what we were, American kids full of clean, we moved back away from them.

"And then one of them, a small man, skin and bones and bloodshot eyes trying to weep, pointed a shaking finger at the Star of David I wore on my blouse. He tried to speak, but couldn't. Then another said, '*Zeit yir a rebbe? Zeit yir a Yid?*' Are you a rabbi or simply a Jew? My Yiddish isn't very good, but my German is better, and I told them that I was a rabbi and an army chaplain. Then they gathered around me, close, these poor, emaciated people, touching me, calling a dumb, twenty-eight-year-old American kid *abba*, the Hebrew word for father. Goodman, the Jewish kid from the Bronx, was still crying, and the other kid with me, who wasn't Jewish, he was crying too, and then one of the men, one of the concentration camp men, he said to me, in Yiddish, 'Please, Rabbi, please,

will you say the *Kaddish* with us for the dead?' For the benefit
of Reverend Carter and his friends here with us tonight, the
Kaddish is an ancient prayer spoken for the dead. It is not easy
for me to talk about this, so I will only say that I took out my
tallis, put it over my shoulders, and I led them in the *Kaddish*.
It was then that I put aside other things and became a rabbi.
So if you will permit me, I will ask you to join me in saying
the *Kaddish* — for the dead in Dachau, Auschwitz, Treblinka,
and all the other places of killing that the Nazis made."

PART TWO
1948

His first death in Leighton Ridge, his first funeral. It was a withered little lady of seventy-nine years, the grandmother of Alan Buckingham's wife, Dora. She had been a shy, silent creature. While Buckingham was one of the fourteen original organizers of the synagogue, he had never been active in synagogue affairs, and after the first few weeks of David's tenure, he ceased to come to Friday night or Saturday morning services. His wife, Dora, however, rarely missed one or another of the weekend services, always bringing the old lady with her, and now and then her children: Jed, who was eight, and Jonathan, eleven. Dora was a tall, slender woman with bangs across a round face and deep, dark blue eyes. The Buckinghams lived in a lovely old Colonial house, which they had restored, and which Dora had furnished with such love and attention to detail that to David it felt more like a museum than a home. Alan Buckingham worked for a burgeoning national magazine with offices in New Haven.

When David and Lucy first met the Buckinghams, Lucy was of the opinion that Dora was not Jewish at all. "She doesn't look Jewish," Lucy decided. "She doesn't even diet, and she has to be at least five feet ten."

Through his laughter, David tried to tell Lucy that she didn't look very Jewish either.

"Don't laugh at me. And even he doesn't look a bit Jewish. I'll bet they're passing."

David stared at her, his mouth open. "That's wonderful. That's positively wonderful."

"I don't like to be laughed at. Hey, that *would* be wonderful, two of these classy Leighton Ridge Wasps trying to pass as Jews. Infiltrating."

"Infiltrating what, Lucy? Did I ever tell you about Father Joey Mulligan?"

"No."

"Funny, I should think I would have. Anyway, he was a Catholic chaplain, and the two of us were together a great deal and we became wonderful friends. He was given a parish in New Mexico, but I'm sure he'll turn up here one day. Well, the way it happened, one of the kids, a G.I., was looking for the rabbi — I think he was from the field artillery — and I tell him that I'm the rabbi, and he says that I don't look Jewish. Joey Mulligan is standing there, and he grabs this field artillery kid by the arm and says, 'I want to tell you a little story, sonny.' The kid is maybe eighteen and Joey is twenty-six, but in that army it was quite a gap.

" 'There was this Jewish feller,' Joey tells him, 'and he liked to travel, and wherever he went, he looks for the local synagogue. This time he's in Tokyo, and it takes a little time but finally he finds the local synagogue, and after the service, he goes up to the rabbi and says to him — that is, he says it to the little Japanese rabbi — "Rabbi, I'm an American Jew and I really enjoyed your service." Then the rabbi looks at him carefully and shakes his head. "You don't look Jewish," the rabbi says.' "

"That's a nice touch for Mulligan," Lucy said. "What did the kid do?"

"He asked Mulligan what he meant."

"There you are. That's why all those nice parables Jesus kept dropping around don't do Christians much good. I finished the Old Testament. I'm on the New Testament now."

Nevertheless, Lucy became quite fond of Dora Buckingham. Dora's family had come to America from Germany in the great migration of 1848. Her husband, Alan, was from an old Virginia family, Episcopalian, his marriage regarded with anger and contempt by said old Virginia family. A bad heart had kept him out of the service, and he bore this as a heavy burden of guilt and remorse, and while he had not formally become Jewish, he pressed Dora to raise their children as Jews.

It was he who approached David about his mother-in-law's impending death, and it was then that he made his position absolutely clear. "Rabbi, I'm not Jewish. I know your wife is friendly with my wife, so you probably know that, but I specify it just in case you didn't know. My wife is Jewish, so, according to Jewish law, the children are Jewish."

"You didn't have to tell me that. I did know, as a matter of fact."

"Well, that's only in passing. The main reason I am here is that my mother-in-law is dying. The doctors tell us another few weeks at the most. She knows, and she desires to be buried in the consecrated ground of a Jewish cemetery. She also knows there is no Jewish cemetery here, but she desperately wants to be buried here, close to her children and grandchildren."

"I can understand that," David agreed. "But you know, Alan, we have a very high water table here on the Ridge. You've seen what happens in a heavy rainstorm. The ground fills up like a sponge, and that's no good for a cemetery. We need a place where the water table is at least twenty feet below the surface and stays that way, and it has to be a fairly flat field — not easy to find in Leighton Ridge. Well, we found a place like that, adjoining the Episcopalian cemetery."

"Oh, yes. I know the place."

"They don't need it. They have enough burying space for the next two hundred years, and all we want is eight acres, and we're ready to pay a very good price."

"But?"

"But we're Jewish. You know, Alan, I have seen such monstrous anti-Semitism in Germany that it's hard for me to adapt to the kind of genteel dislike for Jews that I meet here."

"Like hell it's genteel."

"I looked at the town records. The Episcopalians own about nineteen acres, apart from what they use for their cemetery, and our estimate is that eight acres should see us through the next hundred years. So I took it to their rector. Do you know him?"

"Bradshaw? Yes! I have the misfortune of knowing him. That misbegotten horse's ass has been over to the house three times, trying to bring me back to the church. Oh, he's all right, I guess. He just doesn't have a brain in his head." He paused to stare at David. "He's putting you off?"

"Not so much him as the vestry. They have a treasurer, name of Sudbury, and a secretary, name of Hornblower."

"Tall, skinny cadavers with no lips — oh, yes, I know them. Always had a sneaking suspicion that Hornblower was a lapsed Jew — what is it my mother-in-law calls them?"

"Geshmat' Yid?"

"That's it. He hates Jews with a passion — deep down in the belly. Hornblower. Ten to one that was not his father's name. Sell to Jews? Over his dead body. Sudbury is something else — believes he has a mission from God never to give up an inch of church land. What does the rector say? Would he sell us the land if the vestry agreed?"

"I think so. But you said there's no way to move Sudbury and Hornblower."

"Not for ordinary mortals like you and me, Rabbi, but there are ways. My father was a very dear friend to Charley Gilbert."

"And who was Charley Gilbert?"

"Bishop Charles Gilbert, and he is. I mean he's alive and ambulatory, and top man at the Cathedral of Saint John the Divine — which sits at One hundred and tenth Street in New York and which happens to be the largest Episcopal cathedral in the world, and which thereby has a very large measure of clout. Tomorrow morning I shall drive down there, exercise charm and pleading, and bring the bishop back with me."

"You're kidding."

"Oh, no. I'm absolutely serious."

"I mean, why should Bishop Gilbert come?"

"He loves this kind of thing. Also, there's the simple matter of decency. He's a decent person. He'll come."

He came; he let a few words drop here and there; and he had a pleasant dinner with Sudbury and Hornblower and Alan Buckingham. Votes were changed; the papers were drawn up; and there was a Jewish cemetery at Leighton Ridge. And now, he, David Hartman, was presiding over the funeral of Flora Schultz, the first death, the first hole dug six feet deep into this windswept Connecticut hillside. Somehow, strangely, inexplicably, this passing away of an old woman of seventy-nine years, a passing that was like a blade of grass gently picked up and cast away by the wind, reached into him more deeply than all the deaths by violence that he had witnessed overseas. Perhaps it was the total absence of violence, the coolness and beauty of the afternoon, the trees just breaking into their first yellow-green froth of spring — whatever it was, it gave him a moment of grace, so deep and true and painful that he felt the tears well into his eyes, not for grief but simply because the universe was true at that moment. So should a person go, in the fullness of years. As it was meant to be. But that too was an illusion. The world went on outside Leighton Ridge.

And when he intoned the mourner's *Kaddish*, the moment of grace washed away and he was back at Dachau, with the skinny, starved, hollow-eyed Jewish prisoners.

At home later, Lucy said, "You did very well."

"At what?"

"I mean the funeral service, of course."

"Oh? Well, I don't know. It's not a contest, is it? You look around at the circle standing by the grave, and you wonder who is pleased and who is agonized."

"Pleased? I never knew you to be cynical before."

David shrugged. "I guess I never thought much about old. Old is a sort of nasty word in our society. Oh, what in hell am I talking about? Not with Dora and Alan. They loved the old lady."

He turned away abruptly and went up the narrow staircase to the tiny room under the eaves that he called his study. Directly outside his window was a splendid copper beech, which legend held had been planted a hundred years before by Abraham Stanford, the great Abolitionist leader and agitator, who was parson here at Leighton Ridge before he removed to Boston to head up the antislavery movement there. His presence had made Leighton Ridge briefly famous during the middle decades of the nineteenth century. Beyond the beech, two fine, high white pines framed a view across the Ridge and into the far distance. David sprawled in a chair, staring through the window and thinking thoughts that led nowhere. One old lady dies, like cut grass blown in the wind. He had been witness to a war that left fifty million human beings dead. No mind can grasp it, not the gas chambers of Adolf Hitler, not the atomic victims of Hiroshima, the burned flesh falling away from bones while they spelled out the logic of an eye for an eye with their Japanese screams of pain.

His mind was traveling that path as Lucy entered the room. She stood at the door and asked, "What is it, David?"

"What is it? Me? The world? Leighton Ridge?"

"Come on. You're so low you could eat off your shoe tops without bending." She dropped into a chair. "Maybe I can help."

"Maybe, but not likely." He managed a smile. "You were never cut out to be a rabbi's wife."

"*Rebbetsin.* I hate that word."

"Why ever did you marry me?"

"Dumbbell. I loved you."

"And now?"

"Pushy, aren't you? Now I'm settled in. We have a child

who has begun to walk very nicely, and I'm knocked up again. And I've become a prime Sunday school teacher. David, what has gotten into you?"

"I want to go to Israel." There it was, out and said.

"What?"

"A Jewish state has come into being. A Jewish army is at war with five Arab countries that outnumber them ten to one. Lucy, can you sit here in this damned Leighton Ridge and pretend that the world doesn't exist?"

"I don't pretend that it doesn't exist. I know it exists. I also know that we're connected with it, Leighton Ridge or any other place."

"You haven't heard a word I said."

"Every word. You give up your job here, leave your pregnant wife and son to scrabble as best they may — and off to Israel. Another rabbi is just what they need."

"You can be just lovely when you put your mind to it."

"Why don't you call me a nasty bitch? No one here except the two of us, and nobody lived with the United States Army as long as you did without learning a few proper Anglo-Saxon words."

"You can't understand one damned thing that happens inside of me, not my dreams, my hopes, my agonies."

"Have you ever tried to understand what happens inside of me, David? A fetus is happening inside of me. And incidentally, what would be your mission there? Join the Haganah? Fight? Kill people?"

"You know better than that."

"The strange thing is, I do. You're the gentlest man I ever met. I think that was the most important thing that made me want to marry you. War may bring out the best in some, but when you spend three years with the U.S.O., you can bet your bottom dollar that it brings out the worst in most. You really want to go to Israel?"

"I don't know. Maybe I only want to get away from here."

"There are easier ways. We can burn down the house. I'm

serious, Dave. I don't give two damns if you stop being a rabbi."

"You never did," he said with annoyance.

"So?"

"Oh, what the hell! I never could explain it to you. I've tried for two years, and that's long enough."

"Explain what!"

"Come on, come on," he said. "We're building up to a real fight. I don't want to fight with you."

"Why? Because you're a rabbi?"

"Because it only hurts. It doesn't help."

"Maybe it would help. Maybe it would help if we screamed at each other and let some pus out of the wound. You're a rabbi. I don't know what a rabbi is; I only suspect that he's supposed to reflect some aspect of civilization." She was shouting now. "Fifty million people are killed in that lousy war — fifty million — six million Jews, one third of the Jews on earth! And now again, more killing, and my husband the rabbi tells me he has to be there! For God's sake, go." She stood up and drove a finger at him. "You know something, David Hartman, this thing you and all the rest of the ministers and priests and parsons call God — this thing makes me damned uneasy!"

David sat, staring in astonishment, as Lucy stormed out of the room.

He was astonished, put off, hurt, yet absolutely intrigued by her response. He tried to remember her exact words — this thing, all right, God is a thing, this thing makes me nervous — no, damned uneasy was what she had said, and it put him back to when he was digging a hole, he and a G.I. named O'Brien. A spatter of machine gun fire had thrown them together, and when O'Brien yelled, "Dig, goddamnit, dig!" David obeyed without any discussion of rank. They dug insanely, and when they were three feet down, O'Brien said, "We don't need to go to China, Father."

David dropped his trenching tool and wiped his brow. "We

don't call rabbis father. My name is Dave Hartman."

"Lewis O'Brien."

"Catholic?"

"Not even lapsed, Rabbi. Begging your pardon, I spit when I hear the word. I have resigned. Would you believe it, I was a candidate for the priesthood once? I intended to be the most outstanding, smartass Jesuit the world ever saw, and I even talked myself into the possibility that I would give up women."

"What changed it?" David asked.

"The war — and contemplation on that peculiar thing that you and the other sky merchants call God."

David brooded over the memory, wondering what Lucy's response would be if he asked her why she thought of God as a thing. Then he went downstairs and asked her, trying to be as soft and appeasing as possible.

"Did I say that?"

"Yes."

"I don't know what I meant. You can't talk about God, David. You know that."

"But I do talk about — "

"You were going to say 'Him,' weren't you? And then you stopped yourself. Why did you stop yourself? Isn't it *him* anymore? Then what do I do with that Bible I teach the kids. It doesn't say he made woman in his own image. Too much confusion of gender."

She knew all his weak spots, his confusion and fears. "Why are you doing this, Lucy?" he asked her.

"I'm sorry. Oh, David, I'm sorry as hell. It just put me off and scared the very devil out of me when you started that business about Israel. David, I love you so much and I get so confused."

"I'm not going to Israel," he admitted.

"I'm pregnant again. You know that. I mean, if all you wanted in the world was to get over there, you'd need every dollar we have saved up, but if being pregnant — "

He grabbed her in a bear hug and cut off her words. "Lucy, I do love you so much."

"I'm glad. I have a treat for you tonight."

"Oh?"

"Blintzes."

"You're kidding. Where did you learn to make blintzes? From your mother?"

"My mother? I'm not even sure she knows what one is."

"Then where?"

"Millie Carter," Lucy said smugly. "You see, you don't have to be Jewish. She has a Jewish cookbook, and we worked it out together. And Della Klein brought over a quart of homemade strawberry jam. I've learned to accept anything given. I guess it's a rule of the business that preachers must be beggars — "

"Lucy — "

"Just kidding, forgive me. A gift of love, and I do love Della. She's dear."

David ate the blintzes. They were very good, as was the strawberry jam Della Klein had provided. As a boy he had lived with a mother who disdained blintzes. They were a product of Russian-Jewish cookery, whereas the Hartmans were of German-Jewish extraction. This only added a pleasant zest to the taste of the blintzes.

"Just delicious," David said. "The jam too. Della is talented. I'm glad you've been able to make so many friends here."

"Of course, it's you Della adores. But I do have friends. Do you know why?"

"You're a sweet and friendly person. Why shouldn't you make friends here?"

"No. You're not even scratching it, David. We've been here two years, and you're telling me you don't realize how lonely and miserable most of the women here are, Jew and Gentile alike?"

"I've had indications."

"We cling to each other."

"What are you telling me?" David asked softly. "That you're miserable and unhappy?"

"Sometimes."

"What does sometimes mean?"

"It means — " She broke off and rose and went around the table. "The hell with it," she said. "I love you. I hear the baby crying, and you have a meeting tonight with all the big wheels, and if you want to talk about it, we'll do it some other time."

The meeting with the committee was at Mel Klein's place, about a mile from the old Congregational church that had become David's synagogue. It was a lovely spring evening, the new leaves making a pale, lacy froth over the trees, the sky reddening behind thin strips of cloud, the air as sweet as honey. Bit by bit, the place had gotten to David, in spite of intervals of irritation and boredom. He had to admit that for sheer, quiet beauty, Leighton Ridge took second place to no other spot he had known. His work still intrigued him. On the other hand, being here in this old Connecticut town constantly raised the question of why he was here. When he saw himself in the third person, he would argue that this was David Hartman passing through, only passing through. But never permanently. To live in this place, to grow old in this place — that was inconceivable. Lucy might not believe it, but he understood quite well what she was saying. But where was her understanding of him? She had no inkling of the meaning of his desire to be in Israel. He envied her certainty. Her validity was deep inside her and unquestioned, and that perhaps was a quality of being a woman; his own validity was vague and disoriented, changing from day to day.

Enough of that! It was too beautiful an evening to cloud with vague and unrewarding thoughts. He tried to clear his mind as he strode down the road. He was the last to arrive at the Kleins' place, and as Della opened the door and kissed him, she said, "The wolves are here in the den. Now don't be upset, David."

"What makes you think I'll be upset?"

"I know what's on the agenda. And I know you."

"Everybody knows me these days. I wish I knew myself."

"Terrible thing for a rabbi to say. Next I'll hear you're being psychoanalyzed."

"Hardly."

"But you did have a fight with Lucy."

"You're too wise, Della. I prefer the wolves."

The "wolves" were waiting in what Mel Klein called his den — Jack Osner, president of the congregation, Mel Klein, the treasurer, and Joe Hurtz, the secretary — and as he looked at them and shook hands with them tonight, David toyed with the notion that the governing of the congregation might be helped by the presence of a woman.

They were pleased to see him. After two years, they had the feeling that he belonged to them. They were blessed with this tall, handsome young man who was both firm and amiable; he was theirs; and sometimes they were pressed with the notion that they had created him.

"Sit down, David," Mel said. He was very proud of his den, with its large leather chairs and its entire wall of books. The books were bought and read by Della. Mel was not much of a reader beyond the daily newspaper, and neither of them had enough pretentiousness to call the room a library. "We've been looking forward to tonight."

"Oh?"

"I thought it might be best to call a meeting of the whole board," Joe Hurtz said, "but the colonel thought differently."

Hurtz was the only one who still called Osner "the colonel," and his use of the term irritated David greatly. He had his own opinion of the virtues and titles war pins on people, but there was no way to explain this to fat, easygoing Joe Hurtz.

"I think there may be some contention," Jack Osner said. "Might as well keep it among ourselves until we reach a decision."

"About what? For heaven's sake, let's get down to it and end the mystery."

"No mystery intended, David. But I must review some facts. When you came to us, two years ago, fourteen Jewish families had come together and pledged themselves to the support of a synagogue. When you finished your first sermon, David, twenty-two additional families joined the synagogue."

Della entered with a large tray of cups, a coffee pot, and cakes. David took the tray and helped her to serve. No one else moved to help, and David thought of the attitude Martin Carter referred to as "parsonitis." Della flashed him a surreptitious grin and whispered, "Be stout of heart." She left the room, and Osner took up his narrative while the others munched cake and drank coffee, David thinking, We drink so little alcohol. Marty Carter's board would get themselves loaded a bit, and everything would flow more easily.

"That was two years ago," Osner continued. "Since then, we've grown to over a hundred families, families from Ridgefield and Wilton and even Weston and Westport and Redding — well, I don't have to tell you that, David; you've watched the process. And though it's still insufficient, we've tripled your salary, and earlier this evening we decided upon another annual raise of a thousand dollars, which we intend to place before the full board at our next meeting, three days from now."

"Thank you, that's very kind of you," David said.

"So, you see, things change."

"They do indeed."

"And we have the obligation at the right moment to hasten the change, if the change is needed."

David grinned and said, "I don't need all this prologue, Jack. Let's get to the point."

Osner nodded at Klein. "Mel, the ball's in your court."

Klein cleared his throat, coughed, and said, "David, we have come to the conclusion that we need a new synagogue, a real synagogue."

"So that's it. You know," David said slowly, "we have a real synagogue, a very real synagogue."

"No, sir, Rabbi, if you will permit me," Osner said. "We do not have a real synagogue. We have an old, converted Congregational church."

"We have painted that church, repaired it, reroofed it, scraped the floors and the pews, replaced the broken windows, and built a sanctuary for our Torahs. It's a beautiful building, and except on the High Holy Days, we don't fill it."

"David, David," Mel Klein said, "it's still a church. We are Jews and we worship in a church. Is that fitting?"

"I don't know what could be more fitting. We worship the same God, and you could say that church came to us as an act of love, a hand held out from Christian to Jew — "

"For a nice price," Hurtz put in.

"That's a low shot."

"No, it isn't," Osner put in. "Marty Carter and his crowd had embarked on their own piece of church building, and they had overspent and used up every dollar they raised and still had not finished their new church when we came in as the buyers. We helped them out of a hole. The old church may be a museum piece, David, but nobody else wanted it."

"It's not a museum piece. It's a signature for a great deal of what is best in America. The people who built this church are the same people who created Harvard and Yale, who laid the basis of a country where Jews could come and be free — for the first time, anywhere."

"David, David," Osner said gently, "we are not going to destroy the old church. Do you think that any of us living here on the Ridge are without a sense of what Congregationalism means? We're not that narrow or that foolish."

"I didn't mean to indicate that you were. If I did, I must apologize."

"Don't apologize to us, Rabbi," Klein said, mollifyingly.

"We're not going to destroy the church, David," Osner said again. "There's a group of Unitarians who've been meeting at the Elks Club in Danbury, and since most of them come from Brookfield and New Fairfield, they're delighted at the thought of a church of their own here in Leighton Ridge. They're crazy about our building, and they've offered a very good price, thirty thousand dollars for parsonage and church, which is more than double what we paid."

"So you've sold my home," David said.

"No. We've done nothing, and we won't without your approval."

"I'm afraid you'll never have my approval. On the other hand, I will not stand against any decision of the board. Like the people whose church we are selling, we are congregationalists and we rule ourselves."

"Now wait a minute," Osner exclaimed. "If this goes through, David, we'll build you a good, modern house. Furthermore, I am putting a restrictive covenant into the deed that will prohibit the Unitarians from making any changes in either building without the approval of the Leighton Historical Society."

"Is that legal?" Hurtz asked.

"Entirely legal. Now what do you say, David?"

"I plead with you to change your minds."

"We need some things that we don't have now," Klein said. "We want to start a nursery school, a sort of crèche. We want a gym. We want a reasonable area to expand into. We want some classrooms and an office for you. These are the functions of a synagogue today, and I see nothing so awful about it."

"In one of those ugly modern buildings."

"It need not be ugly."

"We'll have the best and most innovative architect we can find," Osner said. "And you've got to admit, David, that Jewish kids growing up in a Congregational church in Connecticut are bound to be a little confused."

"Such confusion might not be the worst thing in the world. Do we have to go on forever pretending that God changes character every time some sect decides that they own the whole truth?"

"What the devil are you talking about?" Joe Hurtz demanded.

"Come on, come on," Mel Klein said softly. "I know what David means, but that's not the kind of a world we live in. The stink of Hitler's gas ovens is still with us. I spend a day in the showrooms on Seventh Avenue and then come up here to the Ridge, and it's like the rest of the world disappeared. Only it hasn't. My father came here from Kiev, in the Ukraine, and he used to tell me what the nature of anti-Semitism was in czarist Russia, and I grew up on One hundred and fifty-ninth Street and Amsterdam Avenue, so I know a little something about anti-Semitism myself, but my kids grew up here in Leighton Ridge and they don't know one damned thing. They feel comfortable in the old church, and I don't want them to feel comfortable there."

David remained silent.

"David," Osner said, "I never asked you. But you come from German-Jewish people, don't you?"

David nodded.

"Could I ask when they came here?"

"My mother's family in eighteen forty-eight, my father's family a bit before that."

"And Reform since then?"

David nodded. "More or less."

"So your family has a hundred years of the Reform movement behind it. For me, it's my first step, and I think three quarters of the congregation are the first generation of Reform Jews. Those who are Reform. Just remember that we have a few Orthodox and Conservative as well."

"In other words," David said, "you intend to build the new synagogue, and nothing I say will stop you."

"Oh, no. Positively not," Mel Klein said. "You're putting us in a hell of a position, David. We think this is a proper step — but if you're going to set yourself in opposition to it, well, we'll just drop the matter, or postpone it." He turned to the others. "Am I putting it right?"

"Absolutely."

"Why don't you think about it, David?" Osner said kindly. "No great hurry. Meanwhile we're having some drawings made, and you may find it's not as inappropriate as you fear. If we decide to go ahead, we'll put it at the other end of the property, about three hundred yards from the present synagogue. And suppose we meet again in a few days and talk about it? Will the drawings be done by, say, Monday?" he asked Hurtz.

"That's what he promised, Colonel."

At home, Lucy looked at David and shook her head. "No fun with the boys?"

"That's nicely put. If I weren't a rabbi, I might say that those three guiding lights of our religious institution give me a pain in the ass, especially one, our beloved colonel."

"I can go with that. Are you hungry?"

"No."

"What is it this time?"

"They want to sell the church and build a new synagogue."

"Well, you know, Dave, Martin sold it to us, and what's so terrible if we want to sell it?"

He shook his head and remained silent, but as they were preparing for bed, he told Lucy that he had decided to go into New York the following day and talk to Rabbi Belsen.

"Sure. That might be a good thing, you worry so much, David." Her voice was like honey, and David knew that meant she wanted to make love. It irritated him, and he stiffened under her touches; and then his guilt rose up, because she was loving and kind and a good mother, ran the house properly, painted and papered rooms by herself, found pieces of antique furniture for ten and fifteen dollars each and put up with the problem of being the wife of an underpaid country rabbi; and out of this rush of guilt, he entered into the lovemaking. But it was not very good. He had to arouse himself with the erotic images of his boyhood encounters, and if that fulfilled something, it spoiled something else.

Driving into New York the following day, David brooded over his relationship with his wife. As a rabbi, he should have been kind, tolerant, understanding. As a rabbi? And why not as a human being? But he had long ago come to the conclusion that men of the cloth, rabbis or otherwise, were less than saintly, and human beings were not very human. His thoughts wandered and he made a wrong turn through a light, and a police car pulled up alongside and waved him over. When the cop saw his license, his face relaxed and he said, "You got to watch yourself, Rabbi. You make an illegal turn like that, you could end up in the hospital or even dead."

"Then you should give me a ticket," David said firmly.

The cop's big, red, Irish face broke into a grin. "That'll be the day," he said. "Go on, Rabbi, only be careful."

Perks. They brought Lucy food, and cops refrained from giving him tickets he deserved. "Shit!" he exclaimed angrily, using the word as a release he desperately needed. "Shit! Shit! Shit! What in hell am I doing here? What in hell am I doing anywhere? Piousness turns my stomach. So I witnessed the Holocaust! Do I bring any Jew back to life by pretending I'm a rabbi? I'm a joke, a clown!"

"I'm pretending to be a rabbi," he told Belsen, fiercely, challengingly.

"We all are, to some extent," the old man said. He was warming an electric teapot. "A gift from my daughter," he explained. "She's very modern. She couldn't bear that I made my tea in a little tin pot. You want lemon, David? Milk? I don't have any here. But I have sugar."

"Any way."

"All right, David. Plain. You know, I pretend to be a rabbi too. What is pretending? It's passing yourself off as something you are not. But not *anything* you are not. It's passing yourself off as something that is special in your heart and mind, something you want to be very desperately and you feel it's beyond you. When my son-in-law says he pretends to be a doctor, what does he mean? That he didn't go to medical school, that he cheated on his exams? No, absolutely not. He means that with all his learning and degrees, he has not even scratched the surface of the mysteries of the human body. And we who are rabbis, we pretend. We pretend that we know something of the mystery of life and death. We pretend that we heard a whisper of the voice of God. We pretend that we know the nature of worship, the nature of observance, the nature of meditation. Maybe a little. Maybe some of us. Does that make the rest of us liars, cheats, worthless? No. Drink your tea. And about Israel — that is the most glorious miracle of the twentieth century, and to want to be there at this moment is completely understandable. What will you do there, David?"

David hesitated.

"Take up a gun and fight?"

He shook his head.

"Then you're still a rabbi. They have enough rabbis there, believe me. You still haven't mentioned what is underneath all this."

True. He hadn't. He hadn't even spelled it out to himself, and now he wondered whether he could. And what should he say to the old man? The emotion, the passion, the call that I felt in the service is gone, and now I'm a half-baked psychiatrist for a group of middle-class Jews in Fairfield County, and I'm disgusted with it, and I look at my wife and wonder who she is, and even my son brings me no joy. And if he said that, would it be the truth any more than anything else would be the truth?

Instead, lamely, he muttered, "They're going to sell the old church and build a new synagogue."

"Oh?"

"I'm against it. I suppose I could stop it. No, I wouldn't. They want it too much."

"Maybe they need it, David."

David shrugged. "I don't think so. Maybe in five years. The

point is, as far as I am concerned, that we're giving up a beautiful old building, something that's intrinsic to the place, for some modern monstrosity."

"Tearing it down?"

"No, we're selling it to the Unitarians."

"So there you are, David. They'll take good care of it, and you'll have a new synagogue with all modern improvements. Not too bad. Tell me, David, could it be that there's comfort in a church, that it makes you feel a little less a Jew?"

David stared at the old man, feeling anger begin to boil in him, yet knowing he could not exercise anger against Belsen, who wore all the images of teacher and father.

"I know." Belsen nodded. "Over in Israel are heroic figures, a tiny handful of young Jews arrayed against the entire Arab world, and what do you have up there in Leighton Ridge — businessmen, professionals, storekeepers, possibly not even three or four that are noble, heroic, brilliant. What is a Jew, David? Something that wins Nobel Prizes, something chosen for mass murder, something without good manners, something *with* good manners, something supercultured?" His voice became suddenly harsh, angry. "Come, David. We've given you years of study and instruction. Now answer a simple question. What is a Jew?"

David shook his head, mute.

"Then let me explain. When God told Moses to go forth and speak to Pharaoh for our people, Moses demanded God's name. It was a time when there were many gods, with many names, but the Almighty answered simply, 'I am what I am.' Do you understand?"

"I think so," David said.

"So. Finish your tea. You want to give up the rabbinate, give it up. You want to leave your wife, leave her. You want to go to Israel, go. Only get rid of the illusions."

That evening, glum and silent, he helped Lucy bathe the baby. "You know something," she said to David. "This ancient bathtub is impossible and our hot-water system is impossible, and I'm always afraid that the electric heater will blow the current, and I wouldn't be one bit unhappy to live in a clean modern house where there's insulation, and the basement ceiling is more than four feet high, and the windows and the roof don't leak." She saw his expression. "God help me, I've said something wrong again."

"It's nothing you said. It's just the way I feel."

"I think you *should* go off to Israel for a while. Oh, come on, David. I'm only kidding."

He wrapped little Aaron in the towel, handed him over to his mother, and stalked out.

David left the house and walked along the path that led to the old church. Today was Tuesday, the eighteenth of May, just four days since the declaration of independence was announced in the old museum at Tel Aviv, and he was here, trapped in this Connecticut backwater, with a wife who could not for the life of her understand what moved him, and a comfortable middle-class congregation that appeared already to have forgotten that there ever was a Holocaust in which millions of Jews died.

There was moonlight and starlight, and whatever one might say about Leighton Ridge, the air was pure here, and tonight there was enough moonlight to fill the interior of the church with a pallid glow. David opened and closed the door gently, as if there were someone inside to be disturbed or awakened, and then he stood in the aisle, looking toward the sanctuary. The interior, as well as the exterior, was still more or less as it had been a hundred and seventy-five years ago. David's people had painted the chair rail white, the walls above it blue, scraped the floor and every bit of woodwork, oiled the wood, polished it, and repaired the pews; and they had put a new roof on the old church. The Unitarians would get a good, sound building.

David wondered whether Belsen was right, whether this old building helped him to cross some sort of a barrier. And did he want to? Israel was not a Jewish thing, as the world knew Jewish things, a tiny army of strong sunburned young men defying the entire world. Why was he clinging to this church? Osner and the others were right — absolutely right. They needed a new building.

"God help me," David said aloud, wondering then why — and for what? For his sense of loss?

When he came back to the house, Lucy was sitting in the tiny room they had turned into a nursery, gently rocking the baby.

"Are you all right?" she asked him.

"I think so."

"I make silly jokes, David. But if you went off and left me now, I don't know what I should do."

"Lucy, are you happy?" he asked her gently.

"Happy? You mean generally speaking? I don't know. You got me to reading the Bible. Does it say anywhere there that a person should be happy?"

"Why do you do that? Why can't you just answer a question?"

"I know. I'm sorry."

"Why don't you just come out with it and say you're as unhappy as hell?"

"Because I'm not. I have my ups and downs, David. But I'm not as unhappy as hell."

He told himself he was behaving like a fool, a boor, but he was unable to say that to Lucy. Or to tell her that he was a rabbi who did not know why he was a rabbi.

The following morning the door knocker clanged as they were finishing breakfast. It was a rainy morning, a light, steady spring rain, and outside were two men in saddle shoes, seersucker suits, and Panama hats. David opened the door. The two men took out wallets and opened them to display identification.

"I'm Agent Thompson. This is Agent Clark. House Committee on Un-American Activities."

David nodded.

"We'd like to talk to you."

David waited. Lucy joined him.

"You are Rabbi David Hartman?"

David nodded again.

"Can we come in?"

"All right." He pointed toward their little parlor. "You can come in, but I have nothing to say to you."

"How do you know that, sir? We haven't asked you any questions."

"True."

"We've come here with the best of intentions, Rabbi Hartman, and we come to you, not only as a man of God, but as a captain in the United States Army Reserve."

The other said, "We simply want to talk to you about a member of your congregation, a Mr. Michael Benton."

"How do you know he's a member of my congregation?" David asked them.

"We have ways."

"Can we sit down, Rabbi?" the other asked.

"No."

"What!" It was less a question than an expression of astonishment.

"No. I said no, you may not sit down. That would imply a gesture of hospitality on my part. But I can offer you no hospitality." Dropping his voice, he added, "I am a Jew. By our law, I am not permitted to suffer swine in my dwelling place, so the sooner you leave, the better."

They stared at him in amazement. "What is this, Rabbi, a joke of some sort?"

"No joke. Just go."

"You may regret this."

"Just go."

Lucy held the door open for them and then closed it behind them. She stared at David as if she had never seen him before, and then she burst out laughing and through her laughter said, "Oh, David, David, if you could have seen yourself! And so quiet and sweet. I never would have dreamed it, not in a thousand years."

"It's nothing to laugh about. You read in the papers about those bastards and their demented committee and Rankin and Parnell Thomas and all the rest of them, and it could be on another planet, and then suddenly here it is, in Leighton Ridge. Lucy, they are Nazis — here, in my home." He was still trembling with anger.

"I've heard of Mike Benton, but I don't think I've ever seen him."

"He's a member of the congregation, and he makes substantial contributions, but I don't think he's ever been present at services. I met him at the last social evening, big, redheaded fellow, very pleasant, very easygoing. He was an infantryman, out in the Pacific. Good record and some citations for valor. He never speaks of the war, but Arnie Cohen was with him for a while, and it was because of all Arnie's sentimental memories of Leighton Ridge — he had a friend who lived here before the war — that Mike Benton decided to come here and write a novel when he was blacklisted on the Coast."

"That's where I read about him. Was he called before the committee?"

"Not yet."

"Are you going to talk to him?"

"I think I should — although to what end, I don't know."

"Anyway, David Hartman, you did a nice piece of business. My hat's off to you."

"For what?"

She kissed him. How could she say "For not behaving like your normal everyday rabbi?" A while later, driving to the other end of the Ridge, where Mike Benton lived, he mused on the fact that small crises could bring out so many interesting qualities in people. Nothing had actually changed between him and Lucy, or improved, or been settled, yet for a few moments they were very close together. That helped, he decided.

Mike Benton lived in a tiny modern house that he had bought cheaply, for a modern house was the last thing people who set out to live on the Ridge desired. It sat in a cluster of trees, with no lawn and no apparent attempt to make the clump of trees other than what they were, a second growth of scrawny oak and maple. A gravel driveway led up to the house. David parked his car and rang the bell.

"Come in!" Benton shouted.

David entered, calling out, "Dave Hartman!"

"In here, Rabbi."

A girl appeared. She was in her twenties, dark, with large, beautiful myopic eyes, round all over without being fat, dressed in an old skirt, sweater, and loafers. "I'm Miriam," she said, "and why he won't let me answer the door properly, heaven only knows. I followed him from the Coast, and I live with him, Rabbi, if it doesn't shock you."

"It would have shocked my mother," David admitted.

"Who the hell is it, Mitzie?" Benton demanded.

"The rabbi. Didn't he just tell you? Didn't you say 'In here, Rabbi'? Are you drunk? It's ten o'clock in the morning."

"It's fucken raining. You know how I feel about a lousy rainy morning — "

David was looking around the living room, a tasteless mélange of tasteless furniture.

"He rented it furnished," the girl said, her voice listless now. "He's in there," pointing to a door.

Through the door was the dining room, which Benton had turned into his workroom, using the big, ugly table as a desk, piling books everywhere, filling the room with a smell of tobacco from his pipe and gin from a glass and bottle. He sat with an old portable typewriter on a stand in front of him. Table and floor were littered with paper.

"Forgive me," he said to David. "I'm such a slob. I know why you're here, Rabbi. Those motherfucken bastards got to me first. I'm sorry. I shouldn't use that language in front of you, but I spent two solid years in the Pacific, island to island,

and if it didn't make me crazy, it sure as hell enriched my use of the language. Some of the kids out there reached a point where they were inserting motherfucker between every second word. At least I use it as a proper adjective."

David shrugged. "I had four years of G.I. English."

"Yeah, I heard." He began to pour gin into the glass, and then he swept glass and bottle off the table. Miriam burst into the room at the crash, but stopped inside the door and stood watching. "The hell with it," Benton said. "I'm not a drunk. I'm scared. I'm scared shitless."

"Of what?" David asked gently.

"Of going to jail. I know, I'm a big hero. When I got back, my fellow writers, my peers, gave me a big bash at the Beverly Wilshire, a pisspot hotel that's all the class Beverly Hills has to offer. Mike Benton, hero. Judy Garland sang 'Praise the Lord and Pass the Ammunition' all for me. And they were right. We're going into Guadalcanal, and I'm standing on deck, five in the morning, cool as a cucumber, Mike Benton, hero, and we're maybe ten miles out, which is bad, bad submarine water, and there's a guy next to me who's been through everything there is, but he's so terrified of submarines, he begins to shit in his pants, literally. So with me, it's jail. That's my private horror; like his was submarines. I can't go to jail. So help me God, I'll die if I have to go to jail."

"Who said you're going to jail, Mike?"

He sorted through the papers in front of him, found what he wanted, and handed it to David. "Look at it, Rabbi. It's a subpoena from that lousy House Un-American Committee. They dropped it off here before they went to see you."

"Will you tell him it's just a piece of paper and it don't mean a damned thing?" Miriam asked pleadingly.

"She's right. It's only a summons."

"How much you don't know, Rabbi! Sure it's a summons. I go down there to that committee, and first thing they ask me is, am I now or was I ever a member of the Communist Party?"

"So you say no. Mike, it's not the end of the world."

"I don't say no, because that's perjury, and perjury is good for five years in jail. The most they can give me for contempt is one year, and I don't say no because I was a member for three weeks before the war. Hell, I'm blacklisted already, so how much worse can it be in that direction? But then they start asking me to name names, who was at the meetings, is Joe Shmuck a communist? Is Dizzy Dolly a communist? That's the way they did it in Hollywood, and I can't go to jail. I can't go to jail. I tell you, I can't hack it."

"What about this Fifth Amendment thing I've been reading about?" David asked him. "Maybe you could use it. A good lawyer — why don't you talk to Jack Osner about it? I hear he's a first-class lawyer."

"Jack Osner! Come on, Rabbi, you got to be kidding. Jack Osner is a loathsome son of a bitch who'd sell his own mother if the Un-American Committee wanted her."

"Why do you say that, Mike?"

"Rabbi, wake up. Or maybe you don't want to. That shit-head Osner, who sat on his ass in the Pentagon and made it right up to the rank of colonel, turned in Joel Kritsky, the labor lawyer. When they were kids, Kritsky joined the Y.C.L. — Young Communist League to you — and Osner knew about it. Back in 'forty-two, Kritsky was pulled into the Judge Advocate, where the country really needed him, and Osner learned about it and denounced him. And you didn't know this?"

"I'm afraid not," David said. "And I can't make moral judgments about the people in my congregation."

"That's a cop-out."

"I hope not. And whatever I can do to help — well, tell me, and I'll do what I can."

Mike Benton made no reply to that. He sat behind the big table, staring at the mess of papers in front of him, but at the outer door, as he was leaving, Miriam said to David, "I want to thank you, Rabbi, and so would he, if he could. You must understand his situation. Except for me, he's utterly alone. He hasn't made a friend here. You know, he can't. He can't make a friend who hasn't been through what he's been through. His friends are out on the Coast. His life is out there too. He's so alone and so frightened — but what he told you is true. He was in the worst of the Pacific war, and he was a legend. I heard it from so many people, not from him, but from so many others. And now he's as frightened of jail as a little boy is of the dark. So if you could help him — "

"How?"

"Just come back a few times and talk to him. He'll talk to you because he knows about your war record. Rabbi, I don't understand how this crazy business works with men, but it does."

"I'll come back," David said.

Back at the parsonage, David entered through the kitchen door. Aaron was in his playpen, trying his legs, and Lucy was pummeling dough for making bread. Homemade bread had started about three months before, and by now had become something of a compulsion, but when David appeared, she stopped and wiped off her hands. "Surprise," she said. "The Unitarians are going to paint, after all."

"What on earth?"

"David, what's wrong with me? I can't deal with anything except with some stupid wisecrack. Come on, I'll show you."

"Aaron?"

"He'll be all right. We won't be out of sight of the house."

"Where are we going?"

"To the old church."

"What happened?" David asked her, tense already with a sense of impending disaster. "Also, do I engage in male in-security?"

"Sometimes."

"You're kidding. Tell me what happened."

"Better see it yourself than have me describe it."

"The church is there. It hasn't burned down."

"Come around to the back."

At the back of the church, David realized what she meant. Three large swastikas had been painted on the clapboard siding, one in black and the other two in red. For a long moment, David stood silent and stared at the hooked crosses. Then he went over and touched the paint. "Dry," he murmured. "Last night."

"We should have had a dog. He might have barked," Lucy said. "That's a shame."

"It wouldn't have made any difference."

"It scares me. Does it scare you, David?"

"Yes. But it angers me more."

"But who would do it, David? Here in Leighton Ridge — who would do it?"

"Kids, I suppose."

"Why?"

"I don't know."

"What are you going to do? I was thinking that you could paint over them and then pretend it never happened."

"Except that whoever did it would know that it happened. No, I think I'll try to get as many of the board together as I can tonight and talk about it. You know, it's our synagogue, but when we talk about it we call it the old church. It sort of remains a church, doesn't it?"

He put it to the board as he had put it to Lucy, and most of them stared at him blankly. The board now consisted of twelve people, even though the week-to-week business of the synagogue was still conducted by Osner, Hurtz, and Klein. Osner was nominally the president of the synagogue, and though the charter called for election of a president and other officers every two years, the matter had been postponed for three weeks now. Two other members of the board were available on short notice, Eddie Frome, thirty-one years old, a writer who had made the transition from *Yank* to *The New Yorker* magazine, and Oscar Denton, seventy-one years old and the first Jew to live in Leighton Ridge. David invited

Alan Buckingham, which caused Osner to take David aside
and inquire why Buckingham was there.

"I have my reasons," David said.

"You don't want to share them?"

"I will, later."

"That's a little arrogant, Rabbi. I would think that, in a
matter like this, it ought to be kept among our people."

"Alan's a member of the congregation. That makes him
our people." And after calling the meeting to order, David
said to them, "You've all had the opportunity to look at the
swastikas, and I asked Jack to get a few of us together this
evening so that we could decide what to do about it. You see
Alan Buckingham, who's not a member of the board and
who in a literal sense is not Jewish, although his family does
belong to the congregation. Coming out of this ghastly war
that we've all lived through, we named our congregation
Shalom. We could hardly have named it anything else, and
I'd like us to keep that in mind when we talk tonight. We're
all angry, but we have a problem that we can't solve with
anger. I want to point out something else, which touches on
Alan Buckingham's presence. The swastikas were painted
not only on a synagogue, but on a church, and not on any
church, but on a New England Congregational church, one
of a group of ancient churches that defined so much of what
this country would be. And whether or not whoever did
this intended it, a church was desecrated as much as a synagogue."

"I don't agree with that," Osner said. "The bastards who
did the job were desecrating a synagogue, not a church."

"Still and all," Frome said, "the rabbi has a point. The
building was a church, and even though we hold services
there, it remains a church in a manner of speaking. Certainly,
when we sell it to the Unitarians, it will become a church
again — if they call it a church?"

"They do."

"I don't know what the devil we're doing, meeting about

this," Osner said. "This kind of an outrage against Jews is as old as time. To hell with it! We paint over it and forget about it."

"I don't think we can forget about it," Mel Klein said slowly. "We live here. It's too close to the Holocaust."

The old man, Oscar Denton, said, "When we moved in here, twenty years ago, we were the first Jewish family to settle in Leighton Ridge. At first, it never occurred to them. Maybe the thought was impossible up here in the year nineteen twenty-eight. And since I was a builder and worked alongside my men, maybe it didn't occur to them because it conflicted with their concept of what a Jew should be. So they were pretty nice to us until they found out, and then they made life pretty rotten for my kids and uncomfortable for us. But nothing overt. They don't burn crosses on the Ridge, and nothing like this business of the swastikas ever happened. I would not paint over them. I would make a point of them. I would call in the newspapers from Danbury and from New Haven and from Hartford too, and the *New York Times*, yes, absolutely. Let them take pictures so people won't get smug and say it can't happen here."

"For God's sake," Joe Hurtz exclaimed, "why are we making this kind of a fuss over the actions of some stupid kids? Paint it over and forget about it. Kids see things. They imitate. So what?"

"No," Mel Klein muttered. "No — no way."

"I'd like to hear from Alan," David said.

"I've been listening," Alan said, "and of course I saw the swastikas. I'm not Jewish, but I'm married to a Jewish lady whom I love dearly and I have two Jewish kids. It puts me kind of close to the problem, but not as close as you are. At the same time, I can't help being astonished by the calm manner in which you discuss this. I was silent but raging inside myself. Damnit, Joe, what do you mean, stupid kids? If some idiot killed your child, would you dismiss it because it was the act of an idiot? And do you think Nazism was the product of the brains and culture of Germany? I can tell you it was the product of all the stupid, demented rot that existed in Germany. And a church was defaced, not merely a synagogue, so if there was ever a time to bring Jew and Christian on the Ridge together on a very serious matter, this is it. I would bring Martin Carter into this right away. That's only a suggestion. I'm not a member of the board."

"To me, you're making a mountain out of a molehill," Osner said. "This is our affair, not Martin Carter's."

Denton and Klein and Eddie Frome said they agreed with Buckingham, and together with David, they made a firm majority.

"I'll just talk to Martin," David said. "We'll see what he suggests."

"I'm disagreeing with Jack Osner too much," he told Lucy that night as they settled down in bed. "I think he's beginning to hate my guts."

"You have more politics here than in Washington."

"In a manner of speaking — yes, we do."

"Did you think it would be that way?"

"No — no, I never dreamed that it would. I guess the war spoiled me for common sense. The kids were always so glad to see a rabbi — oh, the devil with it, Lucy. If they fire me, they fire me."

"And what about Mike Benton?"

"He's frightened. He could live with war, but jail scares him. He's been subpoenaed by the Un-American Committee, and they'll ask him to name names, same as with the others. It's only three years since Adolf Hitler died in his bunker in Berlin, and we're trying every trick of his on the home ground."

"Come on, it's not as bad as all that."

"It's as bad."

News travels in a small place like Leighton Ridge, and the next morning Martin Carter turned up at the old parsonage. Lucy was feeding Aaron, and David was having his second cup of coffee. "I sometimes do the breakfasts," he explained.

"She feeds my son and heir, although being a rabbi's heir is not much to boast about. Let me cook up some eggs for you."

Carter declined and accepted a cup of coffee. "I heard about the swastikas," he said.

David waited.

"Nothing like this ever happened before," Carter said. "I've been here a long time. *Nothing* like this ever happened before. Sure, we have our Jew-haters, but show me a small town in America that doesn't have them. Ours have always been pretty mild."

"I think it's kids," David said, "but we can't drop it and let it pass just because they're kids."

"Oh, no. It's a very particular desecration. Selling the old church to your people was, I felt, a significant act of brotherhood, very necessary after the Holocaust — but the building remains an old church, a sort of monument to our beginnings here in America. We can't allow this to pass quietly, David, and simply paint over the swastikas and pretend it never happened."

"What do you suggest?"

"I think we ought to have a joint service, perhaps in midweek. We won't use any church. I can get the Board of Selectmen to let us have the meeting hall, and we'll make it an open affair. I think each of us ought to say a few words there."

"Very few for me," David said. "I think you carry the burden."

As with so many small Connecticut towns, the legislative part of the government was the town meeting. Basic changes in the town's criminal and civil code were brought to the town meeting, as well as zoning questions and restrictive covenants. Attendance was never compulsory, but neither was this night's kind of attendance very common, the seven hundred seats in the hall filled, with people in the aisles and standing in back. At this point everyone in town and in the surrounding towns and cities, and in New York too, knew about the swastikas.

Todd Burns, the town manager, opened the meeting by

saying that all of the selectmen wanted to be speakers here tonight, but they decided to leave the issue to the two men of the cloth involved, Rabbi Hartman and the Reverend Carter.

Rabbi Hartman felt strange. He still had to nerve himself to speak to his congregation, and here was a larger and mixed group. "For the first time," he said, "I knew how the Negro felt when he looked out of his window and saw a burning cross in front of his house. But I don't fully know how the Reverend Martin Carter felt when he saw this desecration on the oldest symbol of democracy this country has, the Congregational church. The people and the movement that raised up these symbols, the symbol of the hooked cross, caused the deaths of fifty million human beings and the crippling of a hundred million more. No one can ever calculate the suffering they brought upon mankind. Does anyone want us to create a similar movement here at home? I am still fairly new in Leighton Ridge. Martin Carter has been here much longer. He has agreed to talk about this."

Carter said, "When Rabbi Hartman called us the oldest symbol of democracy this country has, he was quite correct. The Pilgrims built our first church in America, holding that a man needs no intercessor before his God, that each man is responsible for his deeds, his sins, and his cruelties, and that his church is a symbol of a man's dignity, his independence, and his willingness to participate in the democratic process. That is why, years ago, when we were a much smaller town than we are now, the town meetings were held in the Congregational church, which was as often called the meeting house as it was the church. When the time came to forsake the old church, which would no longer hold our congregation, I wondered what would become of it. We are not affluent enough to turn the church and the parsonage into a museum and maintain such a museum — yet this should be done. For the church was built in the seventeen seventies, and the parsonage is even older. How could we face the thought of these two beautiful old buildings being torn down — "

Lucy, sitting with Della Klein, whispered, "He's forgotten what it takes to keep that beautiful old building warm in winter."

" — but fortunately, we never faced that. Three of our Jewish neighbors came to me and asked whether they could buy the church for a synagogue and the parsonage as a home for the rabbi they hoped to find. Of course, I was delighted. It was like an act of hope and faith, a prayer answered, and when I put it to the entire congregation, they were pleased, too. We felt that it was a God-given opportunity to affirm our faith in Christianity, so sorely shaken these past years, and to perform an act of brotherhood toward the most bitterly hounded and persecuted people on earth — yet the same people from whom God chose his Son. And now we have this act of mindless desecration. I think that tonight, by coming here and packing this place, we have performed the first act of an exorcism. As for the second part of the exorcism, that will be performed tomorrow, starting at ten in the morning. I know that most men will be at work, but women can perform it equally well. The Jewish congregation, needing larger quarters for Temple Shalom, have sold the church and the parsonage to the Unitarians, who are quite desperate for a house of prayer. But we cannot hand it over in its present condition. So at ten o'clock tomorrow, armed with paintbrush and good outside white paint, we will meet at the church and complete the exorcism. Frank Hessel, our in-church painter, tells me it will require three coats for a proper job, and he suggests outside white lead. And we'll pray to God that we have seen the last of that unholy symbol."

The next morning, wielding a paintbrush next to Millie Carter, and keeping an eye on Aaron and a dozen other toddlers, being watched over by two teen-agers, Lucy wondered what it all amounted to. "What do you think?" she asked Millie.

"I don't know. I've been a preacher's wife too long. I can't listen, no matter how hard I try. But you?"

Lucy shook her head.

"Come on. Whatever you say to me is privileged. You know that."

"Okay. I would have said, 'We have almost a thousand people here. Let's find the bastards who did this and whale the living daylights out of them and then turn them over to the cops.'"

"You're kidding."

"Am I? Do you know anyone who ever prayed himself out of the gas chambers? I'm all for sweetness and light, but a good kick in the tail sometimes leaves a longer impression."

PART THREE

1951

You're only going for three days," David said. "There's enough there for a permanent departure."

"What's that? Some kind of Freudian slip?"

"Come on, Lucy."

"All right, I'm sorry. I'm packing enough for the two kids and myself. Sarah is only two, but still she has the right to a change of clothes. She'll be the youngest flower girl there, and we may stay a day or two extra. They have a huge house and we'll be very comfortable with my Aunt Dorothy — as you would be too, if you would only come. You have at least a dozen men in the synagogue who are just dying for you to take off so that they can conduct the service and show how classy their Hebrew is."

"I suppose so."

"And I just can't buy your excuse."

"It's not an excuse," he said with annoyance. "Do I have to run through it again? You come from an atheist family — "

"You knew that when you married me."

"I know, and I'm not talking about you. But here's your cousin John, Jewish from the word go, marrying a Jewish girl, and the ceremony is being performed by a justice of the peace."

"He's not just a justice of the peace. He's one of my uncle's best friends."

"It's not the kind of thing I participate in."

"You're not participating. You're just watching. Is there any Jewish law against that?"

"I'm not talking about any law or prohibition. I'm simply asking you to recognize my position and exhibit some understanding. There will be a rabbi watching two Jewish kids being hitched by a justice of the peace."

"So?"

"For heaven's sake, it *past nisht.*"

"Wonderful! You've learned two words of Yiddish, which every German Jew calls not a language but a patois!"

"My word, you are angry."

"Don't I have every right to be?" Suddenly she softened and entreated him, "Davey, why do we get into these ridiculous fights? I love you so much — if you'd only try to be a nice, flexible human being. The kids in my Sunday school class say, 'Mrs. Hartman, first you say one thing and then it becomes something else.' I tell them that's all right, that's perfectly human. And it is, David, it is."

The drive down to the Fairfield railroad station was lightened only by the chattering of the children, who, David had to admit, looked very beautiful dressed for traveling. They were both strawberry blond, both covered with freckles after the long summer, both with David's bright blue eyes.

"They're beautiful kids, aren't they?" Lucy whispered into his ear.

"They should be, with the mother they chose for themselves."

"Oh?"

"I do love you, Lucy."

"Took you eighteen miles to say it."

"Be careful, won't you? And take good care of them."

Both intimations of incompetence on my part, she thought, but said nothing, only nodded and smiled.

At the station, he waited with them, playing with the children until the train arrived. Then he kissed her and the kids and called after her, "My best to your mom and pop."

The train clanked away, and David stood for a long moment, unmoving, thinking that this was the first time in five years that he had been separated from Lucy for more than a few hours.

But what irritated him and plucked at every guilt-ridden cell in his body was the fact that he was happy, free, alone in the world for the next three days, free to do as he pleased and go where he pleased; although he was quite aware that he was going nowhere and that here he was, at almost noon on a Friday, with a sermon to deliver and still unwritten and with the High Holy Days facing him in just another week.

None of which was enough to dampen his spirits. He felt young and vital and alert to everything he saw. The Aspetuck Reservoir was beautiful beyond words; it was as if he had never seen it before, though he had driven past it fifty times. The leaves on the trees were just beginning to turn, dancing before a light, cool breeze, and he had to think What a beautiful, extraordinary place God's world is!

He repressed his feelings of guilt. Is it a sin to be happy? he asked himself, quelling what he knew were the reasons for his delight, but again asking himself, What else could I have done? I'm a rabbi. Could I have gone to that wedding and sat complacently while two Jewish kids are married by a justice of the peace? And suppose questions came. Nothing those characters enjoy better than tweaking a rabbi's nose. "Did you enjoy the ceremony, Rabbi?" "You see, we break God's commandment and nothing happens. Possibly because we are in New Jersey. Sensibly, God doesn't visit New Jersey."

He slipped deeper into his musings. One is always the victim in those things. Even on those increasingly rare occasions when he and Lucy brought the kids down to New York to see her parents, they could not resist working David over, albeit very gently.

His mood of lightheaded joy had vanished with his thoughts, and now he began to think of what he would put into his sermon. No matter how many times he did it, no sermon came easily, and indeed, if anything, each was more difficult than the previous one. There were wealthy congregations where the rabbi could entice a guest speaker every other week, and even pay an honorarium, a word he loathed. But what guest speaker would journey to Leighton for a Friday night audience of fifty?

What else did he have to do today? he wondered. Myron Schillman would be around for an hour's discussion of his *Bar Mitzvah*. The world as Myron Schillman turns thirteen. Myron, if your blessed rabbi used such language, he would tell you the world stinks in this *goyishe* year of 1951 — a strange bit of mentation for a rabbi, and suppose my parishioners could look inside my skull? Just suppose so. Firstly, the use of the word parishioner, even as a thought — heaven forbid that I should speak it aloud, and me, Rabbi David Hartman, with a brand-new *shul*, which of course we call a temple, it would be so old-country and Eastern European to call it a *shul*. But brand new, with a modern red-brick design to replace the little ancient church we started with only five years — can it be only five years? — no, closer to five and a half years ago, and there it stands, Temple Shalom, with three classrooms and an office for myself, Rabbi Hartman, and a tiny office for my secretary — if ever we can afford one — and all of it brought in for a little over sixty thousand dollars.

Now we are a going institution, with eight hundred copies of the Union Prayer Book — no, no, no, that kind of thinking is useless for either my sermon or for Myron, who will step out into the world as a man. Funny thing, you're such a sweet kid, and now at the age of thirteen, you are to step out into this lousy, perverted world. Why am I so bitter and angry at the world, Myron? Well, let us see what the years have brought us. That war to save the world from all other wars — or was that the other one? — well, it's six years in the past and we are at war again in Korea. Why? God knows; I do not. Something about dominoes, Myron. What else? They've purged the Communist Party again in Czechoslovakia. What does purged mean? No, it's not a laxative. It's standing an assortment of people up against an assortment of walls and shooting them. Very popular these days. And let us not forget those two lost souls who have been found guilty of stealing atom bomb secrets, although Herbie Fisher, who is the newest addition to my burgeoning congregation, says he can make an atom bomb with one hand tied behind his back, and so can anyone else who isn't a scientific booby. But I kind of doubt that —

"God forgive me," he said aloud. "I'll get into the habit of talking that way, and then I'll really have to ask God's forgiveness, and poor Myron. If I apologize to him, he'll have every right to ask what on earth I'm apologizing about. Could I tell him? Could I? Answer me, Rabbi David Hartman!"

Only the day before, Mel Klein had taken David aside after a meeting of the board and said, "David, *boychik*, myself I know nothing about politics, and the little bit I know, I don't want to know. I got enough trying to keep my head above the water in that lousy *shmatteh* shop downtown, and taking care of my family, and trying to keep this synagogue from a common religious disease called mortgage-itis. So as far as politics are concerned, I give my fifty dollars a year to the Democratic Party, and that's the end of it."

"Mel, what are you trying to tell me?"

"Politics. It's been in every one of your past four sermons. The congregation don't like it."

"Who doesn't like it?" David demanded, bristling.

"Come on, come on, I say two words, you're ready to deck me. David, I don't want no trouble. You're a wonderful rabbi. It's a miracle we got you here instead of some *shlemiel.*"

"Thank you, Mel. Now who's been complaining about politics in my sermons?"

"I'm naming no names."

"All right, Mel, but these folks, the next time they unload on you about my politics, tell them to read Prophets. A bit of praise the Lord, but ninety percent of the various books of the Prophets is politics."

Still, the message took, and now, driving home, he decided that the subject of the sermon would be Prophets. An evasion, yet a good way out. He would do a biblical sermon, pure and simple, eschewing any mention of current events. It was what Martin Carter did when the going got rough in his congregation, and it always cooled the heat. People felt great comfort going into a house of worship and stepping back three thousand years to a world that did not exist, that was absurdly simple and void of atom bombs, fragmentation bombs, tanks and machine guns. Certainly, he calculated, more human beings were slaughtered in World War Two than the number of the entire human race at the time of Amos. He decided that he must try to work this out. Suppose the entire world population at the time of Amos was, say, ten million; say, twenty million. Less than half the number that died in World War Two. "There, my lad," he decided, "is a sermon. And there is politics," he added ruefully.

"Mel is right," he admitted to himself. "I do it every time."

He was just finishing the sermon, when Myron Schillman arrived. He was a tall, long-limbed boy, with a shy smile and a voice that still cracked occasionally. He entered David's office tentatively. The office had a large, built-in bookcase, a desk, and three wooden chairs that were fair imitations of Windsors. David had a swivel chair behind his desk. Carpeting on the floor, leather couch, leather chairs, and a respectable library in the very large bookcase were all the things for the future. The money had run out.

"Myron, sit down, please," David said to him. "How are you feeling?"

"Pretty good, thank you, Rabbi."

"If you get too many fountain pens, I'll trade for something else." It was his standard small joke to break the ice. Myron knew about it. The other kids told him to expect it.

"Sure, I'll trade, Rabbi," he answered, grinning.

"Well, Myron, this is a very informal hour. I like to have a chat with boys who bear the burden of becoming a man at the age of thirteen years. It's a little early, don't you think?"

"It wasn't in the old days, was it?"

"Not even in the time of the people who first settled Leighton Ridge. But today — well, you do have high school and college still ahead of you."

"Yeah."

"So I guess that the real meaning concerns the taking on of a certain amount of responsibility. After all, the essence of being a kid is being without responsibility."

Myron looked uncertain, and David amended his statement. He never really knew what to say to the kids on these occasions, and frequently his remarks had to be adjusted to the action of the child's ductless glands. There were thirteen-year-olds who were almost six feet tall, the first fuzz of hair on their cheeks, and there were others who were still burdened with baby fat, pink cheeks, and a skin as smooth as silk. Thirteen was an odd age to select as the door into manhood, but as Myron had suggested, it must have been quite different in the old days.

When Myron left, David put his feet up on the desk and leaned back. He had to admit that the swivel chair was a great improvement. He could dispense with the rest of the new synagogue furniture, but the swivel chair, never.

The telephone rang. It was Lucy, informing him that she had arrived safely in New Jersey with the children, that everyone was really devastated that David had not come, and that everyone sent their love. "Did you finish your sermon?" she asked him.

"Yup. Finished the sermon, had a chat with Myron, four o'clock, and I think I'll go home, shower, and drink a martini."

"Who's Myron?"

"Our latest *Bar Mitzvah* boy. Nice kid."

"And what's the sermon on?"

"Amos."

"Who's Amos?"

"The prophet."

"That Amos."

"You sound relieved," David said.

"Well — sort of," she admitted. "I've heard some remarks about politics in your sermons."

"Everyone's heard them except me."

"And there's stew in the fridge. All you have to do is warm it up."

"I'll have a sandwich."

"I made the stew for you, David. Four different vegetables and a decent piece of meat. Your sandwiches are empty calories."

"I'll skip the martini. I'll have a sandwich and a beer."

"Great. There's nothing warms up your breath like beer, and just as soon as you set foot in the synagogue, someone smells it — and there it is, the rabbi's drunk. And as a food, beer is worthless."

"What are we arguing about, Lucy?"

"I know. I know. It's crazy. We say two words to each other, and suddenly we're at each other's throat. David, have your sandwich and beer. I should know you have no appetite before services. I'm sorry."

"Nothing to be sorry for. I love you, dear, and I promise never to die of malnutrition."

"That's a pretty good joke for a rabbi," Lucy said.

David had hardly put down the telephone when it rang again. It was Martin Carter this time, and he said, "David, when are you and Lucy free this evening — I mean when do you finish with your Friday night devotions?" Only Martin Carter called the Sabbath evening services devotions.

"Oh — I'd say nine-thirty at the latest. I decided to do a religious sermon on Amos, and it ran short. Everyone will love me for that."

"I do Isaiah in the Prophets. He's pure gold."

"I've exhausted him, at least for this year."

"Well, nine-thirty, even ten will be great. Millie and I are giving our seasonal bash. You know, we rarely entertain, what with the dinner invitations from the parish members, three or four a week, bad for the stomach and sticky for the mind. So once a year we do a buffet for about twenty of our friends — of course you know. You were here last year. Well, Millie spoke to Lucy last week, and Lucy said you'd both be down in Jersey or somewhere for a wedding, but then I drove past and saw your car sitting in the driveway and thought perhaps the wedding was off."

"No, the wedding's still on. Lucy went with the kids." He explained the problem of a rabbi observing while a justice of the peace married two Jewish kids.

"Yes — yes, I can see where that puts you. Well, come along anyway, David. It's better than sitting alone in an empty house."

"I couldn't get there until almost ten."

"We don't eat before ten. It's our one touch of night life on the Ridge."

It pleased David. He felt truant, fancy free. He recalled the party at the Carters' the year before, and it was rather sedate as parties go, but on the other hand, there were only two other Jews present besides himself, and that was certainly a novelty. This time, there were four Jews and their wives, three of them strangers to him, if indeed they were Jewish. He was irritated by a habit he had fallen into, glancing at a person and deciding whether or not the person was Jewish; but then he was increasingly irritated by the things he did and by the thoughts that ranged through his mind, and he felt increasingly driven by an oppressive sense of his Jewishness. Why, he wondered, had it not been so in the army? But in the army he had been part of a whole; here he was an outsider. He felt that he had come into this room as an outsider; he felt that he came into the Jewish homes of his congregants as an outsider; and he even felt at times that he stood in the synagogue as an outsider.

What nonsense, he said to himself. I am here and these

people are warm and friendly and apparently delighted to meet me.

Millie Carter was a good cook, and the sideboard groaned under a rich assortment of New England autumnal dishes — a bean pot; Indian pudding; a huge salad of red onion, fresh corn, chickpeas, tomatoes, and lettuce; a platter of fried chicken; and a roast ham.

"Both you and Martin," Millie said to him, "are obscenely thin. Please eat and eat and eat. I'll be very flattered. Who have you met?"

"Almost everyone by now." He was looking at a tall, slender woman, a woman of about thirty, at least five feet nine inches. She had a sharply etched face, a high-bridged nose, wide cheekbones, and amber-colored eyes. Were her features not so sharply carved, she might have had a bovine appearance, so wide and placid was her brow; as it was, she was strikingly handsome.

"You haven't met her," Millie said. "Let me introduce you. Be kind to her. She needs a good word and a thimble of kindness."

"Why? Or is it simply what we all need?"

"Some other time. Come meet her. Her name is Sarah Comstock."

Sarah Comstock took his hand firmly. Her own hand was strong and warm. "I'm so glad to meet you, Rabbi Hartman, and so glad that you came to the Ridge. I've looked forward to meeting you. I never met a rabbi before."

"That would make you curious, I'm sure."

"I'm so sorry. That's not what I meant. I've offended you, haven't I?"

"No. Oh, no. I didn't mean it that way either."

"Shall we both start again?" She smiled. She had a remarkable smile that lit up her face and appeared to change it completely, mellowing the angles and planes.

"Please."

"Where is your wife?" looking about the room. "I've heard

so much about how pretty and clever she is. She and Millie have practically finished this cookbook they're doing — *The Parsonage Cookbook* — how to dish up gourmet food on a minister's or a rabbi's salary. It has a whole section on kosher food, and Millie thinks they've found a publisher — " She saw David's expression and broke off. "I don't know what's wrong with me tonight. I don't chatter away like this usually." She shook her head unhappily. "You didn't know, did you?"

"Probably they planned to tell me about it when they had found a publisher."

"Of course. It was to be a surprise. I mustn't monopolize you. It's not my best evening, Rabbi."

"Please, Mrs. Comstock," he said, "you haven't offended me and you haven't said anything out of place. My wife had to be with her family in New Jersey and that's why I'm here alone. Why don't you introduce me to your husband?" for want of anything better to say.

Sarah Comstock nodded across the room to where a rather handsome, blondish man of about forty, with a puffy, high-colored face, sat slumped in a chair, a drink in his hand. Vaguely, somewhere behind him, David heard someone item-izing the furniture in the room, the pieces that were made in Philadelphia in the 1760s, the sewing table from the hand of Hilton, all of them in Millie Carter's family for generations.

"That's my husband, Mr. Rabbi," Sarah Comstock said bitterly. "We got here at nine o'clock, and that's his fifth vodka — on ice, six ounces in a drink. One or two more, and Marty will help pour him into our car and I'll drive us home." And with that she turned on her heel and stalked away. When he looked for her again, she had left.

The following morning, after the Sabbath service, Jack Osner asked David whether they could have a few minutes in the rabbi's study. Once there, he made small talk uneasily until David suggested that he come to the point.

"Judge Interman, the one who's sitting on the case of the atom spies, is an old friend."

David had followed the case in the newspapers, unhappily. Now he nodded.

"We were in the service together — "

David said nothing. He had little love or sympathy for Judge Interman.

"He'd like to talk to you. Well, not as David Hartman. He wants to talk to a rabbi. He belongs to the Temple Emanu-El in the city, but for reasons of his own, he feels he can't talk to the rabbi there."

"There's certainly no shortage of rabbis in New York City," David said without enthusiasm.

"No, of course not. But I know you, and I told him he could trust you. I think he'd rather someone away from New York."

"All right," David agreed, "I'll talk to him. He's about fifty, isn't he? I should think he'd want an older man."

"No. He knows how old you are. Can you see him tomorrow?"

"Tomorrow? I was thinking I might drive down to New Jersey and join Lucy and the kids."

"It's very important to him, David — and to me — that you see him."

"All right."

"About three in the afternoon?"

"I suppose so."

"He'll come to my house. I'll bring him over and drop him off at your place."

All very mysterious, and for some reason distressing to David; but it gave him cause to quiet his guilt about Lucy and to stay away from the wedding in Jersey. He had thought that he might drive down on Sunday and arrive after the wedding. Now he put the thought aside, and when he called Lucy, he explained about the date that Osner had arranged.

"I don't like that man, David. Why must you please him?"

"He's a human being and a member of the congregation."

"Aren't we all? Well, look, don't sit around and brood. Get some kind of dinner invitation. I'm glad you went to Martin's place last night. Did you meet anyone interesting?"

"Not really, no." He didn't mention Sarah Comstock nor did he make any reference to the cookbook.

After the telephone call, he made a sandwich, warmed some cold coffee from the day before, and tried to read. But he was unable to concentrate, and he put the book aside and turned on the radio. Lucy felt that the children should be spared the insidious new diversion called television, and he half-agreed with her, but since they couldn't afford a set, the matter was decided without much discussion. On the other hand, David would have welcomed a TV screen today, something he could watch mindlessly.

He finished his sandwich and had about decided to take a long walk by himself, when the telephone rang. It was Sarah Comstock, and she said, "I didn't know how long your services take on the Sabbath, and I didn't want to disturb you at any personal devotions, so I waited. It's almost three o'clock now, and I must see you and speak to you, Rabbi, please — " All of it breathlessly, the words pouring out as if she were determined to say what she must say before David could stop her.

"Yes, of course," David said.

"Where can I meet you?"

"Come to my study at the synagogue — say, half an hour. Is that all right for you?"

"Yes, I'll be there."

Afterward, he would remember how she looked when he opened the door of his study for her. Her light brown hair was drawn back and tied almost carelessly at the back of her neck. She wore a suit of fawn-colored linen over a white cotton shirt, and her stockingless feet were in sandals. "I should have changed," she apologized. "I don't go to church dressed like this, so I shouldn't come here dressed this way. But you said a half-hour — "

"You look fine."

"Back there," she said, "as I walked past, I saw the girls dancing. They looked so lovely."

"That's Jenny Levine's group. She was with the American

Ballet Theater, and we're lucky to have her in the congregation. She volunteers. We're even more poverty-stricken than Martin, if that's conceivable."

"But the building's so fine."

"Thereby our poverty. Sit down, please, and try to feel relaxed."

She seated herself with her purse held primly in her lap, her legs uncrossed, her glance at the floor. "I don't know how to begin," she said softly, "calling you, so presumptuous; it's arrogant — "

"Then don't begin, Mrs. Comstock," he interrupted. "We'll just talk, and if I can be of any help or comfort — well, it will come out. But there is one thing I must ask you, and only because Martin is a dear friend. Why didn't you go to him?"

"Because he's Harvey's best friend — " She began to cry. "Damnit, I don't cry. I'm not a weeper." She dabbed at her eyes with a piece of tissue.

"Do you want a drink?"

"Yes."

"Sweet wine. It's sacramental and a bit disgusting."

"I don't care."

He poured it into a silver *Kiddish* beaker and she drank it down.

"Thank you. This morning at ten o'clock," she said flatly, still dabbing at her eyes, "I decided to kill myself. I am not a suicidal type. I have never considered suicide before, but this morning at ten o'clock, I decided that this was the open door, and I took a bottle of aspirin and poured about twenty into a glass of water and let them dissolve. That's how stupid I am in the art of suicide. But then I remembered stories I had heard about children who had gobbled down half a bottle and survived very nicely, so I flushed it all down the toilet, and then I said to myself, Marty's been of no damned use to me, but maybe a rabbi is different and possibly he knows things a Congregational minister doesn't, and you have a kind face, and Jesus God, I need a little kindness."

"We'll talk. Kindness is in short supply, but not that short. Let's get rid of the suicide thing first."

"I'm over it. Not because it's a mortal sin — is it with you? I mean a mortal sin?"

"No, not in the same sense. But it hurts too many people — not only the person who dies."

"And who would it hurt if I died?"

"I don't know the people in your life, but it would hurt Martin and Millie — and it would hurt me."

"You hardly know me."

He smiled and nodded.

"Would you call me Sarah, please?" she asked suddenly.

"Yes. It's a fine old Jewish name. It's my daughter's name."

"It goes a long way back in my family — Jewish, yes, I never thought of it that way." Her face lit up with a smile, and, as on the night before, the smile transformed her face completely.

"Why the aspirin and the suicide?" David asked.

"You come to the end of the rope. Or you're the little boy who picks up a baby pony every day. But the pony gets bigger, until a point comes when he can't. That's my point. All the doors are closed, every damned rotten one of them."

"Your husband's an alcoholic and to live with him is apparently very painful and difficult. Why don't you divorce him?"

"I can't."

"Why? You're not Catholic. Is he?"

"It has nothing to do with religion, Rabbi. Have you known many alcoholics?"

"Some, yes."

"I hear it's not much of a Jewish affliction. Maybe it's only our curse. It's terrible. A man turns into something else; you can't reach him or touch him or reason with him or plead with him, and all restraint goes and all decency goes and all shame goes, and this witless, brainless monster is your husband. And then he's sober, and you say to him, I have had it. Enough is enough. I'm leaving. And then he gets down on his knees and grovels at your feet like a whimpering child and kisses your hands and pleads and pleads, and the man is gone and you have a half-idiot child — and even that doesn't touch it, I mean what happens to me, and why I can't divorce him."

"How long have you been married?"

"When he went overseas. That was eight years ago." She shook her head. "I'm not telling you the truth. I'm trying to, but it's complicated and I keep thinking while I'm talking that you have some magic power to help me and release me — " Her voice trailed away, and David waited, intrigued as he watched her battle with herself, give way to her emotions, and then press them back inside her.

"Do you have any idea what I looked like as a child, as an adolescent?" she asked surprisingly.

David shook his head. This was another tack. He had thought before that possibly she was on the threshold of a breakdown, but now he began to see a desperate if disjointed pattern.

"I was too ugly to look at. I am almost five feet nine inches, and I was that height when I was fourteen, long skinny arms and legs like a scarecrow, no breasts, red elbows, red knees, freckles all over my face and arms and legs, and a face like a gargoyle. I still see myself that way. I'll see myself that way until the day I die. Do you know how boys reacted? They laughed. I was a joke, a hideous clown of a young girl. I met Harvey in college. He was the best-looking boy in his house, and he fell in love with me and he married me, and that's why I can't divorce him." The last words came through sobs that wracked her whole body.

David watched her with amazement. She was directing this awful cry of agony at him, and he was unable to respond. What could he do for her? She was out of another world, another culture, something as alien to him as, for example, coming into his mind for some reason, the culture of the Sherpas of Nepal. Had he ever known an alcoholic like her husband? In the service they went off on leave and became sodden drunk to pretend, to forget, to try happiness, and he had done that once himself, turning his mind to mush and his limbs to rubber; but that was not alcoholism. Why had she stepped out of her world into his world? She was sitting and weeping quietly now. She wore no make-up, no lip rouge, and David decided that, in a certain way, she was one of the most beautiful women he had ever seen, and he said to her, "But surely you know how beautiful you are?"

She stared at him through her tears.

"I mean, a mirror and common sense would prove that beyond question. A photograph."

"You don't understand, do you?" she said woefully.

"I'm afraid not."

She rose to go, but David leaped to his feet and pressed her shoulder gently. "Don't go, please."

"Why not? I imposed myself on you. Have you Kleenex or something?" He found a package in his desk and handed it to her. She was in control of herself now, wiping her eyes and saying, "In a way what I did was insulting. I said, You Jews are different. You're not really like other people. You have magic powers."

David smiled wanly. "Even a very few magic powers would have been so useful. Let me be frank with you. Probably the only way I can help you is by listening, if you need someone to listen. But I think you're a fascinating woman, and if you can make yourself free tonight, I'd like to take you to dinner and listen."

"And advise just a little?"

"If it will help."

"I can manage," she said. "Harvey is at the club, and by now quite drunk. I was supposed to meet him for dinner, but I can get out of that. On the other hand, Rabbi Hartman, what about yourself? Your wife is away, and if you're seen dining with me — "

"It will start talk. Suppose we go where we won't be seen. You know the Inn at Ridgefield?"

"Eight o'clock?"

David nodded. She shook hands with him and left. He didn't offer to see her to her car, and he realized that in the normal course of things he would have. But this was not the normal course of things. Whatever his feelings of compassion for Sarah Comstock's suffering, the dinner date was the result of his being attracted to another woman. Well, there it is, he said to himself. No use lying about it. I don't want to let her out of my life.

But if he didn't lie to himself, he had to lie to Lucy. My God, he thought, I'm walking on the edge of a cliff. What in hell am I up to?

He telephoned Lucy. "What are you going to do tonight?" she asked him.

"I have to get out of this place, at least for a few hours."

"Then come down here."

"I can't. Lucy, I can't face your family. Maybe I'll drive in to New York." He was covering his tracks, setting up blinds and emergency exits.

"You know how I miss you — with all this crowd," Lucy said. "If I hadn't found you, David, I would have absolutely remained unmarried. I can't tell you how reinforcing all this is, even if it gets to be a little bit of a bore. You know, we're near Asbury Park, but it's nice. They have this huge Victorian house, and the food doesn't stop flowing. Compared with this cornucopia, our life on the Ridge is positively ascetic. Sarah has the sniffles — "

It took him aback. One Sarah had replaced another in his mind, and for a brief moment, he heard Lucy talking about Sarah Comstock. But it was his own, small, lovely Sarah who had that uncomfortable curse of babyhood, the sniffles. He put down the phone and shook his head. "What in hell am I doing?" he asked aloud. He looked up the Comstock number in the telephone book. He would make some excuse about tonight — no, he would tell her the truth, flat out. He was a rabbi, he was married, he loved his wife as much as most men love their wives after five years of marriage, and he had two children.

He let the telephone ring ten times. There was no answer.

"I knew it was you," she said, facing him at the table that evening, "and that's why I didn't answer it. I knew what you were going to say — that you were a rabbi and married, with children, and that you loved your wife, and that we should forget this."

"How did you know all that?"

Sarah shrugged. "Sometimes you see a person and you feel that you know him, and on the other hand, you can be married for years and know nothing."

"That's rather romantic, isn't it?"

"I feel romantic tonight." She was smiling at him with pleasure. "Here I am at this sinful assignation with a Jewish rabbi — "

He couldn't resist her delight. "As most are."

"Yes, of course. I'm not drunk. I don't drink, which won't surprise you — David? May I call you David? It's a lovely name. As much as I was depressed and suicidal this morning — you're thinking manic-depressive, aren't you?"

"No. I'm listening to you and trying to decide what color your eyes are."

"Of course you're not. You're being sweet and kind and wishing to God you were not here."

"That's half true," David admitted.

"And the other half?"

"I'm very happy that I'm here. I've been bored, depressed, and constantly angry with myself. Tonight, all I suffer from is guilt."

"Why? You're doing nothing wrong, and you're helping me just by being here with me more than anything you could say or counsel. I've been so lonely. And afraid."

There was a long moment of silence before David asked her what she was afraid of.

"Death. I don't want to die. It's all too beautiful, and I

haven't even tasted it, only licked it around the edges. Do you know how good-looking you are, David? Tall, skinny, with those blue eyes like cold water. We are the handsomest couple here, even if there is an ugly little bony girl sitting inside me. I haven't felt this way for years. I actually feel beautiful. I don't want to die."

"You won't die. Not for many long years."

"I try to get Marty to talk about heaven. I don't believe in it. It's too utterly ridiculous. Heaven, hell, how can you believe? But Marty won't discuss it. Pray, he tells me. What kind of a heaven do you people teach?"

"None."

"Just close your eyes and go to sleep. Is that it?"

David nodded. "We do it each night."

"That wouldn't be too terrible, would it? But then I remember Swinburne's lines 'Only the sleep eternal, in an eternal night,' and just the thought of that frightens me so my heart stops beating. I hate Swinburne, a sentimental fraud, oh, I do detest him and all his sloppy, phony hedonism. But there is a God. There must be a God. You know the story about Ingersoll, David, Ingersoll the notorious atheist, and he visited a friend who had a marvelous contraption, a miniature solar system made of crystal and fine wire, and after Ingersoll finished admiring it, he turned to his friend and asked who made it. His friend answered that no one made it, it just happened. But you do believe in God, David. You must?"

"I do, but it's not always easy. You know, Ingersoll was an agnostic, not an atheist. He hungered for belief."

"You're like Marty Carter. You don't want to talk about God or the hereafter. It puts you off. But if I were a Jew, I don't think I'd have much truck with a God who sat back and watched the murder of six million of my brothers and sisters. No! I don't want to get into a discussion about that. I want to order dinner. This is a nice place, David. I think the only restaurants in New England should be inns, and if they run out of inns, they should build careful replicas."

"You're an extraordinary woman, Sarah. But I don't understand this obsession with death and the hereafter."

"Because it frightens me, every minute of every day."

"Now?"

"No, not now, bless you."

"Have you tried to find help for it?"

"I came to you."

"I mean some sort of therapy?"

"No."

"Why?"

"I don't want that. I want to order my dinner. I haven't eaten all day, and I'm starved. I want you to pick out your favorite thing and then I'll select mine, and we'll talk about it."

She was like a charming, wise thirteen-year-old. She was enormously pleased with herself, with David, and with the evening. Her strong, sharp-featured face softened, and the candlelight from the table candle set bits of magic light dancing in her amber-colored eyes.

"It's so hard to be sweet and cute when you're five feet nine inches," she said, "but that's how I feel tonight. What are sweetbreads? Do you know?"

"Only that they come from inside the cow."

"Nobody knows. But I never had them, and tonight's not a time to start. I think leg of lamb, roasted. My maternal grandmother was French, and she worshipped roast leg of lamb. I think it's a national obsession of the French. Do you like it?"

"Very much. Why don't we both have it?"

"No, no, no, dear David. You must have what you love best."

"Hamburger?" very tentatively.

"Really? Thank heavens they don't have it on the menu. Very well, lamb for both of us. Soup, salad, lamb — yes, staunch, plain New England food. Where do you come from, David? Where were you born?"

"In New York City."

"I was born in Boston. My maiden name was Lowell, but not the grand Lowells. We're not even distantly related, but I think that's what got me into college; not denying it, I mean. You look puzzled. Don't you know that wonderful sonnet, Boston, Boston, the home of the bean and the cod, where the Cabots speak only to the Lowells — or is it the Cabots? Well, something like it — and the Lowells speak only to God, and of course I know it isn't a sonnet, which has fourteen lines in iambic pentameter, and is really a dumb way to write poetry. I was a great student. If you're ugly as sin, what else is there? And that's enough. Now you talk."

"I'd much rather listen."

"Oh, no. Then you're doing therapy on me."

"No, not at all. I'm charmed by you. I'm sitting here with a warm glow all over me, Sarah."

"Because we know each other, Rabbi."

"No," David said firmly. "We're not teen-agers, and we don't know each other. Each of us is a mystery to the other one. I've been married for five years to a woman, and each of us — my wife and I — each of us is a stranger to the other. Do you know who your husband is, Sarah?"

"Sometimes, God help me."

"Yet" — he reached over and took her hand — "at this moment, Sarah Comstock, and I'm trying to be direct and truthful, I feel that I would give my whole life up to be with you, but that's not true or real, is it?"

"I'm afraid not," she said sadly, her eyes moistening.

"We both understand our illusions and our fantasies, and they mingle. When I was in the service, kids would go out on a one-day pass and they would come back and say, Rabbi, I'm in love. It was love at first sight. Illusion. It never happened to me, not even with Lucy."

"It would happen to me with movie stars, not with real people." She turned her hand so that the palm pressed against David's palm. "I came to you, dear David, at the moment of my most awful need, and you helped me more than you can imagine, and tonight you're making me very happy. I think you are in love with me — like the little boys in uniform. I am not going to cry. Enough of this. Please order our dinner."

After dinner, they went into the bar, where a good wood fire burned, and David asked for two glasses of port. They sat and watched the flames and sipped the sweet wine.

"I want this evening never to end," Sarah said.

"It must, dear lady. We step back into reality." He leaned over and kissed her. Her mouth parted, as if her whole body was melting toward him.

"But we can stay a little longer. It's only ten o'clock."

"Of course."

"We had a fireplace when I was a little girl. I can't remember anything I loved more than lying in front of it and watching the flames. Did you have a fireplace, David?"

"No, just a plain old New York City apartment. The Hartmans are an old and very wealthy family in New York, but like you and the Lowells, we were only distantly attached."

"And why did you become a rabbi, David? Tell me."

Had Lucy ever asked him that? David wondered. Or were there things that Lucy knew about him that needed no questions and no discussion? He stared at Sarah without answering.

"David?"

"It's not easy to explain," he finally said. "It had to do with justifying to myself that there was some compassion and some decency in the world. Or did it? That isn't all of it either. I don't know how to explain without sounding foolish and presumptuous. You want to help people. You want to find yourself in the universe. We have a legend of the *Lamed Vov*, the thirty-six righteous and compassionate men who must exist in every generation to justify the continuing existence of the human race."

"And if they are destroyed?" she wondered.

"Then the life of man is over. You see, Sarah, the decision

Martin made to become a minister and the decision I made to become a rabbi — these are early decisions in a man's life. We were young enough to have dreams. My family was not a very religious one, and like so many of the German Jews who came here during the last century, my father and mother had almost forgotten that they were Jews. Many of the Hartmans were very rich and had married Gentiles — not that we were rich. I think it was Hitler and his Nazis that reminded so many of us. We remembered that we were Jews. I don't know whether that answers your question or not."

"Probably not. Why should questions be answered? Except for questions that aren't asked. Give me your hand, David." She put his hand between both of hers. "I reach out to you and find God." He shook his head and she smiled with calm satisfaction. "You've passed the magic to me. I know things that you don't know, David. This is the first time I have been without fear in months and months."

"My dear, darling Sarah," David said, "we've known each other a few hours, and each of us has his own hunger and need. At this moment, we feel very close, but we're strangers."

"No, we're not strangers."

"I could love you so easily, but I can't," David said miserably. "You know that nothing can come of this."

"Something already has."

"We'll sit here another half-hour," David said, "and then we'll get into our separate cars and drive home."

"Yes. And not interrupt or shatter our contrived lives, and hang on to this moment. 'The shade by which my life was crost, which makes a desert in the mind, has made me kindly with my kind, and like to him whose sight is lost.' I picked that up far back, back before college, David. There are scraps of poetry that define lives, and I guess I picked that one because of its proper definition. You know, I don't really think I'm ugly. Well, I do and I don't, and enough men have told me how beautiful I am to shake my conviction. But one way or another, how does it help me, David? I chatter like this because my mind chatters."

"The fear will go away," David said gently.

"It has — for tonight."

"You'll have no problems with your husband?"

"He'll be in a stupor, if he gets home at all tonight."

Outside, the cold, clean air of early fall made them press close to each other, and at the cars, David took her in his arms, and both clung to each other in a kind of awful desperation.

"Drive carefully," he whispered.

She kissed him, and again they embraced, and then she got into her car and drove away. She was driving a Mercedes. It was 1951, only six years after the end of the Holocaust. It couldn't have any meaning for her, he told himself, but it increased his feeling of guilt. The romantic glow of the evening began to fade, and as he drove home, it faded even more. He had taken advantage of a troubled, neurotic woman who had reached out desperately for help. It would be assuaging his conscience to imagine that this was one of those wonderful, fatefully appointed love affairs that one reads about in romantic novels, but the brutal fact of the matter was that just about this time Lucy might be singing softly to another Sarah, who had awakened from her sleep. He tried to balance things: How did he feel about Lucy, his wife, and how did he feel about this tortured, beautiful woman called Sarah, whom he had met only the day before? Had Lucy ever woven that same spell about him? But Lucy would have said, matter-of-factly, Come down to earth, Rabbi. Spells are for the birds, as both you and I know. The evening had cost him about twenty dollars. When was the last time he had asked Lucy to have dinner with him at the Inn or some such place? But then Lucy was there. She would always be there, and there would be time for everything later. Procrastination was a salve.

He couldn't get to sleep that night. He tossed and turned and twisted and changed his position again and again, and then, finally, he gave it up and put on a robe. The house was icy cold. He tried to endure it at first, his robe pulled tightly about him, thinking that after spending the price of a week's grocery shopping under Lucy's careful control, he had no right to burn oil. But asceticism had never been one of David's strong points, clerical or otherwise, and after a few minutes he turned up the heat, satisfied that his mental suffering was sufficient to temper his guilt. It was late enough, or early enough, depending on how one regarded the night, for his thoughts to move turgidly, and as he reviewed the events of Saturday night, he tried to frame them in relation to himself.

It was not simple. He was a man who loved women, and he had loved women ever since he could remember, even as a small child. In his manhood, women intrigued him, delighted him, fascinated him, and made him feel, again and again, that the fate of humanity, already halfway down the sewer, was perhaps retrievable through the intervention of women. And, happily, he had been loved by a number of women, but under very special circumstances; for like so many of his generation he had come into his manhood during the bloodiest and most terrible war that had ever been.

Then he had married.

He brooded over his marriage to Lucy. He had never been unfaithful to her. Why should he be? He dispensed the vows of marriage and he respected them, and Lucy was a lovely young woman, bright and totally committed to her husband — which, considering his profession, income, and place in the world, was no easy thing. They had their bleak moments, but all things considered, he had felt that theirs was a good marriage. And then Sarah Comstock had entered his world.

He had tried to help her — or had he? He had kissed her and embraced her. I didn't go to bed with her, he told himself angrily. I helped her. She said I had helped her. She made a point of that.

He walked into his study then, turned on a light, and dropped into his desk chair, tired and miserable. His mail of that day, still unopened, was piled on his desk, and there, on top, was a letter from Mike Benton. Since he couldn't sleep, David decided that he might as well read his mail. He began with Benton's letter.

"Dear Rabbi Hartman," Benton wrote. "Thank goodness I joined your congregation, because I am the most unbelieving son of a bitch in the world, and I don't like Jews any more than I like Catholics or Protestants, except the people and not the cruds who work the pulpits — excluding you, naturally — and as far as God is concerned, if I believed in the stupid bastard who gets his jollies out of things like this war we were in and Shithead Adolf, I'd spend my life writing editorials against him and maybe get a petition out to make him bug off and find some other solar system to work out his lunatic fantasies."

David paused, thinking that it was an amazingly long and awkward sentence, but that hidden somewhere in it was the meat of an interesting sermon, and then said aloud, "Oh, no, Hartman, you ought to go and hand in your credentials. Here's a member of your congregation in agony, which he can only spell out in his own way, and a few hours ago you left a woman in another kind of agony, and all you can do is mine the situation for one of your lousy sermons."

But he also realized that even his act of indicting himself aloud to an empty room was brush and spit and polish for his ego, making him no better and possibly a bit worse.

"All right," he said aloud to the empty room. "Stop trying to be any better, because that stinks too."

He went back to the letter and read: "All of the above being in line with the fact that I can write to you. Who can you write to in a federal jail? Your bookie, mistress, friendly dope pusher — perish the thought. These careful Feds specify: you can write to your lawyer, mother, father, sisters, brothers, priest, minister, rabbi. Since I still owe my lawyer twelve large ones, he certainly does not wish to waste his time communicating with me, and I lack mother, father, sister, and brother. Poor Mitzie, poor dear, is not related to me, and that leaves Rabbi Hartman; but I know you'll read the letter to her, since she has suffered so much more than I have from this demented business. The terror I felt about going in here has gradually diminished, and now, three weeks after I began to serve my sentence, I am a little at ease.

"I think they had good reason for sending me here. By *they*, I mean James Bennett, who is the Federal Commissioner of Prisons, a civilized man laboring in a troglodyte jungle; and *here* is a work prison in the West Virginia mountains. Anything we write about the physical make-up of the prison will be censored out, but I can say that it's fairly civilized as prisons go, and I imagine Bennett would like me to write about it after I get out, five months from now. Six months. One of the cons here says, 'Six months — I can do that standing on my head.' To me, it's an eternity, and it even makes that weird little Wasp village, Leighton Ridge, look good. Mitzie, my dear friend and rabbi, is still living in the house we rented. Please look her up and let her read this. Also, tell her I'm very fond of her. Shit — pull out the stops. Tell her I love her."

David went back to bed then, and this time he slept until he was awakened about eight o'clock in the morning by a phone call from Lucy.

"I thought I'd get this in before the wedding starts. I'm not angry. I love you. Did I wake you?"

"I was up late reading." First lie.

"Hot milk. Did you take a glass of hot milk? You may not believe me, but drink a glass of hot milk and you sleep like a baby. David, you should see the tent they put up here. Not a tent, exactly; a Jewish pavilion right out of the Middle Ages. Are you there?"

"I'm not sure where I am, Lucy. At three in the morning I was sitting at my desk reading a letter from Mike Benton, poor devil."

"Where is he?"

"In some miserable jail in West Virginia."

"Just for refusing to play informer. Dave, it's crazy. We'll be home tonight. I don't like this business of you sitting awake at three o'clock in the morning. The wedding should be over by six at the latest, and we can take a late train. Will you meet us?"

"Of course I'll meet you. Just hang on and I'll get the timetable."

"And get a nap in before the judge comes."

"The judge? What judge?" He had forgotten completely.

He had a ten o'clock adult class on "The Old Testament As History," and he took a cold shower to clear his head. The class had been working on the question of the Samaritans, and David had found himself as fascinated as his students with this strange people of ancient Israel, whose history was so tragic and so little remembered. In spite of his sleepless night, he managed. He had twelve men and women in his Bible class, and since that meant giving up hours of their Sunday morning, he felt that he was doing pretty well.

But as he walked back to the new house the congregation had provided for him, a sort of bastardized ranch house–Colonial creation, his thoughts returned to the incident of the night before. He had to face the fact that not only did he want to see Sarah Comstock again, but his desire to do so was like a hunger.

Waiting for Jack Osner's friend, Judge Interman, to arrive was much more a wait for Sarah Comstock to telephone him. But she did not telephone, and at exactly three o'clock on that Sunday afternoon, Jack Osner drove up with Judge Interman.

David watched them from a window, trying to get some sense of the man before meeting him, but Interman came off simply as a well-fed, very ordinary, and somewhat overweight middle-class, middle-aged man, his thick thatch of hair, gray turning white, his face pudgy. He appeared to have a nervous habit of biting his lower lip, but that might reflect only his current stress.

Nodding earnestly, he shook hands with David. His handshake was tentative, not an unusual thing among those who shook hands with a rabbi, a kind uncertainty which was reflected in the way he studied David.

"Bill Interman and I go back a long ways," Osner said. "We clerked together for the same justice of the Supreme Court, and before that we were at Harvard together. True, I remained a plain old country lawyer, while he's up there on the bench as a federal district judge, but that's the way the cards are dealt."

"Jack's an old friend," Interman acknowledged.

"Suppose I leave you two alone. I'll wander over to the synagogue, and then when you've finished your talk, David will take you over there and I'll drive you back to my house."

Interman nodded, and Osner left. David suggested that they sit down in his small study. Interman appeared to be clamped into silence, and David waited. Finally, Interman asked him how old he was.

"I'm thirty-four, Judge Interman. If you feel that you can't say what you wish to say to a man as young as myself, I can understand that. I won't be offended."

"Still, Jack Osner tells me you've been through all kinds of hell."

"I was overseas during the war, if that's what you mean."

Interman nodded. "If we talk, is what I say privileged?"

"You mean the way it would be if I were your attorney? I'm not sure, but I don't think so."

"It is with a priest."

"Yes. But confession is an integral part of the Catholic faith. That's not the case with ours." And then, seeing Interman's increased state of anxiety, David added, "But I can tell you this. If you wish our talk to remain secret, it will. You will simply have to trust me."

"Do you mind if I smoke?" Interman asked.

"No, not at all."

His hand was shaking as he lit his cigarette. "Trouble is

sleep," he said. "I haven't been sleeping since this began."

David nodded and waited. His previous experience with judges had been limited to several tours of duty as a juror, but that had been sufficient to impress him with the fact that the black-gowned figure seated at the end of a courtroom was both subjectively and objectively a small tin god, more powerful in a certain sense than any other element of so-called civilized society. Now the federal judge in his study was staring at him hopelessly, power and arrogance gone.

"Have you been following the case of the atom bomb spies?" Judge Interman asked suddenly, apropos of no introduction or indication, blinking his eyes as if he had just awakened.

"Only what I read in the papers."

"How do you feel about them?"

"I feel sorry. I feel sad and confused," David said. "I have a member of my congregation, a brilliant screenwriter, who is serving a year in a federal penitentiary because he would not reveal the names of people he saw at left-wing meetings. I feel sorry for him. I feel sorry and ashamed for my country."

"Do you mean that you sympathize with these people?" the judge demanded.

"I'm a rabbi. I sympathize with people who suffer. Do you find that so astonishing, Judge Interman? I also sympathize with you, because you had to sit in judgment."

"No, sir," Interman said harshly. "Not because I was the judge in the case. These people betrayed their country."

"Yes, they did."

"I think," the judge said, "that I may have come to the wrong place."

"Perhaps."

Yet Interman made no motion to leave. He didn't rise; he didn't look at his watch. He simply sat there, staring at David, and after a few minutes had gone by, David said gently, "I'll listen, and I'll try to help. Whether or not I can, I don't know. But I'll try."

"I have some leeway in sentencing them," Interman said. "I suppose you realize that."

"So I've read."

"You don't just sentence two such people in a case like this. God Almighty, no. We're dealing with a death sentence, and that's what I couldn't face. Do you understand why?"

"I think so. You're Jewish and they're Jewish. But you felt they deserved the death sentence?"

"Don't you, Rabbi?"

"I'm not a judge," David said.

"So I asked that I be removed from the case, that some other judge pass sentence. I'm not evading my duty. I sat through the case. The jury brought in a verdict of guilty."

"Why must it be a death sentence?" David asked. "Civilized countries are doing away with capital punishment."

"I thought of that too. Don't think I didn't consider it, but certain things happened."

David waited.

"The President got in touch with me. He asked me to come down to Washington — " He paused, staring past David at the wall. "I was flattered. Anyone would be flattered. Can you understand that, Rabbi? An invitation from the White House, you're flattered. Well, my God, the case had taken the guts out of me, and I handled it. I didn't run for cover because I was a Jew. I did my duty, and it makes sense that I was being invited down to Washington for a pat on the shoulder, doesn't it?"

"It makes sense," David agreed.

"Well, I'm down there. I'm taken into his office. He doesn't even offer to shake hands with me. He just says to me, flatly, 'Judge Interman, I want you to sentence them to death.'

" 'With all due deference, Mr. President,' I said to him, 'I can't pass the death sentence on those two people.' And then he looks at me as cold as ice, Rabbi, and he says to me, 'What in hell do you mean, you can't?' " He paused and closed his eyes. Then he opened them and looked around the room. "You've never been in that office?"

"Never been to Washington in my life," David said.

"No. Well, it does something to you. I tried to explain. I said to him, 'Mr. President, please try to understand the position I am in. These will be the first two people to be executed for espionage in our time, and they're both Jewish. I'm Jewish, and God knows there's talk enough that they've been singled out because they're Jewish.' "

"You said that?"

"Rabbi, you'd have to close your eyes and your ears not to know that."

"What did he say?"

"He was enraged with me. 'You don't spill that kind of garbage in here. They were on trial because they were spies, not because they were Jewish'—or some such thing. I can't remember exactly. I never knew the man could have such anger. I tried to make him understand that if I gave them a death sentence, it would be the end of my existence as a normal human being. I would live on as the judge who had sentenced them to death. Am I right, Rabbi? Tell me, am I right?"

"I think so, yes."

"How would you look at me? I sit here. Here's Interman. He sentenced a Jewish man and woman to death, the first in the twentieth century to be so sentenced. That's what I tried to explain to him, Rabbi. Goddamnit, I am somebody! I paid my dues! He was a political hack from his beginning. I am a judge in a federal court. I'm a human being. Who the hell is he? This is supposed to be a democracy. I stood up to him. I told him, 'No, I will not do it. You want a death sentence, get someone else to do it. You didn't appoint me, and I'm not your errand boy.' Then he just studies me for a while, and then he says, 'It's pretty damn good, being a judge, isn't it?' I didn't know what to make of that. With all that's been written about him, he's not an easy man to talk to. Not for me, in any case. He has that bland middle-America face and those rimless glasses I kept thinking about George Babbitt. Did you ever read *Babbitt*, Rabbi?"

"Yes, when I was much younger."

"Babbitt. Well, you can see the condition my mind is in. Where was I?"

"Something Truman said about being a judge?"

"Oh, yes. Yes, of course." Interman shook his head, closed his eyes for a long moment, and then wiped them with his handkerchief.

"I'd like a drink, Rabbi, if you don't mind," he said almost plaintively.

"Of course."

"Just a little Scotch or bourbon straight, if you have it. No ice or anything."

David brought him the Scotch, and he drained it down in a single gulp. "Yes, he said that it was pretty good being a judge, and then when I didn't know what to make of it, except to agree with him, he says, 'a Jew judge, that's something' — can you imagine, from the President of the United States?"

"I find it hard to imagine or believe," David said.

"I'm not lying. Would I lie to you?"

"Of course not."

"I'm on edge, Rabbi. In my mind, I see myself standing up right then and there in the Oval Office and saying to that little bastard, 'This is the United States of America and I'm a judge in the Federal Circuit Court, and I am Jewish, and I came out of the streets of New York, fought my way out with wit, with intelligence, and I was trained at Harvard College and Harvard Law School — not picked out of a haberdashery by a political boss called Pendergast, and you sit there and sneer at me because I'm Jewish.' "

Then Interman was silent, and after a minute or so, David said to him, "But you didn't say that?"

"No."

"What did you say, if I may ask?"

"I said, 'Yes, Mr. President, it's an honor.' "

"Just that?"

"That's all. He became very sweet and persuasive, and lectured me gently about doing my duty to the country that gave me sustenance. He came over to me, and he patted me on my shoulder, as if I were a kid who had been fresh to his daddy. Yet I kept thinking that I was my own man, and that I would be damned if I sentenced the atom spies to death."

"Then you decided not to pass the death sentence?"

"I don't know. I thought I knew, but I don't, and now I feel that I must do it."

"What?"

"The death sentence. Yet if I sentence the atom spies to death, I will become a leper among my own people, a pariah. God help me, what shall I do?"

They sat for a little while in silence, and then David asked him, "Is it being a pariah among your own people that tortures you — or pronouncing the death sentence on two people who, whatever their sins, perhaps do not deserve to die?"

"I don't follow you," Interman told him. "Would you repeat that?"

"You raise the problem of what will overtake you if you pass the death sentence, if you sentence the two atom spies to death. As you say, they're both Jewish, and they will be the first to be executed for espionage in our time. Then it's almost impossible to separate the sentence from the fact that they are Jews. I'm only an observer of this whole incident, but there are many people who doubt that the government has proved its case — "

"Rabbi, this is damned communist propaganda!" Interman cried.

"Yes — perhaps. I don't want to argue that part of it, their guilt or innocence. I don't know enough to do so. But I do know that a good part of the circus that revolves around them is anti-Semitism, and certainly if we were dealing with a clean-cut, well-bred white Protestant couple, there would be no question of the death sentence. And there is no doubt, I am afraid, that if you sentence them to death, your action will not be praised or even condoned by most Jews. The question I put to you is simply this: Are you agonizing over the matter because you will be despised by many Jews or because you feel the spies do not deserve to die?"

"Forgive me," Interman said with annoyance, "but what in hell are you talking about? I sat on this trial. Those two bastards are guilty as hell, and the fact that they are Jewish doubles the immensity of their crime."

"Why?"

"Because every Jew is tarred by the guilt."

"Every one? Even the six million who died in the Holocaust?"

"You know damned well what I mean."

"And if you weren't Jewish, would you pass the death sentence?"

"In a minute."

David shook his head. "Tell me, Judge Interman," he said, "why did you come to me? To have me praise you? Or to assure you that Jews will not condemn you for sentencing two Jews to death?"

"There's no question about whether or not they will die. If I don't sentence them, another judge will. It's easy enough for you to sit there like some damned stone Buddha. But I have to make the decision and I have to live with it."

"We all live with our particular agony."

"And that's your advice, as a rabbi?" He rose and stalked to the door, where he paused and said, "I shouldn't have come here. I told Osner I shouldn't have come here." He then took two steps back to David. "You are one righteous bastard, aren't you, Rabbi?" Then his pugnacity collapsed and he stared at David, his eyes wet. "For God's sake, help me, Rabbi."

"I don't know how to help you," David said slowly. "I don't know what to tell you. How can I help you when I must speak out of my own belief? In my belief, no man has the right to say who should live and who should die. We have a President who dislikes Jews — not too unusual in our society — but would he undertake any action against you? It wouldn't be easy. You could expose him. He would deny it, but it would still put him in a difficult position, and once you had pronounced something less than the death sentence, no one could change it. But those are just random thoughts. You must do what your own conscience dictates."

After he had taken Judge Interman to the synagogue to meet Jack Osner, David returned home and put down in his diary an account of the conversation as accurately as he could remember it, and then he wrote, "More and more, I wonder about my own function as a rabbi. I know a number of my fellow rabbis who regard their work as a profession. Martin Carter accepts the fact that he has a calling, whatever that is. I must talk to him about that. As for Judge Interman, why have I so little compassion for him? I can see it his way, his fight as a Jew to get into Harvard Law School, the dues he paid politically to get his first appointment, I think as assistant federal prosecutor, according to Osner, and then clawing his way up the ladder. The naked truth of the matter is that I dislike and distrust all judges."

Back home the following day, Lucy and two noisy children set the world to rights. Lucy put on a pale green organdy dress that reached to her ankles and paraded it in front of David. "Gift from the mother of the bride. They sit around nights thinking of ways to spend money. I was a lady-in-waiting. Thank God you didn't come. Flower girls, bridesmaids, groomsmen, or whatever they're called, and ladies-in-waiting, the same as at Buckingham Palace. They had forty-two different varieties of canapés plus a fountain that poured four different flavors of punch. Do you know, it was fun. You weren't there, so I didn't have to be thinking all the time about what you were thinking. It was obscene, absolutely obscene; it created new levels of vulgarity, but it was fun. Did you ever see anything as hideous as this dress?"

"It's not too bad," David said, unable to deny that she looked very young and beautiful. "You are lovely, truly lovely."

"Oh, no, no, no. This color is hideous. Do you know, David, one of my dreadful cousins whom I had never met before came on to me. Would you believe it? An oversized football-player type who decided I was the best-looking woman there. It didn't take any time at all to shoot him down, but I think it was flattering, don't you?"

He was trying to decide whether he should tell her about the dinner at the Inn at Ridgefield.

"David, where are you?"

"I was thinking about Judge Interman." Second lie.

"And you didn't hear a word I said. A big oversized cousin type pawing at me and trying to get me into bed — "

"Your cousin?"

"Well, I finally reached you. Yes, a first cousin, but this is the first time I met him. From Salt Lake City. How would you like to be a rabbi in Salt Lake City, where all the Jews are Gentiles? There was a whole contingent from there, eight of them, with their stupid jokes. Why are families so awful, David? Why isn't there anyone in a family like you? Anyway, it made me think about adultery. Not for me. What's that one Yiddish phrase you know? Yes — it *past nisht*. Not fitting at all. I don't know why I didn't recognize Interman's name — "

David decided he would not mention the Inn at Ridgefield.

" — but then it struck me like a flash. He's the judge who sat in the trial of the atom spies. What did he want?"

"Solace."

"He wants you to take the curse off so that he can sentence them to death?"

Amazed, David asked, "What makes you say that?"

She put her arms around him and said, "My dear, innocent husband, in this stinking world, when you choose the most deplorable answer to any question, it's most likely to be right."

"That's pretty cynical."

"I'm cynical. Let's go to bed and make love."

The following day, David drove over to Mike Benton's house. A quarter cord of wood had been delivered and dumped in the front yard. Mitzie, in jeans and sweater, was carrying it inside.

"Hello, Rabbi," she said. "It's going to be a long, cold winter."

David picked up an armload of wood and followed her into the house. Neat and clean, without Benton's deliberate slovenliness, the house was even less attractive; and Mitzie, noticing his glance, said, "It makes me cringe, Rabbi. Well, he'll be out in six months, and then we'll head for California. I wish sometimes we hadn't taken almost three years of appeals. The end result would have been the same, and he'd be out by now. I never thought I would miss him so, and I never thought I could love a man so much."

"I have a letter from Mike," David said. "You know he can't write directly to you. It's rather terse, but when he settles down, I'm sure his letters will be longer and deeper. Let me bring in the rest of the wood while you read it."

"Oh, no. I can't impose on you."

"Please. I need the exercise."

Later, having finished with the wood, and trying to start a fire, he looked up from where he was stuffing papers under the grate. Mitzie was crying.

"He's all right," David said. "That's the main thing."

"It's crazy."

"Yes. A lot of things are."

"He faced death over and over for his country. Have they forgotten that already, Rabbi? And then they put him in prison. He wasn't a communist. He went to their meetings because his friends went, but suppose he were a communist? Does he have to go to prison for not being an informer?"

"He'll hack it," David said. "Then it's over and done with. I understand you're working."

"I got a job selling stockings in a store in Danbury. It's all right. It's a job, and it's better than waiting tables. And Mike left enough money for the rent and other things."

"Would you come for supper some evening?" David asked her.

"I'd love to. It's the first invitation I've had since Mike went to jail."

At home that evening, Lucy, distracted, nodded and mumbled something about knowing Mitzie and liking her. Lucy was bathing little Sarah while David dried his son. At age four, Aaron gave promise of long limbs and red hair. Both children were articulate, and they were talking a blue streak under Lucy and David's words. Lucy was asking David whether he thought she looked Jewish.

"That's a new one. About this kid Mitzie. Can we have her to dinner next week?"

"Some women at the market decided that I was one of those miserable Jews who are spoiling the place."

"What's a miserable jew?" Aaron asked.

"Let's get them down," David said.

At the dinner table, Lucy said to him, "I miss the old house. I know it was falling apart, but it had some style. This so-called modern house they built for us is so ugly and stupid. It doesn't belong here."

"That's not what creates anti-Semitism, Lucy. You know that. Before the war there was only a handful of Jewish families here in Leighton Ridge. Now there are a good many more."

"It was just a stupid woman, but I never saw her before. It was like putting a knife into me. I had the children with me, and all I could think of was My darlings, my darlings, this was to be no part of your world."

"It's no use thinking that way, Lucy. All the dirt and filth and hate has to be a part of their world. We'll try to shelter them and protect them, but they must live in the world."

"It's a great world. I must say, when that God of yours

fiddles with the planets, he puts together some beauties —
and there I go again. I'm sorry, David. About Mitzie — yes,
of course. I'll invite her to dinner. We'll try to cheer her up."

"It's all right."

She began to cry. He walked around the table behind her
chair and put his arms around her.

But the question came up again at the next board meeting
of the synagogue. Joe Hurtz brought up the issue of increasing anti-Semitism. He had a men's haberdashery store in Danbury, and, as he put it, he had his ear to the ground.

"Still and all," old Oscar Denton pointed out, "Danbury is
not Leighton Ridge. Not only is it a good distance away, but
there were a lot of Jews mixed up in the hat business in the
old days and that might have left some nastiness."

"I hear talk," Joe Hurtz said. "It's not only Danbury. It
reaches over here."

"It's something Jews have lived with a long time," David
said. "Like the weather, we can talk about it, but we can't do
much to change it."

"I agree with David," Mel Klein said. "We got more important things. We got the Israel Bond drive on the agenda, and
we still got the question of a crèche for the preschool kids.
That's going to cost a small bundle."

"Don't drop it so quickly," Jack Osner said. "Anti-Semitism is not like a hurricane. It's not an act of God. The two
atom spies played their part — the two most notorious spies
of our time, engaged in the most damaging piece of espionage,
and both Jewish — "

"Come on," Oscar Denton interrupted, "they did a little
less than that. They passed on some drawings of the implosion mechanism, something I could build myself, given
enough time. They were stupid and disloyal, but so was Ezra
Pound, and no one talks of executing him."

Ed Frome, the magazine writer, was intrigued and said to
the old man, "Come on, Oscar, you're a contractor. I mean
you build houses. This thing — "

"They didn't steal the secret of making the bomb," Denton told them. "That's no secret. What they passed on was a diagram of the mechanism that sets off the bomb. You don't explode an atomic weapon the way you do a charge of dynamite. You have to turn your pellets of uranium into critical mass, and to do that you need what they call an implosion, pellets directed in instead of out. Sure I could make it. Oh, I'd have to hire some machinists for the fine work, but I could make it."

"Goddamnit, Oscar," Osner said, "you're the last person I'd expect to deliver a defense of those two miserable traitors."

"I'm not defending them," Denton said quietly. "I'm explaining what they did."

"Well, I don't buy your explanation."

"Let's get down to business," Mel Klein urged.

Osner persisted. "What I said goes. And it doesn't help that a member of this congregation is serving time as a communist right now."

"Oh, please, Jack," David said. "You know better than that. You're a lawyer. Mike Benton is in there because he wouldn't name names, because he wouldn't be an informer."

"Whatever, he's a communist and he doesn't belong in this congregation. I think it would be a positive gesture to expel him."

"What!"

"I never thought you were a nice guy, Jack," Ed Frome said, "but I also never took you for such a consummate son of a bitch."

"You can't talk to me like that!" Osner shouted.

"Stop it!" Denton snapped. "Grown men acting like kids. We're a board of a synagogue, and we're entitled to different opinions — Jack's as well as yours, Ed. So let's cool this whole thing and talk sense."

"And did they talk sense?" Lucy wanted to know, after David told her about the squabble.

"Not very much. The question of the crèche was tabled for a meeting of the entire board. Oscar Denton, you know, the old man who was the biggest contractor in New Haven, well, he's pretty liberal and open-minded. But on this he just froze up. I think the word itself annoyed him. It's the word Christians use for their models of the Nativity scene — the stable, the Christ Child, and Mary."

"Good heavens, he's not Orthodox."

"People aren't consistent, Lucy, and Oscar is the wealthiest man in the congregation. You know, the Episcopal church has a crèche and so has Martin Carter's church, and Oscar feels we're aping them. It's expensive, not only for the initial establishment, but we need two teachers who have been trained in prekindergarten work. Yet more and more, we're getting young people in the congregation, and when the mother and father both work, it's a problem."

"I don't suppose we could even consider putting our two kids in the Congregational crèche?"

"Over my dead body." David grinned. "And there are at least twenty members of the congregation who'd make sure it was very dead."

It was at moments like this, when they were very relaxed and sharing things, that David considered telling Lucy the whole story of his encounter with Sarah Comstock. He resisted the impulse, just as he had resisted the impulse to ask Lucy about the cookbook. But Lucy told him finally, and he registered appropriate surprise and excitement. They had even found a publisher. His expressions of delight, however, did not lessen his guilt.

Sarah had called David's office at the synagogue twice. The calls were taken by Mrs. Shapiro, David's new and first secretary, part time but kindly and efficient. She was from Bridgeport and had not been around the Ridge long enough for the name Comstock to mean anything, or to be curious as to why a Sarah Comstock was calling the rabbi.

After a week had gone by, David thought that he had to

return the calls. Guilty though he felt, he wanted desperately to see Sarah Comstock again, enough to overcome the guilt. He telephoned her during the day, and she asked him to meet her, if he could, at Brandywine Lake, about twelve miles north of Leighton Ridge. "I'll be at the boathouse at three," she said. "It's closed down for the winter. No one goes there at this season."

David telephoned Lucy, once again with a lie, telling her that he was driving to New York for a meeting at the Institute. It was not only that Lucy was totally trusting; she was also apparently incapable of suspicion, and David wondered how any man could carry on an extramarital affair if he was married to a trusting woman.

He parked at the lake. The weather had turned cold, and he buttoned his coat as he scuffed through the dry leaves. Sarah was sitting on a bench outside the boathouse, wrapped in a huge sweater. There was not another soul in sight. She rose as he came up to her and stood facing him, and after a long moment of hesitation, he put his arms around her and kissed her.

"I want you to know, dear David," she said quickly, "that I understand our situation completely. You will never leave your wife and daughter and son, and even if you were unencumbered, I am not sure you would want to marry me. There is no open door for us, no way out."

He held her face between his palms, staring at her.

"Is there?"

"No," he said.

"Do you love me, David?"

"I think of you day and night. I want to be with you more than anything in the world."

"We're neither of us very strong, and I think we're both frauds. Otherwise, I'd leave my husband, and you — " Her voice trailed away.

"I'm not that strong," David admitted.

"I won't see you again, David darling. Please help me not

to see you again. If I call, don't answer or return it."

He couldn't speak. Hand in hand, they walked over to where their cars were parked.

About six weeks later, sitting at the breakfast table with the *Leighton Clarion* in front of her, Lucy asked David, "Did you know Sarah Comstock?"

"I met her at the Carters' when you were down in Jersey for the wedding. Why do you ask?"

"She killed herself yesterday. An overdose of sleeping tablets. What a shame — such a beautiful woman. There's a picture of her here." Lucy offered him the paper, but he ignored it, rose, and walked out of the room. He went upstairs to the bathroom, locked the door, put his face in his hands, and wept. When Lucy came upstairs and knocked at the door and asked him if he was all right, he managed to say "Yes, as all right as I'll ever be."

PART FOUR

1952

Lucy's father had given David and Lucy a television set, a gift for their sixth wedding anniversary. Lucy was delighted with it; David's view of it was somewhat dim and uncertain, and he had a feeling that this small box was the beginning of a change that was open ended. Tonight, dressing to go to dinner at the Osners', David listened unhappily to the chatter of the box downstairs. His two children and the baby sitter were watching television, silent and enthralled.

"Don't you think your father might have felt the same way about the coming of radio?" Lucy asked, tired of his television-inspired foreboding.

"Possibly."

"And since your congregation is going to have television sets, doesn't it behoove you to have one and know what it does?"

"You have a point."

"I know it has its crazy side," Lucy said, "but so has everything else. Just suppose God sent a messenger to earth."

"God doesn't send messengers to earth."

"How do you know? All right, I don't believe very much in God, but the Talmud is full of stories about messengers to earth. And how about Passover? Isn't the Prophet Elijah supposed to slip down to earth from his heavenly place and join some *Seder* table?"

"This is going somewhere, isn't it?" David said. "I mean we're not having a theological argument — or are we?"

"That's your department. Here, zip me up the back. No, I was thinking Mark Twain style. Did you ever read 'Captain Stormfield Visits Heaven'?"

"No."

"Well, Captain Stormfield gets distracted as he flashes through the universe and he misses the gate he should go to and arrives at a gate where they never heard of the Planet Earth. Well, they got a map about a thousand miles high, and they have angels scurrying all over the map trying to find the earth, and finally one of them locates something, but he can't decide whether it's a fly speck or a planet."

"Well, which is it?"

"It's the earth, but that's not the point I was trying to make, and what was the point?" she wondered.

"Something about messengers."

"Oh, yes. If Mark Twain can try it, so can I. Here's my concoction. God tells this messenger or angel or whatever to coast down to earth and report back, and the messenger says, 'Well, where? I mean where should I go?' And God tells him that one place is as good as another, and where does the messenger end up but in Leighton Ridge?"

"That's interesting. Where do you go from there?"

"Confusing too. Take Jack Osner. He's just been appointed Assistant Secretary of the Treasury — that total shithead is now a part of our government —"

"I hope you reserve the richer parts of the language for you and me."

"Except for Millie Carter. She swears better than I do. We both use it as a buffer against piety. David, why don't you ever get mad at me when I talk like this?"

"Even in the army, where every third word was fuck and motherfuck, the guys would get very upset if I used foul language. The minister and the rabbi are denied the emphatic use of the language. Perhaps it's just as well."

"I didn't want to get into that," Lucy said. "I was just thinking of our messenger trying to make sense out of Leighton Ridge, where the local rabbi and the local Congregational minister are both going to a dinner party in honor of that creep Jack Osner, who has as much compassion and decency as any dues-paying Nazi."

"That's too strong, Lucy. I don't know why you have it in for him," David protested gently. "He's no worse than anyone else in government — "

"And a pillar of the synagogue and a pillar of the community. Did you mean what you just said?"

"Yes and no. For heaven's sake, Lucy, you can't judge people, you can't get inside of people."

"He told the F.B.I. that Mike Benton was a communist. He told Joe Hurtz that he felt we ought to have an older man as a rabbi, someone nonpolitical, and he beat up on Shelly. So much for the famous dictum that Jewish husbands don't beat their wives. And for my money, any man who beats up a woman is pure shit!"

"How on earth do you know all this?"

"Women talk. That's one of the ways we have of staying sane. If you put together a map of how absolutely insane the world of the other sex is, it helps you to stay sane. And, you know, Shelly isn't at all the turd I took her to be. Her life stinks, and she simply does the best she can. You remember his son, Adam — you did his *Bar Mitzvah* a few months after we came here?"

"Yes — nice kid."

"When Jack pushed Shelly around, Adam interfered — a real physical thing between the father and the son. Blows struck. Jack almost beat him senseless."

"I knew there was bad feeling. The boy would not register for the draft, and that drove Jack up the wall."

"Was the boy wrong?"

"No, Lucy. I will not judge the boy and say that he was wrong. When he came to me, I said, 'Do what your conscience tells you to do.' I think this war in Korea is rotten and manipulated from the word *go*. But I'm beginning to think that of every war. On the other hand, the army was the most important thing that ever happened to Jack Osner. A little kid who grew up on the Lower East Side in New York City becomes a colonel, bird and uniform and braid and all the rest."

"What army? He sat on his fat ass in Washington! That's where he fought the war."

"Come on, Lucy. We all fought the war where we were sent to fight it. Jack was sent to Washington."

"Damnit, David, why can't you ever come out and admit that someone in your congregation is an unrelieved son of a bitch?"

"Because they're in my congregation." He grinned and put his arms around her. "You're wonderful, and I love you."

"In spite of the fact that I nag and complain without end?"

"You're my conscience."

"Come off it!"

"You look lovely tonight," he said seriously. "Off to the Osners' to pay our deep respects to money and power. The Lord giveth and the Lord taketh away, and it all balances out. Jack will no longer be president of the synagogue. We have Mel Klein lined up for the post, and he's absolutely an angel."

"And what happens to Osner's house?"

"He's selling it. He bought one of those old houses in Georgetown. He's very serious about his political career."

"And what does he intend to do about Sissy Hart?"

"Who is Sissy Hart?"

"I don't believe you. Well, Sissy Hart is about my height, red hair, blue eyes, and enough curves to make her a big-league pitcher, and is married to Elbert Hart, who is president of the Leighton State Bank and one of the pillars of Marty's church. She has also been sleeping with Jack Osner these past three years."

"And I suppose everyone knows all about it except the rabbi?"

"Not everyone. Shelly caught them at it and blabbed to me, and Sissy poured out her heart to Millie. That was only a few days ago. I thought you knew."

"No. Does Marty know?"

"I doubt it."

"Wonderful. Simply wonderful. The only two people in this town who remain innocent are myself and the Congregational minister. Now off to dinner. It should be interesting."

The dinner party was not very interesting until the matter of the atom spies arose. It was constrained until then. Shelly Osner was tight-lipped and unsmiling. When asked whether she looked forward to living in Washington, she replied that she was still trying to talk Jack into keeping the house and using her as a house-sitter. "After all, it's been my profession for years."

Phyllis Hurtz, thickening around the waist as she made her way through her fifties, said that she and Joe had been contemplating an apartment in Washington. A year ago, Joe had sold his men's furnishings business and had made a deal with a Japanese electronics manufacturer. It had been enormously successful, and Hurtz was already a millionaire. He had donated a new Torah and a gym to the synagogue, but fortunately for David and others, he was so involved in his business that he did not contest the role of president. When Della Klein asked what on earth Joe would do with an apartment in Washington, Shelly said nastily, "Jack can give him lessons in that."

Lucy whispered to David, "Shall I have a headache and work us out of here?"

"The rabbi stays, even after the rest of the troops have fled," David whispered back.

Mel Klein offered a Jewish story to break the tension. He was a gentle, good-natured man who could not bear to be in a situation of contention and anger. "There was this Jewish fellow — "

"Why must it always be a Jewish fellow?"

"It's a Jewish story, so it's a Jewish fellow. So this one owns an antique shop, and a customer comes in, very friendly. I mean it's someone he likes instantly, so he takes out from under the counter an old lamp, you know, the kind you see in pictures from Turkey, and he says to the customer, 'This is a magic lamp. You rub it, and any wish in the world is granted to you.' Well, the customer doesn't believe this and they argue about it, and finally the customer says, 'If this is really a magic lamp like you say, why should you sell it to me?' So the antique dealer, he says, 'What good is it to me? My daughter is married and every week my son calls me.' "

There was a ripple of laughter, and Ed Frome said, "That's a beautiful story, Mel. Beautiful. It's like one of the old classic tales brought up to date."

David had not been surprised to find Frome at the dinner table even though Frome had no love for Osner. The distaste that Frome and Osner had for each other was widely known in the congregation; on the other hand, since Frome worked for *The New Yorker*, it made little sense for Osner, embarking on a political career, to cold-shoulder a writer for so prestigious a magazine. And since Frome was fond of David, he responded to Osner's invitation.

The story broke the ice. Osner was not a sensitive man, except to his own needs, and sitting there with the members of the board, he appeared to set petty feelings and resentments aside. He was totally imbued with the belief that a highly placed member of the federal government must be taken to the bosom of one and all.

"They've finally moved Bill Interman up to the Appellate Division," he said to David as the interested party, but loud enough for the whole table to hear.

"So he's rewarded," David said.

"Are you talking about Judge Interman?" Frome put in. "The same unspeakable bastard who sentenced the two atom spies to death?"

His wife, Sophie, put her hand on his arm and said softly, "Ed, it's done. No one here is responsible."

"If the rabbi here could spend two hours with Judge Interman, you could give ten minutes toward trying to understand his predicament without condemning him out of hand," Osner said.

"The rabbi saw Dachau. I saw Hiroshima. David, did you actually spend two hours with that creep?"

"Perhaps not two hours. We had a talk."

"Did he come for advice?" Oscar Denton asked. "But why here? He doesn't live in Connecticut."

"I imagine he wanted to get away from people who knew him."

"What did you advise him?" Frome asked.

"I couldn't advise him."

Later, at home, Lucy asked him, "Why didn't you tell them the whole story?"

"Because it was told to me in confidence."

"Then you come under the shadow of advising him to do what he did. Of course, I know you didn't. I know how you feel about Judge Interman, and I'm not even sure myself what happened between the two of you, but what are people going to think?"

"I can't help what people think."

"Well, it's not fair."

"Most things are not fair." He was sitting on the edge of the bed in his pajamas. "I'll look at the children," Lucy said. Wrapped in a white quilted robe, her face scrubbed clean, her mass of brown hair braided and controlled for the night, she looked like a teen-age kid. David felt an overwhelming surge of love and protectiveness. How very lucky he was! Even though he often felt that she had more wit and brains than he, it nevertheless satisfied a need to see her as utterly dependent upon him.

He rose and tiptoed after her. In the feeble glow of the nightlights, he saw the faces of angels, Aaron, aged five, Sarah, aged three. How absolutely right to fashion the shape of an angel after a sleeping child; that gave the whole concept of an angel validity. The feeling welled up inside of him, overpowering, and he had to fight to keep back the tears.

"What is it?" Lucy asked him.

"I don't know." He shook his head. "I feel that I've discovered something, and I don't know what I've discovered."

A few days later, Millie Carter called to tell Lucy that one of their parishioners owned a mixed Irish setter bitch that had had pups. Three of the puppies would be given away. Did David and Lucy want one? "Do you know," David told his wife, "when I was a kid, there was nothing I wanted more. My mother couldn't see it in a New York apartment."

"I'm kind of neutral about dogs. I don't hate them, but I don't love them."

"Let's try."

The children were enchanted with the small golden ball. The dog was probably three-quarters Irish setter, with a mysterious fourth quarter that widened its brow and gave promise of a more intelligent animal than most Irish setters. David found himself reading books on dogs and spending their small spare cash on dog food, and then it all backfired.

"What in hell has happened to me?" he asked Lucy. "I've become a sort of preposterous cardboard cut-out of what they call the American Way."

"You mean you've lived ten minutes without guilt."

"That's damned thin. I think you could come up with a little more understanding than that."

"With what, David? You tell me. Suddenly I'm told that because you bought your kids a dog, your world has collapsed. Last night you were playing with both kids and the dog, and an objective observer would have said you were content."

"If that's my goal, what am I doing in this godforsaken hole pretending to be a rabbi with a congregation of make-believe New England Wasps?"

"Is that how you see yourself?"

"Try to understand me," he begged her. "The trouble is,

Lucy, that I no longer see myself. During the war I was part of something. I saw myself in the eyes of every frightened kid in the company. We were sweeping away the filth of Satan. We were renewing the earth. We were threaded together, and when I came back I didn't want that fabric broken. That's why I took the first synagogue Rabbi Belsen offered me. Do you follow me?"

"I'm not sure. What happened?"

"Something turned off. I play with the kids. I play with the dog. I see members of my congregation put up a thousand dollars for a *Bar Mitzvah*. I begin to write a sermon and something inside of me says, Don't make waves — "

"I have two kids," Lucy said. "I shop, I cook, I feed them, I feed you, I make the beds, clean the house, and still teach two classes at Sunday school, and I think we have a decent sex life, and God Almighty, why isn't that enough? It's enough for me, but you and all your mystical, weird beliefs about the *Lamed Vov*, the just and righteous men who carry the weight of the world on their shoulders — well, goddamnit to hell, David, nobody carries the weight of the world on his shoulders, and this stinking, forsaken globe is just what it is and nothing more, a place where morons get their kicks out of murdering Jews and anyone else they don't like, and we're lucky to be here in one of the most beautiful places in the country, and why can't you — " She broke off, burst into tears, and ran out of the room and upstairs to the bedroom. Upstairs, Sarah began to wail. Aaron had taken her drum and was pounding away on it. David went upstairs to where Lucy, still sobbing, was trying to quiet the children. Frightened at her tears, both children became quiet.

"I didn't mean to burden you with all that," David said.

"I know."

He kissed her, and her response was perfunctory. She rose and went into the bathroom to clean her face. David followed her. Watching him in her mirror, she said, "Maybe you would have been happier with Sarah Comstock. Maybe she would have understood you. Maybe she would be alive today if she could have been your wife."

"My God," David whispered. "How long have you known?"

"Since last year. I never meant to tell you. Sarah told Millie, and Millie talked to me about it. Millie thought it would go on and make mincemeat out of our lives and our marriage, but then that poor woman killed herself — and all I knew was that I still had you, and David, I love you so much, so much — " She was crying again. He took her in his arms and held her tightly.

It snowed that night, and in the morning there were six inches of virgin white on the hills of Leighton Ridge. David shoveled a path to the road, followed closely by his two children and their dog, all of them delighted with the rewards of winter. His house was a hundred yards from the synagogue, much of the walk covered by drifted snow over a foot high. David was pleased to see three youthful volunteers clearing the way. For the next eight months, he would be at the synagogue every morning at eight o'clock. In the normal course of things, David, like a good many Reform rabbis, did not hold daily services, but when Dr. Henry Levine's mother passed away, he put the problem to David. "I won't rest easily unless I say the mourner's *Kaddish*. She was very *frum*. I'm not, but I adored her, David. So which is it? Do I drive all the distance to Bridgeport, with my office in Westport, or do we work out a *minyan*?" — a *minyan* being the company of ten men required for a service.

Not only did David like Henry Levine as a person, but each time Lucy called him frantically to minister to one of the children, he stubbornly refused to accept payment. Whereupon, David immediately agreed to the *minyan*. That had been four months ago, each morning a desperate struggle to corral ten Jews of appropriate age and sex. The fact that the ten congregants required for the *minyan* were limited by Jewish law to the male sex drove home the foolishness and waste of male chauvinism; but on the other hand, whenever David brought up the possibility of women being included in the *minyan*, the Orthodox and Conservative members of his congregation objected so violently that he let the matter drop.

On this morning of the snowfall, they were short the proverbial tenth man. For a while, they were at the point of desperation, with Dr. Levine driven to the extremity of calling a number of his patients, but even the sick ones had struggled out of bed to go to work. Then, happily, David remembered the two volunteers who always turned up to shovel a path from the parking lot to the synagogue, each of them fifteen years old — males of an age to be admitted — *Bar Mitzvahed* in this very temple.

When the morning service was over, David went outside to find Martin striding energetically down the road past the synagogue. David called out, "Hold on a bit, Martin. I'll walk with you."

For a few minutes they strode on in silence, kicking through the snow and emitting clouds of frosty breath; then David said, "I don't know how to get into this, so I might as well plunge. Last night, Lucy told me she knew about me and Sarah Comstock, and that she had known since it happened."

"There wasn't much to know, David."

"I've been eating myself up with the question of how responsible I was for what happened."

"It was her seventh suicide attempt in three years. She was gifted, beautiful, and brilliant, and it wasn't Harvey's drinking that drove her to it. He lives with worse guilt than yours. Don't think that you Jews have a monopoly on guilt. I could show you shades of white Protestant guilt that you never even dreamed of."

"Then why did she do it?"

"God knows."

They walked on, taking a path through a clump of woods that separated the new synagogue from the old Congregational church that was now the Unitarian church. The snow began to fall again, small, unhurried flakes that gave promise of a long, deep snowfall. "In Maine," Martin said, "where I grew up, it would begin like this, and then go on for hours. Not a breath of wind. Just a holy stillness."

"It's strange," David said, "how completely you people have united Christianity with winter and snow. Have you ever been to Israel?"

"Someday, David, the four of us will go together."

"I'd like that. But it's hot there, sunbaked and hot. I remember a snowstorm in New York when all the traffic stopped. Nothing moved. What am I doing, Martin? This is a crazy pretense. We're walking through the snow as if it's some impossible stage set. Oh, Jesus Christ, what frauds we are!"

"Jesus Christ — I never heard you say that before."

"Don't make anything of it," David said sourly.

Martin looked at his watch. "In a half-hour, they'll be dead."

"You know Mike Benton?" David asked, as if he had not heard Martin at all.

"I met him once, yes."

"He was an odd case, a valid war hero who was terrified of prison. Well, he made it, all right; got through six months, and it wasn't as awful as he had imagined it would be, except for the first eleven days."

"Why the first eleven days?"

"Because they were spent in Washington, D.C., penitentiary — from all I've been told, an old pesthole of a prison, tier upon tier of cells, electric gates, solitary confinement for any step out of line, prisoners eating in silence in the well at the bottom of the cell block. Well, the warden of the prison has a sense of humor and he hates reds, so for the eleven days Mike was there, a sort of staging period, the warden had him in death row."

"What a rotten thing to do!"

"Ah, yes, there's a lot of rotten around. But the point is that Mike insists that no one who has not experienced something of what he went through those eleven days can properly understand the meaning of capital punishment. He slept very little those eleven nights. The screaming, sobbing, and various vocal terrors of the condemned men kept him awake."

They walked on in silence. The snowfall became heavier. Martin Carter looked at his watch again and said, "Ten minutes more."

"Damn you, Martin!" David exclaimed. "Damn you! What are you, some kind of ghoul?"

"No, David, it's just that there are certain things a *goy* can't understand no matter how hard he tries. Yes, I am sick and disgusted at what is happening a few miles from here at Sing Sing Prison, where in a few minutes two people will be put to death. These two so-called atom spies are not being executed because they are spies, but because they are Jewish. I know it. You know it. And every Jew in America whose head isn't buried under five feet of sand knows it. And Millie's brother Sam, the one who's a congressman from Springfield, he tells us that the F.B.I. at first used the threat of a death sentence to get them to implicate others, and then the President picked it up and pressured the judge. So I know that, and Millie knows that, and probably most members of Congress know that — and yet the Jewish community in America is as silent as the night. Not a word — "

"There have been words," David protested.

"Whispers, whispers. We are less than ten years from the Holocaust, and this symbolic slaughter and sacrifice to all the dark gods takes place in silence — that's what I don't understand, the silence."

David looked at his own watch, and he said mournfully, "They're dead, Martin."

The snow was so heavy now that it was like a curtain between the two men, and David said to Martin, his voice hoarse, "What Mike Benton said about death row, you see, Martin, my friend and Congregational minister, think about it, think about it, because we have been on death row for two thousand years."

Martin stared at David, a ghostly figure behind the curtain

of snow. He started to speak and then swallowed his words. And then, after a long moment, he said, "Let's get home, David. The snow's a foot deep already."

They clumped on home through the snow in silence. David's house was first along the way, and he urged Martin to come in for some hot tea, but Martin said no, he had a lot of thinking to do, and he might as well start on it right now.

Giving David hot tea and dry socks, Lucy saw the grief on his face and asked him, "What is it, David? What happened? Is it the execution?"

"All during the war," he said slowly, "we believed that we were on the edge of change. In one way or another, we all believed that. We had tracked the devil to his lair, and now it only remained to go in and destroy him. Then the world would be different. But, you know, it won't be any different, Lucy, it never will."

"Perhaps not, but you still have your post–*Bar Mitzvah* class in Talmud this afternoon, and you're always telling me what a mind-bender it is. How about a hot bath and a good lunch? Hamburger and home fries."

"You're kidding?"

"No — I have the hamburger in the fridge. You can bet I'm not going out in that snow." But as soon as David was in the tub, Lucy called Millie Carter and asked her, "What on earth happened with the two of them, out there in that snow-storm?"

"I can't get a word out of Martin."

"Same here."

"Give it a little time," Millie said.

Lucy fed the children first and then did something unusual for her. She put them in front of the television so that she might have a quiet hour with David. He had many gifts, but a subtle and sophisticated taste for food was not one of them, and as he once explained to her, he had practically grown up on hamburgers and home fries. But he had no appetite today. "Will you forgive me, Lucy, please. It's wonderful and it smells marvelous, and I can't eat it."

She got up and came around the table and kissed him.

"What's that for?"

"Just one of those things. Coffee?"

He drank the coffee and munched a piece of bread. "No one should have to face an executioner," he said. "It's a mean, ugly vengeance that we exact. I sometimes wonder whether we are sane, any of us, any of the human race." He shook his head. "What are we doing here, Lucy?"

"You know what I'm going to do," she said. "I'm going to put a dollar in the cookie jar every time you ask me that question. It'll pay for a trip abroad."

"It's just that wherever I look, I seem to see something demented. I want it to be them, so that I could say to myself, they're demented, but we're sane. You know Leon Kramer?"

"His wife, poor thing, is constantly pregnant. Four children, and a fifth on its way."

"Appears to be a very nice fellow, but very Orthodox. To him, we are only one step to the left of the Catholic Church — "

"Come on," Lucy said.

"Well — almost. Reform Judaism, in his lights, has already made a pact with the devil. He feels that he's our conscience, and that's why he continues as a member. You notice, he always has a *yarmulke*. Last week he came to me for an *eruv*."

"What on earth is an *eruv*?"

"Well, according to the strictures of the Orthodox Jews, on the Sabbath — from sundown on Friday to sundown Saturday — nothing can be carried out of the house. The act of pushing a baby carriage is considered to be carrying, so when one has an absolute need to give the baby a little sunshine and fresh air, an *eruv* is created, a symbolic area that extends the house. You do this by enclosing an area with a string, say as big as the front yard and back yard, and lo and behold, it becomes your house, and baby can be wheeled out without breaking the Law."

"You're kidding."

"I am not kidding. I am demonstrating insanity — harmless, but still beyond the pale of reason, and no more insane than a thousand laws and strictures of every other religion. There are whole areas of New York that have been enclosed with a string for an *eruv* — well, we're not so special, but God help me, I put myself here. Does God distinguish between those two so-called atom spies and the six million Jews cremated in Hitler's ovens? The world goes on. God is busy trying to sort out the souls of those cremated at Hiroshima and Nagasaki from the ashes of the camps — or does a soul remain after you've been seared into nothingness — "

"Stop it!" Lucy cried. "What are you doing? What are you doing to me, to you?"

"I'm sorry," David said. "I'm sorry."

That night he awoke screaming, and his screams awakened Lucy and the children. Sarah ran into Aaron's room and huddled under the covers with him. Lucy shook David awake and then held him tightly in her arms. She knew about the dream; she knew its content so well she might have dreamed it herself. In life, at the time, David had stood at the edge of the open grave where the bodies of three thousand Jewish dead had been flung, the bodies naked, men and women together, starved almost to death before being murdered, the skin clinging tight to the bones, arms and legs askew, faces like skulls with features ineptly painted, and out of the huge open grave came the dreadful, unbearable stink of rotting flesh. So it had been, as David told her, when Captain David Hartman, chaplain in the 45th Division of the Seventh Army stood at the edge of the open grave; but in the recurrent dream, always the same, David was one of the bodies in the grave, looking up at the American soldiers who stood on the grave's edge.

He opened his eyes, shivering, sweating. "I was in both places this time," he whispered, "in the grave and outside, looking down. That was too terrible."

"It's all right now," Lucy whispered. "It's all right. It's just a dream."

She went into Aaron's room. The two little bodies were huddled under the covers.

"You know about bad dreams," Lucy said. "Both of you have had bad dreams. Now Daddy had one."

"He's dead," Aaron moaned. "That's the way it sounds when you get dead."

"That's the silliest thing I ever heard. David," she called, "would you come in here." To Aaron she said, "You can't see through the covers."

The children poked their heads out. David came into the room and lifted Aaron in his arms. Then Sarah demanded to be lifted. Aaron decided he was afraid to go back to sleep.

"Then we'll all go downstairs and have hot milk."

The children fell asleep drinking their milk, and David and Lucy carried them up to bed. Lucy, who was only an occasional smoker, wanted a cigarette very much now. She lit one and curled up on the bedroom lounge, an ancient upholstered chaise her mother had given her. David got back into bed and lay watching her, propped up on his elbow.

"Women suffer," Lucy said, "but men suffer more."

"Who told you that?"

"I figured it out."

"That's pretty smart."

"I don't think so. I think every lady knows it. That's why we forgive you for fucking up the whole damned universe."

"You have to watch your language, baby. Not only am I a rabbi, but we have two little kids."

"I use beautiful language only when we're alone. You know that. It comes when I am at a loss for other words because there are no other words that fit the case."

"I've never seen you at a loss for words."

"There's a lot about me you don't know."

"Put away the cigarette and come in and lie next to me."

In the morning, the snow had stopped, and Jack Osner's son, Adam, was digging out the Hartman walk — for which he was paid three dollars. "Well, Rabbi," he said to David when David came to the door to pay him, "I guess this is the last time I do this for you. I'm not leaving you in the lurch, though. The Schwab kid is taking over from me. He doesn't have my class when it comes to tossing snow, but there it is. He's the best I can do."

"I'm sure he'll learn."

"Does it snow in Washington?"

"On occasion."

"I hate to go. I really hate to go. I grew up here. My friends are here. You know something, Rabbi, the first kid I ever fought with for calling me a dirty Jew bastard, well, he's my best friend. Now I have to start all over again."

"Oh, I don't know," David said. "That's kid stuff. I don't think it will happen in Washington."

When David got to the synagogue a half-hour later, Nash MacGregor was performing the same function, cutting a path through the foot-deep snow from Temple Shalom to the parking lot. MacGregor was a black man in his forties, tall, wide-shouldered, and strong. He lived in Bridgeport with a wife and three children, and he had worked for years in a box factory owned by a member of David's congregation. The factory was sold three years ago, and the new owner did not employ blacks. David needed a custodian for the new synagogue, and MacGregor was recommended to him. MacGregor was a good, hard-working man. Friday nights he slept over in the basement; other nights he went home. It was still a time when no black was permitted to live in any of the towns on the Fairfield County Ridge, something David became aware of only after he had hired MacGregor. There was a tiny cottage, an old farmhouse, on the edge of the synagogue property, and it occurred to David that this would be a convenient home for MacGregor and his family, sparing the black man the long ride to Bridgeport. It was on sale for six thousand dollars, and MacGregor assured David that he could get it in shape himself. "But they won't sell," MacGregor said; "take my word for that, Rabbi."

David put it up to the board. "No use," Oscar Denton told him. "No way in the world, David. It's over twenty years since I came in here, first Jew, and it only worked because I bought the land first, and they all figured it was a development idea, never dreamed that I was a Jew and was going to live here."

"We could buy the house and then rent it to MacGregor."

They voted him down. As MacGregor had predicted. Mel Klein said, "You're right, David. You're a good man. But the world we live in is the world we live in. Don't make waves."

Then what in God's name am I doing here? David asked himself, as he had a hundred times before.

This morning, MacGregor said to David, "Rabbi, the plow will be here in about an hour; but you know, if I had a blade on my pickup, I could clear that lot myself and save us twenty-five dollars each time it snows."

"What would a blade cost?"

"I can get a nice one for about seventy-five dollars."

"Get it and tell them to bill us."

"I put the book back," MacGregor added. "Can I take another?"

"Any time you wish."

"Curious thing," David said to Lucy that evening. "You know how Nash MacGregor sleeps over in the basement on Friday nights so that he can clean up and have things ready for the morning service? Well, time hangs heavy Friday nights during the service and I suppose later, too, so he asked me could he take a book from the library and read it. He's not a quick reader — has to mouth each word. I think he said he went to the fifth grade and then he had to go to work. But the first book he picked was Faulkner's *Requiem for a Nun*, which I happened to have on my desk. I don't know what he could have made of it, but he read it through to the end, and then he took Hersey's book *The Wall*. It takes him months, but he stays with them and finishes them, and each time he asks my permission to take another book."

"Sometimes," Lucy said to David, "I can see why you want to be what you are. But only sometimes," she added quickly.

MacGregor was indebted. Being treated decently and with respect by whites was not so frequent an occurrence that he could take it in his stride. And he was an emotional man. Therefore, when he called David at eight o'clock in the morning on the Friday following the snowstorm, his voice shook and the words came with difficulty. "Rabbi, you better get over here right away. Something terrible happened."

David was in the kitchen, setting the table for breakfast, while Lucy fried eggs and watched the toast. The children were already gulping their oatmeal. Lucy, one eye always on David's face, reading it, wanted to know what had happened.

"I don't know. Something at the synagogue."

"Breakfast?"

"Later, perhaps." He threw on his old army winter jacket and practically ran to the synagogue, where MacGregor was waiting outside the front door. To the left of the entrance, the brass letters that spelled out TEMPLE SHALOM were defaced with red paint, and all across the front of the building, spray-painted, were swastikas.

"Worse inside," MacGregor said hopelessly.

Inside, the red spray paint was wildly spattered over the pews. The single, small stained glass window, behind the sanctuary, which depicted the tablets with the Ten Commandments, had been smashed, and an icy wind was blowing through the main hall. The curtains of the sanctuary had been ripped off, and the cover of the scroll of the Law, the Torah, had been ripped and defaced with the red paint.

"There it is," MacGregor said woefully. "If I'd a been here, it wouldn't a happened. But I ain't here. I ain't here on Thursday, and I ain't seen nothing as terrible as this in a long time."

"Not your fault, Nash," David said. "It's not your fault at all." He put his arm around the black man and stood there for a while, just staring at the devastation around him. "Tell you what, Nash," he said, "first thing I want you to do is to get something to close up the hole in the stained glass window. I remember seeing some large pieces of cardboard in the Sunday school room."

"They is pictures."

"We can get more pictures. Main thing is to close up that hole as soon as possible."

When the black man had gone, David replaced the scroll in the sanctuary. The scroll was one of the hundreds that the Nazis had taken from German and Polish synagogues and put aside for some future use. Rabbi Belsen had obtained this one through the Institute, and it was a gift to David's synagogue. He was staring at the torn, stained cover of the scroll when Mrs. Shapiro, his secretary, came through the door into the main hall and let out a scream.

"That's enough!" David said sharply. "Go into my office and start calling — " She was sobbing violently. "Please, Mrs. Shapiro, do you have a pencil and paper in your purse?" he shouted.

She found the pencil and paper. The sobs weakened under David's stern glance. Pencil and paper gave her weapons to face this unreasonable and threatening world.

"Call all the members of the board. Mr. Klein first — he doesn't leave before eight-thirty, so catch him — and then Mr. Hurtz, Mr. Denton, and Mr. Frome. And when you've called all of them and made sure they'll be here in the next hour, call the Reverend Carter at the Congregational church and tell him what happened and ask him to join us. And when the people come for morning service, have them wait."

"Shall I tell the others what happened?"

"Briefly. Just say someone has vandalized the synagogue. Don't go into details. Now hurry."

By nine-fifteen, they were all there, Martin Carter included, plus Mel Klein's son-in-law, a Dr. John Ash, who taught psychology at Yale. The mood varied. Hurtz was loud and angry, Klein was deeply worried, and Ed Frome was shocked and bitter. Martin Carter was horrified, and could not conceal his misery, a misery sharpened by the fact that he was the only Christian present. Oscar Denton alone was relaxed and apparently philosophical. "I am seventy-five," he told them, "and past surprises. The human race does not improve, change, or show any evidence of a divine touch. You might say we've come of age in a world that's as uninventive as it is disgusting."

"That kind of talk doesn't help," Joe Hurtz said. "I wish Jack was here, but he isn't. I say we seen a crime, and we call the cops and make the bastards who did this pay for it. This is the U.S.A.; it ain't Germany."

"Cops," said Ed Frome. "We live in a very small town. We have five policemen, three on the day shift, two on the night shift, and they have all they can do to find their way home."

"That's an exaggeration."

"Have you ever seen our police force at work?"

"I say call the cops. Whatever they are, they're still cops."

"What do you think, David?" Mel Klein asked him.

"I certainly don't think we should call in the police, not until we're able to discuss what happened with less emotion. It's not what was done here that disturbs us, but the memories it evokes. I've sent Nash MacGregor out for paint remover. The Torah was not damaged, and the window will be fixed. No one was injured, thank God."

"It's still a matter for the police," Hurtz insisted.

David turned to the psychologist. "How do you react to all this, Dr. Ash?"

"With disgust. On the other hand, it appears to me to be an act of adolescents, high school kids."

"Why kids? Why not adults?"

"Because it's so quick and incomplete. I get the impression of a couple of kids with cans of red spray paint. Were the front doors forced?"

"No," David said, "but we haven't locked them since the synagogue was built."

"My guess is that these kids knew the doors were open. It was more of a prank than a gesture of anti-Semitism."

"Like hell it was!" Martin Carter said vehemently and unexpectedly. "If you don't see this as an ugly, sick piece of anti-Semitism, then your head is in the sand."

"Carter's right," Frome said. "What the devil is wrong with us? I have to ask you that, Rabbi. I am just as angry as hell, and I'd like to take those young hoodlums and beat the living daylights out of them. Do you want to cover this up, pretend it never happened?"

"No, I don't want to cover it up," David said, "but I also don't want it blown all out of proportion. I asked Reverend Carter to join us, not to increase our sensitivity to anti-Semitism, but because, like Dr. Ash, I felt that this was the work of kids, and the Reverend Carter, who knows the community better than any of us, might lead us to them."

The meeting ended with a decision to inform the police chief, as he was euphemistically titled. The matter, they felt, had to be reported. The question of locking the doors in the future arose. David was strongly against it. "It's simply not an appropriate reaction," he insisted. "Even if this should happen again, to lock the doors of a sanctuary is an awful admission of failure."

"Failure for whom and whom do we admit it to?"

"To ourselves."

The argument was short, and David won his point. For the time being, they agreed, they would not lock the doors.

Martin remained after the others had left. "You're damned angry at me, aren't you?" he said.

"Not very angry, no. Only — "

"Only, who the hell is this *goy* to give us lessons in anti-Semitism?"

"Something like that," David admitted.

"Did it ever occur to you that there's a very basic difference between us on this question of anti-Semitism?"

"Oh? Tell me."

"You were never an anti-Semite, David. I was. Rabidly. My father was a bigoted anti-Semite, maniacally so. He and two of his business associates became involved in Henry Ford's terrible swindle with the forged *Protocols of the Elders of Zion.* But my father believed them. In many ways, he was a kind man, but his whole being was saturated with this sickness of anti-Semitism. At first it captured me, then it horrified me, and in the end it was one of a number of things that turned me toward the ministry. That's a long story, and perhaps some other time, but I don't want you to hold against me what I said before. We're old friends, David, and I don't want anything to hurt that friendship."

"Nothing will," David said.

The chief of police came in person, a gray-haired man in his middle sixties, and he prowled around and looked at the damage and nodded sagely. "Kids today," he said, "God only knows what gets into them. What do you want me to do, Rabbi?"

"Catch them, I suppose."

"Won't be easy. Lots of folks have prejudice. It ain't Germany, but lots of folks have prejudice and don't like your people."

"Then I guess you'll just have to sort them out, Chief. You know, our people, as you call them, pay taxes and they vote."

"Not for me. I'm past that age and retiring next fall. That's why I can afford to say it the way it is. A man running for office can't afford that."

The police chief was leaving when Mrs. Seligman, a stout, emotional woman in her late thirties, pushed past Mrs. Shapiro and declared, "I know what a terrible day this is for you, Rabbi, with what happened to the synagogue, but I must talk to you. It's life and death. Alone," she said, glaring at Mrs. Shapiro.

David nodded. "You can go, Mrs. Shapiro."

"I'm only trying to do my job," Mrs. Shapiro said, returning to the refuge of tears. "Everyone wants to talk to you today."

"Of course, and thank you." He asked Mrs. Seligman to sit down. "What's the trouble, Mrs. Seligman?"

"The trouble is that my daughter is pregnant, and she's fifteen years old, God help her."

"Yes, that's trouble." He recalled her daughter, a luscious, lovely young woman, dark eyes and silken hair. "Do you know how it happened?"

"It happened with a football player in high school whose name is Freddy Bliss. Not Jewish. Anyway, how could a girl her age get married?"

"No, we don't want to destroy her that way. Does Bert know?" He hoped he recalled her husband's name correctly.

"I'm afraid to tell him. He goes into rages."

"Suppose I come by tonight, and we'll tell him together. We can't make any decision about your daughter until he knows."

His phone rang then.

"David," Lucy said. "I heard what happened, and things must be a little crazy over there — "

"You could say that."

"But Mom called. Pop had a heart attack. They've taken him to the hospital."

"I'll be there in a few minutes," David said, and then he explained the circumstances to Mrs. Seligman.

"Do you think I should tell Bert?" she wanted to know. "By myself. He'll go crazy, but I can tell him."

"If I can't come by tonight, it will be some time in the next two days. Better wait."

"I hope it's all right at your home. Today isn't a good day, Rabbi."

It wasn't a very good day. By the time David got home, Lucy's father was dead.

"It's so damned unjust," Lucy said. "He was only fifty-five. He was such a good, decent man. Why is the world so rotten unjust?"

A long, long time ago, when he was a student at the Institute before World War Two, David had complained to Rabbi Belsen about the unjustness of God.

"And what has God got to do with justice, David? Man, not God, invented justice." So he had said, or something of that sort. It was long ago, and David's memory might well be failing him. It was said and taught that the God of Israel was a just God.

Della Klein came to take care of the kids. "Don't tell me anything," she said to Lucy. "We'll all survive. Just go."

Lucy sat next to David, crying quietly as they drove to New York. He had no easy words to say to her. He could imagine an Orthodox rabbi saying, "Your father will be among the blessed ones." All the religions had words to say, and no one said simply that death was a rotten and terrifying thing that we understand as little as we understand everything else. For some reason, his thoughts were taken back to a road in Germany, and by the roadside there was lying the head of a young German soldier, just the head, with its blue eyes open and staring and its hair like corn silk. No body, only the head, and the American kids marching by it would see it and pretend not to see it, glance at it and then turn their eyes away. Why the thought at this moment? Why mourn, even in vague memory, one dead of a nation that had inflicted upon mankind a war that left fifty million dead? But his mind was not a single thing. It was split into past, present, and future. Where had he read that when the mind is a single thing, a person is given a state of grace?

Lucy touched his hand on the wheel. "David, David, is it the end? Will I ever see him again?"

"Darling, I don't know." That was a lie. Her question had evoked the terrible finality of death, and it laid its icy fingers over his heart. Never, not when his mother passed away, not during the war, had he responded to death like this. It was not her father; David liked Herb Spendler. He was a good-natured, easygoing man whose years of composing the news in the Linotype room of the *New York Times* had bred in him an unaggressive cynicism. He had tried gallantly to conceal the contempt he felt for the rabbinate, the ministry, or any other aspect of religion, and his affection for David had been very real.

"You didn't know," Lucy said, "but whenever we had a scrap, or when I felt I had come to the end of my own rope, I would call him. Now he's gone."

"I'm here," David said.

She pressed close to him, silent for the rest of the drive.

In New York, it was Lucy's mother pleading for him to unfold mysteries. David had never realized what a young and attractive woman Sally Spendler was, perhaps because one reserves a certain point of view for a mother-in-law. Now she clung to him and told him tearfully, "We don't even have a burial plot. We never belonged to a synagogue. What shall I do, David?"

"That's no problem," David assured her. "We'll bring Herb up to the Ridge and bury him in our cemetery," wondering meanwhile what it would be like with the frozen ground and the winter weather.

It was snowing again, lightly, when they laid Lucy's father to rest. The little circle of family and friends stood mutely in the snow, cold and shivering. Lucy and her mother wept. It was as if death had reached out and touched the whole world with its icy fingers.

But, as occurred to David, life denies death and asserts itself; and the life in question was growing in the uterus of the fifteen-year-old Seligman girl. Or *child*, as David noted, sitting facing Bert Seligman and his wife. Bert had already expressed his anger, stalking back and forth across the room, raging that he would kill "that rotten little slut," demanding that he face her with her "crime" immediately. His wife wept, and David allowed the man's anger to use itself up.

"Would you send her away?" David wondered.

"Send her away? Rabbi," Bert Seligman said, "she's a slut, but she's my kid. I don't send my kids away."

"Then you must understand," David insisted.

"What in hell's to understand?"

"That she needs love and it isn't there. If you'd stop tearing the kid to pieces and take her to your heart — "

"Who are you to tell me what to do?"

"I'm you're rabbi, and either you will damned well listen to me or I walk out of here right now." He rose.

"No. Please," Mrs. Seligman begged him.

"All right. But I will talk and you will listen. Is that agreed?"

They both nodded silently.

"All right. Now whoever the father may be, a child of that age should not be married or bear a child. So we won't discuss that. I want you to take her to Dr. Levine tomorrow."

"And tell the whole world," Mrs. Seligman wailed.

"We will tell no one, but we have to talk about your daughter and how to treat her and try to save her life. Don't you see how important that is?"

It was past midnight when he came home. Millie Carter was with Lucy. It was eight days since Herb Spendler's death, and still Lucy lived with a terror of being alone. David apologized. "The Seligmans are in bad trouble. I couldn't leave earlier."

"You mean the kid and Freddy Bliss?" Lucy asked.

David sighed. "I pledged my word no one would know."

"It's around," Millie said. "This Bliss kid is a damned little monster, and your Seligman child is no angel. Will the family remain here?"

"I imagine so."

Millie shook her head hopelessly. "I'm off now. It would be so nice to be without a congregation for a while, wouldn't it, David? I'm going to find us a tiny isle for R and R, populated entirely by Druids."

About two weeks later, Martin Carter telephoned David and asked him to please come over to the church. The new Congregational church was about a mile and a half from the synagogue and David's home. It was on toward evening, the cold winter sun beginning to set.

"I can't imagine what he has in mind," David told Lucy, "but I'll be back in time for supper."

Martin's office, lit up now, was at the back of the church. His secretary had gone home. Martin opened the door, and inside David saw a man and two boys. The boys were about fourteen years old. The man, about forty, was heavily built, sloping shoulders, powerful arms and hands. He wore a sheepskin jacket and denim trousers. David learned later that he was a builder, living in Leighton Ridge and with his business in Danbury. His name, Martin informed David, was Thomas Hendley.

"Mr. Hendley," Martin said, "is a member of our church. This," indicating one of the boys, "is his son, Robert, and this young man's name," indicating the other boy, "is Joe Menaro. They're here because Mr. Hendley brought them here. They're responsible for the damage done to the synagogue."

"I'm prepared to pay the cost, and they're going to work it off or I'll take it out of their hides. I'll tell you this, Rabbi, and right to your face. I don't like you people any better than the next one, but we don't do things this way in America." Hendley paused for breath. "We're not hoodlums or the Mafia."

"How did you find out that the boys did it?" David asked.

"Robert told his mother."

"Perhaps you could wait outside and let us talk to the boys," David said.

Hendley stared at him suspiciously. Martin said, "It might help, Mr. Hendley. Just for a few minutes."

"Whatever you do, they brought it on themselves. You going to call the police?"

"That's not what I had in mind."

"What the police do," said Hendley, "that's legal."

"I'm a minister," Martin said, "and he's a rabbi. We don't beat children."

"All right — and remember, I can't stay here all night. I'm willing to pay all the damages."

The door closed behind him. Martin pushed a couple of chairs toward the boys. "Sit down."

"We're not calling the police," David said. "Mr. Hendley will pay the costs, and you can settle with him. But nobody gets a free ride, and the price of being able to walk out of here without a police record is to answer some questions I'll put to you."

For the first time since he had come into the room, the two boys raised their heads to look directly at David.

"What questions, mister?"

"Call him Rabbi Hartman when you address him," Martin said.

"Question one: Why did you do it?"

Hendley remained silent. Menaro shrugged and shook his head. "I don't know."

"How many Jews do you know?"

"Some kids in school."

"Do you like them or hate them?"

"They're okay," Menaro said.

Hendley nodded.

"Do you know what a swastika is?"

No response.

"You painted them over the front of the synagogue and on the scroll. Do you know what the scroll was?"

No response. They just sat, silent, and stared at him.

"That scroll we call the Torah — a Hebrew word for Law. In it, hand-lettered, are the first five books of the Bible: Genesis, Exodus, Numbers, Leviticus, and Deuteronomy. It's the Jewish Bible, the Protestant Bible, and the Catholic Bible — all the same. Would you have defaced it if you had known that?"

Still, they were silent.

"It won't do," David said softly. "You answer my questions, or I call in the cops. Now, would you have defaced that scroll if you knew it was a Bible?"

"No," they muttered.

"All right. Let's go back to the swastikas, the hooked cross you painted on the front of the synagogue. What is the swastika?"

"It's Nazi," Hendley said.

"What about you, Menaro? Did you know that?"

"Yeah."

"And I'm sure that both of you know that the Nazis hated the Jews. They murdered six million Jews. In one day, over eight thousand Jewish women and children were put to death, gassed. But the Nazis, the people whose symbol you painted on our house of worship, didn't stop with the Jews. They murdered over three hundred thousand Gypsies. They executed thousands of Italians and French and every other nationality in Europe. In fact, not since God created the world has any group been responsible for as much suffering and for as many deaths as this same Nazi Party of Germany. I want you to know this so that the next time you use a symbol, you will try to understand it. Now you can go."

After the boys had left, Martin and David sat in silence for a minute or so. Then Martin said, "I think you were right. I wouldn't have thought of it that way."

David rose. "Lucy's still holding dinner."

"No time for a drink? One drink?"

"It's no good when I feel this way."

"How's that?"

"Filled with despair."

PART FIVE

1956

In 1956, spring came to Leighton Ridge like a gentle benediction, indeed like a promise of peace and good will. The world was without war — that is, without a major war — and the President of the United States had turned out to be an amiable old gentleman who did not enjoy rocking the boat. Even Senator McCarthy had been brought to bay and silenced, and in a tiny village in an unimportant corner of Connecticut, Lucy Hartman had invited a few people to dinner. The children had been fed and put to bed, where they would by no means sleep immediately, but whisper to each other and sneak down the hall to the staircase and try to pick up the conversation downstairs. Mrs. Holtzman, a stout, middle-aged lady who was the only survivor of a German-Jewish family that had perished in the concentration camps, was there, helping with the cooking and serving, and the dining room table had been extended to its greatest length to accommodate eight people.

Aside from the Hartmans, the dinner guests were Mel Klein, the president of the synagogue; his wife, Della; Eddie Frome and his wife, Sophie; and Millie and Martin Carter. They were the best friends that David and Lucy had made since coming to Leighton Ridge. Mel Klein at sixty-one was a father figure of sorts; Della, twenty years younger, was Lucy's rock and consolation. When she wept, when she had to be a little girl, when she hated Leighton Ridge so bitterly that she was ready to pack a suitcase and walk out, it was Della's bosom that received her, and Della's gentle praise of David that made Lucy look at David newly. Indeed, sometimes Lucy felt that Della was in love with David. Yet this was never a threat. As for Eddie Frome, not only did he bring them his world of *The New Yorker,* one of the very few places where wit and common sense and sanity still survived, but he himself was a source of amiable intelligence. The fact that he had the reputation of consoling certain lonely and unhappy women in the neighborhood did not press David toward judgment. His wife, Sophie, accepted it. She was a very slender, delicate woman who adored their single child, a boy of ten named Philip, and who adored her husband. She said little at any gathering, but she was sweet and sufficiently doll-like to be accepted with her silence. And Martin and Millie Carter were relaxed in the one place they felt they could say anything they pleased and not be rebuked by one or another section of their parishioners.

"We talk from premises," Ed Frome said, after there had been a round of tributes to the spring weather. "If no premises are shared, no conversation is possible."

"But arguments."

"Not conversation. Something else."

"No brotherhood is possible," Martin Carter said.

"I think arguments are conversation," Lucy said.

"Brotherhood is your *shtick*, Martin," Frome said. "I'm a simple semanticist, and I take my hat off to bad weather as well as good weather. You see, we share. Everyone loves a cool, sunny day. Everyone is depressed when it rains. Everyone is cold, everyone is hot. Marvelous shared premises."

"I'll be the silly one," Della said. "Why no conversation without a shared premise?"

"Conversation. You know, the word once meant a way of life, a style of living. But not today — today, Della, it's a relaxed exchange of thoughts. Well, suppose I say to you that the Soviet Union is a good place to live. You believe it's a very bad place to live. We share no premise. That makes conversation difficult."

"It makes jokes more difficult — what you call your premise," Mel Klein said. "In my shop yesterday, two Puerto Rican workers are having a bitter argument. They try to pull me into it. I say, 'Hold on. I'll tell you a story. This fellow's walking down the street and he comes across two men having a bitter argument. He listens to this one, he listens to that one, he listens to this one, he listens to that one — and then he shakes his head, says, "Don't make me crazy," and walks away.' Would you believe these two fellows in my shop, they don't know what I'm talking about?"

"No wonder," Della said. "I don't know what you're talking about, and I'm Jewish." She turned to Millie Carter. "Do you get that joke, Millie?"

"I'm afraid not."

Mrs. Holtzman came in with an apple tart. There was much praise for the tart, which Lucy had created. There was talk about Sanka, real coffee, and tea. Lucy cut the tart and sent the plates around the table. More praise for the tart after they tasted it.

"Still and all," David said, "that question of the premise which Eddie talks about is very important, and I know just what you mean, Mel. Without a shared premise, you can't tell a joke. I was in a little stone farmhouse in France with half a dozen G.I.s, and we were under heavy fire, and in a moment of silence, one of the kids said to me, you know, kind of bragging, 'What the hell, Rabbi, everyone has to die some time.' I said to him, 'I know, I know, but I want to die in a very special way. I want to die in a corner room at Mount Sinai Hospital at the age of ninety-seven, all my relatives gathered around, a bowl of fruit on one side of my bed, a jar of nuts on the other.' Well, by now all the kids were listening. No one laughed. Finally, one of them said, 'Rabbi, what would you want with that jar of nuts, you in there dying?' "

The men around the table burst into laughter. Millie looked at Lucy, "Is it that I'm not Jewish, or do I totally lack a sense of humor, or is it that premise of Eddie's?"

"None. What David told those kids in the farmhouse is an old Jewish vaudeville cliché. In a Jewish hospital, or I suppose in any hospital, corner rooms are the most expensive. Dying in a corner room shows status. Having the family around shows status in the family. And when I was a little girl and we visited someone in the hospital, we brought nuts, fruit, and flowers. And I suppose, David, the kids were from Tennessee or Iowa or some such place?"

"No doubt, no doubt, but you put your finger on so much of it — the shared premise, I mean. Our society would fall apart without it."

"This is delicious," Martin said, taking the last bite of his tart. "David's right. Every social function partakes of a shared premise. Christians share the belief that Jesus was the divine Son of God. But the belief rests on a shared premise. Jews don't share the premise, which makes it almost impossible to convince them."

"And what is our premise, David?" Frome asked.

"That God is one. *Adonoy Echod.*"

"But there's a prior one, isn't there?" Frome persisted.

"Prior?" Martin asked.

David felt a cold chill touch his heart.

"Definitely. Prior."

"God," David said softly.

"Exactly."

Mel Klein, increasingly uneasy, changed the subject. "Did you all read about Jack Osner today? I know David gets the *New York Times.*"

"Haven't looked at it today."

"I've been avoiding mine," Martin said.

"I read ours," Lucy said. "I'm not impressed."

"What is she not impressed with?" Frome asked.

"The fact that Jack's been made Deputy Secretary of Defense," Mel informed them. "He'll be sitting in on Cabinet meetings."

"I don't see him there. Defense? He spent the war at a desk in Washington."

"It makes sense," Frome said. "He's very close to the gentlemen in the Pentagon. I have no love for Osner, but I had to do a story on the Joint Chiefs of Staff, and I had some real trouble getting to them until I mentioned it to Osner. He waved his wand, and I saw them the following day."

"Jack does things that way," Mel said. "He's a smart man."

"He's a pig," Della said.

"Makes him fit for government," Ed Frome commented.

"Oh, come on," Mel scolded. "That's no way to talk about him. It's unfair."

"Ask Shelly Osner how unfair. He beat the living daylights out of her."

"Oh, no," Martin said. "We haven't seen Shelly lately, but we used to be close. I can't imagine."

"His kids won't see him," Della persisted. "They're both away; the girl at college — "

"Hold on, please," David said. "The Osners still belong to this congregation. They're not selling their house, and they'll be spending summers here. As for Jack, we'll wait and see."

"Speaking of premises," Lucy said, "a prevalent one holds that apple pie was created by Martha Washington on an off day when she was not inventing ice cream. You know, as American as apple pie. Now this tart you are all praising so wisely is definitely European, and it might of course be argued this isn't an apple pie. Although I think it is. However, apple pie is eaten in a good many countries. So much for the premise."

"Nobody argues the truth of premises," Martin said. "Only the usefulness."

"Like our being the result of the premise that good is poor. We all want our minister to be good, therefore keep him on the edge of starvation."

"Millie, we're not on the edge of starvation."

"Because Grandpa left me a trust fund. Not because of a minister's wages."

"Hear! Hear!" Lucy said.

"We're not starving," David reminded her.

"Still, it's no path to riches," Martin said. "Yet in a way I find it comforting to accept the fact that I'll never be rich, regardless of what happens and in spite of the trust fund."

"Episcopal ministers do better," Millie said.

"Not in this town. But what about your side of the street, David? You have three sects, so to speak, don't you?"

"Not exactly sects or even divisions. Let's say interpretations. The Orthodox Jew is for the most part a fundamentalist, accepting a literal interpretation of the Bible and living his life, to one degree or another, by a code of Jewish law called the *Shulchan Aruch*. The Conservative group accepts a great deal of Orthodox Judaism, but tempers it to modern life. For instance, many a Conservative Jew will eat ham in a restaurant but not at home. Others are indifferent in religious terms, but unwilling to take the step to Reform Judaism."

"How big is the step?"

"Not very big, but qualitative. We try to do away with superstition and mumbo-jumbo and find an ethical response in religion. We try to go back to the simple worship that prevailed long, long ago, before the stultifying superstition of the Middle Ages and the Pale of Settlement in the czar's Russia."

"The Pale being," Frome explained, "an area where Jews were allowed to live, there and nowhere else."

"To me," Mel Klein said suddenly, yet tentatively, "it's the rejection of Orthodox Judaism. I think orthodoxy anywhere is a terrible thing."

"All orthodoxy?" Millie wondered.

"All of it. My mother died when I was eight years old," Klein said. "My people were immigrants, and like most immigrants they were Orthodox, and every day I had to go to an Orthodox synagogue to say the prayer for the dead. There would be fifteen or twenty old men at the morning service, and they teased me and tortured me with little stupid tricks, like giving me a glass of vodka and telling me it was water. I don't know whether it was malevolent, but even at that young age, I realized that their devotion to prayer was apart from any sensitivity to the feelings of a kid who'd just lost his mother. After that time, I never set foot in an Orthodox synagogue again. I don't pretend to judge Orthodox Jews on my experience as a kid in that one place, but after that, I began to watch every kind of orthodoxy. None of them are good — in my opinion. I don't ask anyone to agree with me."

"Yet it could give you strength and courage at a time when you might need it."

"Orthodoxy or faith?" Martin wondered. "The two are not the same thing."

"But your forebears, Martin," Ed Frome said, "the worthy Pilgrim fathers, were the most orthodox of the orthodox. They may have been a cold and bleak parcel of folk, but they cut their homes out of this wilderness and they survived and they really put their stamp on this place."

"True, and I can't help thinking of the Orthodox Jews who went to their death in the Holocaust with such courage and faith."

"Your own vision, Martin," Ed Frome said. "I'll be damned if I'd vouch for or even try to approximate the feelings of the people who were slaughtered by Hitler. And I'm not defending orthodoxy, and I'm not even sure that I don't dislike your Pilgrim fathers intensely. They're definitely not my crowd. But I will say this — that the handful of Jews who fought the Nazis in the Warsaw Ghetto for over forty days — they were not Orthodox."

"I suppose Catholics are the most orthodox of all," Millie said.

"I did a hitch in Salt Lake City for the U.S.O.," Lucy said. "You can't even spell orthodoxy until you've been around the Mormons."

"Or a Southern Baptist," Martin said. "They're all very

sure that they have God's word and purpose down letter-perfect. All the orthodox share that conviction, and in the name of this crazy, malignant, bloodthirsty God, whether Episcopal, Lutheran, or Catholic or Muslim — whatever religion you choose — they will kill and slaughter by the millions."

"Good heavens," Della said, "is that the kind of sermon you preach?"

"That's the kind of sermon he thinks," Millie said. "It isn't easy to be a minister and know what hell religion has produced."

"Into the living room, please, for our coffee," Lucy told them. "This conversation is getting dangerous."

Mrs. Holtzman lived with her daughter and her son-in-law in Danbury. Usually, her daughter picked her up, but tonight both of them were in New York at theater. Lucy suggested that they make up a bed on their couch, but David said, no, he'd drive her home. When Lucy protested that it was over an hour's drive round trip, David told her that he could use the time to clear his head.

For the first few minutes, sitting beside David in the car, Mrs. Holtzman remained silent. Then she said, uncertainly, "Would it be all right for me to ask you a question, Rabbi?"

"Of course."

But like most people who at last find their important point of reference, Mrs. Holtzman's question was preceded by a lengthy explanation. She herself was the daughter of a lower middle-class Jewish family in Frankfurt. They had owned a notions shop and also sold some specialized fabrics, cheese cloth and netting and stiffening and inexpensive lace. It was a small business that provided no luxuries. They were a deeply religious family. "We suffered," Mrs. Holtzman said, counting on her fingers, "Mama, Papa, my brother Hans, my sister Esther — all of them dead, murdered by the Nazis. I survived Dachau. Why? I don't know why, Rabbi. God decided. I must not question God's decisions. At night I pray

God of my fathers, God of Abraham, Isaac, and Jacob, I mourn the dead and I do not understand your favoring me, but I thank you. But my son-in-law, he has a different point of view. He won't set foot in a synagogue. His son will not be a *Bar Mitzvah*. I can't repeat the words he says about God, the names he calls him, and he says it doesn't matter, because he says there is no God. He says that even a stupid, sick God would not create such creatures as Hitler and Stalin. So I have to ask you, Rabbi, and I don't like to because it shows how weak my faith is, but still I must ask you."

She couldn't frame the question, he realized. She could no more say to him, Is my God a sick, demented, malignant son of a bitch? than she could take off her clothes and dance naked in the moonlight.

"Well, you know," David said, "if you read the Bible, you will read of men almost as evil and destructive as Hitler and Stalin."

"You believe that, Rabbi — just as evil?"

"Oh, yes. Yes, indeed. And in history but apart from the Bible, men like Genghis Khan — yes, even such a man as Napoleon."

"But Napoleon was a great man!"

"Well, perhaps it's how you look at these things. I feel that God has his own point of view," thinking, And if she says to me, "Is there a God?" What am I to answer?

"And you think God has a purpose in all these terrible things, a purpose we don't understand?"

He had to force the words: "I think, perhaps, that God arranged it so that men work out their own destiny."

"And he, the Lord of the universe, watched the gas chambers and stood by? And he watched what happened in the Warsaw Ghetto and just shrugged it off? But why does it say in the Bible that in the battles, he helped the Jews? He made the sun stand still. He made the walls of Jericho fall down. He destroyed a whole Assyrian army that had invaded the land of Israel."

"Yes, well, that was another time."

He was lying. He was sitting next to a poor, stout, uneducated middle-aged woman who had been through all the fires of hell, and who pleaded with him to explain the vagaries of the God she worshipped. After all, that was his function; that was surely one of the reasons why he had become a rabbi, to explain all the bewildering and monstrous behavior of God; and now, he knew, he was expected to explain to Mrs. Holtzman that God gave man free will, and free will included Hitler and all the others — monsters that peopled the pages of history.

"Rabbi — " she said plaintively.

"Yes, Mrs. Holtzman?"

"I shouldn't ask you such questions. I know that I shouldn't ask you such questions."

He brought her to where she lived with her daughter and her son-in-law, and then he drove home, slowly. There were tears in his eyes. A great surge of emotion had produced the tears. And the emotion was the result of the simple questions Mrs. Holtzman had asked.

Lucy was in bed, waiting for him, and she said, "You do know, David, that without Mrs. Holtzman I would be absolutely wiped out. That lady is a treasure. I thought the night went well. Real nifty, high-class conversation." She had Graham Greene's book *The Quiet American* on her lap. "This is dynamite. Your friend Eddie Frome brought it tonight. Is something wrong?"

He shook his head, and Lucy studied him, seeing him consciously for the first time that evening. "You look so sad."

"Yes, I suppose I do." He began to take his clothes off.

"David, something did happen."

He went into the bathroom. Lucy heard the water running, the sound of his tooth-brushing. All the motions we go through, she thought. All the senseless motions.

The toilet flushed. Through all the misery that she had sensed in her husband, still he washed his hands, brushed his eth, and flushed the toilet. She remembered a story by Sinair Lewis, in which a Middle Western farmer, rebelling against the structure of his whole life, refused to brush his teeth. She tried to think of something appropriate to say to David as he opened the door of the bathroom, but nothing she could think of fitted the moment. David, in his pajamas, sat down on the edge of the bed.

"Want to talk about it?" Lucy asked him.

"What can I talk about, Lucy? I'm a rabbi who has lost his belief in God."

"You feel that? I mean, when did it happen? Can something like that happen, just all of a sudden?"

"It's been adding up, one thing and another. Then that talk about shared premises. My own premise was a fraud. I've always counted myself a person of reason and intelligence, and all the horror and cruelty and duplicity I have seen, I've always explained with the handy proposition that God gives man free will. Tonight it didn't work. I drove that poor woman home, and she asked me about God, and all my thoughts and beliefs and devotions turned into a miserable and shameful farce."

"You've never done a shameful thing in your life!" Lucy protested.

"Endless numbers, Lucy." He got up and began to pace the room. "Standing at that pit of horror at Dachau with a full stomach, a well-dressed, well-fed American officer, top of the world, what fine liberators we are when we're not atomizing Japanese cities, and then ten years here in this safe little nest of white Protestant middle-class comfort, where they don't murder Jews and are mostly quite nice to them — "

"David," Lucy cried, "what the devil are you doing?"

"Oh, my God," he whispered, dropping down on the bed again. "I'm not talking sense, am I?"

"Not very much, no."

"I'm frightened."

"Of what, David? Of what?"

"I was never frightened this way," he said slowly, holding out one trembling hand. "The world disintegrates," staring at his hand. "No God and no hope — hairless apes who kill and kill and kill."

"You married an atheist," Lucy said firmly. "I work, I live, I have carried two children, and they're pretty good kids too. I cook and sew and take care of all of you, and I do it without any God kicking my ass around."

"I never believed that," David said desperately. "I always thought it was a piece of bravado on your part. You must believe in something, or you'd feel the way I feel now."

He was pleading with her, and now she gave in and said, "Yes, something. I don't know what it is or if it's inside me or outside me. But I don't believe in the kind of God you and Martin push, and neither does Millie, if you want the plain honest truth."

"Are you telling me that Millie Carter is an atheist?"

"No, that is a dumb word, David. Millie and I have talked a good deal about this. We don't know what we believe in, but not the ridiculous God you and Martin push. God as a man — heaven help us! Can you watch a woman give birth and believe — if you're going to have an anthropomorphic God — that it's a man and not a woman? But that's crazy, isn't it? Do you know why nobody talks about God? Because the moment you start, you descend to the realm of idiocy."

"I never thought of God as an old man with a white beard sitting up in the clouds."

"How did you think of God?"

"I don't know."

"David, David, my dear, nothing has changed from yesterday. It's almost two o'clock in the morning, and in a few hours I'll have to put up the oatmeal and fry the eggs and do the rest of it. Let's go to sleep. Nothing looks as bad in the daylight as it does at night."

Not until there was a touch of dawn in the sky did David sleep. His mind was out of control. It was a separate thing alive, willful, and free of any control he could exercise upon it. It swooped from childhood to the present; it burrowed through history; it pleaded for a miracle — what of Joan of Arc, what of Lourdes? What of Israel? He was transparent and too clever, and he saw through himself. He said to himself, If ever a man sold his birthright for a pot of lentils, the man is myself, and like Esau, I can't get it back.

Lucy waking him gently. "When did you fall asleep?"

"It was beginning to get light."

"I hate to wake you, David. The kids are off to school. It's nine-fifteen. I'd let you sleep, but Mrs. Shapiro called. You missed the morning service, but they managed without you. Now there's a little boy, name of Herbert Cohen, waiting in your office. He was excused from school this morning because he has a tutorial with you."

"Oh, yes, of course. I know the boy. Oh, no, he must not be sent away. Telephone Mrs. Shapiro and tell her I'll be there in ten or fifteen minutes."

"Will you eat an egg?"

"No. No, thank you, Lucy. Just coffee."

Fifteen minutes was too optimistic. It was almost ten o'clock when he got to the synagogue and said to Mrs. Shapiro, "Is he still there?"

"He's there. You're his hero, Rabbi. I'm sure he would stay all day and all night as long as he knows you are coming."

"Please, hold my calls for one hour."

David tried to give at least two hours of individual attention to each of the boys who turned thirteen and faced his *Bar Mitzvah*. Herbert Cohen was a special case, a gentle, somewhat pathetic little boy, one of those children to whom puberty comes late. He came from a family that had joined the Temple Shalom because there was no other synagogue within miles, and his inability to cope with the requirements of the *Bar Mitzvah* and his fear of failure touched David deeply. He could not learn Hebrew. David had encountered this now and again in other children, an absolute block against learning a language so different from any Western tongue. Part of this, David came to realize, was due to the method of instruction. The synagogue had hired a Hebrew teacher, a Polish Jew who was a poor teacher and whose English was completely inadequate. David would have fired him half a dozen times over, but each time he thought of it, he also recalled the concentration camp number tattooed on the man's arm. The result was that the man remained in the job.

When David came into his office, Herbert Cohen, a small, skinny boy in a large chair, looked up and smiled tentatively. "Good morning, Rabbi," he said.

"Sorry I'm so late."

"That's all right. It doesn't matter."

"Oh?"

"It's no good, Rabbi. I can't learn Hebrew — I can't. I told you that, and you wouldn't believe me. I lie to my father. He'll kill me when he finds out the truth."

"He won't kill you, Herbert. We'll do your *Haftarah* in English, and it will be perfectly fine."

"We can't!"

"Why can't we? It's not the language that's important; it's what is being said. You know, in earlier times, the *Haftarah* was read by a small child, and then as now it was a selection from Prophets. Not as a *Bar Mitzvah* thing, mind you. They didn't have the *Bar Mitzvah* ceremony until the Middle Ages, but because" — he hesitated here — "because God might listen better to the voice of innocence. You see, Herbert, the prophets were the defenders of the people. In those days, kings, rulers, generals, were as cruel and crazy as they are today, and only the prophets stood between them and the people. That is why I gave you your *Haftarah* from Isaiah. You will read it in English."

"You're sure, Rabbi?"

"Of course I'm sure. And I think it will be more valid if people understand what you are reading."

"What will I tell my father?"

"Tell him what I said."

"He'll be mad."

The boy's prediction was correct. David and Lucy and their two children were at dinner when Mr. Cohen called. "I want to talk to you, Rabbi," he said.

"Can you come to my office at the synagogue tomorrow?"

"No, I can't. I'm a working man, mister, not one of your rich Jews up there at Leighton Ridge. I want to see you tonight."

"All right. In my office at the synagogue, an hour from now."

"Who was that?" Lucy asked. "He has a strong voice. We heard him in here."

"Cohen. He's a house painter in Bridgeport, and he lives in Fairfield. He's here only because he had a fight with both rabbis at the local synagogues down there, and I imagine he's ready to eat me up because I told his boy that he could read his *Haftarah* in English."

"When I was a kid," Lucy said, "I was convinced that the Bible was written in English."

"Mom," Aaron said, "not really?"

"I'm afraid Mr. Cohen is convinced that it was never translated."

Mr. Cohen was also convinced that the Temple Shalom was not really a synagogue, and he said as much as he stamped into David's office an hour later and, apropos of nothing yet said, snorted, "If there's anything turns my stomach, Rabbi, it's this business of calling a *shul* a temple. I don't like it!" In the nineteenth century in Europe, synagogue and school were combined in one building, called by the Yiddish word *shul*.

Cohen was a short, barrel-chested man with heavy brows. He wore his hostility like a weapon.

"Well, we're not here to talk about what to call a synagogue," David said, temporizing. "Myself, I'm not fond of calling a synagogue a temple. I try to avoid the word temple where I can."

"I should thank you for the opinion."

"Won't you sit down," David said.

"I can say what I came to say standing. In all my life, Rabbi Hartman, in all my life I never heard of a boy being a *Bar Mitzvah* and singing his *Haftarah* in English! In all my life, I never even heard of someone suggesting something like that. You going to tell me my boy can't learn to read Hebrew? That's crap, and you know it is! My son is as smart as any other kid. It's that goddamned idiot Polack you got teaching the kids."

"He isn't the best language teacher, but even with the best, there are children who cannot relate to another language, especially a language as different and difficult as Hebrew."

"I told you that's crap. I've put up with this lousy Reform Judaism long enough. Seems to me you're as Jewish as the Pope. Now you listen, either you get another Hebrew teacher, or I take my son out of here and find a Jewish synagogue."

"You're very angry," David said, "and I can understand your anger. You feel that we are saying that your boy is backward, that he lacks intelligence — "

"That's what you're saying! You're damned right I'm angry!"

"But that's not what I'm saying. The ability to absorb a language has nothing to do with intelligence. Herbert is one of the most sensitive and intelligent children we have."

"Yeah? Well, let me tell you this, Rabbi. I don't want a sensitive kid, not in your terms — and the kid tells me you teach them that war is wrong and somebody don't have the right to defend himself. Well, that's crap too. You're telling me Israel don't have the right to defend itself. So I'm taking my kid out and putting him where he can learn to be Jewish."

"So that's it, and my heart goes out to the boy," David told Lucy after he got home.

"It seems such a small thing. Of course, to my way of thinking it makes a great deal more sense to do it in English."

"No, it's not English versus Hebrew. I had intended to suggest that I do a transliteration for the kid — you know, the Hebrew spelled out in English letters, so that he could read it — I mean if I couldn't convince the father, but he stormed out before I had a chance. No, it's not the English. He probably has memories of a small, warm Orthodox synagogue he knew as a child, where everything was just as it had been for a thousand years, and which was a refuge against the world. Poor man, he's frightened. I can understand that."

"David, why can't you face reality? You don't have to love everyone, and everyone is not a good human being. I saw welts on the little boy's arms last week in Sunday school. His father beats him."

"Frustration."

"Bullshit!" Lucy exclaimed. "Do you beat your kids when you're frustrated? What in hell is wrong with you, David Hartman?"

"I'm a rabbi," he replied feebly.

"Oh, that's a great beautiful excuse. You're a rabbi!"

"You're turning this into a fight. You're shouting at me as if I did something terrible. You're taking the position that it's a crime to understand people instead of hating them mindlessly."

"That's right. I hate people who beat kids. I don't have to understand them. I just think they stink. And let me tell you this, David Hartman, there's a reason for language. Bullshit is bullshit. Lousy is lousy and rotten is rotten. You can even carry it further and say that shit is shit. You and Martin wipe out those words; you wipe out feelings; you pretend to a world that doesn't exist. Oh, hell, what's the use of talking to you!" And with that she fled upstairs, almost tripping over the two kids, who were crouched at the top of the stairs, listening.

The next day, during a slack moment of no calls and no demands, David drove over to the Congregational church. Martin Carter was on the telephone, and he assured David that he'd be with him in a moment. "My own *tsuris*," he said. He knew half a dozen Yiddish words, and he used them whenever an opportunity arose. "My daughter Ellie is twenty-three. She's the perpetual student at Smith. This time it's a master's. Next time a doctorate. And her father's a country preacher. Well, now, at long last, she is deeply, romantically in love — with a Catholic boy, plain Boston Irish Catholic."

"And it troubles you?"

"I don't know," Martin said uneasily. "I told her that if she loved him, that was the important thing. He's a doctor and probably a hell of a nice lad. No, David, it upsets me. I'll get used to it, but right now it upsets me."

"Millie — does it upset her?"

"She doesn't know yet, but she won't be troubled. She considers all religion as more or less of a disaster."

"No — you're kidding." When he had heard the same thing from Lucy, he had simply rejected it.

"Absolutely not. Haven't you sensed it?"

"But you seem to have the best marriage in the world."

"Yes, we're very fond of each other. She simply accepts my attitude toward Christianity as evidence of a sort of brain damage. But that's not what you want to talk about."

"Let's walk a bit," David suggested, and when they were outside, he said to Martin, "In the ten years you've known me, Martin, how many petitions for civil rights have we signed, how many antiwar demonstrations, how many peace vigils?"

"Quite a few. Where do you go from there?"

"Lucy and I had one of our scraps. She said that you and I pretend to a world that doesn't exist."

"Oh? Interesting. Did she elaborate on what she meant?"

"No."

"Funny formulation — we pretend to a world that doesn't exist. Those words? Really, David?"

"Oh, yes. They stuck in my mind."

"Thing is, where is the pretense? Are we pretending — or does she mean that we create in our minds a world that doesn't exist?"

"Or both."

"That's a very bright woman, David, but I wouldn't brood over it. Marriage is an endless succession of small tragedies and new starts. But that's not it, is it? You've been depressed."

"The world is depressing, Martin."

"Come on — on a spring day, the Ridge here can be the most beautiful place in the world. It makes your heart sing just to look around you."

"I envy you."

"It'll work out."

"I wonder," David said. "I just wonder."

"Of course it will. As for Lucy and Millie, God knows, it's not easy to be a minister's wife."

"Do we pretend that language doesn't exist, Martin? I mean the kind of language that seemed to be as necessary to the war as a fifty-millimeter — motherfuck in every phrase, screw, shit, and all the rest of it — and I have to force each word."

"I know."

"Then for the love of God, what kind of a game are we playing?"

"We pretend. But we're not the only ones. I try to work it out some way, David. If I did not believe in God, if I lost my faith — "

"You do believe?"

"Yes, I believe. Do you know, when they were ready to test the first atom bomb, Fermi and Oppenheimer and the other great minds, as we've been told, they raised among themselves the question of whether the explosion might not ignite the atmosphere and, in one horrible moment, extinguish all life on earth. They took bets, and then they exploded the bomb. Is there any doubt in your mind that these so-called great scientists were criminally insane?"

"No, no doubt," David said bleakly.

"I can say this to you, David, but not from my pulpit. So I pretend, so I'm a fraud and a coward, and I ask God to forgive me. I am only one human being at a point in history where mankind's madness has been combined with enough scientific knowledge to destroy the entire human race in moments. If I didn't believe in God, David, I would find the world meaningless and intolerable."

"And you find meaning in it?"

"I try, David. You understand that, because you also try."

"Yes, I try."

"So we are what we are, ministers of a time so awful the mind rejects it."

"On the other hand — "

"I know," Martin interrupted, "on the other hand, life goes on as if nothing were any different, and we play our games. David, we are necessary, believe me. If I didn't feel that, I'd throw up the whole thing tomorrow. Maybe not honest, but necessary. Aspirin is necessary. Same thing. Liddy Delman is a parishioner. Fifty-two years old, intelligent, attractive woman. Husband passed away from a heart attack last year. Now she's dying of cancer in Danbury Hospital, a week or a month left. I get to see her at least every other day. I hold her hand and tell her that she will live again, that Jesus will receive her in his arms, that she will see her husband and loved ones. Am I telling her the truth, David?"

David was silent.

"No answer, my friend? The rabbi will not commit to the Christian minister. But damnit to hell, I give her peace! David, I give her peace! I take away the fear of senseless disease and meaningless death. I help her to depart this life with some dignity. Is that wrong?"

At home Lucy said to him, "If we could only have a fight, a real knock-down fight, and scream at each other and call each other vile names, and then cry and carry on and come out clean."

"I don't understand that. I love you. I can't fight with you, Lucy."

"I know, David. Tomorrow, I have to go into New York and spend the day with Momma. She can't go on in that apartment, all alone, after Pop's death — "

"I told you to persuade her to live with us. I like your mother."

"You don't understand. You're a rabbi. The arguments with my mother would be endless. Anyway, she's decided to give up the apartment and go to California. We have all kinds of relatives out there, including Mom's sister, my Aunt Freda. She wants me to come to the apartment and take whatever I want. I don't really want any of the stuff in the apartment, but Mom will be hurt if I refuse."

"Sure. You can leave the kids with me. No problem."

"I'll be leaving at six forty-five in the morning, before the traffic gets heavy, and then I can be back here at dinnertime. I'll have a roast ready to go in the oven, and I'll write out instructions for stove temperature and basting. You'll have to get the kids up, see that they get dressed, give them breakfast, and pack them off to school. The bus picks them up at eight-forty sharp. Corn flakes and milk and doughnuts. They won't perish from one cold breakfast. They'll have a hot lunch in school, and the bus drops them back here at three-ten."

"I think I can manage that."

"Sure you can. I'm being a pig about it."

It was still night, and he had just fallen asleep. Lucy was shaking his shoulder. "Up and at them, Rabbi. It's six-thirty, and I'm on my way out."

He might have complained angrily that he didn't have to get up at six-thirty, but he never complained angrily. That was part of the burden he bore. He never complained angrily.

He had always accepted as fact that his two children, Sarah, aged seven, and Aaron, aged nine, were an intimate part of his life. Suddenly on this morning, they were strangers. A relationship had shifted. They looked with suspicion on the corn flakes. "Mom gives us oatmeal or Wheatena, and she puts honey on it. You can't put honey on this stuff."

Sarah explained in a hoarse whisper, "He can't make oatmeal. He's a man."

"Why did she go to New York?" Aaron demanded.

"Grandma Sally is moving to California. Mom has to help her clear out her apartment."

"Where's California?" Sarah asked.

"We'll never see her again," Aaron said.

"Why?"

"It's too far."

"We'll never see Mommy again," Sarah wailed.

"She'll be here tonight in time to put you to bed," David assured them. "She's not going to California. Grandma is — to be near her sister, your Great-aunt Freda."

The strange, subtly antagonistic relationship continued until the children went off to school — leaving David to brood over what he meant to his kids. When they returned from school, he had milk and cookies waiting for them, but the first thing they asked was whether Lucy had come back. David's efforts to amuse them were as unsuccessful as the bowls of corn flakes. They tumbled out of the house to go their own way with their own friends, leaving David to wonder what he should do. So long as he remained in the house, he could watch the kids in the back yard, but did Lucy feel, as he did, that she must be there constantly to watch them?

Mrs. Shapiro called from the synagogue and reminded him of his appointments.

"You have to cancel them. I have to stay here and watch the kids."

"We can't cancel now. Rabbi, I'll come over and watch the children. You keep your appointments. Wait for me, I'll be there in a few minutes."

He felt a great sense of relief, released from the responsibility of his two children and entrusting them to Mrs. Shapiro. Mrs. Shapiro was a chunky, solid woman, whose every aspect spoke of dependability. And how brilliant she was to think of the exchange.

"You will keep an eye on them all the time I'm gone?" David said to her.

"Rabbi, Rabbi, what can happen to the kids in this beautiful place? Where I grew up, on Avenue B on the East Side, that was something else. But, you know, even there kids survive. It's a habit kids have."

David stayed at the synagogue until the weekday evening service was over, and then he hurried home. Mrs. Shapiro was in the kitchen with the children, all of them seated at the kitchen table. In front of the kids, plates of scrambled eggs and sliced tomato, which they were eagerly devouring while they stuffed the remaining space in their mouths with bread and butter.

"My goodness, I forgot the roast. Lucy will kill me."

"They're so skinny," Mrs. Shapiro said accusingly.

"That's only because they're very active. Not because I forgot to put the roast in the oven."

"They say you allow them to watch television. Is that true, Rabbi?"

"They don't lie, Mrs. Shapiro. Of course it's true. One hour of the children's programming."

"There you are, see?" Aaron said. "You made us miss it."

"And she fed you an excellent dinner, so don't be a pig about it," David said.

"But I had the dinner in the fridge," Lucy said, when she returned an hour later. "I told you that, David. I specified — roast, oven."

"I know. I mean, I seem to have forgotten. Mel Klein came back from New York early for a finance meeting, and then the sisterhood came in with their argument that we should have a woman for a cantor. Sophie Frome and Dora Buckingham are both gung ho for something they call women's rights — "

"So am I."

"And so am I," David said. "But a woman cantor?"

"Why not? We sing better than men, we sound better, and I hear that there are a couple of places that already have lady cantors."

"Let's not get into a thing about this. Tell me how your mother is."

"All right. She's getting over it, but it's a slow thing. It's four years since Pop died, and you'd think she'd be over it at least a little. Well, maybe a little, but whenever we talk about Pop, she breaks down and cries. Well, they were very close, and I think it's a good thing that she's going to California."

"Why? She'll be so far from you and from the kids."

"Yes, but at the same time California has a kind of mystical significance for her. That's where she and Pop went on their honeymoon. They stayed in a little inn at Santa Barbara. That was right after Pop was mustered out of the army in nineteen eighteen, and from what Mom says, at that time Southern California was as close to heaven as you could get. The family's still in Santa Barbara, where Uncle Bert has his harness shop. Well, not much harness anymore. It's mostly boots and saddles and stuff like that, and they need help, and they're ready to give Mom a job. So that part of it's not too bad."

"And the bad part?"

"I'll miss her so much, David."

"We'll just have to tighten up on everything and put away enough money for a couple of trips a year."

Lucy burst out laughing. "David, you're wonderful. Tighten up? Do you know how tight it is already?"

"We get along, don't we?"

"Barely. If it weren't for Dr. Levine and his free medicine and Della Klein's garden and the sewing machine the sisterhood gave me — well, we'd never make it. And two plane trips to California? I don't know how."

"We'll find a way."

David mentioned it to Martin, who said, "Well, there you are, David. We commit ourselves to a profession that pays nowhere as well as plumbing or carpentry. Fortunately, Millie has the little trust fund that throws off a few thousand a year, but my own feeling is that they should limit pastoring to the children of the very rich."

"You're not serious?"

"No, of course not. But the trouble is that the Pilgrim fathers, who were as poor as church mice, turned poverty into a sin and created a national ideology to perpetuate the notion. If you're rich, God has blessed hard work and intelligence. If you're poor, it's because you're lazy, Godless, and stupid."

"Leaves us out," David noted.

"Leaves out the prophets, the apostles, Saint Francis, and any number of others."

A few weeks later, at the beginning of June, David preached his last sermon of the spring season. For the next four weeks, the sermons would be preached by outside speakers invited for the evening. For his subject, David selected the ancient Jewish legend of the *Lamed Vov*. It was years since he had spoken of the *Lamed Vov*, and he had never been too eager to dwell on the subject, since it was at best a sad and lonely notion. David reminded the congregation that according to the old legend, if there came a point in history when thirty-six men of honesty, integrity, and saintly decency could not be found, the world would simply come to an end. "But," David said in his sermon, "at a time when we are already stockpiling enough nuclear weapons to wipe out the entire human race, how shall we regard the legend of *Lamed Vov?* Is it quaint and pointless? Or is it that thirty-six just men can no longer exist in the kind of a world we have today?"

Afterward, Lucy said to him, "How could you? There were kids listening to you. That was the most depressing thing I ever heard."

He accepted Lucy's criticism silently, avoided people as much as possible, and when the weekend was over, he drove to New York, telling Lucy that he would be back before dinner. His manner was such that Lucy did not ask for reasons or what business he might have in New York, but simply accepted with relief his absence for a day.

Rabbi Belsen, emeritus now, eighty-three years old, still occupied the same small office at the Institute. No one dared suggest that he retire or leave the office, because, as someone put it, no one cared to face the task of moving his books and papers. His books and papers filled the shelves, floor to ceiling, shelves built over every inch of wall space.

"You're early," he said as David came into his office. He was making tea on his little electric plate. "Is it too hot for tea?" he asked. His beard was pure white, his eyes encased in more wrinkles, but otherwise little changed from the last time David had seen him, years ago.

"How are you?" David asked him.

"How long since you have been here, David, six years, eight years? I'm old. God saw fit to give me eighty-three years, but not to attend to other things like my eyes, my arthritis, my memory, not to mention my heart. Well, so what have I learned? Browning was a good poet, but a little foolish. 'Grow old along with me! The best is yet to be, the last of life, for which the first was made.' Rabbi Ben Ezra, God bless him, maybe for him growing old was a pleasure. I don't enjoy it. You want sugar in your tea?"

"No, thank you."

"Don't think I'm heartless or senile, rattling on like this. I'm trying to put you at your ease. You're filled with pain."

"How do you know?"

"The way you made the appointment. The way you look now. Lost weight. Circles under your eyes. No ease — no plain pleasure about you, David."

"My whole world has gone to pieces, Rabbi Belsen."

"Worlds go to pieces. It's an old habit."

David sought for words for what he had to say. "A failed priest" had a ring of history, tradition, but a "failed rabbi" was very flat indeed. He sat facing Rabbi Belsen, who waited patiently, gently stirring his tea, and then David blurted out, "I've lost my faith."

"Oh?" The old man shook his head. "What you lost is unclear to me, David. Faith is a very Christian thing. The dictionary, if I'm not mistaken, usually defines faith as a belief without proof. Did you have such a belief to lose, a belief without proof? If you did, tell me what kind of proof you would have required to turn your belief into a fact?"

"I'm not sure I know what you mean. I believed in God.

Now I don't believe anymore. I'm a rabbi who does not believe in God."

"You know, it's such a long time we've been in America," the old man said. "A hundred and fourteen years since my father came here. Nothing of course to compare with the people who settled Leighton Ridge, but nevertheless long enough to become totally confused. David, I would watch the way the people who came more recently from Eastern Europe drank their tea, holding a cube of sugar in their teeth while they drank. I tried it once, but it was not very satisfactory." He paused and shook a finger at David. "No, I'm not losing my wits. I'm still trying to put you at your ease. I ask myself why you lost your belief in God. Is it because the world shows no indications of sanity anywhere? Or is it because people do terrible things? Both are underlined simply by reading the Bible, which will provide you with chapter and verse of acts of terrible horror consummated without atomic weapons or gunpowder."

"I don't know why I stopped believing. I only know that I don't believe anymore."

"I suppose you know that we say a Jew doesn't stop believing, he simply becomes very angry with God."

"I've heard that."

"You see, David, I am not arguing with you or trying to convince you of anything. At a moment like this, argument on my part would be useless. It would merely serve to sharpen your wit and force you to work out good arguments to support your case. I prefer to leave you confused. After all, you've had excellent rabbinical training, which is, I think, as good as what the Jesuits are said to provide. You know, David, a very wise doctor once said to me that no one who studies the human liver could fail to believe in God. But that would be no solution, would it?"

Smiling, David shook his head. "I'm afraid not."

"Good. You feel a little better. I can imagine the agony you felt."

"It's not simply a question of my own belief. I have to give up the synagogue."

"Why?"

"How can I talk about God and belief and hope when I have no belief and hope?"

"From all I've heard, you're a very good rabbi. That's important. Do you feel that if you go on, you'll turn into a worthless rabbi?"

"Maybe. I don't know."

"If you resign, will they find a better replacement?"

"I don't know, Rabbi. I can't answer such a question."

"And I can't tell you what to do, David. I can't find God for you, and I can't tell you anything that will convince you that God exists. This is something you must discover for yourself. But is it possible that you never actually believed in God — something you have never been willing to face — until now?"

"No, that's not possible," David answered, almost fiercely.

"All right. But think about it."

"And you'll replace me at the synagogue?"

"Well — not yet. I'm not actively involved any longer in the placement of rabbis, but I can talk to the people who are. But not so quickly. You must think about this. Examine yourself more deeply. And don't think it would be so easy to find the proper person for Leighton Ridge. So for the time being, please, David, go on with your work."

David left the Institute annoyed with himself and with Rabbi Belsen in equal measure, annoyed with himself because he had come whimpering to the old man without a shred of pride or dignity, as he saw it, and annoyed with Belsen because Belsen had offered nothing, neither hope nor knowledge. Hands thrust into the pockets of the old seersucker suit he was wearing, head bent, indeed his whole long, bony figure bent, he drifted along the city streets, turning over in his mind what he would have done had Belsen told him that he was through and that he should turn over his pulpit to someone else. He would have to tell Lucy that he no longer had a job and that the house they lived in was no longer theirs. And then what? What else was he fit for? His whole training, his whole competence, was for being a rabbi. He knew of a good many rabbinically trained men who ended up in various universities, teaching Bible History or Hebrew, or the Religions of the Middle East, but none of these speculative futures held any great attraction for him, even assuming that he could ever be hired by a college.

He found himself walking along Riverside Drive, and he paused to lean on the stone wall and look out at the river. There was enough wind to make the water dance in the sunlight, and directly opposite him, a large yawl was making its way up the river, trimming its sails to catch the wind. There were two men and two women working the sails, scampering across the boat, dodging the boom as it swung around, all of them sunburned, young, alive with the exhilaration of the struggle with wind and sails. Watching them, David realized that he had never been on such a boat, indeed on any sailboat, and suddenly his life appeared gray and meaningless, dull, a dullness interrupted only by the years of World War Two, and looking back at those years, he could recall instantly, and not without pleasure, the excitement, the danger, and the horror.

"My God," he said aloud, "is the only way to be alive, to participate in the worst slaughter man ever created?"

He drove back to Leighton Ridge, wondering why he had come to New York, and when he tried to explain to Lucy why he had gone, she said to him, "David, you don't have to explain anything to me. You're a grown man, and you have the right to go to New York or anywhere else without consulting me or explaining to me."

"No, I haven't. You're my wife."

"Yes, and I know what you intend to tell me. You're going to tell me that you went to New York to see Rabbi Belsen or someone else in that strange place and ask them to give back to you the God you lost somewhere down the line."

He was hurt. She could hurt him more deeply and easily than anyone else, and she saw the hurt on his face.

"Oh, I'm sorry," she cried.

"It's all right. That's what I was going to tell you."

"But why, David? Why? Not me — this you do to yourself."

"You know, I want to tell you why, Lucy. You're my wife and I love you, so I should be able to tell you why. But it's so hard to say."

"Try me, David. We've been married over ten years. Isn't it time you were able to talk to me, or each of us to talk to each other?"

"It's not that I don't want to talk to you about it — it's just so hard to put it into words. I guess since I was a high school kid, I just knew that I was put on earth for a certain kind of service. No, that doesn't say it. Let's say I put myself in God's hands, and then whatever happened, it was all right. No matter how terrible it was, it was all right — as the poet put it, God's in his heaven, all's right with the world. And then, all of a sudden, the hands were no longer there."

"David, David darling, they were never there. There are no hands. There are just people — you, me, the kids, our friends — just people. We do everything that's awful and we do everything that's good."

"No!"

"David, look around you. There's an old religion called golf, and a new religion, absolutely ecumenical, called tennis, and the new apostles are the tennis pros. And God? David, he's out to lunch. David, look at what you're in. If you must have a God and if there is no God, what do you do?"

"I don't know," he said hopelessly.

"You and Martin — you've painted yourselves into a corner."

Two months after this incident, about ten days before the

children were due to return to school, David and Lucy were finishing a late supper. The children were asleep, and Lucy suggested that they take their coffee into the living room. "I have something very important to discuss with you, David." She had arranged for Mrs. Holtzman to be there — for reasons David couldn't understand, since there were only the two of them at the table — but she wanted to talk out of Mrs. Holtzman's earshot.

David sensed the chill of what was coming, if not the substance. For weeks now, the cord binding him to his wife had been stretched thinner and thinner. Their lovemaking had come almost to a standstill; their talk was more formal; the silences longer and longer. Tonight, Lucy said, "We must talk, David. We must talk about things you usually don't want to talk about, namely, you and me."

"What good will it do to talk? You'll become angry. You always do. I can't fight you, Lucy. You shred me to ribbons."

"Not tonight. But that's it — the question of becoming angry."

"We've been through that."

"Not really, no. If we could both become angry enough to fight with each other, we'd be alive. No, I don't mean that. I'm trying to say that there's something missing in our marriage, something I need desperately, as much as I need air to breathe."

"And what is that, Lucy?" he asked quietly.

"I'm not sure. Laughter, maybe. Joy. A kind of excitement. Maybe to be eager for tomorrow to come because you know there's something good tomorrow, but not to have tomorrow no less dreary than today."

"And that's how you feel?"

"That's how I've felt for a long time, David. Didn't you know that?"

"No — not the way you put it."

"It's not that I don't love you. You're so good and kind."

"That's not enough, is it?"

"David, I have to get away. Otherwise, I shall go absolutely mad. I'm not talking about a divorce. But I want to take the kids and go to California for one school term. From now until February. I spoke to my mother on the telephone, and she discussed it with my Uncle Bert and Aunt Freda. He needs help desperately in the store, and he'll pay me a hundred dollars a week."

"And that's what you're leaving me for," he said unbelievingly, "to work in a saddle shop somewhere in California? Lucy, I don't even know where Santa Barbara is. And you're taking the children?"

"I'm not leaving you. Well, I am, but I'm not. I'm not asking for a divorce, only to save my — no, I'm not going to say my sanity. It's my life, David."

"I don't understand. I just don't understand what you're saying."

"Did you ever understand what I am saying?"

"That's not fair," David protested. "I listen to you. I always listen to you, and I try to see your point of view."

"Well, here it is, flat out, my point of view," her voice rising. "My point of view is that if I don't get away from Leighton Ridge, I will go insane, I will kill myself, I will scream until my vocal cords part, I will become a mumbling idiot, I will divorce you — any and all of them. Oh, Jesus, I don't know. I don't want to end our marriage. I don't want a divorce, but I can't go on this way. So I worked out this separation. You won't have to send us money. Momma found a nice house with extra bedrooms, and we'll live there with her. She'll help with the children while I'm working — " He was trying to control the pain he felt, and she broke off, trying desperately not to burst into tears.

"How can I explain it?" she asked hopelessly.

David didn't answer. He sat motionless, stiff, in his chair, looking at his wife, and perhaps a minute went by, and then he said to her, "When do you want to go?"

"In a few days, David, so that I can put the kids in school when their term begins."

"Are there any Jews there, Lucy?" with childish innocence.

"Of course, and in Los Angeles, just sixty miles away, about the same distance that we are from New York, there's the second largest Jewish community in the world."

"I could call you. That wouldn't cost too much. And suppose I came out there, say in a month or two, I'd be missing all of you so much," plaintively, hopelessly.

"Sure. We have five thousand dollars put away. I think half of it should be used by you for fare or whatever."

He shook his head. "This is crazy. What happened to us?"

"It happens to a great many people, David."

"But I love you. I always thought you loved me."

"I do — in a way. But it's not enough. It's simply not enough."

"I just don't understand," he said despairingly. "What do I do? Do I go on living here?"

"Mrs. Holtzman will move in and sleep in Sarah's room. I've made all the arrangements with her. I told her I'm taking the children out to California to see my mother and to stay with her for a while, and that's all she has to know or anyone in the congregation. You just tell them the same thing. It's perfectly natural."

"And live alone?"

"For a while, David."

"You spoke of a whole school term, five months. Or is that just to ease me over the hurdle before the divorce?"

"I'm not asking for a divorce, David. Not unless you want one?"

"Why would I want one? Lucy, for God's sake, don't do this. There's no reason to do it."

"Only to save my own life, David."

A week after Lucy and the children went off to California, because he had to talk to someone, he told Martin Carter the truth about Lucy's visit to her mother, and quite understandably, since he was not sworn to secrecy, Martin told his wife. Millie promptly invited David to dinner, and then told her husband, "You be upstairs when he comes, and let me have a few words with him alone."

Millie was in the kitchen when David arrived. He entered through the front door, which was never locked, and Millie called out to him, "Make yourself comfortable in the living room, David. Martin's upstairs, showering." She came into the living room with two tall glasses of gin and tonic. "For the dog days — you do like gin and tonic?"

David accepted the glass and smiled bleakly. He had been studying the furniture in the room, the chintz-covered, over-stuffed chairs and couch, the eighteenth-century sewing table, the mahogany desk, the sunburst mirror that had belonged to Millie's grandfather, the two old family oil portraits — studying them and trying, as he had a hundred times before, to understand Lucy's flight from all this, her statement that everything — certainly beautiful old things like these in-cluded — everything in Leighton Ridge was stifling her, kill-ing her. Yet their lives had not been confined by Leighton Ridge. He and Martin had been in every good fight, walked in demonstrations, signed petitions, preached against war and injustice. But that was himself and Martin; where had Lucy been?

Here now was Millie, as good a friend as Lucy ever had — this according to Lucy — coming right to the point: "David, why did you let her leave?"

"I didn't let her." He was taken aback, trying desperately to formulate his own attitude. "How could I stop her?"

"By telling her that you're her husband and she'd better damned well not run off to California."

"I couldn't tell her that."

"Why? For heaven's sake, why?"

"She's a human being. She's a person. In her place, if I felt the way she felt, I would have gone too."

"No you wouldn't. Now you listen to me, David Hartman.

I've been married to one of you for more years than I care to count, and I know what I'm talking about, and I've been watching you for ten years now. It has nothing to do with religion. People like you and Martin turn to religion sometimes and sometimes to other things, I don't know what, maybe revolutions, but whatever it is, you go into it because you're some kind of damned saint, and God help any one of us who is married to a saint. I know. I've been there, and I know every thought Lucy thought and every feeling she felt, and I had the same screaming desire to run away — not once, but half a dozen times. But I was not brought up to think and act as freely as Lucy, and I had no one in California to run to, and if I had run, Martin's family and my family would have cast me out into the dust. Not Martin, mind you. He would have exhibited that same lousy understanding that you saints are so expert with. Yes, I'm glad I stayed. Life is just as frustrating and meaningless in Santa Barbara or anywhere else as in Leighton Ridge, and underneath all his saintly denseness, Martin is a wonderful, beautiful man — just as you are. And my kids grew up with a mother and a father, which is the way it should be. It is not Leighton Ridge. It's this stinking planet we live on."

"But if you felt that way, what kept you here?" David wondered.

"What kept me here? Closed doors, David. I was a minister's daughter married to a minister. That closes a lot of doors. I was not raised in a free-thinking, open household, as Lucy was, free to doubt and question, and do you know, I thank God for it — because I still have Martin."

"If she still loved me, she wouldn't have gone away. What sense would it make to force her to live with a man she stopped loving?"

Millie sighed hopelessly. "I don't think I've ever known a man who didn't have the brains of a tadpole, not when it comes down to anything concerning emotions or feelings. The few hours you spent with Sarah Comstock, God rest her poor soul, were hours of love. Very wonderful, but hours, David, don't you understand that? In days it cools, in weeks it barely stirs, and in months it's either replaced with friendship and consideration and compassion, or the lovers are ready to destroy each other. And most of them do. And Lucy respects you, honors you, and trusts you, and that's a kind of love a lot better than what they sell us in the movies and on the tube."

"Even if that's true, it's too late."

"Why?"

"She's gone."

"David, David, get on a plane and go out there."

"I can't."

"You must. I love Lucy, but she's crazy. She'll ruin her life and yours and your kids'."

"I can't force her."

"David, get on a plane and go out there. That's all I am going to say. We have meat loaf, poor parish meat loaf. Martin!" she called. "We're eating in five minutes."

David stayed awake half the night, thinking, planning, talking to himself, arguing with himself, sleeping finally out of sheer exhaustion. He didn't get to his office at the synagogue until after ten, and when Mrs. Shapiro came into his office with a list of his calls, he brushed them aside and said, "I'm flying out to California this afternoon, Mrs. Shapiro. My suitcase is packed at home. Reserve a ticket as close to two o'clock as possible. That will give me time to get to Idlewild. Can you drive?"

"Of course I can drive. I drive here every day. I think it's wonderful you should go see your wife and children, but what about Friday night service?"

"Call Mel Klein. He'll lead the service. I'll drive my car to Idlewild. You come with me and drive the car back."

"I'll get lost. I'll never find my way back."

"You'll find your way back. Grown people who get lost in cars are always found. Meanwhile, reserve the tickets. Round trip for me, one way from California to Idlewild for my wife and the children." He tried to say it casually and to feel casual about it, but inside he was sick with doubt and fear. He had split himself in two, and the part in motion and action was shredding every fiber of the part that was David Hartman.

He felt that all the way out to Idlewild, with Mrs. Shapiro reminding him, "You have the Kaplin *Bar Mitzvah*. That's a week from Saturday, which is ten days. Will you be back in ten days, Rabbi Hartman? Do you know, you didn't even give me a forwarding address or a telephone number. You know where your mother-in-law lives, but I don't. Maybe you don't. What should I tell Mikey Kaplin? Or his mother? She gets hysterical."

"Santa Barbara."

"Where is Santa Barbara? I can't just say Santa Barbara. What do I do, call Information and ask for Santa Barbara?"

"Please, Mrs. Shapiro, don't panic," thinking that he was sufficiently panicked for both of them. "My mother-in-law's name is Sally Spendler. You could get that from Information. In fact, when we get to the airport, I'll write it all down for you."

"Oh, my God!"

"What's that, Mrs. Shapiro?"

"You got a wedding. The Silverman wedding. I forgot. God help me, I'm getting like you, Rabbi."

"The wedding is a week from Sunday. I'll be back. If not, call Rabbi Bert Sager in Norwalk, and he'll do it."

"Suppose Rabbi Sager has a wedding from his own congregation?"

"In September?"

When they reached the airport, David was so involved with Mrs. Shapiro's problems that he momentarily forgot his own. After the airplane took off, he began to reconstruct his miseries, and he brooded and worried over them the whole seven hours to Los Angeles.

However, by the time he reached Los Angeles, his doubts

and worries faded into the excitement of knowing that he would see Lucy and the children in a few hours. It was only ten days since they had left Connecticut, but it seemed like an eternity. Mrs. Shapiro had booked him onto a one o'clock flight, which meant that he had no time to do anything but make a mad rush for the airport, and the plane landed at five o'clock Los Angeles time. By six o'clock, David was in a rented car, driving north to Santa Barbara, guiding himself by frequent consultations with his road map. At eight-fifteen, he drove slowly up Acacia Road, looking for Number 432, the house Lucy's mother had rented. When he found it, 432 reminded him of nothing so much as the big beach houses in Far Rockaway, where he and his mother had occasionally visited some obscure relative. It was covered with shingles stained dark brown; it had a porch around two sides; and the door had a stained glass panel.

The last glimmer of twilight had faded. Lights twinkled through the stained glass panel. David rang the bell, and Sally Spendler opened the door, looked at him, cried out in surprise, and then folded him against her ample bosom, whispering, "Thank God you've come. She's lonely and miserable, which she deserves. Why, why, why did you let her do it?"

Against this, Lucy's voice, "Mother, who is it?"

Sarah saw him and screeched, "It's Daddy!"

Sally let go of him, and the two children came running. He dropped onto his knees and embraced both of them. Never an embrace like this before. He looked up, and Lucy was standing in the hallway, staring at him. Then he let go of the children and stood up and walked to her and kissed her. "David, are you hungry?" her mother said quickly. Lucy continued to stare at him without saying a word.

"Absolutely. I am starved."

"Then come into the kitchen and let me feed you."

"I'll put the kids to bed," Lucy said abruptly. Both children protested so loudly that Lucy gave in and allowed them fifteen minutes in the kitchen while their grandmother warmed food for David and then set a heaped plate in front of him. The children chattered away about their plane flight to the Coast, their school — which they disliked — and their rooms upstairs, which, according to them, were always too hot. When Lucy finally led them off to bed, her mother said to David, "I'm going up to my room too. You talk to her. What on earth happened between you two?"

"I don't know."

"Well, it's time you did know. She hasn't smiled since she got here, so I hardly think she's the happiest woman on earth. And for heaven's sake, don't let her put you on the couch. You're married to her, and her bed is wide enough for two."

A few minutes after Sally left the kitchen, Lucy entered and informed David that she had made up a bed on the couch.

"It's ten o'clock," David said, his voice rising, "and I don't usually go to bed at ten o'clock, and I'll be goddamned if I'm going to sleep on any damned couch, and just who the hell do you think you are, coming in here like this and telling me you made a bed on the couch!"

"Then I think you'd better go and find some other place to spend the night."

"No way. I'm here. Right here, today, tomorrow — as long as you're here and as long as the kids are here."

"You mean that?"

"I mean it," he said.

"What about the synagogue?"

"They'll find another rabbi."

She sat down at the kitchen table and put her face on her arms.

"What are you doing?"

"Crying," she mumbled.

"Why? Because I came here?"

"Because everything's all fucked up."

"It always has been. As you told me so often, that's the nature of life on earth."

She raised a tear-stained face and said, "Funny thing is, I'm glad you came. I hate it here."

"How about me?"

"I missed you."

"Will you come back?"

She hesitated; then she nodded. "All right. I'll have to make arrangements."

"I have the tickets — for you and the kids."

"What?"

"I figured I'd just stay here until you came."

"That's sneaky."

"No, it isn't."

"I never thought you were sneaky — like this whole scenario tonight. I always thought you were such a damned saint. Oh, the hell with it. We talk too much. Let's go to bed."

"On the couch?"

"No, it's too narrow. My bed."

"Your bed. Sure."

PART SIX

1960

David had never been to the Deep South before, and in some ways it was the most alien place he had ever seen. The heat was different from any heat he had known, the air heavy and turgid, the jack pines wavering and deformed as the heat and the air distorted the image.

A little while ago the few hundred people behind him had been singing, "We shall not, we shall not be moved. We shall not, we shall not be moved. Just like a tree that's standing by the water, we shall not be moved." But now the singing had stopped, and they walked quietly. The heat seemed to be increasing. Under his suit jacket, his shirt was soaking wet, and a veritable host of insects, apparently attracted by the odor of perspiration, helped to make life even more miserable.

The march was led by three men. In the center was the Reverend Marchand Jones, a tall Baptist preacher, deep black in color and possessed of a booming magnetic voice. On his right hand was Martin Carter, his clerical collar wilting, his face pink, his hair still thick but almost entirely white, a transition that had taken place over the past half decade and that made him look somewhat older than his fifty-five years. On the Reverend Jones's left hand was David Hartman, tall, thin, balding, and a bit stooped already in his forty-fourth year. The Reverend Jones would have nothing else but that David should lead the march with him. He had known very few rabbis, and to have one here with him today gave him a sense of biblical validity. Martin was also a first for the Reverend Jones — the first Congregationalist he had known, and this joined early America to the biblical stance, and when the Reverend Marchand Jones saw eight state troopers, standing shoulder to shoulder, legs spread, blocking the road from side to side, long riot clubs cradled in their hands, and behind them a dozen more troopers and cars with flashing lights, he said to David and Martin, "Just let me handle this, please. I know these folks."

David nodded, wondering whether he was not getting too old for this kind of confrontation with danger.

"Morning, Reverend," one of the troopers said.

"Cap'n Queen," Jones whispered to David, spreading his arms for the march to stop, about twenty feet from where the troopers stood. "Morning, Cap'n."

"Always know you as a law-abiding citizen, Reverend."

"That's what I am, Cap'n, law-abiding."

"Well, no, sir. I got to say you are not, Reverend. You are leading a parade without no permit for a parade. You are blocking a public thoroughfare. You are creating a disturbance and you are fostering a public nuisance."

"Good heavens, Cap'n, how can we be doing all that when what you see here is just a few people going into town to register to vote?"

"Reverend, you got maybe three, four hundred people there in the road behind you. Now what I want you to do is to turn around, just nice and quiet and peaceful, and go home."

"We can't do that, much as we'd like to."

"Why not?"

"Because we told these good folks behind us that we would lead them into town to register to vote."

"Now, Reverend, you know we ain't going to register no niggers and we ain't going to vote no niggers, so don't try to con me. Who are them two white men you got with you?"

"Well, this one here's the Reverend Martin Carter, who is a Congregationalist pastor up there in Connecticut, and this here on the other side of me is Rabbi David Hartman, and he is also from Connecticut."

"Well, you two are a long way from home. I sure as hell don't know what a congrega—— whatever the hell it is, and we don't like Jews down here, not one bit. So I'm going to give the three of you one minute to disperse and start clearing away that mob behind you, and after that, we are going to do the clearing away ourselves. One minute, gentlemen."

"Well, what do you think?" the Reverend Jones asked his two clerical companions.

"We must stand our ground," Martin said.

"A matter of principle," David said, thinking at the same time of how much grief those four words had caused Martin and himself, "but keep your hands over your head, Martin."

"So long, so slow," the Reverend Jones said.

The minute up, the troopers advanced toward them, holding their riot clubs in front of them; and then, with a sudden rush, the troopers were on them. David tried to protect his head with his hands, and that was the last thing he remembered until he opened one eye and found the road an inch away, warm against his cheek, with a small puddle of blood almost bubbling with the heat of the road. Someone was pulling at his shoulder, and a voice said, "Come on, Rabbi. You just got yourself a tap on the head." They helped him to his feet. He felt a trickle of blood running down his cheek, and he took out his handkerchief to stop it. Aside from about a dozen of the black people who had been in the march, and who were now sitting on the road and nursing head wounds, and one other who was lying there unconscious, there were only the Reverend Jones and Martin. Martin had a huge lump on his head that was turning blue. The Reverend Jones had been badly beaten, and he was sitting on the road, his head in his hands, while two of his parishioners, ladies both, dressed in white choir costumes, tried to comfort him.

"He needs a doctor," David told one of the troopers. "Can't you see that he needs a doctor?"

"He'll get one in jail."

"He should be taken to a hospital, not to jail."

"Rabbi, you just be a quiet Jew or we'll put you in a condition for a hospital."

Tugging his sleeve, Martin whispered, "Let it be, David. They're angry now. Let it cool down. Are you all right?"

"I don't know."

"You have some scalp cuts and some swelling. Does it hurt much?"

"It hurts. How about you?"

"Terrible headache. I'm a bit dizzy."

They were driven into town in one of the squad cars. "Separate but equal," the driver told them. "We don't put niggers and white folks together, even when they break the law together."

"Where are you taking us?"

"Jail, Rabbi. Jail."

"We need a doctor, both of us."

"Old Jake, down at the jailhouse, he's fixed up worse injured parties than you two gentlemen. Just don't worry about it."

He was right about that part of it. At the jailhouse, they were put in a cell which they had to themselves, even though it had four beds in it, and Jake came in with a first aid kit. He washed out the scalp and facial cuts with peroxide and taped dressings on them, and he gave Martin a cold wet towel to hold against a large bump on his head. Jake was a man in his middle fifties with an enormous beer belly, a totally bald head, and blue eyes that blinked nervously and rapidly. "I hear you are a rabbi," he whispered to David, selecting him for the absence of a clerical collar.

"That's right."

"Now I don't like a nigger-lover no better than the next man, but I am going to help you. You know why? Because my

Grandma Sadie, she was Jewish, and blood is thicker than water. I'm going to telephone Professor Byron Jackson down at the State University. He's the head of the law school, and when he hears what happened, he'll be here in two shakes of a lamb's tail."

"How soon is two shakes of a lamb's tail?" Martin asked him.

"Maybe this evening. Maybe tomorrow morning."

"I was going to ask for the customary telephone call, to which, as I understand these things, we're entitled. Although maybe you'd better make the call," he said to David, "because when Millie hears what we've gotten into, she'll be so mad she may just decide to let me stay here and rot."

"You know she wouldn't."

"Now you two listen," Jake said. "You was brought here by the troopers, but this is Sheriff Benton's place, and he ain't going to let you get no Yankee lawyer down here until your faces look more human, and that will be maybe a week. So you better let me call Professor Jackson."

"Where's the Reverend Jones?"

"Got him over in a nigger cell. But I fixed him up same as you. He's all right, but we don't mix the races here."

"I think you'd better call Professor Jackson."

He didn't come that night. David and Martin were served a watery oxtail stew with a thick chunk of bread, but neither of them had much appetite; as soon as they finished eating, the lights went off.

"Try to sleep," Martin said.

"I'm afraid to lie down."

"Pain?"

"Bedbugs."

"How do you know?"

"After Pop died, we lived for a year in an apartment where we couldn't get rid of them. I've had a horror of the little bastards ever since."

"If they're in your bed, they're in mine."

"No doubt."

"What do I do about it?"

"Nothing," David said. "Just thank your nice New England parents for raising you in a non-bedbug home."

About an hour went by, and then Martin asked softly, "David, you asleep?"

"Not so you could notice."

A few minutes of silence after that, and then Martin said, "David, did you ever lose your faith?"

"Most interesting question," David replied, after a long moment. "The answer is yes."

"Oh? Did it return to you?"

"I don't know. Maybe some of it, different."

"Well, how do you manage?"

"I might ask how you manage, Martin?"

"Yes."

"When did it happen?" David asked him.

"Probably differently from what happened to you. I could never really swallow the virgin birth. Somehow, I managed the divinity of Jesus, but then that collapsed. Yet I love the story, the Christmas story, the birth of the Christ Child, and all the rest of it. But then I was on a TV show with a Paulist priest who had a lot more brains that I had, and I extolled the glory of Christ's death, dying for the salvation of man, and this priest, who had been a chaplain during the war, like yourself, was just enraged by what I said. He said that only Christ's life had meaning, that his death was a filthy, bloody horror, and that no death is glorious, and that we are fed that rotten lie so that we will support war. That was when it snapped."

"Do you believe in God?"

"You?"

"God the creator — that came back to me, little by little. But God the white-bearded old man, no. Oh, no. God the mother is much more reasonable, and I don't believe in that either. God who cares about us — I don't know. We're a tiny dot on the edge of a star cluster in a universe that has millions of star clusters just like it. Maybe a spirit, a force that knits us together. I'm not very good when I try to think about it or talk about it."

"Better than I am," Martin said. "I tell myself that I serve something, some purpose, some need. At first I was terribly troubled. But then that passed away. I feel a sense of peace now."

"It's a strange world," David reflected, "but most peculiarly strange if you're a clergyman. I'd love to go on talking, Martin, but my jaw hurts every time I move it, and I'm so tired I'm going to lie down on this bed, bedbugs or not. Anyway, there is nothing to be solved. The best thing we can do is to dwell a bit on our unimportance."

Jake had opened the door to bring them their morning coffee and bread, the early summer sun warming the cell, when there came through the door a booming voice: "Don't be the greatest horse's patootie in the county, Benton! You are already in more kinds of trouble than I care to list, not to mention putting the county in a position where it can be sued for five or six million dollars."

"Hell, Professor, it ain't my doing. Them damned state troopers brought them in, and I got twelve niggers too and that big nigger preacher, Reverend Jones, and he is the last person on earth I want in my jail. I am getting him out of here just as soon as I can."

"Were they mishandled? The colored folks?"

"They had their asses beaten off, if that's what you mean."

"Makes it worse, don't you see? Makes it so much worse, I just wouldn't want to be in your shoes."

"Professor, we didn't lay a finger on them. It's Captain Queen and them crazy troopers — Jake, will you close that damned door!"

A few minutes later, the door opened, and Jake escorted Professor Jackson through it, the corners of Jake's mouth twitching with what was less a smile than a controlled smirk of satisfaction. "This here's Professor Jackson," he said to them. And to the professor, "This is Reverend Carter from up there in Connecticut, and this here is Rabbi Hartman from the same place, and he is a real, legitimate Jewish rabbi."

"Thank you, Jake," the professor said, "and now suppose you step outside and see we're not interrupted, and you can't be a witness to what you don't hear."

"That's right, Professor. That's absolutely right."

No more than five feet six inches tall, the professor had a physical appearance that contrasted oddly with his booming voice. He had sparse red hair, turning white, a freckled complexion, and pale blue eyes behind heavy glasses. When Jake left, he looked at the two men sadly and said, "Never known a do-gooder with the sense of a flea. You come down here to show your presence, fine thing. Maybe it'll help to get the colored folk to come forward and exercise their constitutional rights, maybe not. But when a passel of baboons in the uniforms of state troopers tell you to stop and break it up, you do it. They are armed. You're not. Heavens to Betsy, we are not animals down here. We have decent folk and indecent folk. That man, Jake Hunter, he put his job on the line, telephoning me. Now come over here and let me look at those bruises." They stood by the bars and he stared at the cuts and bruises. "Nasty, nasty. Very nasty."

"When can we get out of here, Professor?" Martin asked.

"Maybe an hour, maybe less."

"Will you want bail?"

"For what? For getting beat up?" He turned and left, and they heard him saying to the sheriff, "I'm going down the street and get an order from Judge Parsefal for their release."

"I can't let them go. Captain Queen — he'll skin me alive."

"Now look here, Sheriff, you ignore a court order, and you'll finish your term in that same cell."

"All right, all right. I can hear you. Why is my ass always in a sling?"

"Professor!" David shouted. "Professor, please come back

a moment!" The professor came back. David was taking deep breaths. "Hurts my head when I shout. Professor, you've been very kind to us, but we can't leave here without the Negroes."

"What?"

"We just can't. We were walking arm in arm with Reverend Jones. We can't go out and leave him here."

"Marchand Jones?"

"That's right."

"Goddamnit, Rabbi, I'm letting you and the reverend here walk off free. Why make it more difficult for me? The colored folk will get three months in the cooler, maybe only thirty days. I suppose I can get Jones off, not the others."

"Then I'm afraid we sit here."

Martin came to life, his voice shrill. "Means TV coverage, Professor. Every reporter in the foreign press corps will be down here. I'm just a Congregational minister, but Rabbi Hartman is one of the most important rabbis in America, and they'll make the worst anti-Semitic case out of it you ever saw — "

"That's enough, Reverend. You made your point. God Almighty, why don't you people stay home? You have more inequity up there than we could ever match, but you don't see us putting together delegations of crazy clerics to drive you mad. All right. I'll see what I can do. But you set foot in this state again, I swear I'll let you fry in your own juice."

When he had gone, David turned to Martin and said, "I don't believe it. One of the most important rabbis in America. All he has to do is to call the Central Conference of American Rabbis and ask them if they ever heard of a David Hartman. If they're not too busy, they might find me in their directory, but suppose he calls the Conservative movement or the Orthodox. They'll say they never heard of me, and these people don't know Jews are divided into different groups. He'll wash his hands of the whole thing, and we'll end up on a chain gang somewhere."

"Well, it's no worse than your sudden spurt of nobility. I had to back it up somehow."

"You call that backing it up?"

"Yes. Sort of. I thought you were right and very principled. I had to back you up."

"Martin, you are crazy. Plain crazy."

"Yes — yes. But it's a shared lunacy, David. Remember that."

The dean of the local law school was as good as his word, even to the extent of having the town doctor clean out their cuts and tape them properly; but Lucy did not absolve them that easily. "You and Martin," she said coldly, "are not only two unintelligent men, but two middle-aged men who should have realized that their Don Quixote days are over!"

"I trust you meant intelligent. We are fairly intelligent."

"Not by Millie's vote or mine."

"You knew we were going down there. We weren't the only clergymen. There were over fifty of us enlisted for the registration drive."

"According to the *New York Times*, this Captain — whatever his name was — ordered you to stop. All he had were guns and clubs in the hands of young men. But you and Martin didn't see fit to stop."

"Well, not just the two of us. Aside from all the people behind us, there was Reverend Marchand Jones. You know it was his back yard, so to speak. It wasn't just that we were ordered to stop. The *Times* man got the story from the troopers and from some of the marchers and Reverend Jones. The way he was beaten, he couldn't remember much of anything, but the way it happened was that we were ordered to disperse, to break it up and get off the road. Well, we couldn't do that."

"Why not?"

"I don't know how I can explain it. This Jones fellow, he went up and spoke to the troopers. Then he came back, and very quietly he said, 'So long, so slow.' It was like a total lament for his people, a road so very long, progress so slow. We could say the same about the Jews — two thousand years of it that leads David Hartman up here to Leighton Ridge, so long and so slow. Do you understand?"

Minutes passed while Lucy stared at him in silence. Then she nodded, tears welling into her eyes. "You make me afraid to love you."

He took her in his arms. "Don't ever be afraid. Don't ever be afraid, my darling."

It was not the end of the incident by any means. A new thing had come into the world in the decade and a half since the end of World War Two, and already it was titled *the media* — radio, television, film, and press. The television networks had discovered that occasionally but increasingly their cameras could be where the news was being made, and that if their cameras were not there, it would sometimes happen that other cameras would be there, ready to sell them the footage. It had happened in this incident; the footage was taken and sold to one of the networks, whereupon millions and millions of Americans witnessed the clubbing of three men of the cloth by state troopers. Since things happen in a very ordinary manner from day to day, almost no one observed that it was amazingly odd for three clergymen, one a Baptist, one a Congregationalist, and one a Jew, to be leading a march in the Deep South for the registration and freedom of black voters, and for all to go down together under the troopers' clubs. Something had changed in the world. Clergymen were doing something they had not done before. It evoked a new kind of interest, and both David and Martin found themselves in the position of being momentary celebrities. They were interviewed, they were begged to participate in talk shows — most of which they refused — and Leighton Ridge suddenly, after two hundred years of blissful obscurity, was catapulted into the public eye. Americans were treated to a capsule history of Connecticut, the fifth state to ratify the Constitution of the United States, the settling place of the famous — only now

— *Levelers*, whom Cromwell had decimated and driven out of England.

In all reality, as some Connecticut booster put it, this was the real birthplace of the American Revolution. Along with this, TV viewers were lectured — in short form — on the intriguing topographical structure of Connecticut, ridge after ridge, valley after valley, the low foothills of the Berkshires riding down to Long Island Sound.

There were all sorts of odds and ends of results, one of them being a telephone call from Mel Klein, who said, "David, can you and Lucy come to dinner next Monday? There's a friend of mine, a very interesting man from Germany, and he's spending a few days with us here. As a matter of fact, he's a film producer, the biggest in Germany. His name is Herman Strauss, and he wants very much to meet you. He's Jewish, yes."

They were delighted to come to dinner. Lucy wondered what connection Mel Klein had with a German film producer, and David guessed that he might be related to Della, whose mother's name was Strauss. It turned out that there was a relationship of sorts, but thin and distant. But Della's mother was still alive, and Strauss had come to her and through her, he had met Mel Klein and had been invited for a few days to Leighton Ridge. Herman Strauss was an unimpressive, balding man of middle height, with mild brown eyes behind heavy glasses, wide mouth, small nose, and the marvelously ingratiating manner of a cultured, middle-class Viennese. He wore a three-piece dark gray worsted suit, and as he shook hands firmly, David noticed a very odd thing. In the vest pocket of Strauss's suit were visible the tops of two silver teaspoons.

"I am so pleased to meet you, Rabbi Hartman," he said. He had a heavy German accent, but his English sentence structure was excellent and his vocabulary sufficiently ample so that he did not have to grope for words. "I read about your struggle, believe me, but I also read three of your sermons. I thought they were brilliant and very perceptive."

"Three of my sermons? I'm flattered, but you must be mistaken."

"Oh, no. Printed in the Frankfurt magazine, *Der* — how would I translate it? Yes. *World Views.*"

Della Klein, listening, said, "I can explain it. The synagogue mimeographs the rabbi's sermons for those who want them, and I send copies to Mother. She has a dear friend in Germany who is one-quarter Jewish, and somehow managed to survive in Frankfurt, and Mother has been sending her copies of the sermons."

"So it is explained," Strauss said. "With an explanation everything is understandable. But I am sure they have not paid you a dollar for your writing, and to me that is the worst kind of thievery and not worthy of the magazine. In any case, I have an interest in a small publishing house, aside from my film work, and already I suggested to Hans Kramer, our managing editor, that he should make a book of your sermons — if you have enough, of course?"

"You must never ask a rabbi whether he has enough sermons," David said, smiling. "If we could trade them for bread and butter — "

"That is what we will arrange. You see, in Germany, unlike here, guilt is very deep, very deep, so books of sermons do well." His shirt sleeve had slipped back, the cuff revealing a digit of a number tattooed on his arm. "Guilt," he said, touching it. "Two years in a concentration camp. Well, that's in the past, isn't it, Rabbi?"

"I hope so."

At the dinner table, Mel Klein said gently, "Mr. Strauss, they say you are the largest film producer in Germany. Is it so?"

"And you're wondering how it can be, only fifteen years after the Holocaust. Maybe the largest, maybe second largest. I'm not sure. But you see, I am Viennese, even though I lived many years in Germany, and before the war I produced seven very successful films. To some extent, I saw what was coming, and I managed to hide the prints. So when the war ended and

I came out of the concentration camp, I had the prints of my films, and Germany was starved for film. So it began."

"And yet you stayed in Germany," Lucy said. "After all the horror of the Holocaust."

"Yes," he said softly. "Wherever I am, the Holocaust sits beside me. From that, I can't run away. Also, in this life, I know only one thing, how to produce a moving picture. A shoemaker can make shoes anywhere, but myself — all my memories were Austria and Germany. I love the German language, German literature, German film tradition. So I remain in Germany."

And still no one asked him about the two silver teaspoons. After dinner, David could contain his curiosity no longer, and he drew Strauss off into a corner of the living room, where the two of them, sitting in a pair of wing chairs, could talk with a degree of privacy.

Strauss, nodding with a slight smile, anticipated David's question and said, "No, I did not steal them from a restaurant. They belong to me. They are sterling. Why do I carry them around? You can't imagine, can you?"

"No. And I feel like a presumptuous fool."

"No, never think of yourself as a fool, Rabbi. You're not a fool. I will tell you about the spoons. They are a reminder. In nineteen forty-two, I was in Berlin. I had no papers. As a Viennese Jew, I had no country. I had no money. I had no friend. All I had in the world were two sterling silver teaspoons that I had found in a buffet drawer in the ransacked home of a Jewish family I had sought out. Unexplainably, the Nazis who looted the place and took my friends away overlooked the two teaspoons. So you see, Rabbi Hartman, when you have no papers, money, or friends, a sterling silver teaspoon will buy you shelter and food. So I always keep two teaspoons in my vest pocket. People who know me understand. Others, like you, sometimes ask. And myself — they serve to remind me that I am a Jew; no matter how rich, how secure, I am a Jew, and the only thing in the world I can depend on is God's mercy."

Or two silver teaspoons, David thought, staring curiously at the unimpressive man who sat opposite him. "And you still believe in God," David said.

"I did not — not very much when I was young, Rabbi. In Vienna — and I speak about this to you, Rabbi, because you are Rabbi Hartman — when I was twenty-four years old, I married a young actress. Her name was Gretchen Schwartz. She was not Jewish. She was a fine, honest, gifted young woman, with the face of an angel. What she saw in me I will never understand, but then she was only a child, only seventeen and foolish, so she married me." He paused and took several deep breaths. "Forgive me, I will try not to become too emotional. For five years, she did not conceive. I wanted her talent to mature before she was burdened with childbearing. Then she became pregnant, and our only child, a girl, was born. We should have left, but there were those of us who simply did not believe. If we hung in, as you say, another day, another month, this madman and the animals he led would destroy themselves. Well, one day, they picked me up. I never saw Gretchen again. Then, in the concentration camp, I became close friends with a Catholic priest. He's dead. The ovens took him. He would listen to me dream and plan about finding Gretchen some day. Finally, he said to me, 'Stop dreaming, Strauss. Gretchen is dead.' You see, he had heard the confession of one of the Nazis in the party that came for Gretchen, strangled my infant daughter, and then raped Gretchen and killed her. He knew that he was violating the law of confession, but he felt that he had to tell me so that I would stop dreaming of seeing my wife again and make my peace with God." He shook his head and wiped his eyes. "Why did I tell you this long, unpleasant story? Yes. You asked me whether I still believed in God."

"Yes, I asked you that."

"Have I answered you, Rabbi?"

"I don't know."

"I'm not enough of a scholar or philosopher to make anything out of what I think. There is an old Jewish legend about the righteous man who dies and comes before the throne of God, and out of God's eyes there pours a river of tears. The righteous man asks God why he weeps, and God says, 'I weep for what my children do.' Just a story. Yes, Rabbi. I believe. How could I live without believing? After the Holocaust? No, I believe because if I stop, there is nothing but darkness. You know the custom, Rabbi, of planting a tree in Israel in memory of the dead. Since this custom began, I have ordered the planting of two hundred and seventy-one trees. That's the number of people personally known to me who died in the concentration camps, the gas chambers, starved, beaten, shot, two hundred and seventy-one human beings, my infant daughter among them, my wife among them, thirty-two who I know were Christians, about a dozen I can't decide about, and the rest Jews. It is not in spite of what has happened that I believe in God, but because of it — and that is something I hardly understand myself, so to explain please don't ask me."

It was just twelve days after this dinner which he gave for Herman Strauss that Mel Klein died. He passed away in the middle of the night, a victim of a massive coronary thrombosis. Dr. Henry Levine, living in Leighton Ridge, was the first to reach him; and almost immediately after that, the emergency rescue truck of the volunteer firemen arrived, but it was too late for oxygen or anything else. Dr. Levine called David at five in the morning, an hour after it happened, and he and Lucy drove to the Kleins' home immediately. The Kleins had three children, all of them grown and out of college, one living in New York, a boy, and two girls out on the Coast, one a medical student, the other an actress. Della was talking to her son on the telephone when David arrived. She was a gray-eyed, round-limbed woman of forty-five, younger than her husband by twenty years, and quite beautiful in a very simple manner. She had light brown hair, streaked with gray and sun-bleached strands of corn color, cut in a simple pageboy style, and almost no make-up; and she displayed the easy manner of a woman totally secure in her relationship with her husband.

Now that husband was dead. David had expected her to be utterly devastated by what had happened. He was surprised by her control and calm. "I'm so glad you're here, David," she said, embracing him. "I'll have tears and hysteria later, alone. Right now, I must be controlled for a while. But you know, David, God gave us such love and companionship! How many people have that? I watch people grow old and fear death and become feeble. Mel missed that. I had twenty-seven years with one of the best human beings I ever knew. I had that."

Mel Klein's grave was the eleventh grave in the little cemetery. Standing beside the open grave with Della and her children, David spoke the prayers and then whispered his own farewell to a thoughtful and kindly gentleman. Eleven times he had done this. This was the rabbi's function so little discussed in the seminary, and almost everybody here, almost every corpse in every grave, had been someone he had known and touched. Strangely, it had not hardened him; and he supposed that was one of the great faults of his existence, that nothing hardened him.

Jack Osner had come up from Washington to attend the funeral. It was bruited about that Osner was one of the men most trusted by the President. He sat in on Cabinet meetings; he was the direct link with the Pentagon; and if the fall election brought a Republican victory at the polls, Osner was certainly slated to be Secretary of Defense.

The members of the congregation were impressed with the fact that he had come to the funeral. "But after all," he said, "Mel and I put this synagogue together."

He also ordered and paid for a bronze plaque to be affixed to the wall of the synagogue hallway, bearing the names of the synagogue's founding group, with Mel Klein's name at the head of the list. "Of course," he said to David, "it would make a better impression on the Gentiles if we had a plaque of members who had died in the war. But we can't do that, since we didn't organize until after the war. I got a sketch of the plaque. I want to show it to Della."

"I wouldn't," David said. "Not right now, Jack."

"Figure it might shake her?"

"It might."

After the funeral, Mel and Della's friends gathered at the Klein home. David felt that one of the few decent aspects of the modern way of death was the gathering to eat after the funeral. People brought food, and women in the kitchen arranged it, cooked it, served it. Food was the most ancient affirmation of life. Now the house, large as it was, filled up with friends of the Kleins and their children, and in the crowd Osner found David and said to him, "Can we find a quiet place to talk?"

"Can't it wait, Jack?"

"I'm afraid not," Osner said. "I have to get the five o'clock out of La Guardia, and that's three hours from now. This is important, David."

"All right. Della has a little sewing room upstairs. It's probably empty."

Perched on a small stool, his long, skinny legs drawn up in front of him, David nodded and said, "Okay, Jack. Let's hear it." Osner sat on the only chair in the room, uncomfortable, uncomfortable with the smallness of the room, the litter of sewing baskets, sewing machine, goods, scraps. Osner had gained weight, neck, jowls, and stomach.

"You know, David," Osner said, "I'm very close to the people at the Pentagon."

"So I understand."

"Well, it just happens that there's an opening for Jewish chaplain número uno. That is top dog — for the entire United States Army. Full colonel, very respectable pay, makes what they pay you here look like the gross of a peanut vendor, and perks. My God, David, when you add up the perks, it amounts to what you couldn't buy for a hundred thousand dollars a year. You get a limo — not just a car, but limo and driver, on call twenty-four hours a day, you want him three o'clock in the morning, you got him three o'clock in the morning. And that's only the beginning. Special rental rate, giving it away, on a house in Georgetown that the army owns. Free travel to any corner of the world where our troops are stationed, and that's a lot of corners, and if you slip Lucy and the kids in, no one asks questions. David, there is nothing like this. You want silk prayer shawls — order up a thousand. They're in your office the next day. Anything. No one who hasn't associated himself with the Pentagon can possibly imagine how a job like this pays off, not to mention the pleasure of wearing the old uniform again. Now, when I suggested your name, first thing they did was to order up your war record. Well, I heard things, but I never dreamed that you sported that kind of war record. Aces — absolute aces. It's true that when they checked with the F.B.I. they found a different kind of a file, but I talked them out of that one. I told them that you were as loyal as any man in the U.S.A., and I carry enough clout to make them believe it. But I will say this — no more marches, no more demonstrations, no more letters to the *New York Times*. I wish to God this fracas in the South had never happened. You know, most of the big brass are old Southern boys, and it gets their ass up when they're made out to be Nazis. Well, what's done is done, and everyone's shooting his mouth off today about how the nigger's got to vote, and why not be in a position where he votes for our candidate instead of their candidate? So what do you say?"

"You mean do I want the job, Jack? No, I don't think so."

"You're kidding?"

"No."

"David, David," shaking his head, "a rabbi's a rabbi. I understand that. But if you're a rabbi, you go to whatever's the top for a rabbi, and this is it. That's the name of the game, David."

"Oh, I appreciate your thinking of me and extending yourself for me, Jack, but there's no way I could take that job."

"Give me one reason," Osner said.

"Well, for one thing, I'm a pacifist. I believe that war as a means of settling a dispute or achieving a social end is sheer insanity."

"We all believe that, David. But do the Russians? Do we defend ourselves, or do we say to them, Come over and take it all?"

"I don't like the Pentagon."

"Come on. What's to like or dislike? We got clients I went out of my way not to talk to. Their money talks to me."

"No, I couldn't do it, Jack."

"David, I went out on a lot of limbs for you. I told them I had a package ready for delivery, and now you're pulling the rug out from under me. That doesn't sit well with me."

"Jack, I appreciate what you've done and I appreciate your thinking about me, but I can't take a job simply because you feel it's the right job for me."

"Right job? This is not a job; it's a position, a post, a way of serving your country, a pension at retirement twice what you're making now! Who the hell do you think you are!" His anger mounted. David had never seen him like this. "You're a small-town rabbi making eight thousand dollars a year! A ditch-digger takes home more money than you do! And you sit there and look down your nose at me and tell me you're some kind of fucken pacifist! Well, you have blown it, buster!" And with that, he walked out of the sewing room, slamming the door behind him.

David sat motionless on the little stool for a while after Jack Osner had left. There was a sewing table in the room, the sewing machine open for use, the foot of the machine clenching a seam on a tiny dress of printed cotton, a dress Della had been making for her year-old granddaughter. There was a sense of peace, of creativity and timelessness in the little room. David felt Osner's anger even after his departure. It violated the place.

Finally, David shook his head unhappily, and then left the room and went downstairs.

"What happened between you and Osner?" Lucy whispered, pushing through the crowd of people to his side.

"We'll talk about it later."

Della was holding a baby in her arms — apparently her granddaughter, the child the dress was intended for — and she said, "Isn't she beautiful, David?"

"Very beautiful."

"Don't go, please. Please stay."

"Of course. As long as you wish."

By nine o'clock that evening, everyone had left except David and Lucy, Eddie Frome and Sophie, and Della's three children. The older daughter was upstairs, putting the baby to bed. The son sat with his mother, and his sister sat alone in a corner, silent and staring at the floor. Unexpectedly, Della said to David, "You don't play pinochle, do you, David?"

He was taken aback by the question, and he stared at Della a long moment before he shook his head. "No, I don't."

"I haven't lost my mind, David. Eddie and I were talking about Mel's passion for pinochle. Mostly they played two-handed pinochle, which Mel told me was just a ghost of the game. They needed a third desperately, and Eddie would say, 'Let's ask the rabbi,' and Mel would say, 'You just don't ask a rabbi whether he wants to make a third in pinochle.'"

"No?"

"Mel was right," Frome said. "You don't."

"I'm a rotten card player," David said, "but why didn't they teach you, Della?"

"Pinochle? Good heavens, women don't play pinochle."

"Why?"

"It's an antique game out of a male-dominated society."

"How can you!" the girl in the corner, Della's younger daughter, cried out. "My father in his grave only a few hours, and you sit there talking like that."

"As if he were here," Della said gently. "We must, you know. Otherwise, we forget too quickly." She rose and went over to her daughter. "And, Joan, we must not forget." The girl stood up and her mother embraced her, both of them weeping now.

In their bedroom, a half-hour past midnight, Lucy said, "All right, tell me about Jack Osner."

"I was thinking about Della," David said. "That's a very remarkable woman."

"Which, I imagine, is why you've always been in love with her. You have, you know."

"Lucy, don't do that."

"What amazes me is that with all your preaching about insight, you have so little of your own. Why don't you admit how you feel about Della?"

"Because I don't feel that way."

"Oh, I'm sorry, I'm sorry, I'm sorry. Why do I do it? Wipe it out, please. Tell me about Osner."

Happy to change the subject, he told her all that Osner had offered.

"Wow," Lucy said softly, "that is a biggie, isn't it? Chief of the whole works, the whole, entire United States Army."

"It's not that big — chief chaplain in charge of Jewish chaplains, and this army is not precisely loaded with Jewish soldiers. We're not back in 'forty-two, when we had half a million Jewish soldiers in the army."

"Why just a colonel?"

"That's all it calls for."

"And, of course, you refused it."

"I had to."

"Why?" Lucy demanded.

"You know why. You know how I feel about war."

"You didn't feel that way in nineteen forty-two. You weren't drafted. You enlisted, and when they made you a senior officer, you didn't protest it." He tried to interrupt, but she pushed on, "Just let me say it, David, once and for all. You may be a pure one hundred percent pacifist and you may hate war, but if it weren't for you and millions of other kids in U.S. uniform, we might both be living under Hitler today, only we wouldn't be living, we'd be dead. Tell me I'm wrong!"

"I don't know whether you're wrong, Lucy, and that's not the point here."

"What is the point? I know what a miserable shithead Jack Osner is, but he didn't have to do this. He held out a hand to you and you spit in it."

"No, he didn't," David said softly. "He has to make points with the Pentagon wherever he can. I hate to say this, but for him to hand the Joint Chiefs of Staff a war hero with all the damned decorations they gave me, no less a Jew and a rabbi — that's bonanza time for him. He's Jewish, and don't think they don't know it, and if Nixon wins the election, Osner will be Secretary of Defense."

"David, I'm a rabbi's wife in a congregation that pays you eight thousand dollars a year and a house to live in. This is nineteen sixty. You have been rabbi in Leighton Ridge for fourteen years. You are almost forty-four years old, and what do we have to show for it? I make my own clothes. I save pennies to have Mrs. Holtzman in to do dinner for a few guests, and we're the only family in the congregation who doesn't have a color television. Our car is falling apart — David, do you realize what Osner offered you? Have you ever been to Georgetown?"

"I've been there, yes."

"It's the best neighborhood in Washington. If the army offers us a house in Georgetown, it doesn't come without servants. We both know the army. Not just a car, but a chauffeur-driven limousine. David, it's like a Cinderella story — and the freedom to travel anywhere without cost, all the places we've talked about and dreamed of seeing and never saw. We can send our kids to college — David, it doesn't mean you have to drop your principles by the wayside. Those kids in the service need you. They needed you during the war, you know that. Please — call Jack. Tell him you've changed your mind. He needs you as much as you need him."

David shook his head. "I can't. Please don't go on with this, Lucy. You know that I can't."

"No, you can't," Lucy said. "If you could, it would put you

in step with the rest of the human race and we can't have that, can we?"

"Lucy — "

"Oh, the hell with it, David. Let me go to sleep. I'm tired."

Summer ended and fall came, but the gap between David and his wife was not closed or healed. After their talk that night, she never again referred to Jack Osner's offer. The election day of 1960 arrived, and Nixon was defeated and John Kennedy became President of the United States. But those in Washington who prided themselves in knowing what was going on, and who was making it go on, did not package Jack Osner together with Dick Nixon. It was noted that Kennedy shook hands with Osner in front of the cameras, and Kennedy said, "Jack, suppose you call me Jack." So it went in the seats of the mighty, but then Osner had not run for office. His law firm was known in Washington as power brokers. Members of such firms are never counted out.

So Camelot came to the Potomac, and the torches that lit its golden glow were not unlike the torches that began to burn in Vietnam. It would be called Johnson's War and Nixon's War, and very few remembered that John Kennedy lit the first flames.

In Leighton Ridge, David's son, Aaron, faced his thirteenth birthday. David had never been very fond of the *Bar Mitzvah*, ushering a boy into so-called manhood, and he had been even less delighted with the Reform movement's decision to extend the process to girls. He felt that the potlatch, the tidal wave of food and drink with which the proud parents inundated friends and relatives, was vulgar and unnecessary, and he would just as soon have erased the whole medieval ceremony. Yet, strangely enough, facing the *Bar Mitzvah* of his only son, he was excited and proud, and he found himself looking forward to the day.

At thirteen, Aaron Hartman was a tall, large-boned youngster, already five feet ten inches in height. He played center on the Leighton High basketball team, even though he was still in the junior high, and he was on the high school swimming team, with a preference for the free-style hundred meter. All of this made him a local hero of sorts among his peers and a kind of idol to his sister, Sarah, who might one day be a lovely woman, but who was now possessed of the same build as her brother — long, large bones, skin so heavily freckled that the untouched skin went unnoticed, five feet seven inches tall, with hair bleached by the sun into a variety of shades. Her fine features, well-shaped head, and bright blue eyes reassured her parents, but Sarah considered herself the ugliest living creature in Leighton Ridge and took refuge in her brother's glory. As for Aaron, his long, ugly, bony face bothered him not at all.

As far as David was concerned, he regarded his son with a mixture of love and bewilderment. Aaron was at ease with the world. It was a fine physical world where you did your thing, where you poured sweat, drank great quantities of bottled junk, ate enormous amounts of food without gaining any fat, and gave no thought to anything beyond Leighton Ridge. Times were when David took him climbing on the gentle slopes of the Berkshires. The boy was interested in what he was doing and not much else, yet he was no fool, his school grades were excellent, and when David and Lucy had taken the children with them on a trip to Israel, paid for by the congregation, Aaron fell into Hebrew as if he had been born to it, often translating for his father, whose seminary Hebrew was hardly up to the occasion. Both of his children reminded David of the *kibbutz* children they saw in Israel — the lack of pensiveness, the fierce physical self-possession, the indifference to the intellectual's need to question things.

Yet facing his son now in the synagogue, completing the *Bar Mitzvah* ceremony with the blessing *Baruch she-petarani*, "Blessed is the Lord who has brought him to manhood," David added softly, "Be wise, my son, because without wisdom, there is no goodness."

After she kissed her son, Lucy kissed David, her eyes brimming with tears. She had made herself a yellow dress for the occasion, and she had done her hair in a new way, piling it on top of her head. Recognition came to David as if she were a stranger. She was a very comely woman indeed.

A few days after, alone with David, she said to him, "I don't know how I can live without you, but I must. You know that, don't you?"

He watched her without replying.

"Please don't try to stop me this time, David. Please don't." And then she added, "I have to live, David."

"Yes, you do," he said.

PART SEVEN
1966

When they picked up the last passenger at Norwalk, Father Joseph Kelly, a very fat Paulist priest, David began to chuckle. Martin Carter's old station wagon groaned and creaked with the added weight, and David apologized to Father Kelly. "Forgive me, Joe, I am not laughing at you. I was thinking of Jerome K. Jerome's book *Three Men in a Boat*, and that broke me up."

"Why?"

"I don't know. I can't even remember it properly. I think it was Bert's umbrella."

"It's going to rain," Rabbi Bert Sager said. "Do you know what you people are? You are something out of a Sholem Aleichem story, or divine or maybe not so divine fools out of Chelm, where they bring out all their sieves to gather rain water for the future. I bring an umbrella because it looks and feels like rain, and this rabbi of what they call Reform Judaism, here sitting next to me, tells me it reminds him of Jerome K. Jerome. Not bad, David, not at all bad, when I come to think of it. Tonight, my wife says to me, Bert, will you please tell me where you are going? She is a plain, intelligent, suffering wife of a rabbi who has a congregation in Connecticut, nothing so fancy as David's here, but a simple Conservative congregation. So what should I tell her? Should I say to her, Sylvia, I am being picked up by two skinny Protestant ministers, a skinny rabbi, a plump Catholic priest — plump, Joe, it fits both of us? Never admit to being fat. Plumpness is a virtue that these desiccated Puritans cannot understand."

"That's kind of you, Bert. I've always thought of myself as being substantial."

"Nice, too. Substantial. So they pick me up, I tell my wife, and we drive to New York to Saint Patrick's Cathedral. Not inside — heaven forbid — but outside, where we have pledged ourselves to a four-hour vigil. That's why we are loaded with candles. We will sit down cross-legged on the street and light our candles. Of course, since I haven't been able to sit cross-legged since I was twelve, well, we'll work that out. Anyway, we sit there four hours. I tell this to my wife. So what would Sylvia say?"

"There'd be a lot of truth in what she would say," David decided.

"I don't know," Philip Simpson said. He was a Methodist minister from Westport. "It's absolutely true that if I were to go down there alone and light a candle and sit myself down in the middle of Fifth Avenue, the police would pick me up and cart me away to Bellevue. And I suppose they'd be right to do so."

"They'd be wrong to do so," David said.

"Perhaps, perhaps. But there'll be a hundred thousand people sitting there on Fifth Avenue with lighted candles, and the police have stopped the traffic and the Mayor has sort of given his blessing, and perhaps it will mean something, or change something."

"Very little, I'm afraid," Father Kelly said. "President Johnson is a hard man; unfortunately, a very stupid man, frozen in his lusts and his madness. Only the wise can be good. I picked that up from one of your sermons, Rabbi Hartman. I confess in all good faith that I steal from your sermons without conscience; but to go back to this man Johnson, there is no wisdom there. It's a small matter to him if a hundred thousand people sit on Fifth Avenue through the night burnng their hands with hot wax. By the way, how many of you thought to bring a candlestick?" He twisted to look around the car. "Ah, the two rabbis. You Protestants have lost touch with the magic of candles."

"Not at all," Martin said. "Drip a bit of wax onto the street, plant your candle there, and let it burn. Why hold it in your hand?"

"Touché!"

"None of that," Kelly said. "This is the most interesting ecumenical foray in history. This is a nineteen fifty-two station wagon we're riding in, isn't it, Martin?"

"Fifty-one."

"So God's purpose becomes immediately explicit, since for this car to carry the five of us to New York is assuredly a miracle. Unlike Rabbi Sager, I have no wife to conceal my innocence or insanity from, but I do have my boss at the church, Father Flannigan, and I could hardly lie to him. The look he gave me was completely astonished. 'Do you mean, Joseph,' he said to me, 'that you are driving to New York with a Congregationalist minister and a Methodist minister and two rabbis, and you will all sit down on Fifth Avenue opposite Saint Patrick's Cathedral and hold lighted candles in your hands?' 'That is exactly what I mean,' I told him, and then he says, 'And why are you doing this strange thing?' And I say to him, 'Why, to stop the war in Vietnam. Why else?'"

"He didn't forbid you?"

"Oh, no. No indeed. Of course, I can't say what he was thinking. He's a kind man."

"He would have to be," Rabbi Sager said.

"Of course you can miss the point," David said. "It's in the nature of our culture to see the cleric as an object of ridicule. He is tolerated as a sort of idiot survival of the past in a time where nobody believes in God very deeply, if at all. Yes," nodding at Kelly, "you Catholic priests are a little better regarded, because you work harder at your mythology, though it's not all wine and roses there either. But suddenly something has changed. For the first time in modern history we're involved in the leadership of a great antiwar movement and that is absolutely a fact. There are thousands of ministers, priests, and rabbis joined together to stop this obscene war in Vietnam. And we do not give God's blessing to our side. We cry out that it is wrong."

"No doubt, no doubt," Kelly agreed, "and if you can't see the hand of God in that — "

"Where was the hand of God in the First World War when the fields of France and Flanders ran with enough blood to float a fleet and it was all blessed by our colleagues on both sides?" Simpson wondered.

"Let's not get into one of those God's will things," Martin said. "What I'm doing is my will. My son, Joseph, is in Toronto, working as a carpenter and glad to get the work. When he evaded the draft and refused to go to Vietnam, Millie and I agreed with him that as a Christian he could not do otherwise. Suddenly, it had become very hard to be a Christian. As for Jews — well, it has always been hard to be a Jew. Rabbi Hartman's son is in prison as a conscientious objector."

The others were quiet then. David wondered whether they were praying.

There were not a hundred thousand people with candles burning, seated in the street opposite St. Patrick's, but there were certainly half that number, and among them David sat and wondered, as he always wondered on such occasions, what possible good could come of his action. Lucy used to ask him that.

"It doesn't matter. You do it," he would say.

Why? Why? Lucy's mind was filled with *whys*, as applied to David's view of the world. As far as Lucy was concerned, it was the way it was and always had been and nothing would ever change it. People got what they deserved, not via faith or prayer or God, but through the more effective agency of sheer, unmitigated stupidity and greed.

"You see," Father Kelly said to Rabbi Sager, "it did not rain. God looks after the small things as well as the large."

"If you think about it," Rabbi Sager said, "you will recall that it never rains on Yom Kippur but very often on Saint Patrick's Day."

"I don't believe this," Martin said. "I just don't believe what I hear out of the mouths of two grown men."

Of course, David was thinking, it was Lucy's intelligence, her sharp, incisive intelligence, that brought matters to a close. If she had been a foolish woman or a thoughtlessly pious woman, their marriage might have dragged on for a lifetime; but it was precisely because she could see no sense in what he did, no meaning or point or destination, that the marriage came to an end. That was basic; the amenities missing from her life were merely a necessary argument to herself.

Over five long years since she left him a second time and divorced him. It seemed incredible that so much time could have passed; empty time. And what did he face now? More and more emptiness.

"There's the rub," Rabbi Sager said. "Nobody wants to believe in a divine handle in the weather. Not anymore. Even myself."

It was a very simple and, as they say, civilized procedure. Lucy had taken the children with her to California, and leaving them there with her mother, she had spent enough time in Reno to have an uncontested divorce.

This time, David's world collapsed. He had heard it said that people who become sodden drunk may have little or no memory of what they do during the time, but his own memory of what happened was as clear as glass and as cold as ice. He was not a teetotaler. He would have a drink when the occasion warranted a drink, or two drinks or three, and during the war he had now and again become beer-drunk in the sad and lonesome way that kids do in a war. But this time, when a letter from Lucy informed him that the divorce was complete, that their small bank account was his, that he could visit his children when he pleased and work out any longer periods of visitation that he desired, that she would never fight him on any issue and that she would never turn the kids against him and that she still loved him and probably always would, he found his own existence to be more than he could bear. He took out a full quart bottle of Scotch whiskey, an unopened gift this Christmas past from Martin Carter, and he sat down with the whiskey and with a glass and proceeded to attempt to drink himself into insensibility.

Instead, with two thirds of the bottle in his stomach at two o'clock in the morning, he became very, very drunk. In that condition, he staggered out into the snow, the bottle in his hand, and made his way over the mile and a half of road that separated his house from the Carter house, pausing every now and then for another swallow of the whiskey. Considering what was in his stomach, his feat was a testimony to his physical make-up and his endurance. The snow was at least eight inches deep and still falling in fat, lazy flakes.

Under Martin and Millie's bedroom window, he stopped and shouted, "Carter, you holy God merchant!"

There was no response. The white clapboard house and the white clapboard church stood alone in an expanse of snow-covered fields, defined in the moonlight by the dark blue shadows of the stone walls that divided them, walls raised there long, long ago by tight-lipped Connecticut farmers, specifying where their sheep would graze and where their wheat would grow. And now a drunken rabbi shouted into the cold wind, "Martin Carter, you and I have been — you and I — we, we have been accused of eschewing the life of language, which is what Lucy said! Lucy was my wife! She said I eschew the living language and she left me and took away my children! If I could only say she ripped me off with all her motherfucking smarts, she would not have left me alone in that shitpile we call our house! But I can't say anything that means a damned thing anymore, and she knows it!"

At that point, the door opened, and Martin, in a bathrobe,

his feet in a flapping pair of galoshes, came out into the snow and took David by the arm.

"Come on inside, old friend," Martin said.

"No."

"You're wet and cold and all you're wearing is a shirt, and if you don't come inside, you'll be sick."

"Good. I'll die. It's about time."

"You won't die. You'll just be very sick, and your friends, who all have better things to do, will have to take care of you."

"They don't have to. Who's asking them to?"

He took the bottle from David's hand. "Did you drink all this?"

"You bet your ass I did."

"Was it full?"

"You bet your ass it was."

"You wouldn't want me to get sick, David?"

"Oh, no. No way. You're my friend, Martin. Of course, you could be some motherfucken S.S. man, trying to come off like some kind of Jew-loving priest — "

"David, stop that! You're drunk and you don't know what in hell you're talking about, and now you're coming inside with me." There was a swallow of whiskey left in the bottle, and as David tilted it up, Martin grabbed it and flung it into the snow.

"That's enough!"

"You're shouting at me," David whimpered.

"You are damned right I am!"

"I want to talk to Millie. Millie doesn't hate me."

Martin guided David into the house, into the kitchen, where Millie had a large pot of coffee perking. The kitchen was cold. Millie had a robe over her nightgown. "How is he?" she asked Martin.

"He is as drunk as any drunk I ever saw. He apparently put away a quart of whiskey."

"He could die from that."

"He has the constitution of a horse. He's soaking wet. You

start feeding him the coffee and I'll find a dry shirt and a sweater for him."

A broken groan from David.

"Get him into the bathroom!" Millie cried.

Martin held him as David vomited into the toilet bowl. They were both lean men, but David was taller and heavier, and it was all Martin could do to keep him from collapsing onto the bowl. After he wiped him off with a wet towel, Martin somehow manipulated him back into the kitchen.

"Good and black?" he asked his wife.

"You bet."

"Let's pour it into him."

"I hear that with this kind of thing, you have to walk them too. The alcohol is, in effect, a poison."

"That's right."

They did both. They walked him and they poured black coffee into him, and by the time the first fingers of dawn touched the kitchen, Rabbi Hartman was sick, tired, red-eyed, and reasonably sober — sober enough to feel ashamed and miserable and guilty. "You always do it to those you love," he mumbled. "I'm so sorry. And now I have to add insult to injury by asking for a ride home."

"There's a foot of snow out there," Millie said. "And anyway, you have to have something in your stomach, so I'll put up some eggs and toast. The children are all out of the house for years now, so it's nice to have someone infantile to take care of."

"Millie!" Martin cried.

"She's absolutely right," David said. "What a disaster I've turned into!"

"Nonsense. You've gone through a divorce, which is one of the most awful things a sensitive person can experience, and for you, with the burden you carry, it's worse than it is for most. But it's not the end of the world and it's not the end of your life."

Millie put the eggs and toast in front of him. "Please eat this, David. I'm sorry for what I said."

"You're perfectly right."

"No, I'm not. Now please eat this. You've had a terrible night."

So it had been, a terrible, sick night, over five years ago, yet the taste of that night was still with him. It would always be with him, and even his relationship with Martin would never be quite the same.

"You don't have to hold the candle in that little holder," Martin whispered. "Put it on the pavement. I think Father Kelly is a bit of a nut."

"Do you suppose we actually change anything?" David asked him. "Lucy never felt that we did. It was a bone of contention between us. When the cookbook she and Millie put together was published, I saw a whole window full of the book in Westport. She said that at least she and Millie changed the way people cooked — at least somewhat. What do we ever change?"

"That's a hard question to answer. In Vietnam, the Buddhist monks douse themselves with gasoline, sit down cross-legged, and set themselves on fire. I suspect the thinking is that the pain is so great, the horror so great, and the courage so great that it makes a plea for peace that must be heard."

"But it isn't heard and nothing changes."

"Can we be sure, David? I sit here with this silly candle, and then I think about the song, it is better to light just one little candle than to sit and curse the dark. Well, that's our only choice, isn't it?"

"Yes, our only choice."

There had been a lot of talk in the congregation after David's divorce, and there had even been talk among some members of the congregation that he ought to resign; but nothing came of that. There was a minority group in the congregation who would have liked to rid themselves of Rabbi Hartman, but they were a minority and for the most part they kept their peace. The book of sermons, which was originally published in a German translation under the title *The Outsider*, had become a modest best seller in Germany; it was picked up in Holland and translated into Dutch and then into the Scandinavian languages. Its publication in England in the English language took place about a year after the German publication; and a year after that, David was approached by an American publisher. It was about this time that David received news of Herman Strauss's death. He changed the name of the American edition to *Two Silver Teaspoons* and wrote the story of his evening with Herman Strauss as a preface to the American edition. Although the book was not destined to be a runaway best seller, it was expected to do very well indeed, and, what with the foreign royalties and the American publisher's advance, his income was very substantial. For the first time in his life, David was freed from the niggling worries of poverty.

For this, he was most grateful, since Lucy had decided that the best place for the children to spend their summers was with their father at Leighton Ridge.

It had given him the sensation of meeting his children for the first time, and indeed the change in their appearance in the seven months since he had seen them brought two strangers to him. The boy had turned into a shy young man, but it was with Sarah that the actual miracle had taken place, the burst of puberty changing the ugly duckling into a lovely young woman. For the month of July, David had rented a cabin on the shore of Lake Cobbosseecontee in Maine.

It was a marvelous month. For the first few days, the children were stiff and protective of themselves, closed off; but after that, bit by bit, the three of them found each other. They had a canoe and an old skiff, and they had a shallow corner of the lake where the water was deliciously warm. There were islands scattered around the lake, and they found the best ones for picnicking. They built campfires in the evening, and they roasted corn and frankfurters.

But why had he never done it with Lucy?

And the questions were always the same, the same questions repeated to him when any couple in his congregation got divorced.

"Why did you and Mommy stop loving each other?"

"We never stopped."

"Then why don't you live together?"

"Why can't we all live in Leighton Ridge?"

"What will become of us?"

Sarah was afraid of airplanes. "It will fall down, and we'll all be killed."

They didn't like California. At summer's end, they sat with tear-stained faces, pleading not to be sent back.

A burst of wind in the Fifth Avenue canyon set the candles to sputtering. David's went out. Father Kelly leaned over and lit it for him.

"Why do we do what we do, Rabbi?" Kelly asked him. "Why do we sit here on Fifth Avenue, pleading with the men who rule the world to show a bit of compassion for people?"

"I suppose so that we can sleep at night."

"Do the Johnsons and the Kissingers sleep?"

"I imagine they do," David said.

"So what is left of your argument?" Father Kelly asked genially.

"What is left of all arguments, I suppose."

"I would guess," Rabbi Sager said, "that we sit here because we want so desperately to believe in God, and our silly pleading is that if we were to dispense with compassion and anger and prayer, then who would there be to bear witness to the fact that there ever was or could be a God? Possibly, that's what drove your Saint Francis. We want so much for God to notice us. I was in Jerusalem and I saw a terrorist's bomb explode in a crowd of women and children. I will never forget it, but we drop a very large bomb in Vietnam every minute of every hour of every day."

"The thing is," said Philip Simpson, the Methodist minis-

ter, "that there are people in my congregation, good, decent
people who love their children and who read books and are
literate and tithe properly, who never give a second thought
to the things we're talking about, and who support the government totally."

"Did we — twenty, forty, fifty years ago?" Martin wondered. "When Mark Twain raged about the hypocrisy and
evil of the war in Cuba, was there one pulpit in the land that
supported him? And when the conscientious objectors went
to prison in nineteen eighteen, the pulpits were as silent as
the night, and where were the voices from the pulpits when
the six million Jews were being put to death in Hitler's abat-
toirs? So if we serve God, we do it poorly — poorly."

"There has to be a beginning," Father Kelly said gently.
"Perhaps this is the beginning."

No one spoke now, and they sat in silence for another
half-hour.

A uniformed policeman made his way among them, looking at them curiously, and in the distance a woman's voice,
clear as a bell, singing the old Irish song "I laid my boy away
today, with a bullet in his chest."

The network people were threading back and forth with
their hand-held cameras, and the sound of a woman's rich
voice came, speaking for the television microphone, "We do
what has to be done. It would be better done in Washington,
but nothing is done there, so we try." David craned his head
to see her. She was a tall, lean woman, with light close-
cropped hair, and as things do, she reminded him suddenly
and poignantly of Sarah Comstock. The flash of memory
created an almost overwhelming ache and desire for a
woman, to be in love with a woman, to look at her with
delight, to be in bed with her, to hold her in his arms.

It had happened to him once, the third summer he took his
children to the lake in Maine, and she was working as a
waitress in a hotel around a bend of the lake. She was very
young, a senior at Smith College, a compact, delightful girl

with brown eyes, short black hair, and a skin burned berry brown by the sun. She was not pretty, but healthy-looking and open-faced. She looked very much like Lucy when David met Lucy, and her name was Patience Street. She met him and his children in a canoe, her canoe floating alongside his, and since she worked only the dinner shift, she had time to spend with them. They went fishing and picnicking and swimming together, and she fell in love with Sarah and Aaron, and very likely with David too. There was one night when the children were asleep, and the black-haired girl, her eyes shining, went to bed with David, and after they had made love, whispered in his ear, "Marry me, David, and I will love you all my life."

"And I think I could love you all my life," he whispered back, "but I am forty-six years old and you are twenty-one years old, and I am a tired and tortured old Jew, and you are the essence of life and youth and joy and excitement and anticipation, and my anticipation is gone."

"And you are absolutely crazy," she said. "You are strong and vigorous and you make love better than any stupid boy pawing over me, and I love your kids and I think you're the most wonderful man I ever met, and we're so good in bed together — aren't we? Tell me truthfully, aren't we?"

But in the cold light of day, Patience Street's insistence that they be married faded, and when he embraced her before leaving the lake, David knew he would never see her again.

He spoke about her to Della Klein, simply because he had to speak about her to someone, but Della offered him small comfort. "You always run from it, don't you, David?" she said. "You run from life and you're guilty when you have a little joy."

He had dinner at Della's house a few days after the candle-light protest, which had ended in a downpour of rain. "It's the kind of thing that I want to do," Della said, "but I can't. I suppose I'm afraid. I always wonder whether it does any good at all. But that probably is a sop to my conscience."

"Which is what we all wonder — does it do any good?"

"And did you stay there while it rained?"

"For a while. But then, instead of persistence being admirable, a point comes where it turns ridiculous."

"Yes — "

"A feeling I am well acquainted with."

"You are never ridiculous, David."

"That is kind of you." They were dining together, just the two of them, at Della's house. She had kept the big house after Mel died, mostly, as she put it, out of lethargy, but mainly because the old, rambling Connecticut farmhouse was a place she knew and loved and felt secure in. She was still a handsome woman who had retained her figure and her sense of humor. Her son had turned Mel Klein's small garment business into a national institution, but Della had no desire to become a part of it. She tended her garden, read books, and worked at the synagogue.

"Very kind of you," David said, "but I often feel ridiculous. I have spoken to Martin about it, and he recognizes the feeling — the feeling of someone who steps into a totally impossible position. Think of it, to have the effrontery to believe that you can speak in God's name."

"I never thought of it quite that way," Della admitted. They had finished dinner. "It's turned cold," she said, "and I have a fire in the living room. Can we sit in front of the fire, David? I'll do my best to seduce you without making you feel ridiculous."

"It would take no effort. Do you know that once, in a fit of annoyance, Lucy accused me of being in love with you."

"Without any truth in the accusation?"

"Some truth. You're a seductive and delicious woman. It's no sin to be in love with you."

In the living room, they sat on the couch facing the fire, and Della poured coffee and said to him, "David, why in God's name must you indulge that sin thing? There is only one sin — to hurt another human being. All the rest is utter hogwash.

I am no kid, but I am a woman who is still a woman, and I haven't felt a man's touch since Mel died."

Suddenly she broke into tears. David took her in his arms. "Oh, this is stupid," she said. "Stupid." He touched her face, and then he kissed her, and her passion was like an explosion. Then she stopped suddenly and said, "My God, David, we're making out on a couch, like a couple of kids!"

"I know."

"Upstairs, there's a real bed."

"I feel so damned ridiculous."

"Oh, shut up, David," she said.

Then they went upstairs.

For both David and Della it was a literal outburst of desire. Neither of them had ever made love that way before. For David, her body was like a pot of honey into which he plunged. She was a round woman, round limbs, round breasts, all of her given to him, welcoming him, receiving him, touching him as he had never been touched, kissing him as he had never been kissed — and he gave it back, caressing her, embracing her, biting her, going over every bit of her body, exploring it, as if he had never held a naked woman in his arms before.

Afterward, lying together on the bed, naked, side by side, David said, "It never happened with Lucy."

"What never happened? David, you have two kids."

"I don't mean that."

"What do you mean?"

"I don't know."

"Are you happy now?"

"More than you can imagine," staring at her well-formed naked body, the wide hips and full breasts.

"Not more than I can imagine, Rabbi. I have a Catholic friend who tells me how exciting it is to go to bed with her priest — "

"No. You're kidding."

"David, you are absolutely the most innocent human being

I have ever known. Tell me something, am I the first woman in the congregation you have ever taken to bed?"

"Of course."

"Mother of God! Excuse me, I'm reverting. I'm half-Jewish. My mother was Jewish, my father was a sailor, a bum from Liverpool who walked out on my mother when I was two years old. I met Mel when I was sixteen, and he fell in love with me and took care of me and my mother until she died, and I turned Jewish. The whole thing. I took all my instructions even though I didn't have to, because Mom was Jewish, but I had spent six years in a Catholic orphanage, where she had to leave me. I'm not going to bore you with details, but that's how I can sort of straddle religions. What was I saying?"

"I've lost track of it."

"Yes, no one in the congregation. Unbelievable."

"Is that the truth, about your being half-Jewish?" David asked.

"Why not? Mel wanted it quiet, so I kept it quiet. I adored Mel. And you really think Martin Carter never strayed? Well, he did, you know."

"I don't believe it. How could you know?"

"The lady told me."

He got out of bed and began to dress.

"Are you going home?"

"It might put you in a difficult position."

"Me? Oh, David, you are absolutely wonderful. It's beginning to rain and it's after midnight. Please get back into bed."

Actually, there was nothing in the world he wanted more at this moment than to crawl back into that wonderful warm bed and embrace the ample bosom of this remarkable woman. But, instead, he told her that Mrs. Holtzman, who slept upstairs in what had been Sarah's room, would awaken in the morning to an empty house.

"Oh, no, you're putting me on."

"No."

She was gurgling with laughter now, and David, standing in his underwear briefs with his trousers in his hand, found that irresistible. He had never known anyone like this before, nor was he quite certain about what had convulsed her with laughter, the sight of the rabbi of Leighton Ridge in his underwear and his long skinny legs, or his woeful statement about Mrs. Holtzman. Whatever, he dropped the trousers and fell into bed, embracing her with a bear hug that took her breath away.

"David, David!" she begged him.

"Sorry, oh, I am sorry."

She pushed him back, holding his arm, nodding admiringly at his long, flat muscles. "You are in good shape, aren't you, for someone who carries all the woes of the world on his shoulders. How old are you, David? Is it fifty?"

"Soon. Forty-nine."

"The best time in a man's life. Of course, I'm old enough to be your mother."

"Hardly. You're fifty-two, come January."

"How do you know that?"

"I'm your rabbi, my darling Della."

"Of course. So you are. You're almost fifty years old, you've been divorced for years, and you're afraid that Mrs. Holtzman will come into your bedroom tomorrow morning and discover that the bed hasn't been slept in."

"Oh, come on — the way you put it."

"How shall I put it, David? Doesn't it ever occur to you what an extraordinary person you are?"

"No, it does not," he said firmly.

"Ah, well, we will talk about that another time. Do you know that at least a dozen women between here and Westport have been conniving to put their female offspring together with you in the bonds of holy matrimony?"

"No, I don't believe a word of that. You know, I do believe you invent things like that." He reached out to touch her rounded breast, her straight hair, still cut in the same pageboy style as when he had first seen her, twenty years before.

"It was twenty years, wasn't it?"

"Perhaps a bit more," she said, smiling. "I remember that first day you and Lucy came up here to the Ridge, and we all had dinner at Jack Osner's place. I thought you were just beautiful. I was always so jealous of that wife of his, eight feet tall with cheekbones sticking up like horns. She always made me feel like a fat, dumpy little woman. You know, he'll be Secretary of State. It's in the cards."

"No one could ever think of you as a fat, dumpy little woman. You're marvelous."

"Mother Earth?"

"You keep laughing at me," David protested. "I do remember that hours ago we were talking about how ridiculous a rabbi could be. Am I still so ridiculous?"

"You're a delicious, sweet person, and I'm beginning to be madly in love with you. But I don't resemble Shelly Osner, not one bit."

"Why should you?"

"Or Sarah Comstock, poor woman."

"Good heavens, how do you know about that? It was ages and ages ago."

"Rabbi, there are no secrets in a place like this."

"No, no. I suppose not."

"You have a congregation that loves you."

"Yes, some of them."

"Most of them," Della said softly.

They lay side by side in silence for a while, and then David took her hand and looked at it and then kissed the palm.

"You're a gentle person. You make me feel like a young girl again."

"And you make me feel alive."

"And that is almost everything, to feel alive. *L'chaim*, as we say."

"Almost everything. That — and love."

"I went a few times to hear Martin preach. He's a very good preacher — not as good as you, David, but very good in that restrained *goyishe* way of his. He says God is love. Is that what you believe?"

"I don't know what God is. I hope that someday I will, but not now."

"I want you to make love to me again. Do you think that's somewhat improper for two people our age?"

David burst out laughing, and Della said, "I can't remember seeing you laugh before tonight for ever so long. But I want you to stop it. You can't make love properly if you laugh."

"We'll try," he said, still laughing, and then, after they had made love a second time, Della said suddenly, "I want a cigarette. I want one desperately. I haven't touched one for months now, but you can't make love without a cigarette afterward." She was rummaging in her night table drawer as she spoke. "Got it. Here, four of them," holding up a crumpled pack. "Do you want one, David?"

"Never started."

She lit the cigarette and inhaled deeply. "Ah — that is good. Oh, David, don't go off and pretend this never happened."

"Not likely."

"Oh, what loving words! Not likely."

"Very loving in this context, Della. I loved Mel, I loved you. That went on for many years. Tonight was better than I could ever say. I don't think I'll walk away from you — but on the other hand — "

"Suppose we let the other hand rest for a time."

"Sure. By the way, Lucy's coming to see me next week."

"What!"

"It's all right. She's remarrying. There are some things in the house that she wants, things that belonged to her mother and father. There are also some legal loose ends — "

"Then why didn't she ask you to come to California?"

"She did. I didn't want to go. I think she wanted an excuse to come here. She has good friends here."

Della reached out and switched off the light on her bedside table, and now a pale glow came through the draperies. "It's morning, David." She got out of bed and drew the draperies open. "What a fine morning!"

David joined her at the window. The rain had stopped, and the sun was rising against a thin tracery of clouds. The rain had stripped the great maples and oaks of their autumn leaves and spread a carpet of red and gold across the lawn.

"How do you feel?" Della asked him.

"Guilty and conscience-stricken, but otherwise pretty good."

"Let's feed your guilt some breakfast, and then can we walk a little? I'd love that, David."

"If you wish."

"We'll be seen, but the hell with them! Let them send their kids out to find husbands their own age."

"Ah, well. They tolerate a rabbi who is divorced, so I suppose they'll tolerate a rabbi who sleeps around with married women."

"They tolerate a rabbi who's brainless, which is what you mean. I'm not married women. I'm both single and singular, and I'm a widow and I've been a widow for six years."

After breakfast, they walked down a little dirt road behind Della's house. Two rows of blazing red swamp maples enclosed the path until it rose up to the brow of a hill, where the view was open, rolling pastures and meadows beneath them, and to the north, vaguely visible, the foothills of the Berkshires. The air was pure and clean and full of October perfume, and the golden leaves on a little stand of white birches gleamed like jewels.

"This is the most beautiful place on earth," Della said.

"Almost."

"Why almost?"

"During the war, I flew into Casablanca, and as we were

circling to land, I looked down and saw this enormous swimming pool. I don't know what it was or who built it or why, but there it was. I was sitting next to a tough old regular army colonel, and I said to him, 'That has to be the largest swimming pool in the world.' He looked at me a moment, and then he said, 'No, sonny, it is not. Maybe the second biggest, but not the biggest, because whatever it is, there's something bigger or better somewhere.' "

"That's a nice story, David, and let this be the second most beautiful place on earth, but why on earth can't you tell me that Lucy's coming here to see your son?"

"Divorce is a complex thing," David said after a long pause. "It becomes more complex when you have a son in prison."

Its complexity surprised even David when Lucy called him the following week.

"When are you coming in?" he asked her.

"I am in. I'm at the Carters'."

"You're where?"

"At the Carters'. Millie picked me up at the airport. I'm staying only three days, and by Ben Franklin's dictum, that's permissible for a guest."

"But you could have stayed at the house. We have Aaron's room, and Mrs. Holtzman stays here."

"David, darling, I don't need a chaperone. I simply thought it would be better if we weren't sleeping in the same house."

"Perhaps you're right."

"And when do we see Aaron?"

"Day after tomorrow. I'll drive you over to Danbury, of course. Tell me about Sarah."

"Sarah's healthy and lovely, and she started college two weeks ago, and Martin wants you to join us for dinner tonight. You will, won't you, David?"

His agreement was very civilized. Divorces were civilized these days. He was civilized. Martin and Millie were civilized. Lucy and Della were both civilized — and yet he felt so empty, so terribly empty. What did it add up to? The small house that his congregation had built for its rabbi was the coldest, loneliest place in the world. And his wife? He still thought about her as his wife, but she was gone and lost, and he felt very deeply that there was no way she could ever return to him.

It seemed like only a moment ago that he had walked into the U.S.O. store on Broadway to have her greet him with that smile of hers. "Welcome, soldier — except that you're an officer. There's an officers' club over on Forty-fourth Street, where you'll be much happier."

"I don't want doughnuts or coffee. I was watching you through the window. I want your name, address, and telephone number, and then I want a date."

"What? Are you some kind of nut, Captain?"

"Possibly."

"And what's that thing?" pointing to the Star of David on his blouse.

"I'm a rabbi."

"You got to be kidding. And all that fruit salad?" pointing to the three rows of ribbon on his blouse.

Did she remember? He tried to think of what he had said to that. He had not been in character that day. He was a diffident, shy young man, and standing out in the street, watching her through the plate glass window, he had rehearsed the speech he would make to her. Was he wrong in remembering the beginning as a very happy time? Twenty years was not so long ago, yet the world and attitudes of that time were gone forever.

He tried to conquer and control his anticipation. After all, he had found another woman who was loving and who was concerned for him, and he had found in the single night with Della a kind of lovemaking and sexual exchange he had never dreamed of. He blamed only himself for not having experienced it with Lucy, but responsible or not, there were other roads to happiness than a return to Lucy.

Yet reason with himself as he might, he was still not prepared for the youthfulness of Lucy. He had not seen her since she went off to California a second time, a harassed and agonizing woman; he was not prepared for someone who, five years later, looked younger than he remembered her to be. She embraced him and kissed him, giving him no feeling that she was holding back, and she said warmly, "How good to see you, David. You look wonderful."

"You look wonderful," he countered. "I'm losing my hair, and what I haven't lost is almost gray. You're not a day older."

"No pact with the devil. I work hard and enjoy what I do — which is something you'd hardly approve of," she said quickly. "I'm a theatrical agent — an actor's agent. The man I'm going to marry, Bob Greene, owns the agency. He's divorced." She got it all out very quickly, almost in a single breath. Martin was watching both David and Lucy intently, and as David spoke, he nodded slightly.

"Of course, I approve of it," David said. "Why not? I think it's great that you've found yourself."

"Well, that's putting it a bit loftily. I can't say that I've found myself — not in the way that you and Martin use the expression, not in the way of having found a calling or some esoteric meaning to my life. The best I can say is that I earn a lot of money, more money than I ever dreamed I could earn, and I do put people to work and fight for better pay from people who can well afford to pay what we ask, and I'm lucky enough to have found a man who's comfortable to be with."

"You're happy, and that's what matters," David said.

At dinner, she told them that she would be living in Beverly Hills. She had an apartment there, but after they were married, they'd look for a house. Beverly Hills was a glamour place. They all felt somewhat abashed.

"Here, nothing much changes," David said.

"Not so, not so," Martin put in. "David is becoming quite famous."

"Martin!"

"Well, not as famous as some, but more famous than others.

His book is a real phenomenon — just keeps selling — and he's asked here and there to speak, and believe it or not, there was a piece in the *New York Times* about the rabbi of Leighton Ridge, practically the first time we've come to the public's attention since the Battle of Leighton Ridge was fought here in seventeen seventy-eight — "

"As a matter of fact," David said, interrupting Martin, "there's a lot more coming out of Leighton Ridge than the mouthings of one desiccated rabbi. *The New Yorker* sent Eddie Frome to Vietnam, and he's published an absolutely brilliant analysis, and Mike Benton has a hit play on Broadway, and everyone says it's number one for the Pulitzer Prize."

"I know all about Mike's play," Lucy said. "Bob's his West Coast agent. But he can forget about the Pulitzer Prize. They won't even give used carbon paper to an ex-red."

"Then maybe they'll give it to Freddie Sims. He's in our congregation," Millie said, "and his play finishes its fourteenth week on Broadway."

"You must know we're being silly," Martin said. "Instead of urging Lucy to tell us about a fascinating business that she's become a part of, we're competing like a bunch of kids. I, for one, would like to know exactly what she does. I have only the vaguest notion of what a theatrical agent is."

Relieved, David listened to Lucy's explanation of how she found jobs for actors, of the thousands of actors who lived at a starvation level, of the vast sums paid to stars, and of how the agent took his commission. Lucy sparkled with animation now that she was engaged with the new life she had chosen, and David was able, for perhaps the first time, to watch her very objectively. The last strings binding them together were being cut without his ever knowing that they were cut. She was truly a delightful, intelligent, and attractive woman, but he had lost any desire ever to be her husband again.

Later, while Millie took Lucy upstairs to prepare her room for the night, or as an excuse to give Martin an opportunity to be alone with David, the two men sat down in Martin's tiny study and sipped brandy. Martin lit his pipe and observed David with interest.

"You always surprise me," Martin said.

"What did you expect?"

"I was worried. David, that's a remarkable woman."

"I meet remarkable women everywhere. That's either my fortune or misfortune."

"Keep her as a friend. Our curse is that we're joined to so few others, and from what she says, your daughter will remain in California."

"It's only a few hours away by plane."

"She and Millie are very fond of each other. My wife doesn't make friends easily, David."

"The whole world is spread so thin. I wonder how it was when it took two days to go from Leighton Ridge to Danbury."

"Not better, I think. But who knows? How's Aaron? How is he taking prison?"

"How does anyone take prison?" David wondered. "He's an interesting boy, which I suppose is another way of saying he's a strange boy. He appears to have no anger, and he tells me that he feels prison is a valuable experience. I think I would feel it as a deadly and terrible experience. But of all the people in our lives, I sometimes feel that those we know least are our children."

"And perhaps those they know least are their parents."

"Yes, that too."

Lucy and Millie came into the room now, and Lucy looked about her with pleasure. "What we don't have much of out on the Coast is taste. Nothing like this little room could exist out there, no hand-hooked rugs, no pegged floors, no charming eighteenth-century furniture."

"Come on," Martin said, "I've seen this room in the movies lots of times. Also, no below-zero temperature, no snow, no frozen plumbing."

"And I've been so absorbed in my own misery over Aaron that I never asked you about Ellie and Joe. Did she ever marry the doctor?"

"No, that fell through. As for Joe, he's reasonably happy," Martin said. "He has a job as a carpenter in Toronto and he's found a girl he likes — "

"But can he come back — I mean when all this insanity is over?"

"It will never be over," Millie said hopelessly.

"We brought him up as a Christian," Martin said. "We taught him to comprehend and to live by the literal meaning of Christ's words, to do no violence to any human being. My people came here over three hundred years ago because they found a cruel and mindless government intolerable. He has made the same choice, and I can only respect it."

"But this is our place," Millie protested. "My father's people have been here in Connecticut for generations."

"Still, we're outsiders — just as David and Lucy are. That's our curse — or our blessing."

"I could live without such blessings," Millie said.

"Someday he'll come back," Martin said. "Everything changes, and this will change too. The awful tragedy is that thousands of kids they are sending over there to Vietnam will never come back — except in body bags."

Driving toward Danbury Prison two days later, Lucy asked David, "Do you agree with Martin? Do you feel that his son was right in going to Canada? Aaron wouldn't have to be in prison. He could have gone to Canada."

They had been riding in silence for the past ten minutes or so, David without thought at the moment, utterly enchanted by the explosion of fall colors in the Connecticut countryside. No matter how often he witnessed the miracle of the turning of the leaves, the sudden change of a green vista into a wild, beautiful riot of gold and red and orange and yellow, he could not become blasé about it. It was always new, unexpected, and improbable; and instead of answering Lucy, he said,

"Don't you miss this? I don't think I could go years without seeing it."

"What?"

"I meant the colors."

"Did you hear a word I said? I was saying that Aaron didn't have to go to prison. He could have gone to Vancouver on the coast. There are hundreds of American kids there who fled the draft."

"I didn't tell him what to do, Lucy. He did what he wanted to do."

"Did you ever tell him anything?" she said with irritation.

"We'll see him in a little while. Until then, can't you just relax and enjoy the fall colors? I'm sure you haven't seen them for years."

"You're wonderful, David. You're absolutely wonderful. We're driving to Danbury Prison to see my son, who has been locked up like a common criminal, and all you can think of are these goddamned fall colors. I don't give a damn about the colors! I can only think that those bastards may never let my son go. They can keep him there forever."

"They can't keep him there forever. You're letting your fears run away with you, and this is still a country ruled by law — at least inside our borders — and in eight months he'll be released to begin a work program."

"Yes, and what does that mean? A chain gang somewhere?"

"Probably Danbury Hospital, where he'll do whatever has to be done. The point is, I think, that when we see him, we shouldn't lay our own problems on him. He has enough of his own."

"That's not what I meant to do."

"I know."

"Only if he had gone to Canada — "

"Lucy, Aaron would not go to Canada, and he would not label himself a pacifist. He simply took the position that the war in Vietnam was unjust and violated every principle of his belief. They had to send him to prison. For my part, I would have done anything, said anything, to keep him out of that butchery. You know that."

"Yes."

"He'll be very happy to see you."

"I know." She leaned over and dropped her head against his shoulder. "I'm so tired, David, so damned tired. I was all right, not seeing you. In five years, I was able to blur things, what you looked like, what our life here had been, and then seeing you loused it all up. I can't be married to you, I can't — and I love you so damned much. I can't live in this place. I feel choked here, with all your beautiful colors, closed in and choked. Everything's too small. Bob and I have a little place at Malibu, and when we drive back to Los Angeles, five minutes from the house we're in Malibu Canyon, with its great, towering mountains — no, it's not that. It's not the scenery. That's stupid. It's just the way you and Martin take on the world as some kind of personal responsibility. Well, it's not your responsibility — not yours or anyone else's. You want to know what the world is? I can tell you that. The world is a shitpile. The world is a conglomeration of idiots who let themselves be ruled by a maniac like Lyndon Johnson and who go out periodically and slaughter each other. You know what they call these people in the movie business — the shit-kickers. That's what the world is, the shit-kickers and the mental slobs. No one can change it. You and Martin can't change one damned thing, and you stumble through life with all your faith in a God who doesn't even exist, and what you lose is life itself — " Her voice broke and she burst into tears. "I love you," she said. "I always loved you, and it's no damned good."

David pulled the car over onto the shoulder of the road.

"We'll be late," she whimpered.

"Visiting goes on until three, and it's only nine-thirty now. Come on, baby. You've fallen into a deep hole of emotion, and what else could you expect? We haven't seen each other for years. You've been away from Leighton Ridge for years."

"David, why don't you yell at me? Why don't you tell me what a bitch I am?"

"Because you're not — and because I love you."

"Oh, David," she sobbed, "you do, don't you, and I love you, and it's no use, is it?"

"Whatever use you want to make of it. We'll never live together again, but we have two kids that tie us together. We can love each other. It's better than hating each other or being indifferent to each other."

She took some tissues from her purse and dabbed at her eyes. "What do my eyes look like, David?"

"Very nice."

"You're the dearest man."

"Well — at times. I can be pretty nasty."

"You?"

"At times. How do you feel now?"

"Much better. I had to get that out of me. I could go to jail — believe me, I could if I had to — but to see your kid go through it is a thousand times worse. And he didn't do anything. All he did was refuse to kill people."

The guard at the entrance to Danbury Prison inspected Lucy's purse. She had a roll of Life Saver mints. "I wouldn't try to give him those," the guard said.

"It never occurred to me."

David and Lucy, each of them, had their hands stamped, an invisible mark on the back of the hand. "That's to keep us from switching clothes with desperate characters like Aaron," Lucy said. "I think they get all their ideas from the movies." They were waiting in the very large visiting room, already filled with prisoners and their visitors. A guard brought Aaron to them, a tall, long-limbed, lean young man, nineteen years old, and so much like his father that Lucy caught her breath in surprise. She had not seen him in months, and she had created in her mind a vision of prison clothes, a bowed head, and a shambling gait. Instead, she saw a sunburned young man in blue jeans and a blue work shirt.

He embraced her in a bear hug, and then, unexpectedly, embraced David too.

"I am glad to see both of you," he said. "So glad. Mom, you look absolutely beautiful."

"Because she is beautiful," David said.

"Sure. Absolutely." He was measuring both of them, and David realized that the boy hadn't known what to expect.

"Aaron, listen," David said softly. "Your mother and I love each other. We will always love each other. The fact that each of us must go his own way in his own place doesn't change the fact that we love each other. Can you understand that?"

"Not too well." He stared at them for a long moment. "I'll try."

"All right. Now tell us about yourself."

"Do you have enough to eat?" Lucy asked him.

"There's plenty of food, and it's pretty good. They treat us all right. The prison's on the shore of the lake, so that helps, and we get outside. There are enough kids in here for the same reason that I'm in here for me to have friends and people to talk to. You know, this is the place where they send the crooked politicians, you know, even congressmen like J. Parnell Thomas, who once ran the Un-American Committee — he did time here — so in that way it's considered the real Class A top-dog prison in the United States. That doesn't mean it's any country club, but it's all right. It's not like those places you see in the movies."

"Well, thank God for that," Lucy said. "I had visions of something dreadful."

"It's okay. You go back to California?"

"Tomorrow."

"I have eight months more. Pop is right here, so I get to see him, but will I see you again before I'm released?"

"I promise you. At least twice more. And when you're out, you'll come to California."

"And Sarah? How is she?

"Just great. I didn't bring her because I thought this prison was so much worse. I'll bring her next time."

"When I get out, I have two years of service. I think I start at Danbury Hospital here, but maybe I can get that switched to California. I know, Pop," he said to David. "But I've been seeing you right along. Mom and Sarah are three thousand miles away. Are you still going to marry Bob Greene?" he demanded, turning to Lucy.

"Yes."

"Well, I mean being here — you and Pop are so friendly. You said you love each other."

"We can't live together," Lucy said. "Someday you'll understand why."

"I don't understand," he said stubbornly. "I don't understand it at all. I know that if I loved a girl, I'd want to live with her."

"Suppose she had both feet firmly planted in midair," David said. "How would you ever get her down?"

They all laughed at that. It did David good to watch Aaron laugh, and somehow it shifted the subject to college. Aaron brought that up. "Talk about midair, I've just barely finished one year at Yale. Do you suppose I could do the hospital work and college at the same time? And what college? I'm not sure I want to go back to Yale. You know, if I wanted to be a doctor, the hospital service would make some sense."

"What do you want to do with your life?"

"I think I want to be an engineer. I don't want to deal with philosophy, any kind of philosophy. I want to learn to build something. There are plenty of Jewish doctors and lawyers, but there was a woman here from Israel — headhunters, they call them — and she spoke at Yale. She was recruiting engineers, and what they desperately wanted in Israel was an electric-utility engineer, and do you know she couldn't find one Jewish electric-utility engineer in the United States? I might go to Israel if I could build something there that no one else could."

At three o'clock, visiting hours were over. Lucy clung desperately to Aaron. He was as tall as David, so much taller than his mother, reassuring her, "Mom, I'm going to be all right. Nothing's going to happen to me. When you come right down to it, this jail is the safest place in the world."

"Visiting time is over," a guard called out. "Three o'clock. Visiting time is over."

"I forgot to tell you," Aaron said. "I'm learning another language. Spanish."

"Why?"

"It's the California language. Who knows where I'll be?"

Outside, crying again, Lucy said, "How can he laugh about it?"

"He was laughing because we were there, because it made him feel good. Lucy, he's young and strong and full of the future. And he's alive."

"I know." They were at David's car in the parking lot now. The bright sunshine had gone, and now the sky was covered with heavy, dark clouds. "Oh, David, I think he'll want to come to California, and then you'd have no one here. I mean, why else would he try to learn Spanish?"

"French was his important language in school. He's not going to France. Who knows where he'll go? He might go to Israel."

"Oh, no. David, I'm cold."

He put an arm around her, holding her to him while he rummaged in his pocket for the car keys.

"Let's get away from here. I hate this place. It's an ugly place." In the car, however, she added, "But I will come back. I didn't mean I wouldn't come to see him again. David, all that about the electric-utility engineer in Israel — what makes him so Jewish?"

"He is Jewish."

"I don't mean that. There's something I feel about him that I don't even feel about you, and it's not in anything he says r does. Do you remember, when he was a *Bar Mitzvah*, he handled the Torah with such love. Does he have a girl?" she demanded suddenly.

"He certainly does, a beauty. She lives in New Haven. But for heaven's sake, Lucy, he's just a kid, only nineteen, so this is no candidate for marriage. Just a girl."

"Is she Jewish?"

"I never thought to ask."

"You never thought to ask!"

"Lucy, what difference does it make?"

"You're a rabbi, and you ask me what difference does it make?"

"And you're a self-proclaimed atheist."

"Don't confuse me, David. Being an atheist has nothing to do with my feelings about being Jewish. What's the girl's name?"

"I think — yes, Susan Andrews."

"Susan Andrews. And you don't know whether she's Jewish."

"It doesn't matter. I don't know what you're afraid of, but let me tell you something about your son. Do you remember — I think he was about twelve — he came down with an awful case of poison ivy, all over his face and arms, and he invented some silly story about how it happened."

"I'm not likely to forget that. It was terrible."

"What actually happened was that three boys, three fine young men, each of them a year or two older than Aaron, began to bait him, calling him a dirty Jew and a Christ killer — yes, right in Leighton Ridge, where such a thing could never possibly happen — and when he resisted their pushing him around, they grabbed him and rolled him in the poison ivy. A year later, the year of his puberty, having grown and filled out, he took on each of the three boys separately and beat them. He gave each of them a bad beating."

"How do you know this? Did he tell you?"

"No, he hasn't mentioned it to this day. That was just

before you left for California with the kids. No, I got the story from Martin. The father of one of the boys came to him, knowing we were friends — in a rage, I may say, for the way his son was beaten — and I was so shocked I was sick over it, after a lifetime of living and preaching nonviolence. But then I talked to the boy, and then Martin and I got the three boys together and put all the pieces together. I don't condone what he did. There are moments when it frightens me to think about it. But you asked me why he seems so Jewish, and he is, in a way that's hard for you or me to comprehend."

"You never spoke to him about it?"

"No. It's nothing I could discuss with him, and I can't sit in judgment."

"It's so strange," Lucy said, "so inexplicable. We raise two children and they're strangers to us, and we live together for years with each other, and still we're strangers to each other."

"Is that true of Sarah?"

After some hesitation, Lucy nodded and said, "Yes. It's true of Sarah. There's a wall between us. I try to understand her. I try."

"Was she happy this past summer?"

"I know you wanted her with you, David, but believe me, I didn't influence her either way."

"I know that."

"She wanted the Oklahoma thing. She said, 'Mom, I'm going to be an archeologist, and this is a chance to begin, and I can't miss it,' and the truth is she was as excited as a kid with a new doll about uncovering an Indian mound in Oklahoma. And David, do you know what she took with her as luggage and wardrobe? Four pairs of denims, cut off above the knee, and when I offered to hem them, she said absolutely not — well, four pairs of denims and eight T-shirts and two pairs of sandals, and that was it. No socks, no lipstick even, and she's such a beautiful kid, oh, yes, tampons, and she comes back burned brown, with that marvelous strawberry-blond hair of hers all streaked and discolored by the sun, and when I tried to send her to my hairdresser, she just looked at me as if I were out of my mind."

"And how does she feel about Aaron's being in jail?"

"Didn't she write to you?"

"Not about that."

"He's her hero. Not only that, but it makes points for her, as she puts it, with her friends, a brother who had the guts to go to prison. That's the hero of the moment. She and the other girls hung a huge poster outside their dorm with that slogan that the kids have — *Hey, hey, L.B.J., how many kids did you kill today?*"

"She never told me about that. Why didn't she? Doesn't she trust me?"

"David, you're her father, but you're also the rabbi. The kids adore you, but you're far away. You're always far away. You were always far away from me."

"No, oh, no."

"I'm sorry."

They were almost back at Leighton Ridge when David said to her, "I'll drive you to the airport tomorrow."

"I'd like that."

"I thought you might like to have dinner with me. Mrs. Holtzman prepared enough food."

"David, I wish you had asked me before. I can't. Martin and Millie are expecting me to have dinner with them." She thought about it for a moment. "I suppose I could get out of it. Or you could join us. I'm sure they'll be happy to have you."

"No, let it be. I'll see you in the morning."

At the Carters' he didn't get out of the car. She leaned over to kiss him on the cheek, and by the time he pulled up at his own place, he was thoroughly depressed. In the house, Mrs. Holtzman called to him from the kitchen, "Shall I set two places, Rabbi?"

"One. Just one."

"I'm sorry. I thought Mrs. Hartman would be eating with you."

"No."

"Your telephone messages are on your desk."

He went upstairs to his study, feeling as lonely and abandoned as ever in his entire life. One of the messages was from Della Klein. He picked up the telephone and dialed her number.

"David," she said, "you sound terrible. Did the prison get to you?"

"No. I think life got to me."

"That's the worst, isn't it? Positively the pits, but one can't resign. After all, what's the alternative? How's Aaron?"

"All right. Just fine."

"So the trouble's with you and Lucy. Are you having dinner with her?"

"No. She's at the Carters'."

"Good. Let's you and me go out to some luscious place for dinner. We'll find something elegant if we have to drive twenty miles, and maybe we can take your mind off misery."

"Thank you. You're a nice lady. I'll take a rain check."

"Don't ever call me a nice lady."

When David finally sat down to eat his dinner alone, Mrs. Holtzman brought in a steaming platter and told him, "I made pot roast, brisket the way you tell me your mother made it."

"It smells wonderful."

"Rabbi, I shouldn't talk like this, I have no right to, but it breaks my heart to see you eating here alone like this, night after night."

"Delicious," David said, tasting the meat. "It's not night after night, really, Mrs. Holtzman, but you're very kind to be so concerned. Never more than three times a week. I'm not forgotten. If I accepted even half the invitations from families in the congregation, I'd never have an opportunity to be alone. And I need to be alone now and then."

"I know, Rabbi. Believe me."

He slept poorly that night. He always slept poorly when e had an early rising hour, and in one of those short inter- ls of sleep, he dreamed once again of Dachau. He fre- ently had dreams of the concentration camp — sometimes rrifying nightmares, sometimes more placid dreams. This as a nightmare. In his dream, he was once again at the ge open mass grave where the bodies of Jews were piled ke cordwood. In his dream, as so often before, he was one the bodies in the grave, and though his eyes were open d though he was positioned so as to be able to look up and e the edge of the grave, his body was nevertheless stiff and mobilized with rigor mortis. As he lay there, chilled rough and through with the icy cold of death, American ldiers began to gather at the edge of the grave. He shouted them. He screamed at them. But no sound came, and now saw that the American soldiers had shovels, and they gan to shovel dirt into the grave. This had never hap- ned in the previous dreams of the open grave. David ex- ted every effort to turn his screaming into sound, and sud- nly he was awakened by his own screams, awake and embling and covered with cold sweat.

For all of that, he felt quite refreshed in the morning, ob- rving himself curiously as he shaved. Just short of fifty, he ill was on the better side of baldness. His pale blue eyes were adled in nests of tiny wrinkles, and lines were being etched tween his nose and his mouth. His old army uniform still him, and if he had gained weight, it was no more than a und or two.

Mrs. Holtzman had heard him scream. "You had a bad eam, Rabbi," she said.

"Yes."

"The concentration camp again?"

"Yes, I'm afraid so."

"You remember, Rabbi, I told you that I was at Dachau hen you and the other young men from America came and

liberated us." Her eyes filled with tears. It was always s
when she spoke about Dachau.

"Yes, of course."

She looked at him lovingly. She had created a script in he
mind in which he was sometimes her child and sometimes he
lover. "You know, Rabbi, I also had the most terrible dream
about Dachau, but you know what happened? When you tol
me how you were there with the beautiful young men wh
liberated us, the bad dreams stopped. In my mind, what yo
told me was like a blessing. A blessing can make miracle
yes?"

"Sometimes."

She didn't know how to continue from there, and Davi
sensed she felt she had said too much. She fed him instead, an
he sat regarding with despair the huge breakfast she place
in front of him. He was late and he had to rush off, he ex
plained, as apology for the food he left untouched.

Martin and Millie came outside with Lucy, Martin carry
ing her bags. It was a cold October morning, the air so clea
and fresh that it almost crackled, the frost of the night sti
crunching underfoot.

"We'll be going to Toronto in a month or so," Martin said
"It's been too long since we've seen Joe, and then, since we'r
partway across, we'd like to go on to California. We've neve
been there, and Millie is a dedicated movie fan — "

"What nonsense! Dedicated! But Lucy, if we come, coul
you truly get us into a studio?"

"I think so."

The two women embraced and clung to each other. Marti
shivered in the cold, and David reminded Lucy of the tim
She was weeping again when she sat down in David's car

"But why?"

"You think I have no feelings? Part of my life is her
Maybe some of it was the best part. I don't know." Then, afte
a few minutes, she said, "It's no use. You can't go back. Yo
can't, can you, David?"

"I don't know."

"David, if I ask you a question, could you give me a truthful answer, free of pity or guilt?"

"I think I could."

"All right. What would your answer be if I said, David, I don't want to go back to California. I want to stay here. I want to marry you again. I want to be your wife and live here with you."

David was silent for a while, intent on his driving, while Lucy stared at his profile. Then, speaking slowly, "I'd have to say that I'm very flattered. And excited. Because I think I will always love you more than any other woman. I'm grateful, too, because in all honesty I felt rejected and abandoned. On the other hand, in two weeks or so, you would begin to hate me. You would hate yourself, because nothing evokes self-hatred as much as an act of self-destruction. You would be bored. As you said, you would hate the smallness of everything, the cold, the endless, miserable freezing winter, the fact that you have to drive twenty miles to see a film and sixty-five miles to a theater or a really good restaurant. You wouldn't have the children to care for or to distract you, and since we can't fire the teacher we hired to replace you, you wouldn't have that either."

"Good God," Lucy whispered.

"Perhaps I laid it on too thick."

"Oh, no," Lucy said. "Not at all. You're absolutely right. What a terrifying, dismal prospect! But you are right."

"If it's any sort of consolation, ever since I laid eyes on you a few days ago, I've been ridden with lust, thinking about our nights in bed, years ago — "

"David, you're kidding."

"No, it's the truth."

"How sweet."

"Working out the most intricate and ridiculous schemes to seduce you."

"Why didn't you?"

"Lucy, I'm a rabbi."

"Yes. I tend to forget that. Do you know, I think everything you just said is a lie."

"You know I don't lie."

"All right. There's a hotel at the airport —"

"Lucy darling — that way wouldn't be any good, would it? You know that."

"No, it wouldn't, would it? I'll never know whether you're telling the truth, but it's a sweet thought, and thank you."

PART EIGHT

1971

The tall, redheaded young man had evidently been provided with a description of David, for he pushed through the crowd at Washington's National Airport and with as much a statement as a question wanted to know whether David was not Rabbi David Hartman.

"And you know how I knew you, Rabbi," he said enthusiastically, "aside from your picture in the temple bulletin? Please, let me take your suitcase. No hat. Reform rabbis don't wear hats. That's a dumb joke, isn't it? I recognized you from the picture. This way to my car, and — "

"Stop!" David said.

"Did I say something?"

"Take a deep breath. What's your name?"

"Teddy Berg."

"Good. Now where are you taking me, Teddy?"

"To your hotel so that you can rest up a bit. Then Rabbi Gerson wants to join you for an early dinner. The service starts at eight and you're scheduled to speak at nine. I'm Rabbi Gerson's assistant, but I'm delighted to meet you just on a one-to-one basis. We should have over a thousand people tonight — you know, we're one of the largest temples in the East."

"So I've heard."

"And of course we're thrilled to have you here. If I may say so, you're in good company. Nixon spoke at the temple a few months ago, and in spite of what they say about him, the man comes across to you."

"I'm sure he does."

"We have a divergence of views, but he is the President of the United States."

Sitting in his hotel room, so much like every other hotel room he had ever seen, David wondered why he had agreed to speak here. He had always made it a practice to speak only at colleges and universities, never at other synagogues or at churches, with the single exception of Martin's church.

At Martin's church, the Congregational church of Leighton Ridge, they felt a sort of possessive pride in Rabbi Hartman. After all, he had been at Leighton Ridge as long as anyone could remember, but even there David agreed sparingly to Martin's requests that he preach. "No one appointed me an apostle to the Gentiles, and anyway, you've been hammering away at these particular Gentiles for so long that if they haven't got the message, they will never get it."

It was during that conversation, held at dinner, when Lucy was still his wife and he and Lucy were spending an evening with Martin and Millie, that they fixed on the question of why any man becomes a minister or a rabbi.

"For one thing," Lucy said, "you cut yourself off. David feels he comes closer to people, but I don't see it that way. Oh, there are loads of people here who respect David, and I suppose some of them even venerate him, but you and Martin are our only real close friends."

"Exactly," Millie agreed. "Thank God for both of you."

Martin shook his head.

"Martin denies it," Millie said. "But ask him why he became a minister, and he'll tell you that there were nine generations of Congregational ministers in his family. On his mother's side, of course, not his father's — which to me means absolutely nothing, since his father was something else entirely."

"There was also the fact that I had to live like a Christian."

"Oh, nobody lives like a Christian," Millie said. "You know what Mark Twain said about Christianity — an excellent religion that had never been tried."

"It's been tried," David said gently.

"David, you're not a Christian."

"No. It's one less burden to bear. But Martin and I have talked about this. It's not easy to explain. In some ways, it's an indulgence, since each of us found something wonderful and precious, which brings a kind of selfishness into the picture. But I don't know where man is unselfish in anything he does. The doctor's oath says, Do no harm, but one also helps oneself. It would be very odd for me to say that at the age of nineteen, I faced my own life and found it meaningless; but I don't know how else to put it. I was a sophomore at City College in Manhattan. My father had died, and a younger sister whom I had adored had also died five years before. Just my mother and myself. I walked out of school one day and came home and talked to her; I told her how I felt, empty, worthless, with no hope anywhere. I don't know why I did it. It was cruel of me. She began to cry. She was frightened. So I put my arms around her, and she managed to say to me, 'Do you believe in God, David?' I left the house and walked for hours, and I ended up at the Institute. I think I want to be a rabbi, I said to them, and they told me to come back when I felt more certain about it. I finished the semester at City College and I went back to the Institute, and I was admitted."

"But why?" Millie pressed him. "You don't say why."

"He can't say why," Martin said.

"Oh, don't make it all that mysterious," Lucy said with some exasperation. "One does something. It can be explained."

"Perhaps by some," Martin agreed. "By others, perhaps not. We say a man tries to save his own soul, but what does that mean? We don't know what a soul is and we don't know what saving it means. We are so confused about good and evil that one man's saint is another man's monster. I can't explain why I'm a minister. I only know that I must be."

"There are things that can't be explained," David said. "All we have are words. We use a word like love. It can mean a hundred different things, and all of them are elusive. I have heard ministers and rabbis say that they love God, that they fear God, that they serve God, that they honor God, and truly I don't know what any of them mean. Martin had to be a minister; I had to be a rabbi. It may have been a misfortune in my life, but there it is and I have to live with it."

"Still, neither of you can say why you are what you are."

"I'm not sure any man can."

This came back to him now. He was here in Washington for no other reason he could think of, except that he was a rabbi — and as a rabbi he could not refuse, and this was the result of a strange mixture: the war, his son, himself. He still had an hour before Rabbi Gerson was to join him for dinner, and he drew a hot bath and soaked himself and argued with himself.

The moment he set foot on the plane at La Guardia, he had begun to have a disquieting feeling about this evening. Della had driven him to the airport. "Good luck, dear Rabbi," she had said to him, which had probably planted the seed that started his brooding. In the tub, his mind picked out a tasteless joke, in which one man says to another, "What is your son's profession?" "He's a rabbi," the second man says, and to this, the first man snorts, "What kind of work is that for a Jewish boy?"

When he was speaking at Wellesley, a psychology teacher had gone out of her way in an attempt to seduce him, only to break down and admit that she desired a clinical experience with a rabbi. He told the story to Della, who said, "Clinical baloney. She wanted to be laid, Rabbi. The perks of the road, my dear David. At last I see a reason for being a rabbi."

Now as David dressed in what he always wore on such

occasions, navy blue blazer, gray trousers, white shirt, and striped blue and gray tie, he decided that his brooding and ruminating, and his evoking reasons for his profession arose from the fact that he had accepted Rabbi Gerson's invitation and had sent Rabbi Gerson his speech. Gerson had requested it. David should have said that he never sent a copy of a speech ahead of him, and indeed he had delayed sending it until the previous day. Rabbi Gerson, when he arrived, was sufficiently unctuous to make David aware that he had received the script and read it.

"My dear Rabbi Hartman," he said, "how very good finally to meet you. I do feel honored." Excessive, David felt. Gerson was a large, heavy-set man with a thick neck and intense dark eyes. He underlined things with his eyes. "Shall we eat here?" he said, making it more a statement than a question. "We can talk privately."

The last thing in the world David desired was to be pressed into a private discussion with Rabbi Gerson, but he saw no way to avoid it without hurting Gerson's feelings. To compensate for what David might have regarded as insensitivity on his part, Rabbi Gerson managed to insert in passing that of course his temple was picking up all the costs as well as David's honorarium. Which is no great sacrifice on our part, David. We're a large and reasonably wealthy congregation. We seat a thousand people, and we can put up folding chairs for five hundred more. That's not because the Jews in Washington are necessarily *frum* — and incidentally I must say we have a good many members from Maryland and Virginia — but because any politician who wants to put his message to the Jews finds ours a most useful pulpit. And believe me, we have had the whole spectrum, from President to Secretary of State to Speaker of the House, and most of what's in between We get maximum press and media coverage — all of which brings me to the draft of your speech, which I read this morning."

"Did it disturb you?"

"No, David, it did not disturb me at all. I know how you think, and I agree with most of it. But it will disturb the very devil out of most of my congregation."

"Then perhaps if most of your congregation is inhabited by the devil, it or he or whatever should be disturbed out of them."

"Oh, come on, let's not get silly about it."

"Ernest, I like to think that I am never silly, although I sound silly frequently and even more frequently stupid. Now why don't we get down to specifics. Tell me what will disturb all these good people."

"For one thing, Muste. I have nothing against a rabbi quoting a Protestant minister. We're ecumenical enough for that. But A. J. Muste — he was a red, a wild, crazy radical."

"Oh, no, he wasn't," David said gently. "He was a Protestant minister and a good and saintly man."

"Well, after I read your draft, I called Jeffrey, Cootes, and Herblin — three of the most important Protestant ministers in town, Episcopalian, Presbyterian, and Methodist — and all of them agreed that they'd call the cops before they'd let A. J. Muste use their pulpits. Now just let me read you the quote you use in your draft from A. J. Muste: 'The world waits for a great nation that has the common sense, the imagination, and the faith to devote to the science and practice of nonviolence so much as a tenth of the money, brains, skill, and devotion which it now devotes to the madness of war preparation.'"

"A very simple, straightforward statement. Thousands of others have said the same thing, from George Bernard Shaw to Mark Twain."

"Maybe so, but not in the context of your talk. You take a rigid pacifist position. You say that under absolutely no circumstances is it permissible to arm a man and send him out to take the life of another human being. You say that this is the basis of all ethics."

"I said I would talk about ethics, and you agreed."

"David," he fairly shouted, "this is not ethics! This is madness."

"Ernest, Ernest," David said gently, "the simplest dictionary definition of ethics is the principles of honor and morality. The basis upon which we function as rabbis was specified by our father and teacher Rabbi Hillel. When the nonbeliever came to him and begged Hillel to teach him the Law, Hillel said, 'Do not unto others what thou wouldst not have them do unto thee. There is the Law. All the rest is commentary.'"

"Damnit, David, you insult my intelligence! Would there be an Israel today without the Israeli Army? Would there be a world today without the Allied armies that fought Hitler? Jesus said almost the same as Hillel, but it's not the Christian definition of ethics." He picked up the draft of David's speech and shook it. "You leave no room here. No room for any thinking except yours. I can't have it that way, David. As much as I honor and respect you, I have my own position. And yours. They will hoot you off the *bimah*."

"I don't believe it."

"Take my word for it. This congregation has raised millions for Israel. Our sacred plaque at the entrance has one hundred and seventy-three names of members who have died in World War One, World War Two, Korea, and Vietnam. Are you going to face their relatives and friends and tell them that no war is just?"

David was silent now, studying Rabbi Gerson.

"David?"

Still he was silent.

"David," Rabbi Gerson said, "I heard you speak on the religions of the Semites at American University three years ago. I heard you field the questions. You don't need this draft. All I ask is that you modify your position somewhat. Simply make it palatable."

"But then, it's not my position, is it?"

"For one night, does it make that much difference?"

"To me. In any case, I know you're not in a hole. You made provisional arrangements before you came here."

"I had to."

"Of course. Who is he?"

"Harry Fergerson."

"Chairman of the House Committee on Ethics?"

"That's right. David, we still intend to send you your full stipend."

"Please don't. If you do, I will only return it."

"Give it to your synagogue."

"They don't need it."

"All right. You're the most stubborn man I ever knew. We'll still pay the expenses. You must take that."

"Yes, that I'll accept."

"I wish it could be you. We advertised you. People want to hear you."

"I'm right here," David said without malice. "All you have to do is ask me."

Gerson shook his head. "I can't."

David considered the possibility of returning on the shuttle that same evening, but he found that he was quite tired. He had brought Tolstoy's *War and Peace* with him, a book he had meant to read for years, and which he had started and put aside at least half a dozen times. This time he was well into it, over two hundred pages into it, and lost in the charm and complexity of the wonderful and colorful nineteenth-century Russian families. Strangely, he was not terribly upset by the fact that after his trip to Washington, Rabbi Gerson had decided that his speech would blow the roof off the synagogue, which Rabbi Gerson was careful to call a temple. David did not agree with him, and right now he was much more relaxed sitting here in his hotel room reading *War and Peace*. He thought of how pleasant it would be to belong to one of those extended families that Tolstoy wrote about. His own family was attenuated rather than extended. Sarah had married a very nice Protestant boy. David had thought that he could take that in his stride, but once it happened, he found it quite disturbing, even though Martin had officiated at the wedding ceremony. They were both teachers without tenure as yet at Arizona State, where Sarah taught archeology and the boy taught physics. Sarah had a year-old baby, a girl she had named Priscilla, after the boy's mother. Aaron was happily writing sports for the *Los Angeles Times*. Aaron's delight in it puzzled David a good deal, since once out of prison, his service over, Aaron had dropped both engineering and medicine as career objectives. David got out to see both children at least twice a year, but the distance, both geographic and otherwise, between himself and his children always oppressed him, and since Aaron had fallen out with the Andrews girl, there was nothing to keep him here.

He tried to concentrate on the book and found himself dozing, and rather than go to bed at this hour, he went down to the hotel bar and ordered himself a Scotch and soda.

David had seated himself at the bar, which was rather crowded, just a few empty seats here and there. One of the empty seats was alongside him, and a moment later this was occupied by a good-looking, dark-haired woman of forty or so. She glanced at David once or twice, evidently measuring him before she decided to strike up a conversation, and then she asked him whether he came there very often.

"First time. I'm from out of town."

"Where out of town?"

"I'm afraid you never heard of it."

"Try me. There are few places I haven't heard about."

"Leighton Ridge, Connecticut."

"I never heard of it." She stared at him approvingly, nodding slightly. "What do you do there?"

"I'm the local rabbi."

"You're putting me on."

"No, not at all."

"Rabbis don't look like you."

"How do they look?" David asked, smiling.

"They look Jewish — " She bit off her words. "Good God, I did it, didn't I? I'm so sorry. But people do look Jewish, don't they?"

"Yes, I suppose they do." He finished his drink, said good night to her, and went back to his room. He was very tired but no longer drowsy, and it turned into one of those long, sleepless nights, during which he brooded over his own unwillingness to respond with anger to so many situations that demanded it.

The following morning, striding through the terminal to board the shuttle for New York, he heard his name called and turned to see Jack Osner — the first time David had seen him since Mel Klein's funeral. Aside from the fact that he had put on some more weight around the waistline, he was little changed.

"Glad to see you hale and hearty," Osner said, falling into step beside him. "From what Gerson indicated last night, I expected total collapse."

"Well, we had a rather basic difference of opinion, and he had to have some explanation for his pinch hitter."

"Of course you did. If the damned fool had a brain in his head, he never would have invited you. Now Fergerson, that's another matter. That old whoremaster would sell his own mother at bargain rates if it meant a few dollars in his pocket. Head of the Ethics Committee! He not only has a wife and three kids and goes steady with a gal who works for the Commerce Department, but he visits a massage parlor every week."

"How on earth would you know that?" David wondered.

"Because I have the same masseuse, and she doesn't limit herself to massage. Anyway, Fergerson talks too much, and one day he's going to talk himself into a neat scandal. I can't say that I mind. The idiot's a Democrat. Shall we sit together?"

David realized that Jack Osner had forgotten he had parted from David in anger five years before. Evidently, he lived a very full life, in which each day crowded out the past. Just as well.

"Of course," David agreed.

Settled in the plane and awaiting the takeoff, Osner explained, "In case you've been wondering why the new chief of the Security Council uses the shuttle — "

"It never crossed my mind."

"You're an innocent, David. You always were. Yes, I have an army plane on call, but Dick wants a low profile on that kind of thing until after the election. It's going to be a landslide, and then all stops are out, but meanwhile, some nosy reporter gets his hands on what it costs to push a Seventwenty-seven up to La Guardia and back every week, not to mention a few other places, and it makes waves. Don't make waves when you don't have to. Now I went out of my way to go to Gerson's temple and listen to you, David. That ought to give me a few points on your scorecard."

David realized that Osner was trying to curry favor with him, to find approval.

"How is Shelly?" David asked.

"She's just fine. We're divorced, you know. Perfectly amicable — one of those mutual-agreement things without rancor. The kids are grown, so that's out of the way. I hear you and Lucy have taken the same path."

"Yes. Some years now."

"But you remain at Leighton Ridge."

"Yes."

"David, tell you what. I'm not sure how old that boy of yours is, but any day now they have to be grabbing him to ship him off to Vietnam. You don't want him in that butcher shop. A kid goes over there, his chances of not coming back in a body bag are mighty slim. Now I can work your boy a second louey commission and keep him stateside for the rest of the war. Just say the word."

"Jack, Jack," David said, "my boy went to prison as a conscientious objector five years ago. He served his time."

For a long moment, Osner stared at David blankly, as if David had introduced some obscure joke that was beyond his comprehension. Then he shook his head. "Too many things on my mind, too many. I did hear somewhere that he was in prison up in Danbury, but you forget."

"Of course."

"I was trying to reach out a hand to you, David. Why the hell can't you let me reach out a hand to you?"

They were airborne now and well on their way to New York. "I never turned away from you, Jack."

Silence again for a time while David looked out the window at the landscape below. He had the impression that was his so often when he was in an airplane, of a world far below, inhabited by very tiny creatures. Somewhere in the writings of Lao-tzu, David had read that a man's life falls into two sections, the first fifty years to be concerned with man and the second fifty years to be given to a relationship with the *tao*, a fabric of mind that knit the universe together. The notion had grown on him and led him into a great deal of reading in Chinese philosophy, and it had also led him to a curious feeling about the insignificance of the creatures on this tiny planet on the edge of a star cluster that was only one of thousands and thousands of star clusters. At times, this thought grasped his heart with icy fingers and at other times it gave him a sense of the glory and majesty of what men so easily called God; this was particularly vivid in an airplane, where either mood could take hold of him.

"Jack," he said, "sitting here with you is as close to the seats of the mighty as I'll ever be, and I want to ask you a question that has troubled me enormously."

"Go ahead, David."

"I got the story from Martin Carter, who got it from a very highly placed churchman, whose name I can't reveal. It was nineteen forty-nine, and Truman was President. We had the atom bomb and, supposedly, the Russians did not, and the Pentagon planned an atomic raid on the Soviet Union, calculated to wipe out five major cities, Moscow and Leningrad among them, as well as the Soviet navy's home base. This atom bomb was calculated to have the same effect it had in Japan — to reduce the Soviet government to instant submission. The story was that Truman gave his consent to this, the raid was planned in every detail, and then France, England, and Germany persuaded Truman to call it off."

Osner nodded. "I've heard the rumor for years."

"But you were very close to the Joint Chiefs."

"Not then, David, not then. The story's been around Washington for years. Who knows whether it's true or not, but would it have been such a bad idea?"

"You're asking me?" David said in astonishment. "Seriously?"

"Why not? Look at it from my point of view for once, David, I mean from a global-political point of view. The one deterrent to peace in the world is the Soviet Union. Destroy their power, and you have a world ruled by the United States and its allies. No more war, no power strong enough to face up to us, and we and only we have the bomb. Sure, a lot of Russians would die, but isn't peace worth the price?"

"You've seen pictures of Hiroshima?"

"Sure I have. And do you know how many of our boys were saved by the bomb we dropped on Hiroshima?"

David leaned back, his eyes closed.

"David, I'm sorry. You asked the question. I've had to face the same thing in Vietnam. I've ordered bombings where whole villages were wiped out and cities turned into ruins. Well, that was my job. That was in defense of my country, of our way of life."

After a while, David said, "We are all mad. We are a race gone mad."

"Sure, but it's a complex world we live in. You have to be as crazy as the next fellow to survive — or as smart. Goddamnit, David, you never gave this country a chance, a man of your talent burying himself up there in Leighton Ridge, a little backwater hole in Connecticut. Even a pompous fool like Ernest Gerson pulls down fifty thousand a year. David, it's the name of the game — work hard, get a few bucks, enjoy them — one time around, that's all we get. If God wanted it different, he would have made it different. When I offered you that job with the Pentagon, you would have been on ice, but that would have put you into the mainstream, and that's something you couldn't tolerate. It's easier to blame me and look at me as the scum of the earth."

"Jack, I don't look at you as the scum of the earth."

The plane was landing, and David was thankful that it had been a short flight. Osner offered him a ride into New York in the "company" car, the company being the federal government; but David said no, he'd be going directly to Connecticut. They shook hands. "For God's sake, don't be a stranger," Osner said. "My office is at the State Department. I'll leave word that you're to have entrée whenever you show. We'll have lunch or something. Hell, you're a single man, David. We can have some pleasant company, fine, intelligent women, not sluts. Now stay well."

Della was at the airport, waiting for him. "Was that Jack Osner?" she asked him.

"We met on the plane."

"Yich. We won't talk about him. Come this way. I'm in the lot. Tell me about it. Were you a howling success, and did all the women ogle you? You know, I never heard you speak outside the synagogue."

"Did you know that Nazis loved children? Not Jewish or Russian children, but their own. They loved dogs. Dogs and children."

"What on earth are you talking about? Sometimes you come off talking in non sequiturs or sounding like a dumbbell, and nobody ever thinks of a rabbi as a dumbbell. Except me. What was your talk about?"

"Ethics. But I didn't talk."

"You'd better explain."

David explained, and then Della said, "Do you know what I would have done? I would have agreed to whatever that horse's ass of a rabbi asked, and then I would have gotten up on the platform and said my piece. What could they do to you? Would that dunce Gerson come out and wave his arms and tell people not to listen to you?"

"No. But you put me in a role I'm not suited for."

"I suppose so." Della was threading the car carefully through the traffic outside the airport. "Anyway," she said, "you don't lie. That's an awful weakness. I lie all the time. I couldn't possibly get through life without a gift for deft lying."

"I don't believe you," David said.

"Maybe yes, maybe no. You know, my dear, the great dramas of life are usually played to small audiences. When Mel and I were young, we belonged to an amateur dramatic group in Litchfield. There were nights when our audience consisted of half a dozen people, and you know, we played well on those nights. But here is a case where for over an hour you sat next to the most evil presence on this planet."

"Oh, no — no, Della. You're not talking about Jack Osner. I've known Jack for years. He's a complex and perhaps a very sick man, with a great lust for power and a feeling of inferiority because he's Jewish. But to call him the most evil presence on this planet — by the way, that's a very colorful phrase."

"I didn't read it anywhere, if that's what you're thinking. I made it up. But look at your friend Osner. The crazy, lunatic bombings he ordered in Vietnam killed thousands of men, women, children. He turned a beautiful land into a junkpile of death. He poured C.I.A. agents and millions of dollars into South America, overthrowing elected democratic governments — murdering thousands, establishing torture squads, turning countries over to the secret police."

"He didn't do it all by himself, Della."

"But he did do it. It came out of his warped, crazy mind.

I knew the man long before you did, David. He propositioned me at least a dozen times — "

"What do you mean, he propositioned you?"

"Oh, David, you are dear. He asked me to get away from Mel for a day, a night, or whatever, and go to bed with him. He pleaded with me to join him and Shelly in a three-way sex gambit. He almost raped me once, but I kneed him in the testicles and that decked him. David, there's a filthy, stinking dirty world out there; and Jack Osner is one of the top dogs in charge." She shook her head suddenly. "No, I'm not making myself out to be some sort of femme fatale. I'm a fat, middle-aged, Jewish housewife. I know that. It was long ago, David."

They were silent for a time after that while Della fed the car through the traffic and over the bridge into the Bronx. And then David said, "But where is the guilt, Della? I stopped believing in God, but I had to pray to God, because without prayer, I couldn't exist. I had to pray to God to take this curse off my people. I began to read history, American history. Do you know that in all the history of this country, no Jew has risen to such heights of power as Jack Osner? But who puts him there? Who uses him? I can agree with you that all the precious wonders that our prophets preached have been cast aside by Jack. He is a man without conscience; without pity, without remorse, without guilt, without that sweet thing that a hundred generations of Jews put above everything else, and which in Yiddish is called *rachmones*, a kind of pity that goes beyond pity. But in that, he is like all the rest of them. Should he be specifically cursed because he's Jewish, because he's fat and graceless? Is he worse than Truman, who dropped two bombs and put a million innocents to death? Is he worse than Johnson? Than our current Mr. Nixon?"

"But he's Jewish," Della said, almost in a sob.

"Yes, and that was my prayer — for us not to be made a mockery of before the whole world. And do you know, that way my faith began to return — because if there's a God, there are no Jews and no Gentiles, only people. As for Jack," he said, "it's no new thing. The German dukes and princes had their court Jews, one Jew raised to power while the others huddled in the ghettos, like animals in a pen."

"I sometimes think you could forgive anyone."

"That's another religion, Della. I don't judge and I don't forgive. But how did we get into this discussion? I am so very glad to see you again."

"So? If that's the case, why don't you marry me?"

"Seriously?" David wondered. "Or just in the way of making conversation?"

"I really don't know. I suppose this is at least the tenth time I've proposed to you, so I guess it's just as serious as the other nine times."

"Where would we live?" David asked her.

"What do you mean, where would we live?"

"Well, I live in that shabby little house that the synagogue built for us twenty years ago, and you live in that marvelous old farmhouse that you and Mel made into a museum of sorts, and I couldn't expect you to move in with me."

"Do you know how you're talking?"

"No."

"Like what the kids call a male chauvinist pig."

"Really?"

"Oh, get mad at me or something. Look, the hell with where we'll live. We'll work it out. Do you want to get married to a fat, middle-aged, Jewish housewife?"

"I don't mind your being Jewish," David said. "I don't think you're very fat. I suppose we could work it out."

"Sometimes, David, I suspect you of having a sense of humor. Are you saying you want to marry me?"

"I think so."

"Oh, don't kid around about this. It's too goddamned important. I love you to death. There's nothing else in the world I want out of life. Do you love me?"

"Right from the beginning."

"You never showed it."

"My word, Della, I'm a rabbi. I was married, and you were married, myself to a wonderful woman and you to a wonderful man."

"Why am I looking a gift rabbi in the mouth or eyes or whatever? We've known each other a long time, David. There can't be too many surprises."

"Thank you," he said softly. They both understood that remark, and Friday evening, Sabbath eve a week later, standing before his congregation in his black robe, his father's worn silk prayer shawl over his shoulders, David said to them:

"I tried to calculate last night how many times I have stood here and preached a sermon. Even allowing for guest speakers, it must be close to a thousand times, and that thought is a little terrifying. All those sermons; all that awful righteousness. No matter how hard I try, it creeps in. On the other hand, there were some compensations, aside from the attention of you who have sat so patiently and listened to me again and again. They tell me I am cribbed from a good deal more than most rabbis. My sermons have been cheerfully stolen by Catholic priests, Lutheran ministers, Baptist ministers, Presbyterian ministers, Congregational ministers, and of course rabbis. Mostly either with permission or confession; once by the dean of a great cathedral, with permission. But I suppose the most interesting theft comes from Emil Hostra, who is a Mormon churchman in Salt Lake City. I brought his letter with me. He wrote, 'My dear Rabbi Hartman: I read your sermon on anger in the August issue of *Young Israel*. I am writing to tell you that I shamelessly lifted it, so this is in the way of a confession. Since my city, Salt Lake City, is the only place in the world where a Jew can be a Gentile without apostatizing, my colleagues and I invite you here to taste the experience. I think you may find it highly overrated, but rest assured that we will ply you with food and love in payment for our thievery.' Well," David said, after the ripple of laughter had died down, "I have not yet gone to Salt Lake City, and I am afraid I may have to live out my life without the experience of being a Gentile. But since I have known Martin Carter for a quarter of a century as a warm and enduring friend, I think I may assume that the experience is not too unfamiliar. On the other hand, the fact that a sermon in a synagogue fits so well into a Catholic or Mormon church gives me some hope for an ecumenical future.

"Tonight, however, I have no sermon of my own, and like these good people, I'll tell a story not of my making. It's an old, old Jewish legend, and it deals with God, the Prophet Elijah, and a saintly rabbi. It would seem, according to this legend, that some of God's missions on earth are done by the Prophet Elijah, who sits among the angels, and when he was sent on this particular mission, God suggested that he appear to this good rabbi and take him on the journey with him, as a reward.

"So the prophet appeared to the rabbi and revealed himself, and when the rabbi had recovered from the shock of seeing God's messenger before him, he agreed with delight to accompany the prophet on his journey. They set out on foot and they walked many miles. It was almost nightfall, and the rabbi was very tired, and he asked the Prophet Elijah where they would stay for the night.

"The prophet pointed to a small hut in the distance, and he said to the rabbi, 'We will stay there. A poor peasant and his wife live in that hut. They are older people, and very good. They have never harmed another person. They have never refused a request for charity, and they have never spoken a harsh word to each other. Therefore, God will reward them with our presence for the night.'

"As the prophet had said, they were eagerly welcomed by the old couple, who were very poor, who had a single cow and a tiny garden plot to keep them alive. They washed the weary travelers' feet and gave them their own small supper, going hungry themselves, and then gave the visitors their bed, the two old people sleeping on the floor in front of the hearth.

"When morning came, the rabbi was awakened by the sobbing of the old woman, and when he went to comfort her, the two old folks told him that during the night their single cow had died — and how could they live with their cow dead?

"The Prophet Elijah and the rabbi left the little hut and set out to continue their journey, the rabbi muttering petulantly, until the Prophet Elijah said, 'Rabbi, why do you mutter so? I find it annoying.'

" 'Do you?' the rabbi said indignantly. 'I will tell you why I mutter. All my life I have preached God's goodness and mercy, and what do I see? Two saintly people are punished so terribly while the wicked go free.'

" 'You do not question God's actions,' the prophet said severely.

" 'I must.'

" 'No, Rabbi. You must have faith. Ordinarily, I do not explain God's actions, but this time, Rabbi, I will make an exception. While you slept last night, I was called to the presence of the Almighty, and among other things, he asked me about the peasant and his wife. When I spoke of their goodness, God became deeply disturbed. In the Book of Fate, the peasant's days were numbered, and even as we spoke, the Angel of Death, the *malakh ha mavet*, was on his way with the speed of light to end the poor peasant's days. Not even the Almighty can halt the Angel of Death, but God is not without his own powers, and now he reached out and deflected the thrust of the *malakh ha mavet*. Death was delivered as destined, not to the peasant but to the cow. Thus, the Angel of Death was frustrated, and the old couple could have each other a few years more.'

"After this explanation, the rabbi was so filled with shame that he walked for hours in silence. The weather turned cold. It began to rain, and the rabbi and the prophet walked on in the cold, pouring rain, but the rabbi could not bring himself to complain or protest.

"Then, just as darkness was beginning to fall, they saw before them a magnificent house. They hurried up to the front door and knocked. The owner opened the door himself. He wore a robe of fine silk, shoes of the softest leather, a belt studded with jewels, and on his hand two diamond rings of great brilliance. He looked at the two soaked, bedraggled travelers with contempt, and when they begged for a place to spend the night, he spat upon them and slammed the door in their faces. Not far from this great house, there was an old, broken-down shed, and there, huddled together, the rain coming through the roof above them, the Prophet Elijah and the rabbi spent the night. You can well imagine that the rabbi did not sleep a wink, and with the very first light of dawn, he saw the prophet rise and slip out of the shed. The rabbi followed the prophet. The rain had stopped. The prophet went into a nearby village and awakened a stonemason. He led the mason back to the house of the rich man. A corner of the house was crumbling, near the foundation, and the prophet instructed the mason to repair it. After the mason had repaired the house, the prophet paid him.

"The rabbi hurried back to the shed, and when the prophet appeared, the rabbi pretended to be asleep. They shared some bread and cheese and started on their way, and finally the prophet said, 'Again with the muttering, Rabbi?'

" 'I followed you this morning.'

" 'I know you did,' the prophet said, 'and once again you doubt God.'

" 'What else can I do? Two saintly poor people, and their single cow is destroyed. And now this rich, selfish, heartless man, and you — you, the Prophet Elijah — you repair his house and pay for the repairs yourself.'

" 'Rabbi, Rabbi,' the prophet said, 'you have lost your innocence and you have lost your faith. I will explain once more. Last night I was again called to the Divine Presence, and I spoke of the rich man and his inhospitality. God does not interfere with man's life on earth, but this time he was intrigued. Do you know, he said to me, the corner of that man's house is crumbling. In a few days, after the rain, it will crumble enough to reveal a chest that was hidden there a hundred years ago. The chest is filled with jewels, and the rich man will only become richer and more cruel and more selfish. So go to the village and hire a mason and have him repair the corner of the house, that the chest may remain hidden for another hundred years.'

"Once again, the rabbi was so overcome with shame that he covered his face with his hands, and then when he glanced up, the Prophet Elijah had disappeared, and so ends our fable. I tell it to you, not because my own faith is so great, but because it has been stretched so thin. Other people have accepted the calamities that beset mankind, the pain of being human as a natural part of existence, but we Jews are very adroit and we must work them into God's scheme, and perhaps we are right. Who knows?

"I have always loved this old story, but I am not sure in my own mind that faith is the answer to anything. Doubt is more to my liking. Moses faced God. Who are you? What is your name? Prove yourself to me. There is an old rabbinical belief that the only proof of God is in our own actions, and I most often feel that is sufficient."

They always finished the Sabbath eve service with coffee and cake in the lounge, and this night David was more than usually beset with questions and arguments. They ranged from Eddie Frome's plea that he might use the story in *The New Yorker* to Al Bramer's demand for David to show where in the Talmud the story existed. Bramer was in the pro-Orthodox division of the congregation. Martin and Millie, visitors only, stayed in the background, Millie whispering to Martin, "He made it up." "Nonsense. No one makes up a story like that." "It's a sort of Jewish joke," Alan Buckingham said to his wife, Dora, who pointed out that he was the last person in the world to pontificate on Jewish jokes.

"A Jewish joke is a contradiction in terms," Dora insisted.

"We are a Jewish joke," Oscar Denton said. He was well past ninety-four, and he walked without a cane and read without glasses. "I have been spared to this unholy age in order to understand that, and I suppose that having understood it, I'll be gathered to my fathers, as they say. The *goyim*," he said, raising a hand of apology to Martin and Millie, "invented us at the point that they realized that they were utterly insane. They had spent the first three thousand years of history slaughtering each other, and when they realized they were faced with extinction, they invented us. But their invention went haywire, because we started slaughtering each other with equal delight. Now they're stuck with Jews *and* slaughter."

Joe Hurtz, who had wandered into the group, said to David, "The old man's crazy as a hatter. They ought to put him away. I think he's turned anti-Semitic."

"I think he's got something there," Eddie Frome told David, who had not heard Oscar Denton's version of history. "It needs cleaning up and a few facts, but he's got something there."

"Hurtz!" Oscar Denton said commandingly. "Hurtz, how old are you?"

"Seventy-three, Oscar. You know damned well how old I am."

"All right — seventy-three. Now listen, motherfucker, I'm going to outlive you!" With that, Denton stamped out, pausing at the door to shout, "It's past my bedtime, anyway."

David spread his arms hopelessly.

"When we were kids," Sophie Frome said, "and one of us raised her voice, Grandma said, 'Sha, *a Shandeh for the goyim.*' Well, that's what this is. I don't mind salty talk, but that old man's an abomination."

"Oh, come on," Martin said. "Since Millie and I are the only *goyim* here tonight, it's hardly a — what did you say?"

"*Shandeh,*" David said. "Yiddish for shame."

"Oh, he's a marvelous old man," Millie said.

David grinned at her, and they both remembered the evening long ago when Lucy had invited Denton to dinner with the Carters. Denton's wife was long dead, and Lucy had seated him next to Millie. "He had tiger knees," Millie said later.

"What did he say?" David asked now.

"No way that anyone could repeat or make sense of what he said," Alan Buckingham decided.

"And where did your story come from, Rabbi?" Mrs. Shapiro asked him.

"I really don't know. I remember that I heard it as a boy, probably in a synagogue, and again I read it somewhere."

"A Jewish joke," Eddie Frome was arguing, "is not necessarily a defiance of logic. I heard one the other day. Mrs. Cohen meets Mrs. Levy on the street. Mrs. Levy is wheeling a large carriage containing twins, Arthur and Arnold. But which is Arnold and which is Arthur, Mrs. Cohen wants to know? Simple, says Mrs. Levy. The lawyer is Arthur and the doctor is Arnold."

"Awful."

"Not awful. It's a typical Jewish joke — or it could be Italian or Greek or whatever, the desperate need of poor people, lately liberated, to improve their status. David's story is something else. How does one look at God or fate or the universe after the Holocaust?"

"It's a legend from long before the Holocaust."

"What Holocaust? Human history is a holocaust. I have a friend who was in the Manhattan Project, and he and his colleagues have calculated that an atomic war would destroy two thirds of the human race."

"Or all of it."

Della Klein drew David away. "Let's have some coffee and cake, Rabbi. It's too late for clever arguments."

"Yes, I'd love some coffee and cake."

The cake was not good. It never was. There were certainly

ome gifted bakers in the congregation, but they never volun-
eered for the Friday baking. However, no one complained.
The cake was eaten.

"The trouble with your stories," Della said, "is that they
ack a third act."

"It's a story, not a play."

"Yes. Yes, of course. David, have you ever thought of giving
up the rabbinate?"

"Yes, I've thought about it."

"But you won't, will you?"

"Not as long as they tolerate us. You see, they tolerate
ministers and rabbis. We are the clowns of God, if there is a
God, but everything else is crumbling. People are not very
admirable, but they deserve a chance to survive. Perhaps we
an help with that."

"Remember, you agreed to marry me?"

"Any time."

"You do have a sense of humor," Della said. "I was never
ery sure of that. How about the fifth of next month? My kids
an make it then, and it will be nice to have your kids, if they
an come."

Mrs. Holtzman wept. "It's wonderful for you to be mar-
ied," she said. "A man like you, he should be married. But
what will become of me? I will die if I have to go back and
ve with my daughter, God bless her, but not to live with."

David said that he would work that out, but Della saw no
eason for Mrs. Holtzman to come with him. After canvass-
ing half his congregation, he found another place for her. He
ad a letter from his daughter, Sarah, and between the lines
here was a plea for financial help. If he wanted his children
t his wedding, he would have to send them tickets. And then
Lucy telephoned from California to tell him, through her
ears, that her mother had passed away. "And David," Lucy
obbed, "she wanted to be buried next to Pop, and Pop is
here at Leighton Ridge, and I just don't know what to do."

He could picture it clearly as she spoke to him. This was

the woman he had married and lived with so many years, and
he could picture her grief and her confusion — and this wa
apart from him. Everything that happened to her now wa
apart from him. He took down the name of the funeral parlo
where Sally Spendler's body lay, and he assured Lucy that h
would take care of everything else. "I'll have the body her
tomorrow," he said, "and we can have the funeral a day afte
that. Why don't you take the Red Eye tonight, and that wil
get you in early in the morning. I'll make arrangements fron
here. You can stay with Millie. I'll tell them you're coming.

"David, I'm married."

"Yes, of course. There's no reason why both of you can
stay with the Carters."

Later, David drove to the cemetery, the lovely grass
meadow that they had purchased, aided by Alan Bucking
ham's machinations, from the Episcopal church. There wer
twenty-seven graves now, the toll that time had taken, and a
David walked through the little cemetery, he recalled Mar
Twain's comment on the Jews, that they were just like every
body else, only more so. The little graveyard had bee
adorned. It was surrounded by a hedge of taxus, already eigt
feet tall, and the entrance was defined by an iron gate hun
from brick gateposts. Family plots were marked off by lov
iron rods linked by foot-high granite posts. Flowers and nev
cedars everywhere. David might have preferred the simpl
austerity of the Congregational graveyard; but then Jew
were not Congregationalists, no matter how much Marti
Carter compared the virtues and faults of both groups. Marti
Carter was unquestionably a *Lamed Vov*, one of the thirty-si
just men upon whom the existence of the world depende
The notion made David smile. It would be nice to suggest
to Martin, but it would disturb him too much, and Mill
would certainly be provoked. "What an outrageous notion
she would say to David, and of course, she'd be quite righ
He came to his own small plot, a burial space large enoug
for eight graves. He had brought a handful of colored stick

with him to outline the new grave. All too often, they would dig the grave in the wrong spot. "At least, here's a practical need for someone like myself, a practical purpose of rabbis and ministers," David decided. "Birth, confirmation, marriage, death — all very basic to any society." Mel Klein's family plot was hardly more than a few yards away. "Complications." David sighed. Well, Della was very bright. He seemed to gravitate toward bright women. She would work things out.

Back at his office, Mrs. Shapiro said to him, "I've been on the phone all morning, Rabbi, but I think it's all in hand. The funeral parlor will ship the body to the airport, and then it goes by air cargo, and they come into Kennedy at five o'clock in the morning. I had to make arrangements for the coffin to be held until the hearse gets there, which won't be until eight o'clock. The hearse will get here some time before noon, I don't know exactly when, so you'd better schedule the burial for three o'clock or so. Weather says it will be a very nice day, if you want to have an outside service." Mrs. Shapiro had become older, stouter, and marvelously competent.

He was about to say that the decision would be up to his wife, but he stopped himself. He praised Mrs. Shapiro and then went outside. His invitation for Lucy and her husband to stay with the Carters had been rather cavalier, and he thought he would drive over to Martin's place and apologize. As he came out of the synagogue, he heard his name called from the direction of the old Congregational church, which had housed the synagogue and which had been subsequently sold to the Unitarians. The old church and the synagogue were about a quarter of a mile apart, and now David saw a young man striding hurriedly toward the synagogue.

He came up to David with the question "Rabbi Hartman?"

As David turned to the young man, he became aware that Mrs. Shapiro had followed him. "One moment, please," David said.

"The thing is," Mrs. Shapiro whispered, "that this is going

to cost a fortune, Rabbi. Almost a thousand dollars. Who will pay for it?"

"I will."

"But you shouldn't have to."

"Please," he begged her. "Not now, please." He walked over to where the young man was waiting and said, "You must forgive me. My mother-in-law just died in California. We're trying to make some arrangements."

"Of course, Rabbi. I don't want to intrude at a moment like this. I simply wanted to introduce myself. I'm Steven Woodsman, and I'm the new pastor at the Unitarian church. Since we're such close neighbors, I feel we should know each other. We have many Jews in our membership."

"Do you indeed!" David said coldly.

"I only meant — "

"I know precisely what you meant," David said, cutting him off. "I'm glad to have met you, Mr. Woodsman." With that, he turned around and strode across to where his car was parked. Once in the car, driving toward Martin's house, he tried to understand what had come over him. How many times Lucy and Della had berated him for a lack of anger, and here he was seething with anger.

"And I really can't say why," he told Martin a while later. "I put down this poor young fellow with the most disgusting behavior."

"I'm sure it was not that disgusting, David. You haven't done a quick change into Mr. Hyde."

"But I've always known that half the membership of the Unitarian church were Jews. As a matter of fact, I've lured away at least a dozen families through the years, and the Unitarians, Jewish or otherwise, are very nice people."

"You and I," Martin said, "we do have the right to resort to anger."

"Well, when things ease up, I'll seek him out and apologize. You will forgive me for inviting Lucy and her husband to a night of bed and board at your place."

When Martin told his wife about the incident, Millie said, "Martin, don't you see what's happening? David's in the process of becoming an angry old Jew."

"What a thing to say!"

"I don't mean it as anything derogatory. I adore David. But I think his time of childhood and innocence is over. He's been brought up and has lived as a damned, bloodless Wasp, no different from you and me. That's over, I think. He's converted and turned Jewish, and now he's in the process of becoming a prophet. You know your Bible. There was nothing nice about the prophets. They thundered and raged and denounced greed and injustice. You wouldn't want to have one of them in your living room, but they were something."

Looking at his wife in astonishment, Martin said, "You feel that? It's very interesting, but I wonder."

And at that moment, David was saying to Della, "Yes, I finally figured it out. I don't want any young cub of a Unitarian minister telling me about a congregation full of Jews who haven't enough brains and guts, not to mention grace, to remain Jews. No, sir! I do not want that!"

Della doubled up with laughter, and David said indignantly, "You're laughing at me."

"With you, with you. Oh, David, all those people want is to stop being Jewish without converting. Same as your letter from Salt Lake City, where you can finally be a Gentile and remain Jewish."

"It stinks," he said flatly.

"David, you've never said anything like that in your life. What am I marrying?"

"We'll work that out."

"I suppose we will." Della sighed. "I do suppose we will."

David was in his office at the synagogue the following morning when Lucy arrived, and as he stood up, she went to him and threw her arms around him. "David, David, David." In her forty-ninth year, Lucy was still a most attractive woman, her features hardened somewhat, her skin tighter as a result of a face-lift David did not even suspect, her figure trim and tightened by hours of Los Angeles exercise classes. "Oh, David," she sobbed, "the whole thing is lousy. Life is such a bag of crud. Mom is gone, and I have no one. The kids do their own thing and don't even know that I exist."

"You have your husband," David said gently.

"And so have five other women. Oh, hell, why am I crying on your shoulder? I made my own bed. As for Bob Greene, he's too busy. Too goddamned busy to come to my mother's funeral."

"Death is awful," David said. "It's the black monster that lives with us always, but it's also a part of being. Don't brood over Bob's problems. Your mother had love and a wonderful daughter and two fine grandchildren. By the way, where are they?"

"You think that? I mean, you say a wonderful daughter. The kids will be here. Aaron was in Los Angeles and Sarah in Arizona. David, there was a time, wasn't there, when families stayed together?"

"Yes, but now it's different."

"Everything is."

"We made all the arrangements, Lucy. The casket will be brought here, and your mother will lie beside your father."

She had drawn back, but now she embraced him again. It felt good to have her in his arms, something familiar and comforting out of long, long ago. "David, you were always so good to me. My life stinks, David. I could come back here now. I could hack it here."

"That's an odd way to put it, Lucy."

"I know. Just talk. As you told me once before, a week or two here and I'd go crazy."

He was not going to talk to her about Della, but she picked up on that and said, "Oh, David, you're not going to marry Della Klein, are you?"

"Yes. I didn't want to tell you now."

"And how would you keep it from me here where everyone knows when the rabbi sneezes? How can you do it, David? You're a wonderful man. How can you live out your life in this crummy hole? It's nothing, and Della is a fat, frowsy, middle-aged housewife. There's a world out there. If you want to be a rabbi, there are other places to be a rabbi. There's a temple in Sepulveda Pass in Los Angeles that makes this synagogue look like Martin's church compared to Saint Patrick's Cathedral. Why are you doing this?" She broke into tears again, and David took her in his arms.

"It will be all right, darling."

At the cemetery, at the open grave, David said, "We say goodbye now to a lovely and gracious woman. We are not a funerary religion. We honor life, not death, and the reward we look to is here, in the life we live and the people we love and who love us. Sally Spendler, my mother-in-law and dear friend, was a woman well loved and richly rewarded."

After all the others had gone, Lucy and David and their two children remained at the grave for a time. "Will it be taken care of?" Lucy asked, pointing to the mound of raw dirt. "And who will see to the stone?"

Aaron, tall, lean, stood with his arm around her. "Pop will take care of those things."

"Of course," David said. Sarah was next to him, her hand in his. Even with death, as he told Della later, it was a good moment. Even though Lucy said unhappily, "I've left instructions to be cremated when the time comes, David, so don't save space for me."

At the airport, she said to him, "I don't know when I'll see you again, David. I can't come running once you're married."

"I'm here."

"All right, my dear David." And then she threw her arms around him and kissed him. She was alone on the plane.

Aaron and Sarah had been dropped off by David in New York. They wanted to spend a day or two in the city before they went home.

Almost as if it had never happened. He had once asked Martin, "How often do you see your kids?"

His son, Joe, was established in Canada and a Canadian citizen now. "Eight months ago was the last time," Martin had said. "How time flies!" Martin's daughter, Ellie, was living in Boston, married to an M.I.T. professor. "She tries to get down here with her kids every few months — well, sometimes only at Christmas."

"On the other hand," Della said, "how would you feel if they needed you every moment of the day? They're independent. That counts for a lot."

A few weeks later, David said to Della, "I've been talking to the board, and they feel we should be married in the synagogue in a public sense."

"Oh, the hell with them," Della said. "We're not kids. Let's go to City Hall and get it over with."

"There's no city hall at Leighton Ridge. You know that. There isn't even a judge or a magistrate, only the First Selectman, and I'm not even sure that he has the right to perform a marriage. You seem to forget I'm a rabbi. The first thing you give up when you become a rabbi is the right to say the hell with them."

"Then get a rabbi," Della said. "I'm amiable. How about that old man, Rabbi Belsen, whom you talk about?"

"May he rest in peace — twelve years now."

"I'm sorry. Oh, anyone, David."

David called Bert Sager. "Will I marry you?" Rabbi Sager asked. "Only if you're a woman, and even then I'd think twice about it. You are too old and too skinny. Like our eminent precursor, Socrates, I learned about marriage the hard way. Forgive me, David, I have a primitive sense of humor, and I make childish jokes. As so many in my congregation say, a rabbi with a sense of humor who is funny is an asset, but a rabbi with a sense of humor who is not funny is expendable. So if you want me to perform a ceremony, let's do it while I still have a congregation. By the way, whom are you marrying?"

"Della Klein."

"Blessings. I don't know the lady, but she sounds Jewish."

"I think she is," David said.

"Good, good. You know, it must be seen as a sort of a *Mitzvah* when a Conservative rabbi like myself marries one of the Reform faith. Where will the ceremony be and when?"

"A week from Sunday, noon, at our synagogue here in Leighton Ridge. Please bring your wife. We're planning nothing very grand, my two kids if I can get them to come, Della's kids, and some old friends. We'll have the ceremony at the synagogue, and then a buffet dinner at Della's home, so if you could plan to stay on until late in the afternoon, that would be very pleasant."

To David's amazement, both his children turned up in Leighton Ridge the day before the wedding, each alone, having managed to dispense for a few days with their mates — "just in terms of the cost of air fare," Sarah explained. At twenty-two, she was an impossibly healthy, freckled, clear-eyed woman. Her brother, Aaron, explained further, "Well, it's a kind of a special thing. We always looked at Della and Mel as part of the family. I don't recall Mel too well, but we both remember him warmly." Della's three children were their old friends. "You didn't expect them, did you?" Della said to David. "I mean, so soon after coming here for the funeral."

David nodded, his eyes moist. Rabbi Sager said to him, "You know, Hartman, I've known you a long time, but I've never seen you in this context. With your reputation as some kind of wild-eyed radical, raging at the evil in high places, denouncing war, going to prison, turning up on every picket line within a hundred miles of here for over a quarter of a century — it doesn't jibe. You're a very sweet and quiet man, and these people adore you, and that includes even my wife, who doesn't like rabbis very much."

David nodded. He didn't trust his voice.

He and Della were married on the *bimah*, the platform at the front of the synagogue, where he had stood and preached, ever since the new synagogue had been built in the little village on the Connecticut ridge.

At Della's house, packed with friends, including Mike Benton, who had come in from the Coast, Martin said to David softly, "We've both been privileged, old friend. There are moments when a human being must do what we do as an audience in the theater, enter a suspension of disbelief. It gives us a moment of clarity to thank God for all things."

Later that evening, when all the guests had gone, David told Della what Martin had said.

"I think I understand," she said uncertainly.

"You see," David said, "the disbelief is the crutch for evil — or so some of us see it. Hannah Arendt wrote of the banality of evil, but it's the mindless childishness of evil that hurts us."

"Oh, yes, yes." Della sighed. "On the other hand, it's late and we've had a long day, and all I know, Rabbi, about God or anything else, is that there's a great darkness out there, and a man or a woman should not sleep alone. I'm happy to be your wife, and I love you, and I'm lucky. Shall we go to bed?"

"As you wish, Mrs. Hartman."

"I'll have to get used to that. Do you know, David, in all the years we know each other, I've never asked you a question — well, from myself as a foolish woman to you as a wise rabbi."

"You're far from foolish, and only you would be loving enough to call me wise."

"Anyway, my dear Rabbi, here it is: Does it make any sense at all, this life we live — or is it, as Shakespeare suggested, a walking shadow that struts for an hour, or something of the sort?"

"You can take your choice, my dear," David said. "I love

you very much, if I didn't mention that before, and I'm tired, and, like you, I've slept alone too many nights. So let's go to bed, and we'll talk about philosophy and religion over breakfast."

"Heaven forbid. I've invited your kids and mine for breakfast."

"Then let's just go to bed."

"Amen to that," Della said.